MIDNIGHT PRINCE

JULIE SAMAN

For those of us who believe we all deserve the fairytale, especially when it comes with our midnight prince.

This is a contemporary Cinderella retelling set in a fictitious European country. It is NOT a romantasy or paranormal romance. The series, while standalone HEAs for our couples, has a continuous plot woven throughout. It is best read in order.

Content Warning: *This book and series have darker themes and suspenseful elements. Please go to the End of Book Note for a list of potential triggers if you're at all concerned.*

MARCELLA

One of the first things I was ever taught was the power of invisibility. Or maybe it's less of a power and more of a necessary survival skill. The defining talent all assassins carry. Existing in the shadows while others play in the light. Except I don't exist, therefore, I can play wherever I want. Like I plan to tonight.

Sucking in a sharp, frostbitten breath, I hold it tight in my lungs as I scan the crowd of celebrities, dignitaries, world leaders, and royalty for my mark. Since I first saw the guestlist, he's the one I narrowed in on. The wedding reception for King Sebastian of Messalina and his new bride, a much younger American, is about to begin.

And I plan to crash it.

The chalet entrance is only about fifteen meters in front of me, but it might as well be a thousand for how inaccessible it is. My phone buzzes in my sparkly wristlet, but I ignore Antonia for now, unwilling to miss my moment.

Minutes pass, and the chill I'm fighting sinks deeper into my bones until I see him. I step out of the shadows, slipping around a royal attendant, followed by another, until I seamlessly glide in beside the former American president and his wife, who are chatting with a high member of English nobility.

"What a stunning gown," I praise the former first lady, speaking to her in unaccented English.

Her head swivels in my direction as I place myself between her and Sir Robert Blake. A smile attempts to pull up her face as she gives me a quick once-over, approves of what she sees enough to speak to me, and glances down at the gown in question.

"Thank you," she replies softly, though there is genuine gratitude in her voice. "It's Barucci."

"No doubt it was designed specifically for you." I turn to Sir Blake. "Isn't she exquisite in it?"

Ever the gentleman with centuries-old ingrained manners running through his blue blood, he gives a small head bow. "Absolutely," he commends, though his eyes are all over my gown, including the ample cleavage I have on display. "And may I extend the same compliment to you in your gown?"

I preen, batting my lashes and even going so far as to blush ever so slightly. A hand lands daintily on the exposed skin just below my neck. "Are you flirting with me, Sir Robert?" I intentionally use the familiarity of his first name and let the smile on my red lips hold.

He lets out a hearty chuckle, not the least bit ruffled. "Can you blame me when I'm in the presence of such beauty?"

A tinkling of a laugh tickles past my lips, and I give the former first lady a playfully conspiratorial *men* roll of my eyes as if we're ancient friends. She returns my look but carries on with her husband, leaving me here with Sir Robert, who falls in line perfectly as he offers me his elbow.

"May I escort you in?" he asks, and I can tell he's searching for my name without asking for it. He doesn't want to be perceived as rude and admit the faux pas that he doesn't know it. I don't take the bait.

"I'd be honored," I tell him, slipping my hand through the crook and resting it on the black of his tuxedo jacket. I keep my head angled toward him and away from the attendants watching everyone closely. "Such a wonderful occasion. It's lovely that the king of Messalina has found love again. Don't you agree?"

This is the second security checkpoint after everyone has already gone through metal detectors, had their bags searched, and been tagged in with facial recognition at the first. I haven't gone through any of that. Instead, I scaled a legit stone wall last night to get inside the grounds, camping without the benefit of a fire, thankful a fucking wolf didn't find me and make me his dinner. I had to get ready for tonight, full-on wig hair, colored contacts, and makeup, in the goddamn woods with no electricity.

As all women can appreciate, thank God for battery-operated devices.

But this is where Sir Robert Blake comes into play.

"Completely," he exclaims earnestly. "I've known Sebastian since he was born. His father and I were close mates and attended the same boys' school in France growing up."

"I had no clue." My lips part, and my expression turns somber as I place my other hand on his chest, allowing the side of my breast to brush his upper arm. "The former king's death must have been such a painful loss for you."

He nods as we step over the threshold and into the chalet, which is more of a castle in the Alps on the border of Messalina and Switzerland. This entrance leads to the ballroom, and no one stops us or even pays us the least bit of attention. After all, Sir Robert Blake is very well known in this country to this family, as he just said.

"I was. It was heartbreaking. But time moves on, and Sebastian has grown into a wonderful king."

"Yes," I agree, removing my hand and taking in the landscape of the sprawling room, dripping in crystal, glowing with endless candles, and fragranced with white and delicate pink flowers. It's regal yet simple and elegant without being pretentious. Inwardly, I wonder if that's the new bride's touch or if she's simply a yes girl to the beast king. Not a lot is known about the American nanny who stole the king's heart.

A server floats by with flutes of champagne, and I snatch one and take a sip. It's delicious. I've never had champagne before. The bubbles tickle my nose, and with them, a giddy sense of temporary freedom vibrates through me. In the corner, an eight-piece orchestra plays Mozart, and the room hums with money and power.

But I don't care about any of that. It's not why I'm here.

Sir Robert puts his hand on the small of my back and leans into me. "How about we find a real drink and some place quiet to talk?"

The man is more than twice my age, but that doesn't matter to him. He's a notorious womanizer and favors women who look exactly like me: young, curves in the right places with dark hair and eyes—hence the wig and contacts. It's why he was so perfect.

I twist back to him with a smile. "I need to run to the ladies' room. Please go ahead, and I'll be sure to find you."

He's not happy about it, and he can likely tell I'm brushing him off, but those manners are incredible weapons I love exploiting, and he simply gives a firm nod and moves on his way. *Good boy*.

With that piece done, I float through the ballroom, keeping my head high while not making eye contact with anyone. My job is to listen. To hear but not be seen. To grab intel so we can plot the next course. So far, it's proving dull and useless. I can't get near the king and his new queen. They're on the opposite side of the ballroom, and their reception line is hours deep.

Plus, I don't exactly want them to see me. Not tonight. Not yet.

Turning the corner, I spot Prince Rowan engaged in conversation with a woman and her daughter. The moment he dismisses them, he takes a sip of his drink and yawns.

For some reason, it makes me giggle, and he hears it, his handsome face bouncing up into a self-deprecating grin, and I get a half-shrug when our eyes meet. Tall and broad, he's devastatingly handsome with short dark hair that's a bit longer on top and coiffed back off his face. He's in a blue royal suit that's perfectly tailored to him, with gold trim and epaulets, as well as medals of honor for service to his country.

"Bored, Your Highness?"

His eyes sweep languidly over me. "Not anymore."

I dip my head but don't engage. "Maybe a splash of espresso will help perk you up."

"Maybe it's the right company I'm lacking," he volleys.

"Best of luck finding it then." I wink and go to leave when he stops me.

"No, wait. Come back. Please come back." He holds his hands up in supplication and gives me a sad puppy dog face with a crooked smile. "I don't even know your name. At least give me that?"

I wave. "Goodbye."

With that, I slip back into the congestion of the room, resisting the urge to turn around and see if he's watching me go.

Unfortunately, I'm stuck with bullshit and not the sexy smirk of the prince. Men talking politics I'm not interested in, nor will they speak candidly with a woman. Women sneering about the new queen—*she's not that pretty; she can't be that interesting; did you see how chubby she is? How quickly did she spread her legs to ensnare the king? How hideous is the scar on her neck?*—that sort of catty bullshit jealous women like to gossip about.

Even their whispers are useless. This wedding is proving to be a waste of my time so far.

Naturally there are murmurs about the former prime minister and his attack on the king and his bride on the night of their engagement. But it's nothing new. Nothing factual. More banal gossip and useless speculation that don't further my cause.

"I bet she's pregnant," a woman in harsh red and too much makeup chides her friend. "Why else would a king, a man like Sebastian, marry crass American trash?"

God, I hate these people. I roll my eyes and turn away from them before her friend can respond, only to lock onto a pair of bright blue eyes aimed directly at me. I start, surprised by how boldly and unapologetically he's looking at me, and when he holds a finger up to his lips, I can't help but smile. He caught my eye roll.

Prince Rowan returns the wink I gave him earlier and polishes off the last of whatever it is he's drinking before he addresses the ladies in French, since that's what they were speaking. "As my new sister-in-law, I can attest Bellamy's actually quite wonderful and enchanting," he interjects. "Hardly..." His face scrunches up. "What did you call her? Crass American trash, was it?"

The women are appalled, instantly dropping into deep curtsies. "Your Royal Highness," they whisper in unison, their voices now demur. "You misunderstood," one continues after she rises to her full height, giving him come-fuck-me eyes without the least bit of shame. They all want to be the next to snag royalty and force him down the aisle. "We were simply reiterating the ghastly things we'd overheard others saying about her this evening."

"Mmm. Yes. Ghastly and petty, I'd say. I hope the next time you hear such lies, you pass along my message about the new queen of Messalina."

Savage. I like it. If only I weren't here to ruin his brother's life.

But I shouldn't be part of this, and I shouldn't have caught his attention.

I start to move away, only for a hand to wrap around my elbow, stopping me. "Running off on me again so soon?"

"Yes," I tell him bluntly, speaking in French as I shirk his grip. "Gossip and female bashing make me thirsty, and I'm in search of a drink without bubbles."

"Allow me to assist." He holds up his hand, and magically a waiter appears at his side.

I give him an unimpressed look, though that was impressive. "Do you always have people at your beck and call?"

"It comes with the uniform. What can I get you?"

Great. No getting out of this now. "A vodka dirty martini." I've never had one of those either, but it was what my father always drank.

Prince Rowan steps in front of me, standing annoyingly close. "You can't dance with that in your hand."

I arch a brow as I lift my chin. "Who said I was planning to dance?"

"I did. And since you now know people are at my beck and call, I'd like to dance with you."

"That's very high-handed."

"That's not an answer," he parries.

I curtsy. "Thank you, Your Highness, but I must respectfully decline your request."

He grins, mischief dancing in his blue eyes. "If that were a request, you'd know it."

Well then. I puff out a laugh. "Then I must respectfully decline whatever you're deciding to call that."

His gaze wanders about my face and body. It's a move I shouldn't care about. A move I should automatically dismiss as I have with every other male who's done it in the past. But something about him doing it, the look of not just heat but of actual fire and seduction mixed with a dirty promise, makes my chest flutter and my skin hot. And let's face it, my untouched vagina is both of those too.

"Make that two," he says to the waiter, who bows and scurries off, anxious to get away from us so he can make our drinks. "Now you can tell me your name."

Except I can't. Not that it or I would be familiar to him, but he still can't know my name. Instead, I go with a version of it, even when I likely shouldn't.

"Ella." I practically whisper it.

"Ella," he repeats, and it's almost sinful how my name moves across his full lips. "See, I'm not bored anymore." He steps into me and wraps his hand around my waist. "Dance with me. It's not a request."

I narrow my gaze defiantly. "I don't follow orders."

His face dips until we're inches apart, and for the first time all night, despite all the moves I've made and the risks I've taken, nerves hit, and adrenaline floods my veins. I can feel his breath, sweetened by bourbon, against my lips, and the scent of his expensive cologne surrounds me. It's heady and intoxicating, and I hate that my body responds in kind, inching in ever so subtly.

"I wonder if that's true," he muses, almost to himself.

His words ghost over me, and my insides twist painfully. My entire life is about following orders with nothing for myself. It's almost as if he can see through me, and I don't like it.

"Beautiful Ella, would you do me the great honor of dancing with me? At least until my beck and call returns with our drinks."

Damn him for being so charming and leaving me no option but to say yes. Because much like how I exploited Sir Robert's manners, Prince Rowan is exploiting me with charm he's wielding like a weapon.

Still, I don't curtsy. "Thank you, Your Highness, I'd be honored."

His lips twitch. "Liar. But I don't care. I want to dance with you."

He should care. He has no clue who or what I am.

Beyond my silver-blue gown, my dark hair perfectly placed, and the real diamonds sparkling in my ears, he has no clue. He sees me as a guest of the royal wedding. An attendee. An easy fuck like the rest of the women in here.

The reality is, I'm a ruse. An assassin doing her research before I strike. This family is the nightmare of my nonexistent life.

His large hand slides around me before it comes to rest on my hip, where he gives me a squeeze. His eyes are glazed as they hold mine before his lips shift to my ear.

"Where did you come from, and why have I not seen you before tonight?" he whispers, his voice sending shivers up my spine that I fight.

The answer is not so simple.

"I'm here on behalf of someone else."

"Who?" he presses when I let it die there.

"My fairy godmother," I tease. And she's as wicked as they come.

He gives me a wry grin. "Then that makes you mine until at least midnight." He moves my hand onto his forearm so he can escort me to the dance floor in the center of the freaking room, and now all goddamn eyes are on us.

Prince Rowan has a reputation as a bit of a playboy.

He's fucked his way around Europe a time or two.

So I don't take this all that seriously. I doubt most people here do. He's had more photographs with women than *Playboy* did in the sixties. But they're still looking, wondering, questioning, and that's the last thing I can afford. Then again, if anyone has intel, it's him. Maybe Prince Rowan is the piece I've been missing all night.

Perhaps a dance or two won't hurt anything.

This entire night has been a bore. Person after person shaking my hand and bowing and trying to impress me while asking when I'll be the next to settle down. Then there are the women. The same old women in the same old gowns with the same old look. Women of money, power, and influence. Their daughters, too.

Vultures who came here tonight to gossip, make connections, and try to snag a prince as their prize.

Yawn.

I've turned it into a bit of a game. With every new introduction, seductive look, or flirty remark, I take a sip of my drink. I've upped the ante to add drinking to every snarky remark made about Bellamy. By the end of this night, I'll either be too drunk to have fucks left to give or start speaking my mind instead of taking the diplomatic route as I've been trained to.

It's the Bellamy shit-talking that's throwing me over the edge more than the advantageous women. I thank the heavens daily for my new sister-in-law. She not only broke the curse but also brought my asshole of a brother back to life. She's sunshine and beauty, and these women have ugly, greed-darkened souls.

They're all the same. Every single one of them.

Until her. Ella. Raven hair, dark eyes, come-fuck-me red lips, and a sharp-as-a-knife tongue. She was right there watching me, catching me yawn in the middle of a royal wedding party. After casually calling me out for being exactly what I was, bored, she simply sauntered off as if she hadn't just made it impossible to take a breath.

I watched her go, irritated she didn't so much as look back once. The one woman in the entire place I actually wanted to talk to, and she wasn't interested. It took me another hour to find her, but I did. Now I have her in my arms with no intention of letting her go tonight.

The orchestra throws me a bone and picks some version of a popular song and plays it to a soft tempo. I bring her into my arms, one hand on her lower back and the other holding her hand. Her hands have a texture. Like fine sandpaper. It surprises me. These aren't the hands of a lady. These hands are no strangers to work. And her eyes. There's something about them. About the particular shade of black-brown.

Still, even as the questions mount, I can't stop staring at her. It was actually her skin I noticed first. It's creamy white and such a contrast to her hair, eyes, and dark makeup. It's so damn pretty and almost glows silver like her gown. She also smells good. Like fresh air and winter nights and heat. Not like perfume but like skin.

Inwardly, I chuckle. I'm fucking drunk. When the hell have I ever noticed a woman's *skin* before? A woman who is also visibly unhappy to be dancing with me and making sure she keeps a solid bubble of space between us.

It makes me smile like a devil.

"Do you think the space you're forcing will keep you safe from me?"

I get a quirked eyebrow. "Do I need safety from you, Your Highness?"

My hand on her lower back slips a notch, and I draw her in where I want her. This time, she doesn't fight me. Her hand on my shoulder slides to the crook of my neck at my collar as I spin us around the dance floor, ignoring the annoying tickling sensation of eyes on us.

"Call me Rowan."

"Are you safe for me, Rowan?"

The way she says my name in that sexy voice of hers makes my cock twitch.

"I'm the safest person in the room."

A small tinkling of a laugh hits her lips, so light and sweet. Such a contradiction to everything dark she appears to be. "There's nothing safe about you, Your Highness."

I twirl us in circles, both of us good enough dancers that we don't have to mind the steps, and I can focus on her. "Does that thought excite you?"

She stares up at me as if she's giving this genuine thought. "Perhaps. But before you start getting ahead of yourself with me, I'm not safe either."

"Noted." Challenge accepted. "I like the way you said my name."

"Don't get used to it."

"But what if I can make you scream it?" I whisper into the shell of her ear, and before she can answer, just to play with her a bit and keep her off guard, I use the hand I'm holding and spin her out onto the dance floor before I snap her back into me. She gives me a dismayed head shake for that move, especially as there's applause around us, but I catch the hint of a smile on the corner of her lips. It's there underneath all the red and sass.

"You're the worst sort of flirt, aren't you?"

"You're the only woman in the room I want to flirt with."

I get an eye roll that makes my lips twitch. I don't think a woman has ever rolled her eyes at me. I'm starting to understand why Sebastian found Bellamy's back talk and cheek so appealing.

"You just proved my point," she says. "I have a feeling we were photographed."

Ah. So that explains her sour expression.

"Maybe one or two photos," I agree, shifting my hand so I can use her lower back to press her back into me. "Phones aren't allowed in here tonight, as you know, but there is the royal photographer."

"Lovely. I'll be sure to use it on next year's holiday card."

"You'll have to send me one then. Maybe we should smile and pose to make it extra special." I move us between the other dancers, looping us back to the edge of the dance floor so we're not the center of attention.

Her head tilts. "Is that why you're dancing with me? For the fans?"

I chuckle lightly. "Not even close." I bring my mouth to her ear. "You don't have to worry. I won't let any photographs get published. I've got you. Try enjoying yourself with me. A wedding party is meant to be fun, and I want to have fun with you."

Her eyes sparkle up at me, twin pools of midnight, and her hand finally comes up to my neck. It's different than holding her hand. Hotter. Sharper. Like static electricity. It makes me wish I could touch more of her, but her dress goes up her back practically to her neck.

"What do you say?" I press when she doesn't respond. "Can we have some fun with each other tonight?"

"Tonight?" she questions, and my insides quicken. It's an odd feeling. Like excitement when I haven't been excited about anyone in a very long time.

"Tonight," I confirm, my eyes on her lips before I slowly

trail up to her eyes. I can't kiss her here, and I have to keep reminding myself to maintain boundaries. "All night. Tomorrow morning. Through the weekend. Honestly, I might not want to let you go."

Her fingers tickle the ends of my hair. "I don't plan to give you the choice. But I can have fun with you for now. I don't very often, so let's give it a try."

I bring her hand to my lips and kiss her knuckles when I spot our waiter on the outskirts of the dance floor holding our drinks.

"Perfect timing." I move us that way, thanking him as I release her hand so I can pass her one of them. She takes it, patiently waiting for me to take mine. "Cheers."

"Cheers."

Our glasses clink, and we each take hearty sips, our eyes holding because I can't seem to look away from her. Hardly even for a moment. She winces slightly and gently coughs.

"Not what you wanted?"

She clears her throat. "A bit stronger than I'm used to."

"I don't particularly like dirty martinis. I'm more of a whiskey man. Where are you from, Ella?"

"Messalina," she deadpans.

My brows bounce in feigned surprise, and I point at my chest. "No kidding? Me too."

"Har, har, Your Highness."

I wink, but she's a tough one to soften up. "You're not going to give me any details about yourself, are you? You'll make me work for everything I get."

She shifts her weight in her heels but stands up straighter, the stiff fabric of her gown rustling against me as she turns serious. "You could have any woman in this room, Your Highness. Why are you bothering with the one who doesn't want any part of the world you come with?"

"Probably because that's what I like most about you," I tell her honestly. "If I wanted those other women, I'd be with them instead of with you."

"Except I shouldn't be here with you," she states bluntly. "I should turn around and walk away and leave this place behind."

My knuckles brush her cheek. "You don't want to do that." It's all over her face. The reluctance. The inner battle. "Are you married?"

"No," she answers quickly, even if she seems unsure and out of sorts for the first time all night. "Not married. Not engaged. I've never even had a boyfriend."

That's...surprising. It has to be her choice. Any man who looks at her would kill to have her on their arm and claim her as theirs. My guess is she's a sheltered girl from an aristocratic family. The kind of girl who gets paired and married off for money and station. Her parents are likely in this room but don't seem to care that she's dancing and talking to the prince enough to interject. Hell, they're probably loving it.

"Then why shouldn't you be here with me?"

She emits a humorless laugh and takes another sip of her drink. "You mean other than the fact that you're the prince?"

I narrow my gaze. "How old are you?"

"Twenty-three."

"I'm thirty-three."

She smirks mockingly. "I know how old you are."

"So other than the fact that I'm the prince, why shouldn't you be here with me?" I challenge her attempt at a rhetorical question as I stare her down. I don't want her to go. I want her to stay with me. I can't explain it. Maybe that's foolish. Maybe I'm drunk and simply like the way she looks and how she's entirely different from every other woman in this room. Whatever. I don't exactly give a shit if that's my reason.

There's something compelling about her. A siren in a sea of boredom.

She puffs out a breath and twists a piece of her long, dark hair, glancing out into the room, at all the people around us, before returning to me. "Oh hell. It's just for tonight, right? Fuck it."

A laugh bursts from my chest. "I'm good with that. Do you think we can risk more dancing?"

"Sure." She finishes off her drink in two large gulps. "Let's dance, Your Highness."

"Rowan," I correct as I finish off my drink, take her glass, and set them on a nearby table before I retake her hand. This time it's a traditional waltz, and I twirl us around in perfect step. She keeps up easily, a sweet smile on her face for the first time all night.

Her head moves around, studying the crowd on the dance floor until she stops on the far side, her head swiveling around so she can continue to watch Sebastian and Bellamy talk quietly with each other, laughing and touching the way they always do. Their mutual obsession has only gotten stronger now that she's pregnant with twins.

A frown tugs down her lips. "They look happy," she notes.

I glance over and smile, especially when Zayer climbs onto Bellamy's lap and tucks against her, more than a little exhausted at the late hour and the long day. She kisses his chubby cheeks and rubs his back. It makes my heart swell.

"They are happy. Happy to be together. Happy to be a family again. Happy to be alive."

She returns to me, her brows furrowed. "You mean after what happened with the prime minister?"

"It was brutal," I admit, a shiver racing up my spine as I think back to that night. "I've had some pretty rough moments in my life, but that's right up there with losing my father."

I can't believe I just said that aloud. I don't know this woman, and I'm saying too much, alcohol loosening my lips.

Her hand touches my cheek, forcing me back to her. "Your

family has endured a lot, as have the people of Messalina. I'll admit, we're in a bit of turmoil after the attack. Strange how such a beloved prime minister could turn out of nowhere on the king and his fiancée."

I search her eyes. "People aren't always who you imagine them to be. What you see isn't always what you get. A lot of hatred and evil lived in his heart."

"Particularly toward the king, it seems. It's just difficult to wrap my head around it. Samil Batorini always seemed so kind. So fun-loving and full of life with a deep sense of honor for his country, whereas the king was cold and distant. A beast king. Isn't that what they called him?" She licks her lips and looks back over at them. "In any event, I'm relieved the king and his new bride are well, and that we're able to celebrate them and this wonderful occasion."

The soft chime of a bell tinkles through the clatter and causes the orchestral music, along with our dancing, to come to a halt. "Your Majesties." The master of ceremonies bows at Sebastian and Bellamy before addressing the rest of the room. "Honored guests. Dinner is served. We ask that you kindly join us in the dining room."

Everyone starts to shuffle their way toward the entrance, but if we go in there, I'll lose her. That'll be it. She'll sit at whatever table she's supposed to sit at, and I'll be at the head table with Sebastian, Bellamy, Althea, and the children. And while I was looking forward to that earlier this evening, now it feels like the last place I want to be.

Before she can take so much as a step, I lean into her and whisper, "Come upstairs with me."

A breath catches in her lungs, but she meets my eyes, even as hers are pinched in confusion. "Just like that?"

"Just like that." My knuckles drag along her soft cheek. "I don't want to go to dinner. I don't want lobster or chateaubriand or whatever they're serving. I want you. Come upstairs with me."

My blood is thrumming through my veins nearly to the point of pain as I watch her deliberate my offer. I'm desperate for her to say yes. Desperate in a way I'm not sure I've been where a woman is concerned.

It's insane. I know this. It makes no sense, and I can't make heads or tails of it. I just met her, and I don't know anything about her. Not her last name or even which part of my country she comes from, or who she came with, since she seems so different from everyone here.

She doesn't seem interested in me beyond tonight, and that should be a red flag, because everyone wants to fuck and marry a prince, even if they don't give two shits about who I actually am beyond that. Months ago, when I came home to Messalina and watched Sebastian fall in love, I quickly realized fucking my way from one woman to the next had lost its appeal. Then there's the not-so-small issue that I'm expected to be the next to marry. That's how this works in our world. In our country. Especially now that the curse has been broken. It's why every woman was hot on my heels all night.

So I shouldn't be doing this.

But I fucking *want* her.

When she still hasn't given me an answer, my hand slips up along her cheek, and I adjust her face until I have her the way I want her. Without warning or even giving a shit about who sees this and who doesn't, I lean in and press my lips to hers. I rest them there, waiting for her to push me away. And when she doesn't, when her large, dark eyes are bold and wide and locked on mine, I repeat myself for a third time.

"Come upstairs with me, Ella."

3

———

MARCELLA

I need to say no to him. I'm not a friend. I'm not going to be his lover. I'm a woman sent here on a mission by some truly evil people with a connecting revenge agenda of my own. It's a mission that involves his family, not in a kind of fluffy way. They believe the ancient curse on the royal family has been broken, but if my stepmother and her niece, Antonia, have their way, the curse is about to get a second act, and I'm the villain who will make that happen.

I'm a pawn in a bigger game of chess controlled by a ruthless hand.

So I should say no.

But I don't want to. I wasn't lying when I said I don't have fun. I have nothing for myself. I never have. Not since my father died when I was a girl, and I was forced to see the life I thought I knew ripped away from me. I quickly came to realize the cold, unfathomable truth about who and what I am. My father slept around, and I'm the result of one of his trysts. A daughter not even worthy of sharing his last name.

Now I'm a servant. A slave. A snake hiding in the grass, waiting to strike with fangs and deadly venom. That's not only who I had to become to survive, but also what I've been trained to be.

But that night is not tonight.

The wedding was a bust in terms of recon, and there's something about the prince that's annoyingly irresistible. He gives me ridiculous girlish butterflies. The kind I've read about but never experienced. One night with him won't change anything. I'll still do whatever I have to do. Sex is sex, or so I've been told, and that's all this will be.

What my stepmother and Antonia don't know won't hurt them, so it won't hurt me.

I push Rowan back until his lips are no longer touching mine and stare up into his oh-so-blue eyes, ringed in thick, soft, dark lashes. His expression is intense and earnest. Hopeful. It almost makes me smile. It certainly makes my heart beat faster.

My fingers pad along the lines of his straight nose and smooth, sharp, square jawline and full lips that I bet can kiss me into next week. He leans into my touch as if he's anxious for more of it, and I wonder if one day I'll ever have a moment to be free like this again.

I doubt it.

Regardless, he's so good-looking it hurts. "All right, Rowan. Take me upstairs."

His eyes shift around my face, his hand on my cheek going near my hair, and I freeze. Shit. My wig. Then there's my back to consider too.

He misinterprets my freezing and whispers, "Don't worry, it's just us left in here."

With that, his lips meet mine, only now they're not resting, they're taking. Claiming. His lips split my own, and his tongue slides inside. I don't know exactly what I'm doing, so I do my best to follow his lead. He tilts his head and groans when our tongues touch and he gets a better taste of me.

"Fuck, that's good," he mumbles against me, stealing

another kiss, then pulls back, his lips a little wet, and his eyes smoky and dark.

He takes my hand and walks us through the empty space. The sound of dinner in the neighboring ballroom filters in, and a hiccup of unease hits me. I was supposed to leave by now. I had no place at dinner, and I knew it. The cocktail hour was my time, and I feel as though I failed, even if I was able to break in and bypass royal security. I learned nothing except useless gossip and baseless jealousies. Other than one strong sticking point.

The king and his bride actually seem to be in love.

Which means we won't be able to use Queen Bellamy as a weapon. If anything, she could be leveraged against him, but the former prime minister already tried that and failed. It wasn't a stretch to believe the king fell for the beautiful younger nanny. But the reverse, that the younger, beautiful American nanny actually fell in love with the king, was. Now it seems we may need to figure out another angle.

Rowan takes me onto the elevator, and the moment the doors close, he pushes me up against the wall and buries his face in my neck. My head falls back against the wall, and my eyes close as my hands find the soft strands of his hair. He kisses and nips and licks at my skin, and my head spins.

He's good at this. At seduction. He's not mindlessly groping and ripping at clothes to shove himself inside me the way I imagined men did. At least that's what the men who have tried with me in the past did, only they didn't make it all that far before I either killed them or ruined them.

The elevator doors open, and with reluctance, he draws back from me so he can lead me down the hall.

"Your dress is a lot of dress," he grumbles, his lips on my neck, his chest to my back while he attempts to get under it.

I can't help it. I giggle. His struggle is real as he pulls and tugs and lifts and adjusts a million layers of fabric. Finally his hands locate my thighs and glide up until he reaches the globes of my ass.

"I knew it. You're perfect." He gives me a firm squeeze and a soft smack. "Shit, I'm so fucking hard for you. Your ass…"

He lets it end there as we reach a door, and he swipes a plastic room key against the keypad. There aren't many rooms on this floor. Two other doors, but that's it. The lever swishes down, and he holds the door open for me, allowing me to enter first. It's a suite, of course, spacious and luxurious with every trimming and refinement you'd expect in a five-star hotel and fit for, well, royalty.

On the bar is a bottle of champagne on ice, two flutes, and an assortment of chocolate truffles, but that has nothing on the red rose petals scattered everywhere. I turn and arch a brow only to be treated to a shrug and the most outrageously boyish smile, complete with fucking dimples.

"It was supposed to be Sebastian and Bellamy's honeymoon suite, only they decided to stay at our family's chalet up the road, so I took it over. For security, we told no one."

"Oh."

He chuckles and goes for the bottle of champagne, removing the foil and cork with a loud pop. I take the glass and drink half of it down, nerves striking me in a very innocent, virginal way.

He takes a sip of his drink, his eyes all over me, adding to those nerves to the point where I can hardly stand it. I head toward the bedroom, finishing off my drink as I go. I hear ice shift around against metal, then suddenly he's behind me.

"Another?"

I shouldn't. I'm already rocking a fierce buzz or am perhaps drunk. But I think I need it all the same. I nod, and he refills my glass, the head of white fizzy bubbles effervescing, blanketing out the rush of blood in my ears against the otherwise quiet of the room. I force two more gulps down, ignoring how they tickle and burn my nose, before I set it on a nearby table and turn to face him.

I don't want him to see my back. I don't want him to touch it.

Reaching behind, I work the zipper down, and he stands before me, his eyes hooded. His thumb glides along his bottom lip, the tip of his tongue following the motion, and it's so fucking sexy, I push aside my nerves and let the dress fall to my waist.

He sucks in a rush of air as his gaze drops to my bare chest, and when he fully takes me in, he curses under his breath in Russian, of all things.

Firm hands cup my breasts, lifting them to test their weight and thrusting them together. His thumbs brush over my nipples, and my head falls back of its own volition because holy fuck. How can his touch feel infinitely better than when I do it myself?

His lips meet the soft skin of my neck, his breath hot and heavy against me as he toys with my tits, squeezing and pinching my nipples. His lips are all over me, kissing and licking my neck and shoulder and up to my jaw. I move my fake hair over one shoulder and work the dress lower. The bottom half is another matter, clasped around my waist with a hook and another zipper. Before I can do it, his fingers catch the hook. I freeze, hoping he doesn't venture north. Thankfully, he doesn't, and I breathe out a sigh of relief.

He removes my dress, helping me step out of it until I'm in nothing but a thong and heels. Pretty underwear. Pretty shoes. Pretty diamonds in my ears. None of them are mine to keep.

His lips trail down my chest, sucking and licking at my tits as he moves lower and lower until he's kneeling before me. A prince on his knees for me, and I shake my head, utterly at a loss. I should tell him this is my first time, but I don't. I can't force the words out, and I don't want to have the conversation that will inevitably come with it. He gazes up at me, giving me a wickedly sinister grin as he tugs on my nipples and kisses my mound over my thong. His hot breath tickles the wetness pooling and makes my clit throb.

Holy fuck! I nearly collapse. As it is, I make an embarrassingly loud moan.

"So beautiful," he rasps against me. "You're so fucking beautiful. And you smell"—he takes a deep inhale of me over my thong, and my eyes roll back in my head—"so fucking good."

I comb back the thick strands of his hair and stare down at him, shaky and bewildered by all of this. Men have called me beautiful. I have a pretty face and good-sized tits. I've never been insecure about that. Honestly, I've never given my body much thought until now, but I'm far from perfect. Scarred back and muscular thighs and arms. But his saying how he thinks I'm beautiful when I'm standing in front of him like this hits me differently than any man who's said it to me before.

Probably because I've never been nude in front of anyone.

One by one, he removes my shoes, followed by my thong, and here I am completely naked while he's still fully dressed. He's aware of this contrast and anxious to remedy it because while he playfully kisses and licks at my pussy, he's shucking off his formal jacket and works the buttons of his shirt.

My gentle fingers in his hair turn into a vise grip when his tongue flicks my clit. I stumble backward, my knees practically giving out on me, even as he cups my ass and holds me to his face.

He chuckles against me, the vibration insane on my pussy. "You still with me?"

I laugh. "I won't be in a minute if you keep doing that to me while I'm standing."

"Come here, gorgeous." He takes my hips, picks me up, and sets me down on the bed. I crawl back and prop myself up on my elbows. "Better. Damn, so much fucking better. Shit." He rakes me in as he finishes getting his shirt off. I return the favor, memorizing the cut lines of his chest, shoulders, and abs. "Spread your legs. I want to see you."

A flash of girlish insecurity runs through me, but it burns off into nothing with the heat of desire in his eyes. I slide my legs along the silky duvet, shuddering as the fabric runs along my skin.

I spread my legs for him and gasp when I feel his hands on my inner thighs, holding me there.

He's glued to my pussy, utterly rapt as he slips a finger inside me as if he's testing me out. He groans and rubs his cock with his other hand over his trousers. "Fuck, you're tight. Jesus. I'm going to come so fast once I'm inside of you if I'm not careful. Come here."

He crooks a finger at me, but I don't have the chance to obey as he slips his hand under my ass, grips one cheek, and yanks me down until I practically fall off the edge.

His mouth covers my cunt, his tongue shoving up inside me, and I automatically throw my head back and let out a cry that would embarrass me if I could think past the wet heat on my pussy.

"Shit. Fuck!" he groans, low and loud, holding me against his mouth with his hands. He's moving. Grinding. Rubbing into the bed, and I prop myself up higher, curious as to what he's doing when I realize he just came. Holy shit. He came from tasting me.

He doesn't seem to care.

If anything, it's made him more feral because his arms loop around my thighs, and his face buries in me. His tongue thrusts up inside me, fucking deep and fast. It's so wet. The sound is so fucking wet, and he's groaning and grunting with it. He shifts one hand and uses it to press down on my mound so his thumb can rub my clit.

"Rowan!" flies from my lips, my hand ripping at his hair,

and it sets him off. He digs deeper to the point where I don't know how he can breathe. I grind into him, riding his face, unable to stop my body's reaction. He's rubbing my clit, pinching it, pressing down on it, but his mouth…his wicked, diabolical, delicious fucking mouth is feasting on me. He's ravenous, licking and fucking and sucking. It's so much. *Too much*. I can't control or slow the climb.

"So good," he murmurs. "I need you to come. I need to taste your cum."

I nod. I don't know why I'm nodding. He can't see me do it, but it's more of an affirmation because I'm so close. My hips roll into him as my eyes roll into the back of my head. One hand is in his hair, the other balls up the blanket in my fist. I feel. That's all I do. I'm consumed by it. I don't think about anything other than what this *feels* like. How incredible it is.

A curl of heat and tingles starts deep in my core, like his tongue is tickling it, urging it on, stoking the flame and giving it life to breathe until the sensation spreads. It takes over, making my limbs seize and my pussy clench, and holy shit, I'm coming. I'm coming so fucking hard I can barely think through it as it robs me of everything.

It's insanely intense. So unlike anything I've ever given myself.

"Oh god. Oh hell. Oh fuck!" I'm all sounds and thrashing movements.

"Fuck, yes. That's it. Make me take it. Give me all of it. So fucking good, Ella."

My back arches and my body splinters, and that's all it is. Sparks and heat and sensation. Rowan doesn't stop. He doesn't let up. He licks and sucks and rubs me until I can't take it for another second.

I sag, my limbs boneless, and for a moment, I can't move. I'm winded, my eyes closed while a heady, hazy swirl colors my mind. I hear him moving. Shifting. Chuckling. I crack open an eye, and he's staring down at his slacks where his cock is already hard again, straining through the fabric and wet with his cum.

"I came in my pants like a fucking teenager. That's never happened before, even when I was a teenager." He climbs over me and kisses me deeply, his hands on my face and his tongue in my mouth. I taste myself on him. Clean and salty and a little sweet. The sweet part, I think, is him and champagne, and I'm drunk. I'm so drunk right now. On alcohol. On sex endorphins. On him. That last one I'm trying very hard not to think about.

He gets up off the bed, removes his pants and boxer briefs, and walks naked over to a suitcase on a stand in the corner. He fishes through it, and I stare at his rock-hard ass, still in shock that I'm here in the prince's hotel room. He locates a condom, rips it open with his teeth, and slides it on. I need to tell him. I need to say something.

I fold my lips and bite almost to the point of drawing blood.

I don't challenge him. I don't mention that I have an IUD because my stepmother doesn't want me to get pregnant or even have a period, or that things are good on my end because I've never done this before. This is already giving him a piece of myself I'll never get back, and the idea of feeling him inside of me with nothing between us...yeah, no.

Not gonna do it.

With his eyes on mine and a cocky smirk on his lips, he's back on me, kissing me, touching me, licking my tits like a man who can't get enough. Like a man who's just getting started. His face hovers above mine, and his hand slips my thigh over his hips. I'm trembling, and he feels it.

"I've got you."

It's all he says. He doesn't ask if I'm ready. He simply watches my face as he plays with my pussy using the head of his cock. And when he reaches the point of no return for both of us, he rams into me, giving me all ten thick inches at once, and I cry out at the top of my lungs, my body seizing as stabbing pain shoots through my lower abdomen.

"What the fuck?!" His hand is on my face, shaking it ever so slightly to try and force my eyes open. Tears sting, burning the tip of my nose, and those alone would make me laugh if I had humor in me at the moment. "Ella, what the fuck?"

I blow out the tense breath and slowly open my eyes. He's right above me, concern in his black-as-midnight eyes.

"I'm a virgin."

He stares at me and stares at me and stares at me. He's still inside of me, but he hasn't moved. Something I appreciate. Still, the word doesn't seem to make much sense to him.

"A virgin." It's not a question. He can feel it as much as I can, no doubt. "You didn't say anything."

"I didn't want you to know."

He chuckles mirthlessly, his tone incredulous. "You didn't think I'd figure it out?"

"I knew you would, but by that point, it'd be too late."

He shifts to his side, digging one elbow into the mattress so he can caress my face. He wipes an errant tear that somehow escaped and kisses me. "I would have been gentle. Eased in. Taken it slower. Checked in with you."

"You would have stopped," I accuse.

He grins devilishly. "Don't be so sure about that." He glances down at the space between us and groans. "Fuck, look at that. I made you bleed." His voice is tinted in awe. "All of this is mine now, isn't it? I'm the only man to be inside you. You have no idea what that's doing to me." He kisses me and comes back over me. "Can I move? Are you ready for me to move?"

I don't think I'll ever be ready for him to move, but I nod all the same.

Slowly, he pulls mostly out only to roll his hips back in. It burns, but I think the worst is over.

"Jesus fucking Christ." His eyes roll back and close, and he bites his lip, his body stilling as his fists clench. It's so fucking hot I can hardly take it. The way he's falling apart over simply pushing into me. Over tasting me. It's undoing parts of me that can't be undone. That must stay rigid and relentless and unyielding.

But when his forehead falls to mine, and our lips meet, and he slides out only to shove harshly back in, I know it's too late. He's breathing life into parts of me that never existed before tonight. Parts that were stifled and smothered and killed before they ever had a chance to live.

"Hell, Ella," he hisses, his face still pinched up. "How?"

That's all he asks. How. I don't know what he's asking, and yet I do. How can it feel this good? How can it only be tonight? How are we here together like this, and how can we make it last just a little longer?

"Are you okay? Does it hurt still?"

"No."

That's all I give him. It doesn't hurt anymore. It's starting to feel otherworldly good.

My hands find his firm-as-fuck ass, and I hold on, squeezing, urging him to start fucking me because if he doesn't right now, I might die. That's how amazing his cock inside of me feels. Full and deep and perfect. So incredible words can't even begin to imagine this. I moan as he starts to pump, his hands planted into the bed on either side of my head, his fucks deep and penetrating. His hips undulate, rolling into me, massaging something inside of me that has me angling up, desperate for more.

My hips thrust up to meet his, my body taking over, going on instinct instead of practice or knowledge. I keep my eyes closed. He's watching me. I know he is. But if I look at him right now with him inside of me like this...I can't.

His arms wrap around my shoulders, pressing my tits to his chest, and he drops his mouth to my neck. My thighs shift higher, going up to his hips, and feeling delicious friction on my clit as I do. Over and over, he takes me, ripping cries and moans and whimpers from my lips. From his lips. We're sweaty and loud and fucking like we have eternity. On and on, he doesn't stop. The bed bangs against the wall with a constant *thump, thump, thump.*

"Rowan..." I can't go beyond that. I'm on the brink of something, and I don't know what it is or how I'll get there. I just know that I have to.

He seems to know what I'm asking for without me having to say anything else. He puts his thumb in my mouth, and I suck on it, getting it nice and wet before he pulls it free and uses it to rub my clit. That, combined with the way his cock pummels me, massaging every nerve ending in my pussy, catapults me right to the brink.

A shudder racks through me. My head falls back. My eyes pinch shut. My pussy does things I didn't know it could do, growing swollen and tight, with an ache that's so perfect I never want it to stop.

His hot breath pants against my ear. His sweat tickles my cheek. "Ella. Ella. Do you feel this?"

The pure pleasure and wonderment in his voice is what does me in, and I detonate, going to another plane of existence. My nails tear at his back, my teeth dig into his shoulder, and I come so hard I hardly know how to manage it.

"Fuck. God. Yes. That. You."

He follows me over the edge with a roar, his back arching, and the muscles in his neck and jaw growing taut. I realize I'm watching him come. I never imagined something like that would be as hot or sexy as it is, but hell, if it's not. He's coming inside me. Into a condom, yes, but he's having an orgasm inside of me, and I don't know what it is about that, but it does something funny to my insides. It's like I want him to do that again and again when I know perfectly well that can't happen.

His body jerks and spasms two more times before he collapses on me, breathing raggedly even as he touches, kisses, and praises how good that was.

He pulls out of me, and I wince at the small burn that creates. The condom is removed and tied off before he tosses it into the trash and immediately puts on another. This time I fuck him from on top. It's hard and hot and heavy. My tits bounce while my body takes him as deep as I can go. I come two more times on his cock. He makes sure of it.

And when he passes out, kissing my neck and snuggled against me as I lie flat on my back, I allow myself this moment. I pretend and daydream. It's sweet and weird and ridiculous and not the least bit smart. But it's just me. No one else will ever know of these thoughts. So I let them run wild, and when he falls asleep, looking so sated and peaceful, I kiss his lips, slip out of bed, and go.

I sneak back into the cold night, the hour late, as I camp out deep in the woods. It isn't until I pull off my wig to get changed out of my gown that I realize one of my earrings fell out. And was likely left behind with my midnight prince.

ROWAN

I wake to sunlight stabbing through a gap in the curtains, a precise beam of torture that finds my eyelids like it was aimed there on purpose. My head throbs in rhythm with my pulse, and my mouth feels like it was stuffed with cotton, my tongue like sandpaper. Fragments of last night swim through the murky waters of my memory. The diplomatic small talk. The women vying for my attention.

Her.

Ella. A vision in a silver-blue gown with hair and eyes like midnight. A smile cracks across my dry lips, and despite my headache, I roll over and feel the bed beside me, anxious to grab onto her and pull her into me for another round. For another hundred rounds. I'm here through the weekend, and there's nothing I'd like more than to spend it in this bed with her.

Except she's not there, and the place where her body was when I fell asleep is empty. Cold. My eyes pinch closed, and I release a breath. Did she run out on me? Maybe she's in the bathroom? But even as I twist my head in that direction, I don't have to see the open door or note that the room is dark to know she's not in there. It's too quiet in the suite.

She's not here.

Fuck.

I scrub my hands up and down my face and push away from the bed with my elbows until I'm sitting, my feet on the floor and my head in my hands. I feel like shit. But it's got nothing on waking up alone after the night we had. She gave me her virginity. A piece of her no one else will ever get, and she's gone. The sex was incredible. But so was she, and I'm extremely disappointed she fled without a word.

I chuckle humorlessly. My pride is also more than a little wounded.

I suppose I deserve it after all the women I screwed around with and walked away from without a backward glance. But that was before, and this is now, and...shit. I wanted more of her. It was just sex, but I felt a connection with her. I did. More than taking her virginity. From the moment I saw her, I wanted her. And when she opened her smart mouth, she had me.

Clearly it wasn't the same for her.

"Motherfucker," I grind out, more than a little bitter. Definitely angry.

Who was she?

Pushing myself out of bed, I head for the bathroom when a sharp pain slices up the bottom of my foot and something hard presses into the soft flesh. I step back and glance down, squinting at the object nestled into the threads of the thick carpet. Bending, I pick up an earring. Heavy for its size, the diamonds are substantial. I rest the twisted teardrops in my palm. The facets pick up the sunlight, casting tiny rainbows about.

I close my eyes and try to remember the details of her face that aren't coming in all that clear. I drank too much, and it bothers me now that I did.

Setting the diamond on the nightstand, I chug a bottle of water and get in the shower. The hot water helps to clear my head but not that much. I never got her last name. Never knew where she came from. She spoke in French, and I assumed she was the daughter of a member of parliament or some French dignitary. We danced and teased each other, and she wasn't all that interested in doing either with me at first, but she still came back to my room.

She must have snuck out sometime after midnight, leaving me with her earring and no last name, like a modern-day Cinderella. I laugh. I'm going to catch such shit for this.

I get out of the shower, wrapping a towel around my waist when the clock on the nightstand catches my eye: 10:08. Damn. I was supposed to be at the post-wedding brunch over half an hour ago.

I dress on autopilot in dark slacks and a gray shirt, but just before I fly out the door, I snatch the diamond up and tuck it in my pocket, unwilling to leave it behind.

The chalet's corridors are quiet, as is the elevator ride down. Likely everyone is already back in the ballroom, eating off their hangovers and gossiping about whatever nonsense they can. A staff member nods as I pass, and from here, I can hear the tinkling sound of silverware against china and fake laughter.

An attendant opens the door for me, and I search around the room. Not for my brother or Bellamy or even the children, but for her. In the sea of over three hundred people, there is no one who comes even remotely close to matching my muddled memory of her.

But I do spot the event coordinator with her iPad in hand and march myself over to her.

"Your Highness," she greets me with a deep curtsy and a small blush on her cheeks. "How may I be of service?"

"I'm trying to locate one of the guests from last night. A woman by the name of Ella."

She pulls up her iPad and taps through until she has the guestlist at hand. "Do you have a last name for her, sir?"

And this is where I look like an asshole. "No. Just Ella. She was wearing a silver-blue dress. I didn't see who she came in with."

The woman presses her lips together, her expression switching from business mode to apologetic as she scrolls through the list. "I'm sorry, sir. I don't see anyone with the name Ella on the official list, nor do I see anyone who was checked in by that name." She keeps going through the list. "We have three Elizabeths, an Eleanor, and an Ellen, but no Ella."

My stomach tightens. "What about staff? Could she have been working the event?" Maybe she was security or someone placed by security to blend in as a guest.

"All staff were in uniform, sir. Black-and-white dress clothes with name badges. You can certainly speak to your head of security, but all staff on the event side were dressed as I mentioned."

"Thank you," I say with my patented smile when what I really want to do is pick up her iPad and chuck it. Instead, I walk away from what is becoming an awkward conversation. Mostly from my foul mood. That's what happens when the woman you had no business wanting to stay runs out on you in the middle of the night. Unease slithers through me. Who was she?

I didn't make her up. I wasn't that drunk, and I have her earring.

Javier is along the far wall talking with his wife, Emily, as they stand, eating from plates in their hands instead of sitting amongst the guests. It's tactical, and I know this because Sebastian, Bellamy, and the children are two tables over from them.

I cross the room to Javier, and when he catches me heading his way and notes my expression, he whispers something to

Emily, sets his plate down on a nearby tray, and meets me halfway.

"What's wrong?" he asks, his Spanish accent thick.

"It's nothing to be alarmed about." I don't think. "I was hoping we could scroll through the security footage from last night."

"Of course, sir. May I ask why?"

I glance around us, and while no one is paying us any particular attention, I don't want to discuss this out here. "Can we go somewhere? Is there a room we can use? Or even my suite?"

"Do you want me to get Sebastian?"

I think about this for a minute, but he's smiling and happy with his wife and children. He doesn't need to know about this. Not yet.

"That can wait."

He gives me a nod. "Your suite is likely the safest place if you're at all concerned about that."

"Perfect. Thank you."

I flip around and, without making eye contact with anyone, grab a muffin from the side of the buffet and leave the same way I came in. My fingers work to tear at the top of the pastry, shoving pieces of cake and blueberry into my mouth while I get back onto the elevator.

The keycard snicks on the pad, and after I open the door, I swing the latch out so the door catches on it and doesn't close all the way. My suite is a decent size, and I drop down at the dining table that seats four, only to get back up. I didn't grab coffee downstairs, but thankfully, there's a small espresso maker in here.

The sound of gears grinding and water moving through the machine fills the room, as does the aroma of strong coffee. I down my first cup that's as bitter as I am, not even caring if it's burning my tongue because it's already been a fucking day. One that would have started miles better if I'd woken up to a warm body instead of a cold bed.

I make myself a second cup and carry it back to the table to eat the muffin, my stomach roiling from too much alcohol and uncertainty.

A moment later, the door opens, and Javier joins me, his laptop bag slung over his shoulder. He takes the seat beside me at the table and sets up his computer.

"Tell me what I'm searching for."

I don't have to tell him this is confidential. This is Javier, and he's forever on the short list of people I trust.

"I met a woman last night," I begin. "Dark hair and eyes, wearing a silver-blue gown. She spoke in French and was sort of floating around the room. I talked her into dancing with me, and we had a drink together. Once dinner began, I brought her up to my room only to wake up alone with this." I dig into my pocket, pull out the earring, and set it on the table. "She told me her name was Ella. I never got a last name or even who she came with, and there's no record of an Ella on the guest list, or so the event coordinator claims."

His lips thin. "Do you feel she was a threat?"

"No," I reply automatically, only to think better of it and amend my statement. "I don't know. She was just kind of there, listening to other women gossip about Bellamy and rolling her eyes at them."

"You said this was before dinner, si? So during the cocktail hour?"

"Yes."

He nods, already clicking buttons on the keyboard. He tilts the laptop toward me so I can see the screen, and he puts in a time for the video to begin.

"We had cameras throughout the cocktail room and the ballroom. If she went through security, we'll have her face and name on file. It's possible she gave you a nickname."

"Or an alias," I quip, though there isn't much humor to it. I swallow a piece of muffin and chase it down with coffee. I had more to drink last night than I have in a while, and I'm paying for it now in several ways.

"Sì. There is also that possibility." He scrolls through footage of people entering the chalet, person after person, until I spot her dark hair.

"There!" I point at the woman on Sir Robert Blake's arm. "I think that's her."

I can feel him throwing me a side-eye at the use of the word "think," but yeah.

"We can't see her face here. Did she mention Sir Blake to you?"

"No." I lean back in my chair and take my coffee with me, sipping on it some more, hoping the caffeine will clear the cobwebs from my brain. "She mentioned no one, but she definitely knew who I was. She addressed me as Your Highness without me having to introduce myself."

Javier makes a sarcastic noise. "Everyone in the world knows who you are."

I glare but don't comment. We watch her enter the chalet with him, her touching his arm and chest. A weird sort of heat scorches the skin at the back of my neck at seeing that, but a moment later, she says something to him, and they go their separate ways. She moves along with purpose, keeping her head angled furtively, but it's not obvious. No staff challenged her. She simply coasts along as if she belongs.

He fast-forwards until he finds us on the dance floor. "This is her?"

"Yes."

He clicks a million keys, and the video stops with her face clear and centered on the screen. There she is. Ella. As beautiful as I remember her being and then some. A web of lines covers her face, the computer thinking, until a pop-up message appears that says, "No match located."

Shit.

Our eyes meet, both of us thinking the same thing.

"She didn't go through security."

I set my mug down and level him with a look. "How is that possible?"

"Honestly? I'm not sure. We had attendants lined along the only entrance and exit. Both in uniform and posing as attendees. No one could have slipped past them there, and everyone was funneled through both security checkpoints. She went through the second, but that was after we'd already searched everyone and taken their face ID."

"Do you think she came with Sir Robert?"

He shrugs. "It's possible, but she didn't stay with him for long and doesn't seem to meet up with him again during the course of the night."

"Jesus, Javier." I cover my face with my hands. "I brought her up to my room. I barely thought twice about it." I took her fucking virginity. "What the fuck is wrong with me?"

"In fairness, sir, you had no way of knowing she didn't go through security. Like everyone else in the room, it seemed as though she was supposed to be there."

I nod, my hands falling to the table with a heavy thud and rattling my mug. "Except she wasn't supposed to be there. What time did she leave?"

I get a raised eyebrow.

"No, I don't know. She was gone when I woke."

He clicks more keys and fasts forward through the night until her image appears coming off the elevator. She slinks through the first floor as if nothing is amiss and back out into the night, where we lose her.

"Timestamp reads 11:58 pm."

I choke out a laugh. "What, she was afraid her carriage

would turn back into a pumpkin?" I gripe sardonically. "Jesus, I'm a fucking cliché." She must have left almost immediately after I fell asleep. "Can we run her face through our database?"

"Already running it. It'll just be another minute or so."

My forearms fold on the table, and I drop my forehead onto them as we wait.

"No match found," he says. "She's not in our database at all."

I pop my head up. "Nothing?"

"Nothing. That means she has no driver's license or passport in Messalina and hasn't been employed in this country in a position where facial scans are taken."

"She said she was from Messalina." Clearly, she lied. My brows furrow. "Could she be from outside the country?"

"She likely is."

"I need to know who she is," I bite out.

"Sir, with respect, what we need to know is how she bypassed security at the royal wedding," he counters, his expression the stern mask it always is. "This represents a serious breach of security. We have no idea what she was after or what her motives were."

"She didn't act like a threat." But even as I say the words, they sound weak and childish. I have no clue who she really was, and everything she told me was likely a lie. I sit up straight, pulling my head out of my ass. "We need to talk to Sebastian about this."

"Sì. And I'll start a full background check into everything. Every camera she came across. I'll tap into French facial analytics as well since you said she spoke to you in French. Is there anything else you can remember? Anything that would be useful?"

I think back to last night, about how we verbally sparred, and how I made her dance with me. How I liked that she didn't seem to give two shits about who I was. She had disdain for the women speaking negatively about Bellamy. But that was it. Simple things that add up to nothing. Other than the way it felt to touch her. The way she smelled and tasted.

"No. I can't think of anything."

"Then we'll start with what we have and go from there."

"I guess that's all we can do for now." But even as I say the words, something internal snags. Last night I came alive with her. I've never felt that with anyone before. The thought of letting that go, of letting *her* go, hits like a two-by-four to the chest. I fucked up. I have no clue who she is or the dangers she poses.

Yet, I don't have it in me to regret it. Even so, I worry my mistake could be costly.

5

———

MARCELLA

The earring is going to be a problem. Aside from the fact that the diamonds were real, they belonged to my stepmother, Signoria Batorini. That's going to be a bitch to explain. I shudder at the thought of what I'm about to face with her, my back tingling at the memory of Antonia's cane.

Antonia always does her dirty work. She's Signoria's niece from a much older sister, but they're more like best friends. Partners in crime and evil. Signoria doesn't like to get her hands dirty unless she has to, but Antonia loves it.

The drive back from the Messalinian Alps down to the southeast part of the country is long. I didn't dare leave before dawn, which meant I had to camp out in the woods again. I end up stopping twice. Once to use the restroom and another to force some food into me. I'm not hungry, but I also haven't eaten anything since yesterday afternoon, and I can feel my body getting shaky.

I have all the windows down, even though it's barely fifteen degrees Celsius, and music is blasting. Anything to drown out thoughts about last night. About *him*. About how my body is sore in the most perfect and unexpected way. But mostly so I won't think about how the conversation will go when I get home. Or the fact that I'm going on zero sleep.

The exit for Bellezza in Riva al Mare is up ahead, and I speed up in anticipation of the hairpin curve, challenging the cornering Ferrari Purosangue. She handles like a dream, and I hope I can find a way to take her out again.

The drive into town winds along the cliffs high above the Mediterranean Sea. Quaint shops and restaurants are on one side, and on the other is the sprawling, sparkling blue-green water, dotted with sharply rising islands in the distance and boats of various sizes. The smell of salt and herbs fills the air, and if I weren't trapped here, locked like an eternal prisoner, I'd think this was the most special piece of earth on the planet.

People strolling the street notice me as I pass through, some offering timid smiles, others wincing. Very few know my name or, frankly, much about me other than as one of the servants to the Batorini family. A name that once garnered respect and even love. They were revered.

Then Samil had to go and fuck it up by attempting to kill the king and queen, and now the Batorini family, what's left of it, has a perpetual scarlet letter on their chests.

Not that I'm part of the family. Not technically. At least not in a way anyone knows about. Being the bastard child of an affair, Signoria always hated me. I was a reminder of her husband's infidelity, and though I lived in their house since my mother was dead, I was never treated as part of the family. Samil was my older brother, Signoria, and my father's only child together. He was my best friend. My lifeline. Years later, shortly before he died, my father had a second child with a mistress, and now it's Jaqueline and me, stuck in this house with no option of escape.

I plow through town, picking up speed as I hit the country-side once again, and five minutes later, I'm rolling into the grounds of the Batorini estate. The massive Spanish-style palazzo appears like a mirage once you pass the olive groves and towering cypress trees. I drive to the back of the building and straight into one of the garage bays. The car shuts off, and I'm locked in suffocating silence. The kind that hits your pulse and prickles your skin in the worst of ways.

I'm not even out of the car when Antonia steps out. Fuck. Here we go.

"You're late," she says to me in Italian, since that's the only language spoken in this house other than during language and dialect lessons.

I shake my head as I pull my bags from the trunk. "I'm early. I promised three if I couldn't get out of the woods without being spotted, and I couldn't with how tight security was. It's not even two."

"Marcella, did you get what we needed?"

I pause. "I lost an earring."

Her jaw pops. "You know you'll be punished severely for that."

I hold in my wince. "Yes, ma'am. I know."

"It might not be as bad if you have information we can use."

I see we're not wasting time or mincing words, and the urgency in her voice and even her expression raise the hairs at the back of my neck. So much was riding on this wedding, and all of it was disappointing. Well, at least in terms of intel.

I sling my duffel over my shoulder and carry the other large tote bag in my hand as I walk toward Antonia and the back entrance of the estate.

"They're in love. It's real."

She hisses out a curse, her dark curls sprinkled with grays all over the place. "That's unacceptable."

I nearly snort a laugh, but the last time I made a mocking sound at her, I received five lashes.

"Regardless, I can't change that."

She steps back, and we enter the back foyer that divides into two wings, one toward the kitchen and servants' areas and the other toward the family section of the palazzo. Instead of going toward any of that, we veer a sharp right and head to the back before taking the dark, narrow flight of stairs to Jaqueline's and my quarters, which abut the wine cellar and two storage rooms.

And yes, it's in the basement. Complete with no windows, spiders, and other critters.

I chuck my bags onto the floor, noting the worry in her eyes. She should be worried. Signora Batorini will be pissed. I wish Antonia had gone, but it was impossible. The only two who wouldn't have been discovered by their facial recognition were either Jaqueline or me, and Jaqueline is a teenager.

"It's real. It was all over them. Bellamy Wright loves King Sebastian and his children. There was no act. The gossip was useless. Same tragic bullshit story about Samil and useless trash about the new queen. It was catty and based on jealousy instead of facts. We'll have to find another way. The queen won't betray her king."

"Are you sure?" a voice comes from behind me, and my insides chill over. Antonia is a fucking monster. Make no mistake about it. I am too, if we're being honest, because I learned from the masters. But Signoria Batorini, my stepmother, is a special brand of evil, and it makes me miss her son even more.

I turn and place my eyes at chest level with her Chanel blouse before I curtsy. "Yes. I'm certain. On a positive note, I was able to bypass their security and get in without any issue, so now we know it's possible. All in all, I'd say this was a successful mission."

Her expensive heels click lightly against the travertine as she makes her way over to me. Ice-cold, bone-thin fingers lift my chin until I meet her dark brown eyes. Then her other hand flies and smacks my face with brutal precision. I don't wince. I hardly exhale a breath. But fuck, does it sting. She's wearing her eternity bands loaded with large diamonds and made sure that was the hand she struck me with.

The diamonds and metal tear a straight path up my cheek and cut me open. A warm trickle of blood runs down my face to my chin before it drips onto my shirt and the floor.

"Successful?" she sneers. "How dare you use that word to cover your failure. That information is useless to me." She seethes, her eyes narrowing into slits as her red lips that match the soles of her shoes continue to lash out at me. Another slap, this one harder than the first, and my vision pops with stars. "We sent you to the royal wedding, and all you return with is that their affections are real?" She's incredulous, her voice rising an octave, but it's feigned. It's all part of her warfare. "I should have had Antonia kill you like the useless trash you are when your father died."

But you didn't, bitch.

"If it weren't for my son and how he adored you, I would have."

If it weren't for your son and how I adored him, I likely would have done it myself when I learned the truth all those years ago.

"Must I remind you that you don't exist?" she continues, her tone shrill. "That you have no last name. No birth certificate. No national identification number. As far as the world is concerned, you are nothing. I could throw you off the cliff straight into the sea, and no one would care."

Another slap that makes my vision grow fuzzy. I try not to flinch, and for the most part, I succeed.

I've stood at that cliff edge many times, contemplating the very thing she just said. Samil saved me. Loved me. Doted on me. Made me believe that I wasn't nothing. He taught me so many things. He spent time with me. To him, I was someone. I mattered.

My life wasn't exactly singing with the birds and chirping out songs all day long, but it was bearable. It was okay. I lived in the shadows and followed their instructions to the letter. If I didn't, I was tortured. So I adapted. I studied and learned how they wanted me to. I did their bidding and followed their orders, even when I often felt sick from them.

Then Samil died.

I could point out how she's used me and the fact that I don't exist to make an untold fortune from murder, corruption, and blackmail. The amount of fucked-up shit that goes down in the world of the stupidly rich is obscene and would turn any normal person's blood cold. But since she and the rest of her world are already cold-blooded, to them it's simply another day at the office.

"Do you have anything of use for me?" she asks, poison on her breath as she bears down on me. I steel my spine, ready for her reaction when I tell her that I have nothing. Now is definitely not the time to mention that I lost one of her earrings. Why they insisted I wear real diamonds in my ears is beyond me.

"She lost your earrings," Antonia jumps in, and what the fuck?

"You what?" Signoria cries. It's technically one earning, but I don't correct her.

"I'm sorry. It must have fallen out when I was—"

Another slap. This one knocks me to the ground. Out of the corner of my eye, I spot Jaqueline hiding in the shadows. Dammit. I hate it when she sees this sort of stuff. She's stricken, her teeth caught in her lip and her hands pressed into her chest. I toss her a wan smile before I'm hauled to my feet by the back of my shirt.

"Ten lashings," Signoria instructs. "Be thankful it's not more. You certainly deserve it."

My shirt is ripped off my back, and I'm shoved into one of

the support poles. My chest slams into the cold metal, knocking the wind from me. My hands grip the cylinder, my eyes closing, and I work to regain and steady my breathing even as my heart hammers.

I knew this was coming, but it never gets easier. Especially when she hits the scars I already have.

Antonia moves, and I close my eyes, bracing for the first strike.

Air whistles around the cane, which is really a long bamboo stick with striations on it. *Slap.* My back bows, and I whimper, biting into my lip to suppress it. They love the sound of my agony, and it's why I try so hard to fight my reaction.

Fuck them. *Fuck you!*

Slap after slap, my skin is ripped apart, and blood oozes down my back. Fire burns through me, weakening my knees. My hands grip the pole, my knuckles white, and my muscles shaking as I work to stay upright. It's brutal, and I keep my eyes pinched tight and my jaw locked.

"Ten," Antonia announces, barely out of breath. Conversely, my lungs are shredded, and I can hardly catch my breath.

I know Jaqueline saw and heard everything. She's only thirteen. merely a teenager, she feels everything. I don't cry for that reason alone. My tears would break her further. More than that, again, I won't give them the satisfaction. I can't remember the last time I cried, and if I have my say, I'll never cry again. Tears are a weakness.

"Now what do we do with you?" Signoria asks without actually expecting an answer. She wants me to fall to my knees and beg for forgiveness while showering her with undying devotion. Fucking narcissist.

"Signoria, it was two hours at a wedding," Antonia states, which shocks me. She's never one to come to my side on anything, which means there's something she wants and needs me alive for it. What that could possibly be, I have no clue. "We need another strategy."

Signoria Batorini has had a difficult couple of months. Her son was killed when he was shoved out a window at the hands of the king. I never saw the video. I only know that the entire encounter is about as damning as you can get if you don't know the details. But details are inconsequential.

Samil tried to kidnap the king's fiancée, and when that didn't work, he tried to kill the king. Self-defense or madness, it doesn't matter which angle you take. The country hates us, and we want our revenge against the king who killed Samil without a second thought.

A beloved king at that, despite the fact that he had been a notorious beast and gone into seclusion for three years following the death of his wife. They said it was grief that drove him there, but we know the truth. It was fear of the curse, not love for the queen.

My father hated the royal family and used to tell me stories about the former king. How he'd spend tax money like it was nothing, siphoning it away from charities and schools. He'd take bribes and play favorites, allowing votes and policies only on things he was paid off for. My father was a member of parliament for years and often talked about the greed and corruption that lived in the royal family.

Samil carried that torch. He was a classmate of King Sebastian and used to call him a ruthless, arrogant prick, though they were friendly enough back then. That all changed when the king became jealous of Samil. He resented him for where his future was headed, and the freedom he had with it. Out of spite, the king set his sights on marrying Nora, Samil's girlfriend. Pressured by her family, she had no choice but to accept the king's proposal.

It devastated Samil. Especially because the king didn't love her.

He was the same cold, ruthless, corrupt shark his father was. He went after Samil from the start. Did everything he could to destroy him, even holding him back professionally. If the king hadn't been so cutthroat and grudging of Samil, Nora would have married Samil, and he'd still be here. Hell, maybe I would have gone and lived with them. Been a nanny or a housekeeper there.

My life could have been so different if it were not for the bastard king and all he did to hurt my brother. Now my life is worse than it ever was.

Last night, the king married his new bride, and the country is magically healed and beyond joyous. And the great unifier beyond the king's new love and the people's snark over it? Their hatred of their former prime minister.

Oh, and the fact that they believe the curse has now been broken.

"I'm listening," slithers past Signoria's bitter lips.

"We get Marcella into the palace. Not the way we did last night. Not simply for a few hours. We get her a job in the palace. Plant her there from within and allow her to gain their trust. To learn all their secrets. Then we take them out from within."

"Yes. I like it," Signoria agrees. "A Trojan horse."

My insides plummet.

The last place I want to go is the palace, but it seems I don't have a choice if this is what they want. How I'll avoid the prince once I'm living there, I have no clue. I just know I have to.

6

ROWAN

Six months later

"Emily is getting her right hip replaced," Althea announces as she joins us in the breakfast room, and Sebastian, Bellamy, and I all stop eating mid-bite to look at her. The children don't stop, though. Phaedra and Sabrina are going back and forth about who's better at a game they play on their iPads, and Zayer is busy shoveling eggs and ham into his mouth.

Sebastian comes to faster than us. "When is that happening, and why haven't we been notified about it until now?"

"It's happening in two weeks, and she didn't inform us about it because she kept pushing off her doctor, telling her she was fine, when she actually wasn't. The woman can barely walk at this point. You can't tell me you're shocked."

Sebastian swallows his bite of sourdough and wipes his mouth with his napkin. "No. I suppose not. I'm glad she's finally taking care of herself."

Bellamy places her hand on her large pregnant belly and leans back in her chair. "What can we do to help?"

Althea points a stern finger at Bellamy. "You are to keep off your feet. You're growing twins and are scheduled to deliver them in two and a half months."

Bellamy's lips twist. She hates being sidelined because of her pregnancy, but it is what it is. Currently, they don't have a nanny for the children. After what happened with Charlotte two months ago, when she kidnapped and attempted to kill Bellamy, they're extremely trigger-shy about hiring anyone else. Bellamy is already spent, and Emily and Althea have been helping as much as they can with the children, but now it seems they're down another set of hands.

That's going to be a problem, and everyone in here knows it.

"I don't see how I'll be able to do that," Bellamy admits, and Sebastian scowls.

"We should work on hiring a new nanny."

Bellamy's eyes close, and she releases a heavy breath. "I... no. Not right now."

Sebastian rests his hand on her belly. "We're going to have to figure something out. The twins will be born before you know it."

"Sebastian..."

"I know." He leans over and kisses her hand. "It's not what I want either, but you're already struggling to keep up with Zayer and Sabrina."

Bellamy's eyes open, and once again, she's resolute. "We'll discuss this later. Let's figure out how to help Emily first."

"Emily has been reviewing current employees' performance and considering who she'll appoint to oversee the staff and take on the main family responsibilities."

"Does she have any candidates in mind?" I ask, shifting my eggs around on my plate. "There was that one woman—"

"That narrows it down," Bellamy teases.

I chuck a tear of my toast at her. "You didn't let me finish."

"What was her name then?" she challenges.

"If I could remember, I would have used it."

"So sad to be so quickly forgotten by the dashing Prince Rowan."

I roll my eyes at her. "Har, har."

Althea is unimpressed. "Honestly. These are the people living and working in your palace. You'd think you'd at least know their names. And you better not have done anything—"

"I'm going to cut you off there, Aunt," I say, my tone serious. "I've never done anything with one of our incredible staff."

Bellamy holds up a hand. "All that aside, we should meet with Emily to discuss this together. All of us. If this person is to take over for Emily, that means they'll be in our private quarters."

Althea lifts her mug to her lips and takes a sip of coffee. "I agree, and Emily isn't taking this lightly or without serious consideration. There are four people she's narrowed it down to. One works on the family side but has never managed others and isn't always thorough, and one works on the kitchen side, so they have never done much in the residences, and two are guest services attendants."

That's a fancy term for the person who takes care of the guest quarters as well as the guests themselves. Somewhat like a concierge service combined with housekeeping responsibilities. This is the largest palace in our country and has over seventy-five guest rooms alone, and none of those include the family's primary quarters, which are located on the other side of the palace.

"And they've gone through the necessary background checks?"

Sebastian gets a raised eyebrow. "Of course, they have. They're working in the palace. Javier was diligent."

Sebastian and I exchange glances. Javier has doubled down

on background checks after what happened with Charlotte and after my Ella broke into the wedding. Anyone who's been hired since the wedding hasn't only had background checks. They've also had full family reviews and extensive rounds of interviews.

I give him a shrug. If they're good enough for Emily and Javier, that's good enough for me, but I don't have a wife who's pregnant with my twins and three other children. Nor am I the king. I do think the Charlotte situation was an anomaly, and there was no way to know what her ulterior motive was or who her mother was, no matter how much digging we could have done.

He swivels back to Althea. "Yes. I think we'd like to discuss the candidates with Emily and meet with them. Just to make sure things continue as smoothly and seamlessly as they do with Emily in charge."

"And what about what Emily needs from us?" Bellamy persists. "A hip replacement is no small thing. Will she be rehabbing here at the palace or elsewhere?"

"Here at the palace," Sebastian insists before Althea can reply. "We'll turn a ballroom or parlor on the main level into her temporary quarters. That way, she won't have to bother with stairs."

Bellamy touches his cheek. "I love that idea. I agree that if she's comfortable, she should rehab here. Obviously, Sebastian will get her whatever she needs."

He chuckles and leans over to kiss her lips. "Sweetness, you continue to forget that you're the queen and can make that decree yourself."

"Fine," she concedes. "Whatever Emily needs to stay here at the palace with Javier and be comfortable, we'll provide. So let it be written, so let it be done."

I choke out a laugh. "Who are you? Yul Brynner as Ramses?"

She shrugs and returns to her eggs, shovels a bite into her

mouth and talks through it. "Something like that. It always sounded so good when he said it. Plus he was sexy."

Sebastian tickles her side, making her laugh, and it's the best sound in the world. Since the kidnapping, Bellamy has struggled. It's been a rough seven and a half months for her. First Samil nearly killed her, then her father died, and after that, the woman they hired to care for the children betrayed them and tried to kill Bellamy.

Honestly, I don't know how she gets out of bed most days. I give her so much credit. She's stubbornly strong. Both for herself and the children, and she's brought that strength to all of us.

That said, sadness lingers in her eyes, and she has horrific night terrors. Screams that pierce the air and make your bones chill over. I can hear from down the hall. I want her to find peace again, and I know Sebastian is desperate for that.

No one has mentioned the curse since she came home, but I'd be lying if I said we all weren't still feeling its weight on our shoulders. After almost losing Bellamy more than once, Sebastian is adamant about not letting it affect him, and for the most part, he's succeeding.

We thought it was broken, only it seems like it's just warming up, preparing for its next act. I'm not sure how much more we can take. It's been keeping all of us up at night. I'm determined to change all our fates. It's not just Sebastian and Bellamy. It's Phaedra, Sabrina, Zayer, and the twins too.

What Bellamy doesn't know is that Sebastian and Javier brought in a dozen extra guards to the palace and installed more cameras. He's terrified about when the twins are born. About other dangers creeping out of the darkness.

I never believed in the curse. Not once. Not even when our father died when I was a boy or Nora went down in the helicopter. But these last months have challenged that belief.

Something is coming for us, and unless we can stop it, it won't relent until it wins.

I don't have it in me to leave. I have a residence down on the Messalinian coast, not to mention my yacht, but I can't make myself go.

I have to be here. It's my job to fix this.

I can't explain it. It's a gut instinct.

I have to see Bellamy deliver the twins safely. I have to ensure that my brother, my nieces, and my nephew are okay. There are already too many variables hanging over our heads, and until I can locate Marie Elonaise and put her behind bars along with her daughter, Charlotte, I won't rest.

I haven't since the night Desta was taken, and our father was murdered. I'll never forgive myself for what happened. I didn't go into Desta's room with my father. I never woke up my mother. I never alerted the guards.

So many costly mistakes, and our family hasn't been right since. None of us has been. I have no sisters. Desta is gone, and Brea is fragile, living in a place I don't even know about. I've never even had contact with her. She was sick as a new baby, and we weren't allowed anywhere near her, and that was it. Our mother is cold and distant, locked in a grief so thick it's cost her everything and hardened her soul. We haven't spoken to her since she came here several months back and lied to us about who stole Desta and killed our father.

She said everything she did was to save our family and avoid scandal, but at what cost? Plus, she doesn't approve of Bellamy, so there's that.

"Excellent." Althea taps her iPad a few times, drawing me out of my reverie. "Now that that's taken care of, there is a summer festival in Tourin."

"No," Sebastian cuts in sharply. "Absolutely not."

Bellamy is finding it impossible to contain her smile.

"I think the children would love it," she says gently.

My brother throws her his best attempt at a scathing look, but he doesn't sell it anymore. He's a beast king no more when it comes to the softness in his heart for his wife.

"The last time you took the children to a festival in Tourin, they came home with a rodent."

Bellamy rolls her eyes. "A Mustelidae and don't pretend you don't love Arthur."

"I will neither confirm nor deny my affections for the rodent, but what pet will they steal for their own next time?"

"We didn't steal Arthur, Papa," Sabrina protests.

"Yeah," Phaedra chimes in, more than a little indignant. "He was going to die if we left him. He was so cold out there and all alone."

"I love Arthur," Zayer tacks on. "He sleeps in my bed with me."

And just like that, Sebastian is a puddle of mush. "I know, my darlings. But I don't think we need to add anymore potentially dying critters to our family."

"Why don't you come with us and stop them from heisting a new pet from the grounds?" Bellamy suggests.

Sebastian grunts. He still hates leaving the palace. He hates his children leaving it even more, but he's trying.

"Maybe we should all go," I add, only to be cut off by someone entering the breakfast room.

"My apologies for interrupting." The woman's head is cast down, and she does a curtsy toward Sebastian and Bellamy without making eye contact with any of us. She comes over to Althea and whispers something in her ear. Her long, blonde hair is pleated into a neat braid behind her head, stopping at her mid-back. She has no makeup on her face and is wearing a housekeeper's uniform, which consists of a basic gray dress that goes to her knees.

I can't see her all that well, but there's something about her that catches my attention, and I study her a bit closer, even as she speaks in hushed tones with my aunt.

"Mon Dieu!" Althea exclaims, covering her lips with her hand. "Emily has fallen."

The three of us shoot up from our seats, and the children stop moving as if they've been simultaneously frozen.

"Where is she? Call nine-one-one."

Sebastian places his hand on Bellamy's shoulder. "It's not none-one-one here."

"Like I care. Call your Messalinian equivalent," Bellamy bites out.

"She's doing okay, Your Majesty," the mysterious woman states, still skirting our eyes. "She's in a parlor on the second level. She was giving me a tour of the family quarters when she tripped and fell on her bad hip. I moved her to the sofa and rang Javier, but she's in a good amount of pain. I felt I should notify you at once despite her protests."

Sebastian is wrought with worry and displeasure. "Of course she protested. It's why we're learning of her hip replacement only now," Sebastian growls out. "Stubborn woman."

"Yes," Althea agrees. "That was smart thinking. This is Marcella. She's one of Emily's candidates who has been working over in the guest quarters."

Marcella gives a deep curtsy, but when she lifts her head, and I get a shot of her green eyes, something strange tickles the back of my mind. She's beautiful. I mean, that's an understatement. She's fucking gorgeous. But there's something about her that's almost...familiar.

Likely that I've seen her around the palace and never registered her. But damn, looking at her now, that feels impossible. She's the sort of woman you can't help but notice and remember.

"Marcella." Bellamy goes over to her and extends her hand to shake. "It's lovely to meet you. Thank you for all the care you've given our home."

Marcella reluctantly takes her hand and shakes it before she gives her another curtsy and murmurs out, "Your Majesty," but that's not how Bellamy works.

"Call me Bellamy. As you'll soon see, I'm not that formal. Please, take us to Emily."

I move closer to her, anxious for another glance at her face. Strange visions hit me, but they're wrong. Off. She's blonde. Green-eyed. Not dark-haired and dark-eyed. It pisses me off that once again I'm thinking about the woman who ran out on me in the middle of the night after the best fucking sex of my life.

Six months, and I haven't been able to get her out of my head or let her go.

One night has completely corrupted my mind.

I looked for her, but she didn't exist. How do you search for a woman who gives a fake name? Who was she? What was she doing there? And more importantly, how did she get in? We were at a private hotel that has nothing but forest on one side and mountains on the other. Not to mention, we took a million safety precautions.

Was this simply a thrill break-in, or were her intentions more sinister? After all these months without anything else from her, it's difficult to imagine the latter, but not impossible. She was skilled and trained. No doubt about that.

I have more questions than answers.

The one good thing to come from Charlotte and my mystery Ella is that the pressure to find a woman and settle down has eased. Our trust in anyone is nil.

And yet, that's not the only reason I'm anxious to find her. Sebastian teases me. He says it's the excitement of the chase.

That a woman has never rejected me, and it's my pride that's wounded.

Perhaps that's all it is. I was pretty drunk, so it's possible she wasn't everything my mind conjured for her. But she seemed...different. Fun. Special.

Not that it matters. I'll never find her. Not unless she wants to be found.

7

MARCELLA

What an absolute clusterfuck of a situation. On the one hand, this is exactly what Antonia and Signoria Batorini are after. I'm potentially gaining direct access to the family, and if that happens, by extension, so are they. On the other hand, freaking Rowan is still here with no signs of leaving.

I can feel his goddamn eyes on me, and it's not a good thing. When Antonia suggested they get me a job in the palace, I tried not to balk. A one-night stand is by definition supposed to be just that. You're not supposed to see that person again. I knew fucking the prince was a bad call, but it didn't stop me.

Now I'm paying for the mistakes I made that night.

I assumed Rowan wouldn't recognize me if I ran into him in the palace. He was drunk, and it was dark when we were naked, and I was in disguise. But you never know. There is always the risk that he could. Thankfully, the palace is the size of a small village, and it's easy to avoid people if that's your goal.

Which is what I've done for the last four months. I've stayed out of his way. Kept my head down and low and evaded his attention. Until now.

It took us two months to get me into the palace.

Javier is very good at his job, and the security on the royal family's computer systems is tight. I managed to hack it and alter the facial recognition they had on me from inside the chalet so that it wouldn't match when they scanned my real face. But in doing so, I discovered they'd been searching for me. So that was a problem too, and I couldn't tell Antonia or Signoria Batorini that because then they'd ask why.

And probably kill me when I answered.

We had to create documents that would pass muster and an alias that would hold up. Luckily, there's a family about twenty kilometers from the Batorini estate, and they owe Signoria a lot of money they can't pay. They were only too willing to help if it meant their debts were wiped clean, even if they had to lie to the royal chief of security and act like they were my loving, doting family.

I was placed on the guest side of the palace with limited contact to anyone within the royal family, especially the children and the pregnant queen. Those were my instructions from Mrs. Lids when I first started, and I kept to that.

For the last four months, I've made myself the perfect employee while noting every corner of the palace I was allowed in. Every camera. I kept my head down, did my work to perfection, and didn't gossip with other staff, though I was friendly and sweet enough to engage theirs. Not that there was a lot. The staff are extremely loyal and protective of the family. I met Charlotte, the nanny who fooled everyone into believing she was an angel on earth, only to kidnap the queen.

What happened during that time was kept under wraps, only whispered about, though most didn't know the details of the actual kidnapping or why Charlotte did it. Most speculated that she wanted to get rid of Bellamy so she could cozy up to the king and become the next queen.

It never made the news. The palace kept it a secret.

When I told Antonia and Signoria about this, they just about lost their minds and demanded every piece of gossip I could unearth. Even the smallest detail. Unfortunately, that was the only dirt circulating about it, and most don't want to talk about Charlotte, who she is, or what she did to the queen.

Then Mrs. Lids's doctor demanded she get a hip replacement. When she came to me, the new girl, and said I was in the running to take over some of her responsibilities, I was floored. But I didn't exactly jump for joy.

Being here has been a breath of fresh air in an unexpected way.

I have freedom for the first time in my life. I don't have to worry that any mistake I make will result in abuse of some kind or even my death. I'm earning a paycheck that gets deposited into a bank account with my name on it—fake or not, who cares? It's my money, and neither Antonia nor the Signoria has access because they can't give the situation.

Other than missing Jaqueline terribly and worrying about her being there without me, it's as if I can take a deep breath for the first time in over a decade. I'm not tense or always looking over my shoulder. My stomach isn't twisted into a million knots.

But I'm not here on a goodwill mission.

I'm a Trojan horse, exactly as Signoria said.

The king drove my brother to madness and then killed him. Yes, Samil tried to kidnap the queen. Yes, the things he did were wrong. But the source of his imbalance hasn't paid any price for his culpability, and his misdeeds were many and without care. I intend to make him pay for that. After my father's death, I only had Samil and Jaqueline, but Jaqueline was a baby. Samil was the only adult who loved me. Who cared. He saved my life. He was my best friend. My confidant. My family. He made sure I had basic necessities. I owe him my life. Literally.

These last seven months without him have been hell on earth.

I hate the king for taking him from me. For the world not knowing the truth. For all the things that could have been.

I know why Samil wanted the king dead. I know what truly happened between him and Nora. I know how she died. The pain and torment that ate away at Samil's soul because of it.

Which makes Emily's injury, her impending surgery, and me potentially taking over her role the break we've been looking for. Even if it's already creating issues with some of the other staff. Particularly, the three other candidates.

Only standing here in the breakfast room, shaking the hand of the queen and overhearing their worry for Emily, while Rowan eyeballs the back of my head like he's trying to figure me out, isn't how I wanted this to begin.

The queen—because I can't call her Bellamy, not even in my head—places her hand on my forearm, and now it seems I'm leading the charge.

That is until she pauses. "Wait. What about the children?"

The king makes a displeased noise and taps his wife's shoulder. "Nanny."

"I told you not to call me that anymore," she quips.

He rolls his eyes, but his lips are twitching. "You know very well what I meant."

I bow to him. "Your Majesty, if it would be helpful, I can take the children to the playroom so you can go be with Emily."

Sebastian eyes me hard before he shakes his head. "No. We need you to take us to her."

Code for: he doesn't trust me around his children, which isn't a surprise. This is the first time he's meeting me.

"Yes, sir," I reply.

"I'll stay with the children," Althea announces, and I was hoping Rowan would volunteer, but alas, I'm stuck with Rowan freaking standing beside me as we leave the breakfast room and head upstairs toward the parlor.

"Marcella, is it?" Rowan asks.

I dip my head toward him. "Yes, sir." I'm using a bit of an Italian accent even though I'm speaking in French. I have since I started here because it's what the daughter of the Russo family would have. When I met him at the wedding, I had no accent, and my French was flawless.

He chuckles. "Is that all you say? Yes, sir."

"It seemed to be the most appropriate response to your questions. *Sir*." I try not to let any bite cut into my tone, but I doubt I accomplish that.

He continues to laugh. "I suppose it is. You're very formal."

"Yes, sir."

He arches an eyebrow, and I fight my smirk.

"I work for you, and you're the prince of my country. It's how I was raised," I continue, playing the part. "My mother was responsible for my education. She instilled a strong sense of duty, loyalty, and love of country. Your family is one of the hallmarks of that."

Except all of that is a lie. I don't have a mother. Signoria doesn't tolerate me except for when I'm useful to her, and Antonia has treated me like a slave, a servant of the house with no income, since my father died. Not to mention I never had any love for the royal family—only a deep-seated, well-ingrained hate fed to me nightly like a child's bedtime story.

"Where are you from?" the queen asks as we make our way across the first floor toward the winding staircase on this side of the palace.

"Mordeli. It's a small village near the Italian border," I answer, leading the way as we reach the second level.

"Emily must think very highly of you to consider you for this level of a promotion after only four months of working here," the king jumps in, his question more than a little pointed.

I bow toward him. "I'm very grateful to be considered, Your Majesty. Mrs. Lids has been a wonderful role model, and I've learned so much from her. I hope she recovers quickly, and if there's anything I can do to help you and your family during that process, I'd be honored." I pan my hand toward the parlor. "She's in here, Your Majesties."

The king and queen rush into the room, but Rowan stops before entering, his gaze on mine. "Aren't you joining us?"

"It's customary for you to enter before I do, sir, but I felt you all might want some time alone with her." *And I'd like to get away from you.*

He steps closer, standing over me, and I'm hit with the scent of his cologne. It's the same one he wore that night, and it tickles my insides, making me want to squirm and shift. I hold steady, keeping to the role I'm playing.

His head dips toward me, making my pulse quicken. "I think we'd all prefer it if you joined us. And it's Rowan."

My brows scrunch. "Pardon?"

"My name. I never cared for being called 'sir' or 'Your Highness,' especially by people I interact with daily. That's my brother. Not me. I'd like you to call me Rowan. I'd like to hear you say it."

"Why would you want that?"

He squints. "Humor me."

I straighten my spine, but I don't pull away or draw back. I don't want him to know he's affecting me. "I don't believe that's appropriate, sir."

He moves in until there are only mere inches separating us. It sets me on edge and makes my stomach flip.

His lips thin in displeasure. "Probably not, but Bellamy goes by Bellamy, so why can't I go by Rowan?"

"I have no intention of calling the queen by her first name. We should likely get in the room and see how Mrs. Lids is doing."

I start to move when he grabs me by my upper arm, stopping me. He releases me immediately, but it doesn't matter. He doesn't have to touch me. His proximity is a force all its own. And his gaze? It's all over me. Studying. Analyzing.

"Marcella. Marc*ella*," he repeats, though his tone changes, emphasizing the last part of my name, and I wish I hadn't told him my name was Ella that night. Yet another mistake that could cost me everything. "It's a beautiful name."

Fuck. My throat thickens, and I can't move. He has me paralyzed. "Thank you, sir."

"There's something familiar about you, Marcella."

"Perhaps I have one of those faces." My heart stutters in my chest, but I don't flinch. Hell, I don't even breathe. If he realizes who I am, there will be questions. An investigation. I'll be thrown in jail and likely charged with treason.

My one night with the prince could be my undoing. My downfall. The piece that unravels everything, more than it already has.

He scours my face feature by feature, his lips twisting in contemplation as he muses, "No. It's not that. It's as if we've met before."

"Your Highness," I start, not bothering to hide my curt tone, hoping my attitude will properly deflect him. "You likely saw me in passing but didn't take notice because I'm the help, and it's my job to remain invisible to you."

His lips untwist and curl up into a crooked smirk that makes his left dimple pop. "Marcella, there is nothing about you that could be invisible to anyone."

Let's hope that's not the case.

"I'm positive I've seen you before."

"I've been working in this palace for four months. I've seen you on three occasions other than this one."

A smile spreads across his lips. "Have you now? You've been counting?"

Fucking flirt. I knew that night meant nothing to him. I knew he was a practiced seducer, and I'm wholly inexperienced when it comes to, well, anything related to men. I was weak and admittedly lonely, and I stupidly, so fucking stupidly, gave my virginity to the wrong man.

I puff out a breath that rustles my long bangs back from my forehead. "You mistake me, sir. There is nothing specific to you that I've been counting or keeping track of. I've seen His Majesty five times. The children twice. Her Majesty four. Coming from a small village, you can imagine how it's not common place to see any members of the royal family. Keeping track is simply how my brain works. Now, if you'll excuse me, I'd like to go check on Mrs. Lids."

Without waiting for his reply, I leave him standing here in the hall and enter the parlor. Mrs. Lids is propped up with a pillow, her face ashen and glistening with a sheen of sweat. The queen is fussing over her, insisting that she go to the hospital immediately.

I hear Rowan enter behind me, but I don't turn to acknowledge him.

"Marcella." Mrs. Lids offers me a wan smile. "Perfect timing. I've just spoken with His Majesty and the queen, and I'd like to officially offer you the role of interim palace manager."

Well, shit.

I feign surprise, though I'm not, given the circumstance. I should be rolling in joy, yet something about this sits all wrong with me. And it has nothing to do with the prince, who I can still feel on me like a hawk.

I curtsy for the thousandth time in the last fifteen minutes. "I'd be honored. Thank you for your trust in me."

And now it all begins.

8

ROWAN

Emily is loaded onto an ambulance with Javier riding along with her. The moment the doors shut and it drives off, Sebastian throws me a look. A look I know. A look I've seen with more frequency over the last seven months.

He turns to Bellamy and kisses her forehead. "Are you okay if Rowan and I talk for a bit before we meet with the new woman?"

Bellamy is hardly one not to read between the lines, but she's also wasted with fatigue. She had a night terror last night, which means both she and Sebastian got little sleep. She needs a nap. She can fight it, but she needs one.

"Althea said she'd stay with the children," he tacks on, reading his wife so perfectly.

She sags and drops her face into his chest. "I don't want another nanny."

He kisses the top of her head and holds her close. "I know. I don't either. But I can't watch you run yourself into exhaustion either. Will you consider therapy?"

"Not now. Please...just not now. Charlotte is in prison, and

Samil is dead. I know this. I'm fine. They're just nightmares, likely from hormones. Let's see how things are after the twins are born."

Sebastian's hand reaches down and cups her large belly. "What can I do to help you?"

She sighs contentedly. "This. This is what I need."

"My sweetness, you need more than me holding you."

"Sometimes yes, sometimes no." Another heavy breath. "A nanny. Fuck, Sebastian. First Emily needs a hip replacement, and now we need to find another new person? I'm not sure I have that in me."

"Go rest." He tilts her chin up and kisses her lips. "Rowan and I will talk. Do you want us to wake you before we meet with Marcella? That won't be much rest for you if we do."

"Wake me after. I'm less concerned about her than I am about hiring a new person to watch our children."

"You'll need someone," I say, agreeing with Sebastian. "Especially after the twins are born, so I don't know what else to tell you other than we'll do everything we can to ensure she's not another psycho."

Bellamy emits a small laugh, but she's smiling, and that was my goal.

"What he said. No psychos allowed within the palace walls again."

She drags her fingers through his hair. "You're very cute when you say things in English to me."

He holds her face and kisses her softly. "I'd do anything for you."

"You're my heart."

"You're my soul."

Another kiss, then she walks back toward the entrance, too tired to continue their back and forth.

"I don't like it," Sebastian says the moment she's out of earshot. "Rowan, when did everything become so fucked?"

I don't have an answer for that. "Not all fucked. You have her. You have your children."

He nods, but the creases in his face are unmistakable. He brushes back his hair and curses in Latin. "It's been one thing after another since I brought Bellamy into my life. I won't make the same mistake of pushing her away as I did after she fell in the kitchen, but I won't lie and say that I'm at ease with anything. And now we need a new Emily."

"There's something familiar about her."

His brows dip. "Who?"

"Marcella."

Sebastian makes a sarcastic noise in the back of his throat. "Familiar? How so? She looks like every other housemaid. Honestly, most of the time I can't tell them apart, and don't tell our aunt I said that, otherwise, she'll rake me over the coals."

"You're blinded by your wife, brother. Marcella doesn't look like every other housemaid we have. Even in that frumpy uniform with no makeup on and her hair in a drab braid, anyone could see that."

I get a raised eyebrow, and there's a challenging glint to his eyes. "Oh? Noticed her hair and lack of makeup, did you?"

I roll my eyes. "Stop. That's not what I meant. Don't say you didn't notice how beautiful she is."

He laughs and nudges my arm with his elbow. "Actually, I didn't. I was a bit too preoccupied with the fact that Emily fell to notice the girl. But clearly you did."

I almost laugh, pushing up my sleeves against the summer heat. "Clearly I did."

"You can't fuck her."

I grunt. "Thanks for that. As if I didn't already know it."

"I'm serious, Rowan."

"I have no intention of trying. She's to be the new Emily. She just has something about her. A spark. An energy. I felt it with Ella too. I'm telling you, there's something about her. It worries me. It makes me not trust her."

"Ah. Now it's making sense. It's not about your nerves or trust. It's that you're attracted to her, and you don't like it because the last time you were attracted to someone, it ended badly."

"No. It's more than that. She's familiar to me."

He sighs and clasps my shoulder. "They're not the same woman, Rowan. You know this. If they were, facial recognition would have caught that and flagged it. Marcella was scanned as part of her background check. Everyone is."

He's right. I know this. It's not the same woman. I wish I could say my odd fixation with Ella has dissipated over the months, but it hasn't. It's the curiosity of her. Yes, she was beautiful, and yes, she seemed different from all the other women. Yes, she gave me her virginity, which felt like a piece of her that only I got to possess. But it's my unanswered questions that keep her on my mind. The lack of closure from that entire encounter.

Or, perhaps, I simply have been alone these last six months, watching my brother with the woman he loves above nearly anything else, even hearing them fuck on occasion. Maybe I simply need to find someone real and stop chasing ghosts that don't want to be found.

"Fine," I concede, dropping the Ella thing. "Talk to me about what I can do. Right now, all of the Marie shit is a dead fucking end. We have nothing new. No leads on her or Desta. I'm living in your palace—"

He squeezes my shoulder, giving it a small shake. "Rowan, you are the prince of Messalina. It's your palace as much as it's mine. This is your family. It is where you always belong. Having you here has kept me sane when insanity seeks my mind. I don't want you to leave. I want you to stay as long as it makes you happy."

My hands meet my hips, and I shift my weight again. "I can't help but feel that if I could find Marie, find Desta, that—"

"I don't want to say this, but I'm going to, because I think you need to hear it. Not because I'm being cruel, but because I love you and I hate watching your torment. We have to assume that Desta is gone. That she is exactly as our mother said. Dead."

My throat thickens, and I attempt to swallow, but it's futile. I'm suffocating.

"You can't hide a person like that anymore. Everyone has a trail. Marie might be found, or she might not be. But Desta is likely not with her, and this search will only lead to more heartache."

My insides seize up, but it's still what I need to hear. I've had the same thoughts, but...fuck. "What about Brea?"

His brows furrow. "What about her?"

"Where is she?"

Sebastian tosses his hands up. "Down south somewhere."

"Yes, but *where*?" I press. "You realize we've been going based on our mother's word about her."

He looks off into the distance. "I remember Mother and Althea talking about how Brea was sick from the moment she was born. I remember Mother talking about a heart condition and surgery. How Brea couldn't be around us. The only time we saw her was right after she was born. Do you remember?"

I shake my head, then think about it, my face twisting up as I dredge up the memory. "Vaguely. She was in an incubator in the hospital, hooked up to a million wires."

"Yes," Sebastian agrees. "This was three months after Father died and Desta was taken. Mother was beside herself with grief and worry. I can't blame her for that. Her husband died, her child was taken, and by that point, Mother had met with Marie about the tiara, so Mother believed Desta dead. Then her new baby, her youngest princess, was deathly sick. I became king and moved out of that palace and you—"

"I was sent to a boarding school."

I was alone after losing more than half of my family. Sebastian would come to visit on occasion, or I'd go home to his palace on holidays, but it wasn't home. There wasn't much there. It was empty, and we were too young. And I hated myself. I blamed myself for all of it. For everything that happened to us. I filled that emptiness with useless pleasure. Expensive yachts, cars, and pretty women.

It's a wonder I never became an alcoholic or a drug addict.

Nothing has been right with our family since the night our father was murdered. It's been endless lies, secrets, grief, sadness, and this fucking curse.

The night I spoke to Sebastian about what a hot pain in the ass his Bellamy was, I came home. Something in his voice made me do it. I flew all day to get to them. It was the first real spark of life to hit any of us since that fateful night killed it all those years ago. But now...

"Mother never mentions Brea. She hasn't in years. I don't want to say this either, but I'm sure there's a reason for that too."

I close my eyes, that thought sending the worst sort of chill through me. Especially as I think about my growing niece and nephew in Bellamy's stomach. What if something happens to her or them during delivery? What if something happens to Phaedra, Sabrina, or Zayer?

It would end us all. I couldn't handle it, and I'm positive Sebastian couldn't either.

I scrub my hands up my face. "Desta is gone. Brea is gone. Sebastian—"

"Don't." He cuts me off. "I can't. I truly can't. Bellamy is the link. She's the curse breaker, even if the curse isn't broken yet. You said this to me yourself."

"What if I was wrong?"

He shakes his head adamantly. "There's a reason she survived Samil and a reason she survived Charlotte. Hell, there's a reason I survived Samil when I shouldn't have. I died on that floor, Rowan, and yet here I am. I have to believe there's a reason for that."

I release a heavy breath and get myself back in line. "I do too." Otherwise, I'll go mad. Maybe I already am. I just want to fix this for all of us. I want my family to be safe. To be happy.

"Let's just hope this Marcella woman is as sweet and loyal as she seems," Sebastian says, pulling me from my thoughts.

I nod in agreement. "Let's go meet with her."

Sebastian and I walk inside and go right to the stairs. We had instructed Marcella to wait for us in the parlor where Emily was, and when we enter, we find her standing by the window that overlooks the back gardens and pool.

She's not on her phone. She's not pacing. She's not impatient. She's simply standing there, lost in her own introspection, a soft song humming from her lips. Before I can stop it, my gaze locks on her profile, admiring the pretty lines of it.

Sebastian throws me a side-eye. He knows me and can read me better than anyone. Yes, I'm attracted to her. I can't imagine there's a man alive who wouldn't be. She's seriously fucking gorgeous in a very sweet, girl-next-door sort of way.

But so what? It doesn't matter.

I won't fuck her.

She's only been here four months, and I don't trust her. I don't care how polite, loyal, and demure she seems or what the background checks showed. Hell, Charlotte was the daughter of the head of the guard and a former schoolteacher, and she turned out to be as fucked as it gets.

That's the look I give him.

What I told our aunt is a fact. I've never messed around

with staff, and I have no intention of starting now. Especially when she's going to be the primary keeper of the palace.

With that thought, something inside me catches.

I won't let what happened with Charlotte happen again. I'm going to watch this woman like a fucking hawk. Sebastian has enough on his plate with running the country, the children, and a pregnant wife.

It's up to me, and I won't fail us again.

I've been standing at the window watching the children play with their aunt since Emily was taken by the paramedics, and I was told to stay put. They're smiling and laughing with each other as they splash in the pool and jump off the diving board. They seem happy, and I hope they are.

They're just children. Children who have already known unspeakable pain.

I'm hit with a pang of...guilt? I don't know. I've never felt that before, but I can't find any other word for it. I think about Jaqueline. Could she have been like this if she were born into a different family? If Samil had married Nora and they'd taken us with them?

I'm here to ruin their lives, but I don't want to hurt children.

Their father I don't care about. Despising him comes as naturally to me as breathing.

Antonia and the Signoria hate the royal family with a vengeance. It's why I'm here. Even if I have my own skin in this particular game. They snap their fingers, and I dutifully go because I have no options in my life other than to obey. I do their bidding, sometimes with my own adjustments or flourish, but the job still gets done.

When my father died, my stepmother became the matriarch of the Batorini dynasty. A legacy built on money, power, and intimidation. Who am I to argue how anything gets done? No one. That's the point. I'm nothing. No one. I'm not allowed to have my own thoughts, make mistakes, or bother with regrets.

I never met my mother, so I know what it's like not to remember someone who is supposed to be so vital to who you are. From what I've heard, Bellamy truly loves them and cares for them as a mother would. It endears me further to the queen. There's something so inherently likable about her. Like...if the world were a different place, she's someone I'd want to be friends with.

I nearly laugh at that. How ridiculous a thought or notion.

My father loved me and did what he could, but there wasn't much to be done. He wasn't leaving his wife or creating a scandal. My mother died, and my stepmother hated me. I wasn't allowed to even have their last name, which is why I still technically don't have one. They didn't give me my mother's, and to this day, I don't know her first name or anything about her.

I lived in the basement and served the family, but occasionally my father would play with me. He'd read with me or buy me dresses I had no place to wear.

Samil too. On his breaks from school, he'd coax his mother into letting me swim with him or have an ice cream on a hot day. We'd play chess and Monopoly, and after my father died and my training really began, we'd spar and fence and fight each other with fucking knives. He taught me how to code and hack. How to appear one way when you're actually something else.

A noise at the door draws me out of my introspection, and I

turn to find the king and prince watching me. Fabulous. What did they see that I don't want them to?

I curtsy. "I hope Mrs. Lids got off okay?"

"She did," the king tells me as he pans a hand toward the sofa as they enter the room. "How about you sit with us for a few minutes so we can discuss everything, including the new position?"

It's a question, but it's not. His tone isn't brokering any negotiation. Not that I'd ever turn him down, but his wariness of me is pouring off him in waves.

"Of course, sir." Without hesitation, I take the offered seat.

The king sits across from me, the prince in a chair beside him, and the interrogation begins.

"You understand that Emily can promote you, but ultimately the final decision for that goes through my wife and me," the king begins.

"Yes, sir. I didn't take her moment of duress as a promotion."

"But she did add you to the pool of candidates despite the fact that you've only been here a short time."

I offer a simple shrug. "I don't have an explanation if that's what you're after. I'm quiet. I keep to myself and do my work with excellence. I care about what I do and how I do it. I don't gossip. Beyond that, I can't speak to her reasoning."

"What made you want to work in the palace?" the prince questions.

I look down at my hands. "My parents have a farm with a bed-and-breakfast attached. It's been in our family for generations. Last year, my mother hurt her back. Unrelated to that, a large hotel chain opened not far from our home, so more people are staying there, and fewer are staying at our bed-and-breakfast. My brothers left school, and now they both work the farm, but my family needs more income than they can earn in order to keep the house and farm. I've spent most of my life tending to the bed-and-breakfast. To the guests we had. I wanted to help in any way I could, so I started applying for positions, and this one came through."

I keep my head down, but I can see from this angle that they're exchanging glances.

"Emily runs more than simply the housekeeping on the family side."

"I'm aware, sir." Now I look up. "She was walking me through the family side as well as what's required to oversee the staff when she fell. Emily is personally responsible for your offices, studies, and suites and attends to the family, including occasionally helping out with the children when there's no nanny in place, in addition to managing all of the house-keeping staff."

"And you feel this is something you're able to do? It's a big job."

I can't help but laugh. The king's automatic dismissiveness of me shows just what an arrogant asshole he is. "Yes. I'm positive that's something I'm able to do. Your Majesty, I was the sole concierge for all of the members of parliament during their last two visits. I managed the housekeeping staff and made sure everything ran efficiently. I understand why the family side as well as managing the overall housekeeping staff isn't something Mrs. Lids takes lightly, but I don't feel it will be an issue. You already have people in place you clearly trust and allow access. It's simply employee oversight, which I'm more than capable of supplying. If you need help with the children, I'm happy to do that as well. I love kids." I straighten my spine and pin the king with a serious stare. "Sir, I'm here to help in any way I can. Mrs. Lids took a chance on me, and I'd like to return the favor by showing her and you that I'm worth the risk."

The king is quiet for a long moment, and the prince hasn't removed his eyes from me once. I give in. I can't help it. My focus swivels over to him, and there it is. An annoying charge.

An electric spark. A sizzle that fills my belly with heat and makes my skin prickle with awareness.

His gaze is nothing short of intense. Unrelenting. I don't think he recognizes me. If he did, I wouldn't be sitting here discussing a new position within the palace. He might be suspicious. He certainly doesn't trust me. That much is clear, and he's doing nothing to hide it or the warning in his gorgeous features.

If he's going to be watching me this closely, I'll have to be extra cautious. Always on top of my game. I can't slip up. I already made that mistake with him once.

"Hmm. I think—" The king's phone pings and cuts him off. He pulls it out of his pocket to read the text. "Althea needs me to come out to the pool. The girls want to show me something."

"Go ahead," Rowan offers. "I can finish up here."

Sebastian nods, stands, and claps his brother on the shoulder, even as he keeps his focus on me. "Thank you for your help this morning," he says and ends it there as he exits, leaving me here with Rowan. Awesome.

"Did you go to university?" he questions as if he's checking off a list of interview questions from a clipboard.

"No. It wasn't an option for me."

"What would you have done if you had that chance?"

The question catches me off guard. I've never allowed myself to think about my life in terms of what-ifs. Most of the time, it was moment to moment. It was survival. Plus, no one's ever asked or cared before.

"I'm not sure," I admit honestly. "What would you have done if you hadn't been a prince?"

He chuckles and rubs his jaw as if no one has ever thought to ask him this either. "I have no clue. This is all I've ever known. What I knew my life would be."

I nod in agreement. "Same. My family needed my help, and I stepped in."

Oddly, we're not so different in that. Neither of us had authority over our lives or situations.

"I'm sure they appreciate it."

"It's necessary, and that's what matters, sir."

"Not sir. I want you to call me Rowan. Remember?"

"I still think it's inappropriate. Why are you asking me to do that?"

His lips bounce, and he rubs his finger along his bottom lip. "You're going to call Bellamy *Bellamy*."

I shake my head. "I never agreed to that, and I have no plans to do so."

"But you will," he says with assurance. "She'll wear you down.

"You won't."

He smirks, his eyes raking down my body, making tingles explode along my skin. "We'll see, Marcella."

The way he says my name curls through me and tightens my belly. I need to get out of here. Away from him. "If you have no further questions for me, I should get back to work."

"I do have further questions for you. I haven't decided yet if you should take over Emily's position."

I push out a silent breath. I don't want to sit here with him. The more time I spend with him, the greater the chance that he could recognize me. If he hasn't already. I feel like he's playing with me, and I don't like it. I don't know how to outmaneuver him.

"Your Highness—"

"Rowan."

My exasperation comes out in a heavy sigh. "Rowan—"

"See. I knew I'd wear you down. That didn't even take much work." His eyes glint with triumph and something else. He was baiting me, and he won. "The way you say my name...your voice...not much of an accent that time."

Oh god. It's the first time I've said it since that night, and a trickle of fear hits me because I knew that's why he wanted me to say it, and I fell into his trap.

I straighten my spine and meet his gaze. "*Your Highness,*" I emphasize. "I'm not sure what else—"

He sits back, crossing his legs at the knee as if he's settling in for a long chat. "What's your favorite food?"

"Pardon? I don't see how that's pertinent to anything."

His hand twists through the air, encouraging an answer. "Humor me."

"Salad."

His eyebrows bounce in surprise. "Salad?"

I arch an eyebrow in return. "You're rating my answer."

"When your answer is *salad*, I am."

"Sorry it's not lobster, Your Highness. We grow fresh vegetables on our farm."

He laughs and points at his chest. "You're rating my censure?"

I puff out a relieved breath, and with it, some of the tension that's been sitting on my shoulders since I walked into the breakfast room ebbs. I know how to do this. How to be tactical. Patient. Read my opponent. If I want to survive here, survive him, and do what needs to be done, then I have to keep my boundaries. Maintain my façade. Even when he seems to have some obscure way of cracking it without much effort at all.

Just as he said.

"Yup."

"Fine. Salad is your favorite food. Boring." He exaggeratedly yawns. "Moving on. How many siblings do you have?"

The answer flies past my lips from practiced memory. "Three. Two older brothers and an older sister."

"What's your favorite book?"

"I don't have time to read for pleasure."

He swipes his thumb along his bottom lip. I have no idea

what that move is, but it's unfortunately as entrancing as the rest of him.

"What do you do for fun?"

I laugh. It comes out as sardonic as the last one. "Again, sir, I don't have much time for fun."

"Humor me."

What these questions have to do with anything, I have no clue. I try not to shift, but he's rubbing at me. I don't like answering personal questions, and I never practice bullshit ones related to my character.

I do my best to maintain my polite, professional disposition, but I'm struggling, and he knows it. I tug down the end of my ugly dress as I recross my legs. "I go for long walks, play chess, or swim."

"Again boring."

I try so hard not to roll my eyes. "Yes, Your Highness, I'm sure compared to you, my life is rather boring."

His lips twitch. "That sounded like sarcasm."

"Not at all. It's the truth."

"Fine. How old are you?"

I squint at him. "Twenty-three."

Except the moment I say it, I instantly regret it. Especially when he comes back at me with...

"I'm thirty-three."

"Yes, sir. Though I don't think our age difference matters all that much."

His playful and cocky demeanor shifts, turning frosty. Almost hostile while his bright blue eyes sharpen as if all of that between us was a game I just lost. I realize all his banter, his teasing comments, his flirting are all a ruse. A weapon he uses to disarm and hide what truly lurks beneath his charming smile and handsome face.

"Did you already know that?"

My pulse thrums in my neck and palm. "Yes, sir. I did."

"Thought so. What else do you know about me, Marcella?"

Jesus. This guy. I hate the way he says my name.

I know how you smell. How you kiss. How you fuck. How you feel. How you look when you come. I know that you're the most dangerous entity to my being here, and therefore, I need to stay far away from you.

"Not much else, sir. Only what's public knowledge."

He looks eerily calm. "If you say so, though something about you makes me believe you know a hell of a lot more about everything than you let on."

I sit up straighter, my expression and tone even. "I don't believe that to be true."

He's silent for a long moment, his eyes all over my face and body as if he's trying to see through me and find my secrets.

"You're all business, and I respect that. You tell us you'll do a good job, and I'm inclined to believe you because I know and trust Emily, and she wouldn't have put you up for the position and given it to you if you didn't. That said, you should know I'm all business too. You're a citizen of this country, so you're aware of what the former prime minister tried to do to the king and queen. You've also been in this palace long enough that I have no doubt you know about our last nanny. Hell, you likely met her once or twice."

"I did."

"And do you know what she did?"

"Yes, sir."

He leans forward, planting his elbows on his thighs as he levels me with his cold stare. "Good. Then you can imagine what little trust I have in anyone in a position to interact regularly with my family and the need for constant scrutiny and oversight."

I bite back my smile. Not just a pretty face, Prince Rowan has a set of balls and knows how to dole out pretty-worded threats.

I fold my hands on my lap. "I understand that, sir, and you have no reason to trust me. If I were you, I wouldn't trust me either. But that doesn't mean I'm not excellent at my job and can earn your trust in due course."

He stands, and an unsettling silence descends between us. Finally, he speaks, his tone chilling. "Then I guess you just won yourself a promotion. Get used to seeing me, Marcella, because I sure as hell plan to watch you."

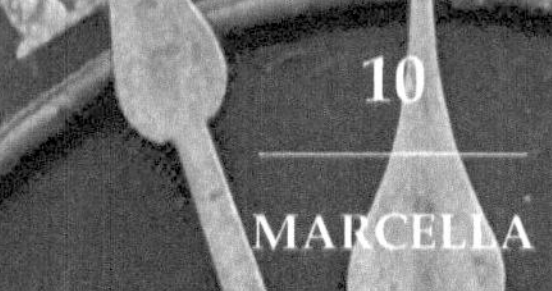

Rowan leaves the room without another word, his threat hanging heavily in the air. I listen as the echo from his shoes on the floor grows quieter and dissipates into nothing. Once I'm positive he's gone, I stand and tug at my scratchy gray uniform as I debate my next move.

I slip my work phone from my pocket and stare at the dark screen.

I decide not to notify the Signoria or Antonia of my new position. Something has me waiting, and I hold to it. I pull up the housekeeping group messenger app. I have no clue if the king or anyone else will make an announcement, but no doubt the gossip mill is already churning. If I'm temporarily taking over for Emily, I need to let it be known.

This should go over well.

Yet as I start to type, a message comes through.

Emily: Some of you may have heard that I fell this morning or saw that I was taken out by ambulance. I'm at the hospital and will be having surgery in the next few days. I've asked Marcella to take over my position until I've completed my rehab and am able to return to work. I've spoken with King Sebastian and have the royal family's approval of my choice.

Emily: Marcella has my utmost confidence, and I expect you all to help her out and make this transition as easy as possible for everyone. I will update you on my condition as soon as I have more information.

I blow out a breath. Well then.

I send Emily a private text.

Me: Thank you so much for your message. I sincerely appreciate your faith in me, and I promise not to let you down.

She replies instantly.

Emily: I'm positive you'll do a fantastic job. I spoke to Prince Rowan and King Sebastian, and you have their confidence as well.

I can't stop the snort that climbs out of the back of my throat and nose. Right. I have no doubt they do.

Emily: Javier will send you a link to everything you'll need to manage the team and learn their assignments. There is also an iPad in my office on my desk. Everything is already logged in on it. The code is 4-5-9-0 to unlock it. It'll have everything you need.

Me: Perfect. This means so much to me. Rest up and get better. You don't need to worry about a thing.

I go back to the group chat.

> Me: I appreciate Emily's and the royal family's confidence in my work and am grateful for this opportunity. I hope we can work together and make this brief change a smooth one for all of us.

Shoving my phone back in my pocket, I head out of the parlor, down a flight of stairs, and across the palace to Emily's office. I've never managed this many people before, but I know how to read people, how to tell them what they think they want to hear, and how to work them if necessary.

I enter Emily's office and find the iPad she mentioned sitting on top of her desk.

"Stealing from the top already?" A voice comes from the door. I don't glance up. It's Esme, a guest staffer like me who was on the short list of candidates. She and I were friendly until Emily approached me about the position. She was one of my main sources of gossip. She and the two people who are flanking her were. It's amazing how fast the three of them turned on me over this.

I've never had friends before, so I honestly don't know how this all works, but the reality is, I don't care all that much. I'm not here to be their friend.

I get it. They're jealous and upset. They sort of have a right to be. They've been here longer than I have. But unlike them, I'm not known for being a gossip. I'm discreet whereas they're not. I also do double the work in the same amount of time as all of them. Call it a byproduct of getting the shit whipped out of me if I didn't work quickly and efficiently enough or that I wanted to appear as the model employee. It doesn't matter.

The facts speak for themselves, and when Emily and I were discussing the position before she fell, she hinted at her reasons for including me in the pool.

"I heard she pushed Emily," Raul claims.

I don't bother to acknowledge his comment. He's testing me to see if he can get a rise out of me, and that's not something I'm known for. Thus far, the only person who seems to exacerbate me and ruffle feathers I didn't even know I had is the fucking prince.

I unlock the iPad and look over everything that I need to familiarize myself with.

"You're not even going to gloat?" Marsha, an American with an annoyingly nasal voice, goads. "Little Miss Perfect got the job. How nice for you. Too bad no one will take orders from you."

"That's so wild since Emily and Prince Rowan made it clear that I can let anyone who doesn't go."

They obviously didn't give me that power, but these assholes don't know that.

I search through the schedule. "Hmm. Marsha, you're supposed to be on the family side, tending to the children's rooms." I glance up at her. "And yet you're here." I turn to Raul. "And you're responsible for the library today, along with the third-floor guest quarters. And you"—I shift to Esme—"are supposed to be on the second-floor guest rooms. And yet you're all standing here."

"You're a bitch," Esme snaps.

"Right." I roll my eyes. "*I'm* the bitch."

"This isn't done." Raul points at me like the tough guy he's not. "Don't think us going back to work is a sign of that."

God, he's a moron.

"Noted." I smile sweetly at them.

Shockingly, they leave, though I take them at their word when they say this isn't over. It would be nice to have someone in my life other than Jaqueline that I didn't hate or was adversarial with. I had two people, and they're both dead. Maybe this is just how it is in the world. I can manage being alone. It'd be an improvement.

I only wish I could bring Jaqueline here.

With all this set, I get myself to work, and the rest of the day goes smoother than I was anticipating. For the most part, there are no major fires to put out or attitudes to manage. Most people are friendly and eager to help in Emily's absence. Esme, Marsha, and Raul, from what I can tell, get their jobs done.

Not all of the staff live in the palace. Some do, but many commute from Tourin, which is about a thirty-minute drive from here, or Aosla, which is about forty minutes away. It makes the evenings quiet, and I like that. Evenings have always been my only breath of air, and I take them gladly.

I spend it going over staffing and schedules. Emily said I should be on the family side, tending to the family's suites as well as their studies. Tomorrow is going to come with a lot of eyes on me.

My phone rings on my nightstand, and I wince only to relax when I see it's Jaqueline. For the first time all day, a smile lights up my face.

"Hi," I answer. "How's it going?"

"It's going," she chirps. "I studied English for most of the day."

"That's great." Even if the reason they have her learning English isn't to make her more worldly. It's to turn her into someone like me. Yet another assassin.

"When do you come home?"

I move to the edge of my bed and look around my small quarters. There's barely anything in here, and it's still a million times nicer than any place I've ever slept before.

"I don't know," I answer honestly. "I wish I could come home and see you. Or better yet, have you come here."

"I wish for that too. I hate sleeping down here by myself."

My eyes close. "I know. I don't blame you. How has this week been with Signoria and Antonia?"

She's quiet for a very long time. "Fine, I guess."

"Don't lie."

She sighs into the phone. "The reason I did English all day was that I think they broke a rib or something."

I hiss a curse under my breath.

"I'm sorry. I didn't want to tell you."

My lungs seize with fury and guilt. "I always want you to tell me."

"They won't live forever," she whispers, and I laugh. It's our saying. One day we'll have freedom. The problem is, with no identity, it's damn near impossible to make it in this world. We're slaves to them with no other options.

"You're right. They won't. I'm in a new position now. One that gives me direct access to the family. Hopefully things will move along faster and I'll be back home in no time."

Only I don't want to go home. Rowan aside, I want to stay. The thought of going back to that palazzo gives me nightmares and makes my insides shudder. On the flip side, I hate leaving her there alone. More often than not, I've been able to take the brunt of their force and keep it off her. Without me there, she's got no one to protect her.

"How's the prince? Still dreamy? Did you finally talk to him now that you got that promotion?"

I smirk. She loved hearing about my wild night with the prince, and though I kept the details PG, she still swooned. "Wow, you didn't even put any bait on that reel, did you?"

She laughs. "Nope. Tell me."

"Yes. He's still dreamy. He's also an arrogant jerk and very suspicious of me in this new role. I have to be extremely careful with him."

"He didn't recognize you though, right?"

"No, but today was the first day I interacted with him. Hopefully, I can keep that to a minimum." Even if he did threaten the opposite.

She sighs wistfully. "Imagine if you and the prince fell in love and got married. Then I could move into the palace with you, and we'd all live happily ever after."

I snort. "I wouldn't hold your breath on that fairy tale. The prince already doesn't like me, and the feeling is mutual."

"Don't burst my bubble. A girl can dream. Especially when that's all we've got."

11

MARCELLA

Emily has the palace honed into a well-oiled machine that I can't allow to lapse, even for a moment. Truthfully, I'm in over my head, and as a result, I wake early after going to bed late. All that aside, somewhere near midnight, with Jaqueline's conversation still lingering on my mind, I had a thought.

I can keep the money I earn here.

I can keep my new name and credentials too. And when I'm done at the palace, I can take Jaqueline, and together we can leave Messalina, Antonia, and Signoria Batorini behind.

I can go out into the world. I can get a real job. How can they stop me? What are they going to do? I was beholden to them with no way out, but now, my options are open. They're the ones who paid off the necessary people in order for me to get the credentials, so it's not like they can say or do anything about it.

Their hands are just as dirty as mine.

The truth is, they'll kill me if I attempt it. But maybe I can broker our release. Maybe I can work out a deal. I have to try. If I can't, I'll complete my assignment here and kill them. I can't go back to that life. Not after living in this one and knowing what's out there.

Once that thought took residence within me, that small taste of eventual freedom, I fell asleep. I can do this job. I can do anything I set my mind to. I can deal with petty assholes and avoid Rowan easily enough. Adding to that, the chief of security, Emily's husband, is with her at the hospital, so I'll have a bit more freedom from that to get things done.

The king, queen, Rowan, and Althea rise early. The king and Rowan go to the main gym or run the trail while the queen and Althea have regular yoga sessions together. The children get up shortly after that, and they all have breakfast together in the breakfast room most mornings.

It's during that time that I'm to ensure that the king's office, study, and Rowan's office are ready for the day. The bedrooms are done after that. I have my trolley full of supplies and tackle the king's quarters first. I don't have access to his computer, nor can I even attempt that now, and the documents he has out aren't of much interest. Simply matters of state that require attending to. Nothing scandalous or even juicy. I also don't take pictures or read anything all that carefully.

I don't know where—if there are any—the cameras are in this room. Snooping will have to come later once I'm more comfortable that I can get away with it.

After I finish with the king's space, I move on to Rowan's study. This and his bedroom are the two places I'm least excited to enter. I don't want the view into his life any more than I already have.

On first breath, it's not what I expected.

It's simple without a lot of fanfare. It has a large mahogany desk with things strewn on it, a comfy-looking brown leather sofa, two chairs, an open gas fireplace, and a table and chairs by the window. His wooden bookshelves that match his desk are mostly empty save for a few ancient-looking tomes about

Messalina that I surmise are ubiquitous on every bookshelf in the palace.

I don't like being in here. It smells like him, first of all, but touching his stuff feels like I'm touching him. It wasn't like this in the king's space, and his was far more lived in and filled with things like family pictures and paintings on the walls and an old mug of half-drunk coffee.

I start with dusting, making sure everything is pristine, but mostly so I can wash out the scent of his cologne with beeswax and citrus. But when I get to his desk, I can't help but study it in ways I didn't the king's. Papers are scattered across his desk that appear to have been ripped out of a sketchbook, along with pencils and charcoals worn down to the nubs. I look at the torn pages, trying not to disturb them as I clean.

They're sketches, which I didn't expect. Most are objects or landscapes. There are a few of the children, and one is with the king and queen. All of them are incredible, so lifelike, and I had no clue that Prince Rowan had an artistic side, let alone real talent. I continue on, going from paper to paper when I spot a leather portfolio tucked beneath his laptop and some other items.

I shouldn't touch it.

My job is to clean, but I'm not exactly a maid, am I?

I glance at the door, curiosity taking over common sense as I listen for footsteps and hear nothing. Then I mark the walls and ceilings, searching for anything that could possibly be a camera, and when I come up empty, I slip it out and carefully open it.

God, this is so stupid. And I hate that I care enough to do this. I hate that there's still a part of me that thinks about him. Is intrigued.

It's more charcoal sketches, but when I get to the second page, my heart stops, and my jaw drops. It's me. Or rather, it's

Ella, the version of me from the wedding, complete with dark hair, dark eyes, a lot of makeup, and a beautiful gown. Jesus.

It looks like me, and yet, thankfully, it doesn't.

With a tremulous hand, I flip the page and find another, this one of me holding my martini and smiling. The next is... holy shit. It's me, naked on his bed, my head thrown back in ecstasy, my legs spread, and my tits high.

Heat crawls up my skin, and I rub the back of my neck as I look at it closer and see his fingers in my pussy and the top of his head hovering close. My empty core clenches, and my nipples tighten. He drew me coming. I remember what that orgasm felt like. How intense it was. The next page is of me on top of him, riding him. I have a blissed-out smile on my face, and I look...happy. Lust-drunk and happy.

I can't believe he drew these. Drew me. Drew us from that night.

With my heart pounding in my chest, I quickly shuffle the papers back in line, close the leather cover, and put the portfolio back where I found it. Only in my haste, I step back and knock into a large vase on the floor behind me that I hadn't noticed.

Shit.

It begins to topple over, and I lunge for it, grasping it at the last second before it smashes. I manage to set the white vase with blue paint back upright and release a relieved breath, only to start and practically drop the thing again when a voice from the doorway says, "That's a Ming Dynasty piece. Glad you didn't break it."

Fuck!

I face Prince Rowan, my heart beating so hard and loud I'd be shocked if he couldn't hear it. "Me too. Probably smart that you keep a priceless object on the floor where anyone could bump into it."

Crap. I need to watch my mouth. But damn him, those

photos and him finding me have me so flustered I can hardly catch my breath.

A ghost of a smile touches his lips. He's leaning against the doorframe, arms folded over his broad chest as if he's been watching me much longer than I hope he has been. I didn't check. I got sidetracked by his drawings. He's dressed casually in dark jeans and a loose white shirt with the sleeves rolled up, revealing strong, tanned forearms.

"Emily never seemed to have a problem with it."

"That you know of."

He pushes off from the doorway and stalks toward me. So much for all that beeswax and citrus.

"What on my desk made you so jumpy that you knocked into my vase?"

My mouth goes dry. "Nothing, Your Highness. I was just cleaning around your desk."

"Were you?" He takes in his sketches and other papers, the ones I left mostly untouched and in place.

"Of course. I didn't—"

"You didn't what?" His tone sharpens. "Didn't look? Didn't touch?"

"Actually, I did both."

He chuckles lightly and angles toward me, his eyebrows raised. "Where did you look and touch?"

His voice is a soft purr, decadent like velvet or melted chocolate. The way he asks that after the drawings I just saw is not helping my nipple situation. I can't tell if he saw me looking at his portfolio or not, so I point to the visible papers, my gaze holding firm on his.

"Do you make it a habit to touch and look at things that don't belong to you?"

Asshole.

"No, sir. I don't. I apologize for overstepping." I shift away from him. "I was about finished in here anyway. I'll let you have your study."

I grab my trolley and head for the door when he stops me.

"Marcella?"

My eyes close. "Yes, Your Highness."

"Did you like them?"

I turn back to him. "Yes. I liked them. They're very good."

"Even the ones in the portfolio?"

Shit. He did see me.

"Yes. Even those." There is no inflection in my tone, and my features stay neutral.

He rounds his desk and crosses the room to me. I swallow thickly as he approaches, standing over me, the weight of his gaze heavy on my face. I fight the urge to bite my lip or shift my position. It's also one hell of a battle to maintain eye contact, the tension so thick between us you could cut it with a knife.

"Maybe next time a little more cleaning and a little less touching." He dips in toward my ear, and I swallow thickly. "Unless that's what you're after here." His warm breath ghosts across my skin.

My jaw locks, and my fists ball up.

Cocky fucking ass.

"No, sir," I grit out. "It's not."

"You wouldn't be the first to try."

I step back and nail him with my ire. "While I'm sure you've had women throw themselves at you, you won't get that from me. I'm not the least bit interested in that."

His blue eyes pierce into mine. "And yet my pictures made you blush so pretty."

Bastard. He's testing me again, but I'm more than done with him. This is the real Prince Rowan. Not the charming drunk guy I met at the wedding who made me feel decadent and special.

"Your Highness—"

"Rowan," he corrects. "It's not 'sir' or 'Your Highness.' Say it, scream it, yell it, whisper it. I don't care—"

I shake my head, cutting him off. "I'm not calling you that again."

"We'll see. You're dismissed."

I spin on the balls of my feet, grip my trolley, and hightail it out of here.

With how he drew me, despite the disguise, I can't help but wonder just how much the prince knows about me and isn't letting on.

"Oncle Rowan, watch me jump off the high board!" Phaedra calls out, her hands waving wildly through the air, her long blonde hair wet and clinging to her small body.

"I'm watching, my darling."

Without a second of fear, she jumps, plummeting like a knife, straight down into the water, where she slices through it and comes up with a jubilant grin.

I clap for her, then Sabrina and Zayer get in on the attention-seeking. It's all Oncle Rowan this and Oncle Rowan that.

"Watch me, watch me!" Zayer cries, his arms flailing, fighting against the restraint of the swim vest he's in. Sebastian and Althea are sitting at the table in the corner under the umbrella, deep in conversation while continuously throwing side-eyes at the children in the water. All three are excellent swimmers, and Zayer is in his floaty. Plus, I'm here.

Poor Bellamy had a bad headache this morning and didn't even make it down for breakfast. Marcella brought it up to her in bed since that's what Emily would have done for her. That's what Sebastian and Althea are discussing. Help for Bellamy, who is an *I can do it all myself* kind of woman.

I respect that about her, but she genuinely *can't* do it all by herself.

I haven't seen Marcella in two days. That doesn't mean I haven't been tracking her on the cameras, because I have been, but I haven't been in her presence again since the other morning. I can't be alone with her. It's become my new rule I promise to heed. I get near her, and I react.

I flirt, I tease, I prowl. The one thing I haven't done is touch, but I've come so close. Hell, I fucking smelled her hair when I whispered in her ear. It has to stop.

She found my drawings. The ones on my desk aren't anything. They're just sketches for passing the time.

But the ones in my portfolio are different.

And she saw at least one from my night with Ella.

I got there just as she opened it, and I watched her expression. The heat and lust that climbed up her face and darkened her eyes. It got me hard. Almost instantly. I couldn't help but wonder if it made her wet. If she imagined that she was the woman on the bed with my fingers and mouth on her cunt or riding my cock until she came.

I taunted her. I couldn't help myself.

I wanted to pin her to the wall, lift her frumpy gray dress, and touch her the way she had touched my drawings.

So since that moment, I haven't been near her.

Watching her is simply because I don't trust her and nothing more, though all I've seen is her doing her job. I also checked the video from my night with Ella. It's not something I've done in a few months, but I did look at it for comparison.

There are similarities there.

The slope of their noses and the lift of their chins. The paleness of their skin, though, Marcella has more of a sun-kissed glow to her. But Ella's face is wider, longer, and the shape of her eyes is different—even different from what I remember.

She looked different than the mental image I have of her, which is odd to me. The image I have is closer to Marcella's, but then again, I was drunk that night, and memories warp with time like water-logged wood.

"Come swim with us!" Sabrina demands, doing flips underwater as many times as she can before she has to stop to catch her breath. They're bored. They haven't left the palace much since Charlotte. I know Bellamy is pushing for the summer festival, and I think it's a good idea too. Maybe the curse attacks in threes, and now it's done.

Samil, Bellamy's father dying, and Charlotte.

My father dying, Desta being taken, and Brea getting sick.

Then again, there's what happened to Nora. Shit. Fuck if I know how this works, but we can't stop living either.

I pull off my T-shirt and chuck it onto a nearby lounge chair, kick off my flip-flops, and drop to the edge of the pool before going all the way in. The water is cool, but not cold, and feels refreshing against the blazing summer sun. The children take turns swimming up to me, splashing me, and daring me to chase them, which I do. I become the shark, and they're the fish. They're all smiles, climbing on me and dunking me under the water. Even Arthur gets in on it, swimming and swirling around the children.

Being with them warms my heart like nothing else.

They have no clue Bellamy was taken by Charlotte. All they were told was that Charlotte had to leave and that, for now, they wouldn't be getting a new nanny. As much as we can maintain their innocence, I'm in. I don't like bringing in new people, and something about Marcella is triggering that.

Well, she's triggering a lot of things in me that I wish she weren't.

"It would be so cool if we had a waterslide," Sabrina says, doing twirls in the water.

"A waterslide?" I question.

"Yes." She swims over and climbs up me until I'm holding her in my arms with her little legs around my chest and back. "A giant one that spins around and around." She mimics the motion with her hands.

"I want a waterfall," Phaedra states, getting in on this. "But it has to have a secret grotto behind it."

I chuckle, shifting Sabrina in my arms so I can brush some of the water back from my face. "How do you know what a grotto is?"

"Mommy and I read it in a book, and she told me what it was. It sounds magical, and I want one. If Sabrina gets a waterslide, I want a grotto."

"What about you, lad?" I ask Zayer, giving his floaty a push that sends him spinning in circles. "What do you want in the pool?"

"I want more swimming."

"And you, Arthur?" I question teasingly.

"He wants more swimming too!" Sabrina answers for him. "And the waterslide. He really wants that."

"I think those are all excellent choices," I say to them. I give Sabrina a kiss on her forehead and drop her back into the water. "Sebastian, your children are asking for some improvements to be made to the pool."

He glances up at me, his eyebrows raised, but there's an amused smile on his lips. "Oh, are they? And what sort of things are they asking for?"

One by one, they start to shout their demands.

Sebastian throws me a *what the fuck are you getting me into* look, and all I can do is shrug at him. The pool area is a bit boring. It was built for swimming laps, featuring two diving boards, one high and one standard height. But that's it. And if this is where the children will spend most of their days during summers, I don't think their requests are beyond reason.

"Come now," I say to him. "I think a waterslide and a waterfall with a grotto would be incredible."

"Personally, I wouldn't mind adding in a spa with therapeutic jets."

Sebastian quirks a brow at Althea, but the woman has never asked for anything in all her years, so if she wants a spa, I think she should have a spa.

I pull myself up and out of the pool, water running down my body and causing gooseflesh to prickle my skin. My hands drag back through my hair, pushing it off my forehead, and I rub the excess water from my eyes as the back door opens and Marcella comes out.

Our eyes instantly lock, but hers don't stay on mine for long. They move down my body, noting my wet chest and abs, continuing south to my trunks that are clinging to me. Cold or not, if she keeps looking at me like that, I'll be hard in a second with no way to hide it. A blush stains her cheeks, and she quickly clears her throat and averts her gaze.

For some reason, it drags a smirk to my lips. Glad to know I'm not the only one affected here.

"I'm so sorry to interrupt, Your Majesty," she begins, coming over to Sebastian. "I was cleaning your study and saw your phone. It buzzed when I picked it up and felt you should have it immediately."

Sebastian stands, shock all over him. "Thank you. I can't believe I left it in there." He takes it from her hand. "Shit," he hisses. "Bellamy texted twice, and the prime minister rang."

"Go tend to all of that," Althea declares. "Rowan and I will stay out here with the children."

Sebastian nods and briskly heads inside.

I grab a towel from the caddy in the corner and wipe myself down. "Marcella, tell us what you think."

"Sir?" she questions, turning to me before she can escape back inside. Why can't she call me Rowan? And why do I care so much that she doesn't? Because I made Ella call me that. It's all I can come up with. I never correct the other staff. I've never asked them to call me by my first name.

"Sabrina wants a waterslide, Phaedra a waterfall with a grotto, Zayer simply wants more swimming, the good lad that he is, and my lovely aunt would like a spa with therapeutic jets."

Marcella tilts her head, even as her gaze stays glued to the top of my head. "I'm sorry, sir. I don't think I understand."

I wrap my towel around my waist and fold my arms over my chest as I move to stand before her. "Do you think we should make these changes to our boring old pool?"

She blinks, perhaps surprised I'm asking or simply uncomfortable with the question. Either way, I want to watch her squirm a bit and see how she reacts.

"It's not for me to say—"

"Perhaps not, but Emily would have an opinion. I can assure you of that. So I'm interested in yours now that you're the new Emily."

Annoyance clouds her eyes, but she does her best to hide it. "I think if you're able to manage the financial implications of such a renovation, then the children and Lady Althea should have what they want."

"I agree." I glance down at Althea. "I don't want it to come from taxpayer funds. I'll pay for it." Lord knows I have plenty through investments and real estate. More than I'll need for ten lifetimes.

"You're serious?" Althea throws at me, a serious look on her face.

"Absolutely." I shake the top of my head, shooting drops of water every which way and managing to get some on Marcella. "My apologies."

"Not at all, Your Highness." She wipes her cheek and forehead.

Yeah, Marcella doesn't like me. That's fine. The feeling is mutual, though my dislike merely comes from the fact that I'm stupidly attracted to her and inherently distrustful of her. She doesn't like me because I push her buttons and get under her skin. She most certainly has trouble looking at me. Is it because of the pictures she found or because I'm essentially half naked? I don't know. Either way, I like her reaction a little too much.

"Let's do it, Aunt. Let's get an architect or landscape designer or whoever deals with such things and get it going."

"You don't want to speak to Sebastian about this first?" Althea challenges, though there is amusement in the curve of her lips and lift of her brows.

I grin. "I will, but you know he won't say no. The moment the children start to work on him, he'll be putty in their hands. Same as I am with them."

"True," Althea concedes. "It would be nice to make some improvements to the palace. We haven't done that in quite some years. Fresh carpet, refinishing the floors, fresh paint, maybe a kitchen upgrade." She turns to Marcella. "From a housekeeping standpoint, are there things that would improve the function of the palace?"

Marcella doesn't like being the center of attention or being asked these things. "I'm sure Mrs. Lids would have a better understanding of that than I would."

"Yes, but her surgeon told me that she'll need six to twelve weeks of physical therapy and that full recovery and muscle healing will be closer to three to six months."

Marcella looks stricken. "I wasn't aware of that."

"Is that a problem for you?" I press. "Filling in for her for that length of time?"

She narrows her eyes at me, only to remember herself and

return to a servant's mindset. It infuriates me. It's as if she's hiding who she is and what her real thoughts are. It only makes me want to push harder, dig deeper. And I shouldn't. With any of that. I shouldn't push, I shouldn't dig, and I definitely shouldn't care.

"No, sir. Certainly not. I was just surprised. In that case, I think an updated elevator system would be quite useful. Currently the freight elevator is small and only on one side of the palace, which makes it difficult for staff with large or heavy equipment to get up and down. I feel this may also be useful for Mrs. Lids with her recovery, as well as others with physical disabilities who find stairs or long walks difficult."

Althea is impressed by this suggestion, and frankly, so am I. It's thoughtful and conscientious of everyone.

"We need Sebastian for this," Althea grumbles with a twist of her lips, even as she does something on her laptop and begins typing. "I'm making notes, though. These are all important elements we must address. Anything else you can think of?"

"Honestly, My Lady, and I hope I'm not speaking out of turn, but much of the electrical, plumbing, and boilers are quite old."

"Yes," Althea agrees. "I've seen the heating and electric bills for this palace. It's ancient, but we must modernize it and make it more efficient and sustainable. I wouldn't complain about better air conditioning either, but now we're talking a large-scale renovation."

"Likely worth a discussion and an assessment, and if Sebastian and parliament agree, we should do the lot."

"Perhaps," Althea agrees. "I'll address it with Bellamy and Sebastian this evening. Hopefully Bellamy is feeling better by then."

"I have to go potty!" Zayer cries from the pool, frantically swimming toward the steps to get out.

"Oh, boy." I chuckle. "I'm coming, lad. Hold on and hold it. Arthur, you watch the girls."

I hear a small giggle behind me, the sound tickling my brain and causing a flash of déjà vu. I cast back over my shoulder and see Marcella smiling and covering her mouth, her attention on me. When she notes me looking at her, all amusement dies, and she quickly makes her escape.

I reach Zayer in the pool and haul him out, unsnap his vest from him, wrap him up in a towel, and quickly bring him inside for the bathroom. It's not near here, so that might be another thing we add to the pool reconstruction.

But her laugh. Marcella's laugh.

No. I have to stop this already.

Am I so obsessed with a woman I'll never find or see again that I make everything about her? Because I'd fucking *swear* I know that laugh. I'd swear it's the same as Ella's. But how can that be?

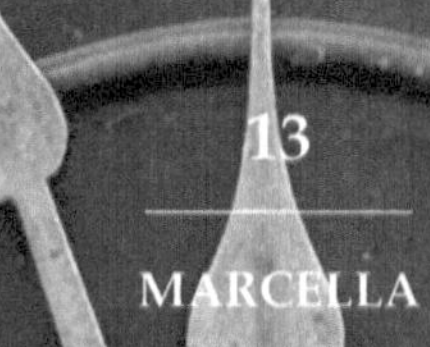

13

MARCELLA

This entire week, there have been small sabotages. Minor things that build and are designed to ruin my day, get me in trouble, or have me fuck something up. I don't have access to the cameras. Not anymore. After I broke into the palace system, did what I had to do in order to alter my face from the chalet and change the facial recognition, and made my background check go through without a hitch, I pulled myself out.

The last thing I wanted was for Javier to notice someone had infiltrated, which he would have. It wouldn't have taken him long to figure it out.

So I can't know who's fucking with my trolley or creating a mess in the king's study that looks like either I created or left behind. They also cut up my uniforms. All of them. I can't exactly tattle that someone is intentionally doing these things because they're petty fucking assholes, because it's, quite frankly, a bad look, and snitches get stitches and all that.

Except the ones to get stitches might be these twats if they continue to fuck with me. I want to retaliate so badly, but I don't want them to know they're getting to me, and I don't want it to backfire. I have too much riding on this.

The master key dangling from my waist bangs into the side of the wall as I turn into the family quarters.

Shit. I stop and make sure I didn't leave a divot. Another thing that needs changing around here? The key system. I understand that the palace is old, perhaps even ancient, but actual keys? They're not the small kind that fit on a regular old ring either. These are the kinds you see in horror films that take place in the nineteenth century.

I'm in a foul fucking mood today, and it's not the kind of mood I enjoy being in.

"I'm sorry, Your Majesty," comes a voice from down the hall that I'm positive is Esme's. "I don't know what to say. She's obviously new at this and is still learning. I suppose we just have to be patient."

"Patient?" the king echoes. "You're telling me to be patient with the fact that my bedroom is in total disarray? How could this have even happened?"

"I'm not sure, Your Majesty. Marcella is responsible for your quarters now. I understand this would never have happened under Emily, but I'm sure there's an explanation for this other than incompetence or oversight."

That fucking cunt.

"Find her and tell her to get it fixed. Now!"

Heavy steps storm down the hall in the opposite direction, and I round the corner, after blood, except Esme isn't here anymore. The hall is completely empty. I go into the king's bedroom that I already tidied this morning and gasp. The clothes from the dry-cleaning hamper are strewn everywhere, the bed is unmade, drawers are open that shouldn't even be touched, and some of the queen's personal items are on the floor.

Bitch is going to die. I've killed people less deserving of it than her.

Jesus Christ, I don't have time for this.

Yesterday, two completely different versions of the schedule were posted to our board—the one I posted and the one someone else posted from last week. It was total chaos in the morning as I had to remove one and redirect people. I've had to restrict people's posting to requiring approval now. Unfortunately, I don't have proof that it's the three of them other than their obvious dismay over me getting the position instead of one of them and their threat.

Dammit, I can't fuck this up. I need this position for more than one reason.

I set to work cleaning up the mess and making sure everything is as perfect as it was this morning, the first time I did this. My mind drifts, thinking up delightful revenge schemes to get back at the three stooges, when I snag on one of the photographs on top of the king's dresser.

The children each have one, there's one of the king and queen from their wedding and one of the king with Rowan on what looks like a yacht, and that's the one I get stuck on.

The king is extremely good-looking. Fiercely so. All hard lines and rough edges, whereas Rowan has a softness to him that the king lacks in the form of full lips and cheek dimples. Those stupid bastards never fail to disarm a girl when she least wants it.

Maybe that's why the king is labeled a beast and Rowan a charmer. Maybe it's more about appearance than demeanor because Rowan has not been charming this week. Not at all. If anything, he's been an ass. Regardless, I can see why the queen fell for the king. Unfortunately, I already know why women all over the world are endlessly eager to spread their legs for Rowan, myself stupidly included.

I was like a blushing schoolgirl the other day by the pool,

all because the man was shirtless and wet. Pathetic. I'm not one of those women. Not again. I hate the way he looks at me. I hate the way it makes me feel like a woman—a beautiful woman. Argh!

Stop thinking about him and get back to work!

I finish off the king's room and lock the door. I'll unlock it later this afternoon, but I want to make sure no one else fucks with it.

My personal phone buzzes in my pocket, and I pull it out to see it's from Signorina Batorini. Awesome. Because this day hasn't already started off like shit.

> S.B.: I've been informed you have a new position there that should further our agenda. Give me an update on your progress.

Fuck. Antonia was all up my ass last night, talking about how they need something concrete to work with and how they're losing patience, etc. I had to give her something and told her about my new position.

> Me: My plan is to hack the king's system when I'm able to. I need direct access to it, though, so it doesn't trigger anything. That takes time, and I just started with this new position on this side of the palace. Once I figure out all of the cameras and triggers, I'll move in.

> S.B: Get it done. I don't have to remind you of what he did to your brother. Or what it means for you and Jaqueline if you don't follow through with this.

> Me: I'll get it done.

I leave it at that. Maybe that's the best way to do this. Get what I need on the king, plant the things Signoria and Antonia have been working on onto his computer, and get the fuck out of this palace. Nothing good will come of my staying here. Rowan will figure it out eventually. I'll get fired, I'll literally kill someone, end up in prison for what I'm plotting to do, or all of the above.

Now that all of the bedrooms and studies are done, I get going on the long hallway outside the royal bedrooms. I start with the duster, going over gilded frames holding paintings with eyes that follow me as I jump from one to the next.

When that's all finished, I set up the large mop with the microfiber head. The children shouldn't be back here for a couple of hours, giving everything plenty of time to dry. I can't wait to be done with this so I can take my walk along the path that leads through the back of the palace grounds and into a wooded area. It's quiet and peaceful and is the only place where eyes aren't always on me. Where I can find some freedom.

The silence of the vast hall wraps around me, broken only by the distant tick of a grandfather clock and the soft swish of microfiber on stone floors. A melody flows through my head, and I follow it, singing the words. I don't listen to music while I'm working. I don't have headphones or wireless earbuds the way everyone else does. I don't have music apps or decent cellular or internet on my phone—it's old and functional.

I don't have luxuries. Hell, I barely have the basics, and this is the first time I've ever earned a paycheck.

So singing whatever song is in my head is the best I've got, and most of my songs are old Italian croons the Signoria likes or more modern angsty rock that Samil used to enjoy. I end up morphing into his favorite song, the words flowing effortlessly past my lips as I swish the mop back and forth.

"That's beautiful."

Startled, I whirl around, the mop dropping from my hand and clattering to the floor. Princess Sabrina and Phaedra are standing before me, holding a large box between them. Arthur is by their feet, peering curiously at me with his glowing eyes. I've never been a fan of animals, truth be told, but there's something adorable about the ferret. Probably because he's always with the children—their loyal guard.

I instantly dip into a deep curtsy.

"Your Highnesses, I apologize if my singing was too loud."

"It wasn't loud at all," Phaedra states.

"I liked it," Sabrina chimes in. "We got our chess game from our room. Aunt Althea is going to teach us how to play."

My face lights up. "I love chess. It's my favorite. My brother taught me how to play."

"Are you good?" Phaedra questions.

I shrug. "I think so."

"Girls, here you are," Althea exclaims from behind me. "Zayer is asking for a snack, so perhaps we'll play later."

Both their expressions fall.

I twist toward her. "If I may, I'd be happy to teach them while you tend to the prince."

Althea studies me, and then after a long beat asks, "You wouldn't mind?"

"Not at all. I was about finished here anyway and was going to go on my break, but I'd be happy to play chess with them instead."

"If you're sure, that would be great. I sent Bellamy for a nap. She ran around with them all morning, and I don't want her to overdo it."

I nod. "Of course. I understand. Truly, it'd be my pleasure."

"Yeah," Sabrina chimes in, jumping up and down. "It's her favorite game."

"Is it? Fabulous. Marcella, if you could take them to the playroom and get started on the game, that would be a huge help."

"Absolutely." I curtsy to the princesses. "Lead the way, Your Highnesses and Arthur."

This makes the girls giggle, and they happily take me along. I remove the box from their hands, carrying it for them, and once we reach the playroom, I set it down on the large coffee table bracketed by two sofas.

I open the box and pull out the board while the girls eye the pieces.

"My brother told me that if you can master chess, you can outmaneuver and out-strategize anyone."

Sabrina scrunches her nose, not fully understanding, but Phaedra gets me.

I start explaining each piece as they touch and examine them. "The king is the most important piece on the board, the one you're trying to protect, but the queen is the most powerful."

Phaedra, who is set to become queen one day, definitely likes this.

"My favorite is the knight."

Now Sabrina's in on it. "I want to be a knight when I grow up."

"Sabrina, we don't have knights anymore."

She pouts. "Then a warrior."

"I love that. Chess will help build your thinking muscles, which any knight or warrior would need. Also any queen." I wink at Phaedra and show them how to set up the board. Arthur is on a soft cushion in the corner under the window, basking in the streaming sunlight, taking a nap as we begin our game.

Phaedra picks white and Sabrina black—thankfully no fighting to be had—and I help them with their moves, talking strategy and how each move will affect the board and other pieces on it.

"This is hard," Sabrina whines, pouting when Phaedra takes one of her bishops.

"I know. It takes a lot of practice. Don't get discouraged. You're doing such a good job for your first time."

Playing with them makes me miss Jaqueline even more. She's had it so tough, but so have these children. At least they have each other and their family and are swaddled in love.

The sound of someone clearing their throat from the door startles all of us. Rowan is standing there with the queen, and he doesn't look happy I'm here with them.

I finished a meeting with Sebastian and the prime minister, where we discussed renovations and improvements to the palace. Parliament will put it to a vote, but it's reasonable to think it'll all go through. The pool and grounds alterations I'm going to take care of, and I'm excited for that to happen. The plan is to start in the early fall, so it doesn't disrupt the children's summer.

Sebastian stayed, having other issues to discuss, but when I left, I ran into Bellamy, who was on a hunt for the children.

"I want to take the children to the festival tomorrow."

I throw her a side-eye as we head toward the playroom.

"I'm down. I'll go with you."

She nudges me. "I think we need someone else with us. Even with the two of us, we're outnumbered, and I can't chase as well as I used to."

"I think Althea has to stay here. I know they have a bunch of meetings lined up."

She twists her lips to the side as she thinks about this. "I really, seriously don't want another nanny, Rowan."

I toss my arm over her shoulder. "I know, but I think you also know that you need one."

"Fuck my life," she mutters in English, making me laugh. "Fine. Maybe. But that won't solve our problem for tomorrow."

"We'll talk to Sebastian about it. Maybe he can move some meetings around."

She sighs and we continue on, but the moment we reach the door of the playroom, both of us freeze. Me in dismay, she in delight.

I get another nudge to my flank as Bellamy juts her chin toward the scene in front of us. Marcella is sitting on the floor with the girls on either side of her as she teaches them chess. They're laughing at something, but shit, how did Marcella end up alone with the girls?

"What if we ask Marcella to come? The girls obviously like her."

I frown. The girls do obviously like her, and listening to them now, Marcella is being sweet and patient. It's her break time, and she's spending it with the children instead of on one of her walks. And yes, I know her schedule. I know her routine.

She's easy to follow on the cameras, and I won't lie and say I don't spend way too much time doing it.

I should discourage Bellamy's idea for no other reason than it's not smart for me to spend more time with Marcella. But the reality is, I have no reason not to trust her.

My fixation is my own. My wariness too.

That said, I want the children to be able to go to the festival and enjoy themselves. I have no intention of letting my guard down with her, but I can't deny that it would be easier to have her there with us tomorrow. Plus, we'll have royal attendants watching our every move. They'll be safe.

"I suppose we could ask her."

Bellamy smirks knowingly at me. "You like her."

I roll my eyes. "I don't trust her."

"Yeah, but you also like her. I'm not blind, Rowan. You look at her the same way Sebastian used to look at me when he thought I was a hot pain in the ass."

I grunt. "Different. Very different, and I don't look at her that way."

She snorts. "Okay, sure. Since women don't know these things about men or anything."

"You're a brat."

She wiggles her hips, doing a little dance. "I'm also right. Even now, you can't take your eyes off her. You think she's pretty. You want to kiss her," she sings.

I flip her off. "You sound like a dying cat."

"Rude!" she exclaims in English, but she's also laughing at my expense, which draws their attention over to us.

"Mommy!" the girls cry in delight.

"Look, we're playing chess," Sabrina continues.

We walk into the room and sit on the sofas. Bellamy is all smiles. "I see. Looks like fun! Oncle Rowan and I were talking about the summer festival."

The girls light up like Christmas trees. "Are we going? Did Papa agree?" Phaedra climbs up onto her knees, hope gleaming in her eyes.

"That's something we need to speak to Marcella about," Bellamy tells them. "Do you girls want to go find Tante Althea and Zayer? I think Zayer went straight from his snack to lunch."

Both girls rise. "Thank you for teaching us," Phaedra, ever the queen-to-be, says to Marcella.

"It was fun. We'll have to do it again."

The girls take off, and Marcella stands, adjusts her black pants, no longer wearing her ugly gray uniform, and starts to put away the chess set. I scooch to the edge of the sofa and help her, which surprises her. Probably because it's not something a prince would typically do.

"Thank you, Your Highness. That's very kind and unnecessary of you."

Our fingers brush as I pass her the rook, and tingles shoot through my hand that has me drawing back. What the fuck is that?

She must feel it too because her eyes round and she murmurs out an apology.

"Well, I'm glad we found you," Bellamy starts. "Tomorrow, as you know, is the summer festival in Torin. Unfortunately, Sebastian and Althea have meetings with the prime minister and members of parliament thrown on their schedules. Rowan had the idea of you joining us to help with the children since that's what Emily would have done if she were here."

I throw Bellamy a look, but she simply beams a smile at me. Such a meddling little thing. No wonder Sebastian is so fond of spanking her. The woman is playing with fire, and she doesn't even know it. Or perhaps she does, and that's her intent.

"Unless, of course you don't want to come with us," I challenge when she stiffens and a look of unease crosses her face.

She licks her lips and finishes cleaning up the set, putting the lid back on the box. "It's not that, sir."

"Tomorrow is Saturday," I continue. "Half the staff have the day off. The other half has Sunday off. Not a whole lot gets done here on weekends as I'm sure you know."

She shifts her weight. "Right."

"It'll be nice for all of us to get out of the palace," Bellamy states. "I know the children are looking forward to it. The girls will drag Rowan on all the rides I can't go on, so it'll be us and Zayer, except he's fast and I'm slow these days." She pats her large belly. "I could really use the extra set of hands. What do you say?"

The fact that she's even asking instead of demanding shows just how new she is to all of this and how different her upbringing was. Americans don't have royalty. They don't have centuries-old ingrained stations of wealth and aristocracy.

Sebastian would have demanded, and I likely would have too.

Regardless, Marcella can't say no, and she knows it. She curtsies because that's what she does. "Your Majesty. I'm honored you thought of me for this."

"It was Rowan."

I sigh. Seriously, I'm going to have my brother punish her later.

"Regardless of whose idea it was," I cut in, "now that we know how long Emily is to be out, I think it's good for us all to get to know you better."

"I appreciate that. Truly. But I'm not sure how much more there is to know other than what you already do."

"Oh, I doubt that. I'm sure there's plenty about you we don't know."

Our eyes lock in a silent duel, and a dangerous electricity hums between us. I'm being an asshole. I know I am. That doesn't mean I know how to stop either. I no longer trust myself or trust my instincts the way I used to. Or maybe I never thought about it before Ella played me.

My anger at the hand my family has been dealt, the fear at not knowing what's coming next, and the frustration at not being able to fix it are making me resentful. Marcella Russo is an unknown entity, and when you don't know who your enemies are or the full extent of their reach, being cautious is the only option.

But I'd be lying if I said part of the allure is how she reacts and fights back.

"Unless," I continue softly, "you're uncomfortable with the idea of spending time with us beyond your professional duties."

Yep, Marcella really doesn't like me.

She gives me a smile that doesn't touch her eyes. "Not at all, Your Highness. I'm simply surprised by the invitation."

"Is that a yes?" Bellamy asks with hope in her voice, her hands folding up in supplication.

"Of course, Your Majesty."

"Excellent!" Bellamy exclaims. "But please, you have to call me Bellamy, especially when we're out tomorrow. I understand you feel more comfortable being formal here, especially given your new duties, but tomorrow will be more casual and relaxed. We'll have royal attendants dressed in civilian clothes close by at all times, so you should dress casually too."

"Understood, Madam. I'm looking forward to it."

"Great! Same here. We'll leave sometime after breakfast."

Marcella curtsies and excuses herself, leaving the playroom. Tomorrow's going to be hell.

15

MARCELLA

Truthfully, this isn't quite what I expected when the queen mentioned a summer festival. I've never been to Tourin, and I've never been to a festival, but I expected something more along the lines of period costumes and people dancing to folk music or something.

This is not that.

This is sensory overload with flashing lights, the roar of fast rides, the screams of excited children, and the pervasive pinging of games. There are dozens of rides ranging from roller coasters to things that go up and down and side to side. Food trucks and vendors divide the games area from the rides, the air thick with the scent of fried food and sweets. It's hot today in Tourin, nearing thirty degrees Celsius, but the children don't seem to care a whit.

The queen, on the other hand, is already feeling it, and I give her a lot of credit for coming here and smiling a happy, excited smile, which I don't even think is put on, for the children who adoringly call her Mommy. I didn't expect that, and it seems to be a common thread for my time in the palace.

It's so easy to like Bellamy, it's almost infuriating.

The moment we step into the festival, all eyes are on us. You can almost hear the murmurs in the air, the whispers, the questions. The queen takes it all in stride, smiling and holding Sabrina's and Zayer's hands, pointing out fun things she thinks they'll like and nodding hellos and sweet greetings to everyone who curtsies and makes eye contact.

"I swear, no matter how long I live, I will never get used to people treating me this way. A year ago, I was a schoolteacher here, caring for my father with no life to speak of. Now I'm a stepmother to three and soon to be a mother to another two, and people curtsy for me and call me Your Majesty."

"Your Majesty, while I understand it's a bit strange for you, your people are very happy to have you as their queen. They love seeing the children and the king happy again, and they're excited about the twins."

All of that is true and has been bitched about and lamented by Antonia and the Signoria more than once. The horrible things they called her, I wouldn't ever repeat.

She offers me a warm smile. "Thank you. That helps."

I return her smile, but my gaze slips past her and lands straight on Rowan, who is observing me with an indecipherable expression.

"I want to go on the pirate ship!" Phaedra cries, tugging on Rowan's hand and thankfully drawing his attention away from me.

Sabrina jumps up and down. "Me too, me too!"

"All right, my darlings. Let's go." But before he takes a step, he stops and checks in with Bellamy. "Are you good with Zayer?"

Bellamy laughs and waves him away. "I'm great with Zayer. Right, little man?"

He nods up at her, sucking on his fourth and fifth fingers.

Rowan doesn't look so sure.

"We'll be fine. I have Marcella here to help if I need it at all."

Rowan's lips dip down into an uncharacteristic frown, eyeing me once again. He steps into me, his mouth coming to my ear.

"Take care of them with your life."

The fierce way he growls that automatically has me saying, "I promise."

Only I can't promise that, can I? Not really. Not to any extent beyond this festival. Now I'm the one frowning. I don't like how that thought makes my insides squirm.

His lips and nose drag along my cheek, and he takes a deep inhale as he does. My breath hitches, and my body tenses. Holy hell, what is he doing? But just as quickly, he's gone, taking the girls and talking animatedly about the rides they want to go on as if none of that happened.

I can't get a read on him. The man I met at the wedding is different from this one. He was so quick to trust that night, whereas now he doesn't trust me at all. Despite the background check and assurance from Emily and Javier. That night, he didn't even know my last name or where I came from, and yet he brought me up to his room.

Here I'm Marcella Russo, a poor country girl.

I don't know what to make of it.

I have to keep reminding myself that if he knew who I was, I'd be in jail. I'd never be allowed near the queen or the children. Maybe he was simply drunk and looking for a quick and easy fuck and figured the wedding was the safest place for it. I don't know. All I know is that I wish he weren't so pervasive in my thoughts. I wish I didn't go to bed every night thinking of him, touching myself to memories, and wondering if there's any possible way this doesn't end with me either being killed or arrested.

"Should we go play some games?" Bellamy asks Zayer, who is already tugging her toward that area. "He's a bit too small for the rides," she tells me. "I think there are some he can go on, but I can't take him."

"I can if that's what he'd like."

She waves me away. "Thank you. Maybe later. He likes the games." She glances down at him. "Let's go win some prizes. We can show Papa later and tell him about all the fun we had."

She glances up at me. "It's good for Sebastian to hear that. I understand his worry, believe me, I do, but the children have to be children. They can't live in a bottled-up existence. It's stifling."

That hits me hard, and I release a shaky breath. "You're an incredible mother to them," I say before I can stop it, but she is, and she should know it. A pang hits the center of my chest. What would I have been like if I had a mother like her? Someone who cared that way. What would Jaqueline have been?

For the next hour and a half, I stand back and watch the queen play game after game with Zayer. He throws balls and rings, fishes for ducks, and shoots water at clown faces. It doesn't take long before I get wrapped up in it too, cheering and clapping for his accomplishments and offering hugs and good tries at his failures.

He's adorable and so sweet despite the fact that he looks so much like the king, unlike the girls who look like Nora. It makes me wonder. With all their blonde hair, if they are actually Sebastian's or if they're Samil's, and the king simply doesn't know it.

Was he aware his wife, the former queen, was having an affair?

An affair that lasted for years, through the birth of all three children?

"Mommy, I'm hungry."

The queen laughs. "Little man, you're always hungry. Probably because you're growing like a weed and will one day be as big and strong as Papa. But I'm hungry too so let's go find us something yummy to eat." She glances up at me. "Are you good with that?"

My eyebrows lift. This is the second time in a week someone from the royal family has asked my opinion on something. It's a first in my life. Not even my father or Samil ever asked for my opinions or thoughts. I was simply there to do the only thing I could do. Learn, fight, kill, and survive. And occasionally be a silent set of ears to listen.

"Sounds lovely."

"Zayer has a big sweet tooth, and so do I, but I think first we need some lunch. Something with some protein."

She searches around before she stops on something. "Oh, they have calzones."

I follow the direction of her gaze and see the vendor selling traditional calzones. "I can go get them for you, Your Majesty. That way, you and Prince Zayer can find a place to sit, and you can get off your feet."

She touches my forearm, pulling me back to her. "That would be amazing, but please call me Bellamy. I understand it's not your norm or custom, but you're only a year older than I am. You don't know me, and I don't know you, but we live in the same palace, and truth be told, I've never had a girlfriend my age."

"Neither have I," slips out.

She nods in understanding, and something hot and liquid pools in my chest, making it difficult to take in a breath.

She laughs. "The only friend I ever really had was Charlotte, and she was a decade older than me and tried to kill me, so I don't have the best track record with that sort of thing. But I'd really like to start getting past that and trust someone again."

Guilt slams me once again, churning acid in my gut. It's

becoming an all-too-familiar feeling lately. "I understand," is all I can say.

"I'm glad. If you wouldn't mind grabbing us three calzones, and possibly some waters, Zayer and I will go find the perfect place for us to eat them."

"I'd be happy to, Bellamy."

I get another smile, something she gives out easily and freely, and a squeeze to my forearm before she takes Zayer on their mission. She talks with him, asking him questions and pointing out things for them to look at and explore. And I realize I want everything she said. I want to be her friend. I want to be someone she can trust.

Sadness sits square on my shoulders, heavy and dragging, but I press through it.

I purchased the calzones using the money that was given to me before we set off this morning, though the owner of the stand tried more than once to give them to me for free since they're for the queen and prince.

By the time I return, both of them look exhausted. Zayer climbs off Bellamy, walks around the table, and straight up into my lap. Just like that. It's...adorable.

I unwrap his calzone for him, and he wastes no time digging in, not caring in the slightest if he's covered in meat, cheese, or sauce.

"God, I'm starving." Bellamy unwraps hers, and for a few minutes, we eat in comfortable silence. Well, comfortable for them. Tense for me. I can't take my eyes off it. "You can ask," she says, startling me with her directness. I hadn't realized I was that obvious. Clearly, I keep fucking things up left, right, and center.

"I'm sorry. I didn't mean to stare, and I hope you don't take it as rude. I'm simply curious about it, is all."

"It's fine. Really. You can ask."

"Does it hurt?" I can't help but question. It's a long, diagonal slice across her neck, starting from beneath her chin to the center of her throat. It's white and slightly indented. Hardly noticeable under most circumstances, but here in the direct sunlight, it's a glaring reminder of the madness and heartbreak the king drove my brother to.

"No. It doesn't hurt. Not anymore. It hurt like hell when it happened, and it hurt for a while after as it was healing. Now it's just something...there. Something I see every day. A permanent reminder."

"I'm so sorry. I didn't mean to—"

"No, it's okay. No one asks about it. It's sort of the elephant in the room, and people don't know what to do with it. They look, they don't look, and they pretend they're not looking. I'm just glad I didn't know I was pregnant when he took me."

"Why's that?"

She picks at a piece of crust, tearing some of it away and popping it into her mouth, but she's looking at Zayer on my lap, clearly making sure he's preoccupied and not listening. "He told me he was going to k-i-l-l me. He was going to toss me out the window to the rocks a hundred or so feet below. That my body would be unrecognizable, so he could torture me a bit first, and no one would know. They'd think I jumped."

My eyes close. *Jesus, Samil. What the fuck?*

"He wanted to punish Sebastian anyway he could. He loved Nora, the former queen, you see. You likely know he was responsible for her death."

I gulp and nod.

"He gave me an ultimatum. My life or Sebastian's. I chose mine to save his. I didn't want the children to lose another parent. If I had known I was pregnant..." She trails off. "I don't know. Samil wasn't...sane," she finally utters, her voice low and soft so it doesn't carry to nearby ears. "He told Sebastian that he tampered with the helicopter because he wanted him and the children d-e-a-d."

That startles a painful, shocked breath straight from my lungs, and my hand covers my mouth. "No," slips out. Because... "That can't be true." It's impossible. Samil told me... "Are you sure? The children?"

She nods solemnly, her gaze casting down to Zayer, who is contentedly sitting on my lap, eating away, thankfully oblivious to all we're discussing. "He knew Sebastian and the children were supposed to be on the helicopter. That was the plan all along, but then at the last minute, Nora decided to come back to their summer palace instead."

I look away, my insides revolting and my body trembling. She has to be wrong. She has to be. But why would she tell me this if it weren't? She has no clue who I am or my relationship to Samil.

"I can't understand that."

"Nor I."

Except she's misunderstanding my meaning.

Samil would never hurt children. He told me he wanted to kill Sebastian because, despite the fact that Nora was pregnant, this time with Samil's baby, she wasn't going to leave the king. That's what she told him the day she died. That's what they fought about that morning when he traveled to her parents' home to see her. He was beside himself. Rightfully so. She was pregnant, and they loved each other.

When he told me what happened, what he'd done to the helicopter, he said Sebastian was supposed to come to her parents' alone. He told me the children were set to stay behind with the nanny. Did he lie to me about that? Did he knowingly try to kill three small children so Nora would have no further ties to the king or the crown, and therefore, he could have her and their baby?

In thinking about it, Zayer was an infant at the time. It doesn't make sense that the king would leave them behind with a nanny when they were that little. Does it?

Bile climbs up the back of my throat.

Marriages of convenience or arranged marriages aren't uncommon in the royal world, and I understood why Nora had to marry the king. I also understood why she and Samil continued to see each other. But I can't understand this. The notion of him killing children so ruthlessly, so callously. Like they'd simply be collateral damage in his quest to win Nora.

I'm a lot of things, and very few of them are good, but I've never killed a child, and I never would. Not ever. Adults make their own decisions, and their actions will sometimes get them killed. But innocent children? Samil told me the king deserved to die and not Nora. I believed that. Hate for the king and the royal family was indoctrinated into my soul with an unquestionable vehemence. But now...

What else did Samil lie to me about? The thought that he did burns me up. I trusted him unequivocally. Listened for hours as he talked and told me everything.

For the first time in my life, I don't trust my brother. It's soul-crushing.

All these months, all these plans, all these years of believing one thing when it was actually another.

I've done some pretty fucked-up things in my life, things that haunt me at night, things I can't unsee whenever I close my eyes. I was told a hundred evil things about each one of them. Hell, I often saw some of their malevolence for myself. All the reasons they deserved the hand I dealt them. That's how I justified my actions. I was young and trained, and it was all I knew. Defiance wasn't an option. Obedience was the only way. I always told myself it was their life or my own, that I didn't have a choice, and that they had it coming.

But what if some of them didn't? What if I were fed lies and misinformation so I wouldn't question my orders? What if I killed people who didn't deserve to die?

The thought makes me hate myself.

"That's..." I have no words. "You're positive?" I question again, this time firmer.

"Yes. I'm positive. Are you okay?" Her brows crease in concern.

"I'm..." I clear my throat. "Yes, Bellamy, I'm okay. I'm simply in shock. He was such a beloved prime minister. I can't imagine anyone wanting to hurt..." I point down at the sweet little prince on my lap.

"Me neither. I break for them that Nora is gone. No child should lose their mother. I should know."

"Me too," I whisper, only to stiffen. Shit. Marcella Russo still has a mother. Marcella of no last name is the one who doesn't. "I mean, I agree, no child should have to endure that," I quickly correct.

She waves her hand flippantly in the air. "Enough of this heavy stuff. All I know is that as far as I'm concerned, this c-u-r-s-e nonsense is over, and I'm over it. I can't live my life in a bubble. In a gilded cage. And I won't allow my children—Nora's children—to either."

"I think that's very brave." I meet her gaze head-on. "I think *you're* very brave."

I envy that about her.

"Living in fear is no way to live at all."

I swallow past the lump in my throat.

"Now, tell me more about you," she says, her tone and demeanor shifting faster than the tide. "Because I know I shouldn't say this, but I think my brother-in-law has a small thing for you."

I choke. On nothing. Like actually start hacking up a lung, and poor Zayer is bouncing about on my lap and throwing me *what the fuck* looks. Can three-year-olds give that look? I don't know, but he's mastering it as well as his father does.

"Sorry, young prince. My apologies, Little Highness."

He shrugs and returns to his lunch, but Bellamy isn't having it.

She laughs, a knowing gleam in her eyes. "Ah. I see. The feeling is mutual."

I shake my head adamantly. "No, Madam. It's not. I was simply shocked you'd say that. I'm no one. A housekeeper. He's not even particularly kind to me. The prince doesn't like me at all."

"Sebastian didn't like me much either at first. But it was only a matter of time before all that tension and chemistry we'd been fighting snapped."

I spot Marcella first. Her blonde hair glimmers like wheat fields against the sun. She laughs, her head thrown back as Bellamy's hands wave wildly in the air. Zayer is on Marcella's lap, tucked against her like it's the most natural place for him to be. This shouldn't affect me. Zayer has sat on Emily's lap numerous times, and Marcella is simply a temporary Emily.

But like everything with this woman, it does.

I smelled her, brushed my lips along her cheek. She didn't smell like Ella. Ella smelled like a cold winter's night, and I needed to test that for myself because, where so many other things about that feel uncertain, I remember how she smelled.

Marcella smells like soap and shampoo. Clean and a bit floral with something underneath it that I liked way too damn much.

"Mommy!" the girls scream, running up to Bellamy when they find her.

"We just went on the biggest roller coaster ever!" Sabrina is practically vibrating with excitement and adrenaline.

"Yes, and now they're *starving*," I dramatize, imitating their voices.

"We just had calzones," Bellamy tells them, wrapping an arm around both girls. "They were delicious. Would you like that or something else?"

"Calzone!" they both chip.

"I'd be happy to get you all some," Marcella offers.

"Marcella, you haven't gone on any rides," Bellamy interjects.

Marcella laughs it off. "I didn't expect to, Bellamy. It's fine. Really, I'm happy to get everyone their lunch. It's my duty here."

"Nonsense. Rowan, take her on a roller coaster or something. She's never been on one."

That catches my attention. Sheltered or not, even the children have been on rides.

"Is that true?"

Marcella looks away, possibly a bit put out that Bellamy outed her that way.

"Marcella?" I press.

"Yes, it's true, but honestly, it's fine."

"What do you think, girls? Should we take Marcella on a ride before we all eat and let Mommy and Zayer have a rest?"

"Yes!" they both squeal because these girls have boundless energy. Being cooped up in the palace will do that. I can't wait for the new renovations on the pool to start. I plan to have them help me with all of the planning.

"Your Highnesses, that's really not—"

"Come now, you don't want to disappoint princesses, do you?"

If Marcella could flip me off right now, she would. "Of course not, sir."

"Zayer, lad, how about you sit next to Mommy and the two of you hang tight for a few minutes? If you're good and stay with Mommy without trying to run off, I'll get you one of those incredible pastries from the stand we just passed. What do you say?"

He nods enthusiastically. "Yes! Yes!"

"I thought so. All right, one last ride before lunch."

Zayer climbs off Marcella, and she stands, throwing daggers at me with her eyes. Bellamy gives her a wink I don't understand that makes Marcella's lips thin.

"Which roller coaster should we take her on?" I ask the girls. "I'm inclined to really get a scream from her, so I'd say the upside-down one."

"Yes! The upside-down one," Sabrina agrees, coming on the other side of Marcella and taking her hand. It startles Marcella, but she recovers quickly and offers her a kind smile. "If you've never been on a roller coaster before, it's a fun one to start with."

"No way!" Phaedra chimes in. "I say the up-and-down one that has the twist. That's better." Phaedra glances up at Marcella inquisitively. "Do you get sick on rides?"

Marcella pales. "I don't know. I've never been on one before. And I just ate. Is it common to get sick on rides?"

"Oh." All three of us pause.

"Maybe, we shouldn't—"

"No," Marcella cuts me off. "I want to go on the biggest, scariest one you've got. I can handle it."

"All right," I agree. "Let's do it."

We get back in line for the upside-down one, and because people are kind and genuinely awed that the royal family—particularly the children—are here, they allow us to cut. Even when we try to tell them no over and over again, they insist, and somehow we end up at the front of the line in the first car in record time.

"I'll ride with Marcella," I tell the girls. "You two go behind us."

The girls are in on the plan, wanting Marcella to have the best first experience possible, and something about that hits me.

"You're a virgin," I state as we get into the car and are harnessed in place.

"Excuse me?!"

I chuckle. Wow, that came out wrong. "I meant a ride virgin."

"Your Highness, if this is your way of trying to distract me—"

"Rowan, and I'm not trying to do that. I simply realized you're a virgin."

She rolls her eyes at me. "Not anymore. You've officially popped my cherry."

It makes me smile, only for it to slip as I study her. "Are you sure you want to do this? You look a bit...sweaty and gray."

She gnaws on her lip. "It's ridiculous, isn't it? I shouldn't be nervous. It's just a ride."

I can't tell if she's talking to herself or me.

"I've done a million things. A million dangerous things and yet..." The ride starts to move, heading toward the rail that will slowly take us to the top. "Oh bloody fuck!" Her head swivels in my direction. "I hate you. You need to know that, and I likely shouldn't be telling you this, but if I die on this ride, I can't die without you knowing it. I hate you. You did this to scare me or make me sick or whatever twisted plot you had in your head. It's why you asked me to come with you all today. You're trying to sabotage me."

There are a million things in that speech to focus on, but they get cut off when she repeats herself.

"Your Highness, respectfully, I officially hate you."

I smile like the devil. "You don't. You just want to."

"I wouldn't be so sure about that," she grumbles under her breath as we trickle up and up, the festival growing smaller and smaller beneath us. "I suppose if you have your princesses on here, I have nothing to be concerned about."

The wind whips her long bangs and heavy blonde hair back

from her face, and I get a perfect shot of her profile. She's easily the most beautiful woman I've ever seen. It sucks to finally admit that to myself, but there it is. She's fucking stunning and sweet-looking, even if she's not sweet at all. A total knockout. A heartbreaker.

There's a snarky side to her that she covers with manners and formality, and it's annoyingly intriguing. It's also fun to try to get her to bite instead of curtsy, but right now, she has an unexpected vulnerability that's not only surprising but oddly irresistible.

"You have nothing to be concerned about. Rides are fun."

"If you say so. I think it's the harness. I don't like being locked in."

This is the most relaxed and conversational she's ever been with me.

Maybe I've been too hard on her. Maybe I've been combining everything Ella with her because they physically have some similarities. Maybe I should trust her the way everyone else seems to.

"Are you ready?" I ask, still watching her instead of the track.

Her eyes close. "I can't believe I'm afraid. Like it's actually comical given my life and all I've endured. I feel like such a wimp, but holy crap, my heart is going to beat itself out of my chest."

"Hey!" I remove my hand from the handlebars by my head and cover hers that's locked in a vise grip around the metal. "It's fun. I promise. Have fun."

"Fun." She tests the word. "There's a new one for me."

"Good, because here we go!"

The car goes over the arch, and we race down at top speed, chasing a fierce angle that makes everyone on the ride scream at the top of their lungs, including Marcella. In a flash, we're heading straight up into the first loop, and she shifts to grip my hand, holding onto me and the bar for dear life.

"Oh my god!" she screams, but now she's smiling and laughing, and her eyes are wide with wonder.

It's a ride. A roller coaster. Nothing major.

But she's holding my hand and smiling at me, and I saw the look in Bellamy's eyes. Bellamy likes her. Then again, she liked Charlotte. We all did.

The ride continues until it comes to a fast and sharp end, and she blows out a giant breath. The restraints lift, and I stand, helping her out. Her hand slips from mine almost instantly, and it has me turning back to her.

"Wow. That was something."

"Fun?" I question.

She tosses me a smile that immediately has me wanting to do that again and again just to get this same smile on her lips.

"Amazing!"

"Yeah." I take her jaw in my hand, mentally giving myself a *WTF*, but not stopping either. Her eyes round and her lips part, and I don't know what I'm doing, but my head is angling toward hers, and I'm staring at her lips like I want to kiss her.

Because I do.

I want to kiss her so fucking badly.

"Marcella!" the girls scream, jarring me away from her. And thank god for that.

That was almost a seriously stupid mistake.

They're all over her, asking if she loved it and telling her all about the other rides. They make her promise to go on it again after they eat, and we do. This time, she rides with Sabrina, the two of them fast and easy friends, sharing secrets and giggles. But I haven't been able to take my eyes off her. Or stop watching her. She's a magnet I'm helpless to resist.

I can't even explain it. There's nothing about her that should be this compelling to me. I almost kissed her. I smelled her. I dragged my lips along her cheek. What the fuck is all that?

Yet she looks different. She feels different. She's shed some of her formal layers.

Most importantly, the children had an incredible time.

We pile into the large black SUV, exhausted and sticky from last-minute cotton candy and candy apples. Zayer passes out in his car seat the moment the car sets in motion. He went on three rides with the girls, which Sabrina whined were for babies, but had fun on all the same. They won prizes, and I'm proud to say we have no critters hiding away in knapsacks.

Marcella is quiet the entire way home. She's had her face glued to the window and the passing landscape, but it's clear she's not seeing any of it. I exchange looks with Bellamy, but all she does is give me a simple shrug as if to say she's as clueless as I am.

As much as I want Bellamy to have friends, I worry about her easy trust. I worry about how easily Marcella has sucked the children in. Has sucked *me* in.

I don't know.

The Ella shit is messing me up. Still. Because I acted on impulse. I went with my gut, and she was a lie. A fabrication. A woman I never should have touched, though at this point, so many months later, it seems unlikely she was after anything with me. A random foreigner who snuck into the royal wedding for a high and got nailed by the prince.

Except I took her virginity.

Who does that? Who sneaks into a royal wedding loaded with security, gives a fake name, fake everything, but then gives a man she just met her virginity? How do I stop thinking about her? And how do I stop connecting her to Marcella?

17

MARCELLA

I jolt awake to frantic knocking on my door. My room is pitch black, and I can tell the sun isn't rising yet. More knocking, and I practically fall out of bed, calling out an "I'm coming" as I snatch my sweatshirt from the chair in the corner and throw it on before I open the door.

"Thank God you're up!" Jennine, one of the cooks, exclaims.

"What time is it?" I ask, rubbing the sleep from my eyes.

"Half past five. We've got a situation that requires immediate attention."

"Okay. Give me five minutes, and I'll meet you down in the staff room."

"Perfect! Thank you!"

She races off, and I shut the door to get myself dressed and ready. I've taken to wearing black pants and shirts—what Emily typically wears—since my dresses were cut up. I slept like shit last night, my thoughts impossibly heavy. I never snuck out to the king's office. I never went to hack his system. Instead I lay in bed thinking over and over about all the things Samil told me over the years about King Sebastian and the royal family. All the things Antonia and Signoria Batorini have told me. Even things my father told me.

I was also stuck on what Bellamy said. The king relayed to her what Samil had said about wanting the children dead. Who's to say he's not lying to make himself look better after what happened between them?

I don't know who or what to believe anymore. It's rattling me. I need to believe my brother didn't lie to me. I'm not sure I can handle the alternative.

I make it down to the servants' quarters and find four others here, including Raul and Marsha.

"What's the problem?" I ask Jennine since she's the one who came to me first.

"The laundry delivery that was supposed to come in last night never came," she tells me. "And it appears the order was changed to arrive tonight at nine."

"What? I didn't change it."

She shrugs. "They said you did. It's on the form in their system, order changed by Marcella Russo."

Motherfucker. You've got to be kidding me.

"The prime minister and his aide are still here," Raul jumps in. "How are we supposed to care for them and tend to their rooms if we don't have fresh linens and towels?"

"Let me get on the phone with them and see what happened. I'm sure we can make something work. For now, we can take from unused rooms, do a quick wash, and reset everything in those two rooms."

Sara, another housekeeper, nods. "Yes. Good idea. I can get started on that now." She leaves us, and I release a tense breath. At least someone is willing to help and get things right.

"Fine, but what are we supposed to tell the prime minister when he comes asking for fresh towels?"

I squint at Raul, one of my three stooges. "We replaced

them yesterday, Raul, and typically we supply enough towels for them to get through the morning without an issue."

"I don't know why you had to go and change the order," Marsha mutters under her breath, though intentionally loud enough for everyone to hear.

"I didn't," I press, my tone firm. "Clearly there was an error."

She makes a dismissive noise. "Yeah, another error. How many does that make this week?"

"I agree. These continued mistakes only seem to have started since you took charge."

"Marsha, Raul, while I appreciate that you're both puppy hurt that you didn't win best in show, how about instead of standing here petulantly whining about it, you get to work and do your jobs? And no, that's not a suggestion, it's an order."

"Fucking bitch," Marsha snaps, again under her breath, but thankfully, both she and Raul leave.

"I didn't want to say this in front of them because they've been talking all kinds of trash about you behind your back, but the lunch order for the king, the prime minister, Lady Althea, and the prime minister's aide didn't populate this morning either, and when I refreshed it, it was completely different and included a dish with peanut sauce, which the prime minister is allergic to. We also don't have enough linens to get us through lunch and dinner service."

I close my eyes. "Linens aside, I double-checked the menu yesterday afternoon when I returned from the festival."

Jennine shrugs. "I don't know what to say."

I grit my teeth. "I went over it with Margarite, so she should hopefully have an idea of what was on the original menu. I'll go into the system and see what I can figure out, and I'll get on the phone with the linens company immediately."

"Great. Thanks." Jennine scurries off, likely to handle breakfast for the royal family and our guests, and I get to work on all the fires that need putting out.

Something is sticking with me, though. This is the third or fourth issue that's happened in the system, but they're showing up as changes I made. I'm logged into Emily's iPad under my credentials. Who else knows the code to unlock Emily's iPad? Once they're in there, it would be easy enough to make changes under my name.

Emily had her surgery on Friday and is still in the hospital. The last thing I want to do is burden her with any of this. She's set to come home to her new quarters by the end of the week. I can change the login code on the iPad and tell her about it then. I also need to make a thousand percent sure that everything is set and in place for her.

Dammit! I never should have gone to the festival yesterday. I knew it too.

After I change the password, I set to work on fixing all the issues. Thankfully, Margarite had already printed out a copy of the lunch menu because she is, and I quote, *old school and works better with paper than a tablet*. Works for me. Lunch crisis averted, but how fucked is it that someone tried to give the prime minister something he's allergic to?

I'm far from an innocent lamb in anything, but that's beyond trying to make me look bad. That's straight up potentially killing an innocent. Maybe they assumed it'd be caught, and I'd simply look incompetent? I don't know. But it's still fucked.

The linens are another matter, and the owner of the company says he can get them here by twelve. Let's pray he's on time because lunch service is at twelve-thirty. Once that's all done, I head across the palace to the family side, keeping my eyes and ears open for Esme, Marsha, or Raul.

I have no proof that it's actually them doing this. Just my suspicions, but damn do I wish I did. Revenge would be so sweet.

I finish the king and queen's suite and the king's office and study without any issues. The king's laptop isn't here. It must be with him, so I don't have the option to snoop or hack. Sara managed to wash two sets of towels and linens she took from empty bedrooms and has made up the prime minister's and his aide's rooms. Just as I start to relax, a voice in the hall stops me.

"Hey, can I ask a favor?" Alice, the housekeeper who typically does Rowan's, the children's, and Althea's rooms, questions.

"Of course."

"I have a massive migraine hitting me. Lady Althea's and the children's rooms are done, but would you mind attending to the prince's for me? I can't handle the smell of cleaner and just need to lie down for a bit. I have medicine in my room I can take, which should help, and I swear by tomorrow—"

"It's fine," I cut her off, even if it's not fine. "I understand. Go rest up and feel better."

A grateful smile partially turns up her lips. "Thank you so much. I changed the sheets on the prince's bed yesterday, so he just needs the bed made and the room tidied."

"Got it."

She takes off for her quarters, and now I'm stuck having to clean Rowan's room. A place I've avoided like the plague. His study is difficult enough.

The door opens, and I'm instantly assaulted with the scent of him, all masculine and woodsy and freaking delicious. It's one thing to be near him and smell it. It's another to be immersed in it. I start with his bathroom, hoping to find it disgusting so there can finally be something about him that turns me off.

But no.

It's not disgusting. The toilet seat is up, but that's about as far as it goes here. Everything is neat and organized, and it doesn't take me longer than five minutes to clean and reorganize his space.

His bedroom is large with a light wood four-poster king-sized bed, two nightstands, a brown leather bench at the foot of the bed, and a dresser and desk that match his bed. I pick up the couple of items he has on the floor and put them into the laundry bag to be sent down, give everything a fresh dusting, and lastly, make his bed.

The drawer on his nightstand is slightly open, and I go to close it but stop when something inside catches my eye. After checking that no one is here and there's no sound, I open the drawer wider and gasp. Holy shit, it's my earring. Or Signoria Batorini's earring, I should say.

I told Antonia I had lost one of them, but she said "earrings" to Signoria—meaning the pair—and I never corrected her. I was getting a beating anyway. Might as well keep what I had. Call it payment for fifteen years of indentured servitude and years of abuse.

I assumed it had fallen out in his suite, but I was hoping it happened after I made my escape. No such luck. I pick it up, holding it in the palm of my hand. Heat prickles the back of my neck. He kept it. And he drew pictures of us from that night. I'd figured it meant nothing to him. He is Prince Rowan after all. The very definition of a playboy.

But the earring...the pictures.

I hate how much I like that he drew those pictures. That he kept my earring and has it in his bedside table. No condoms in here. Not even lube.

I can't take it. He'll know.

I wish he hadn't kept it. I wish he hadn't drawn those pictures. I wish I didn't feel the way I do when I'm around him.

With a mental headshake, I put the earring back and close the drawer.

The sheets are a bit rumpled, and his pillows are in disarray. My hand runs along the silky sheets where he slept, feeling like a total creeper, but not stopping either. Memories of him from that night swarm me. He teased me yesterday about how I was a ride virgin, and I teased him back about popping my cherry, but that's exactly what he did.

The way he thrust inside me makes me shiver. His mouth. His hands. His voice. His words. I've made myself come over and over to thoughts of that night, and being in here now is doing things to me.

I force myself to get back to work and finish making his bed. His pillows are large and soft, and like a girl who knows better, I bring one up to my face, smiling softly to myself in the way you do when you're doing something naughty, something forbidden, and no one knows about.

Except that's the moment Rowan enters his bedroom and finds me with my face in his pillow.

"Well, well. Look at this."

Oh god.

The pillow falls from my hands, landing with a gentle thud. My heart takes off at a sprint, and my adrenaline-frazzled mind works circuits to come up with a plausible explanation, only to fail. He saw me. He knows what I was doing. There is no talking myself out of that.

"Sir—" I stop short as he enters and shuts the door behind him with a deafening click.

I don't move. I hardly breathe. He steps deeper into the room. The tap of his shoes on the wood becomes softer as he reaches the carpet beneath his bed, and my body stiffens.

My hair being swept over one shoulder makes me jump, and his hot breath by my ear has me biting into my lip.

"Were you smelling my pillow?"

"Your Highness, I—"

A hard smack to my ass jolts me forward, my hands planting into the mattress to break my fall, but now my ass is pointed back to him like an offering. It's funny, in all the ways I've been hit, no one has ever spanked me before. But the thought of him hitting me, punishing me, sends a frisson of fear through me.

I hold bone still, not even my chest rising or falling with the need to take in extra air.

He moves in behind me. His hard cock presses against my ass as he leans over me, eliciting a gasp I attempt and fail to suppress. I was wet and turned on before he walked in, but feeling him like this...

His hands are on either side of mine, and his body is completely against me as he brings his mouth back to my ear.

"I've asked you to call me Rowan."

I gulp. "Yes, si—Rowan," I correct. I'm trembling. I've been hit by women, and their brutality is fierce. I've never experienced a man. His sheer muscular strength alone could tear me in two.

"Better. Did you like how I smell?"

My eyes pinch tight, my fists clenching the bed. "Yes. I liked it."

"I like how you smell, too." He takes a deep inhale of the space beneath my ear, and I whimper, half aroused, half in fear, unable to stop my reaction to him. He chuckles, the sound warm as it rustles my hair. "Marcella, Marcella, such a beautiful name for a beautiful woman. Where is the person who normally cleans my room?"

"Sick, Yo—" I stop myself. "I filled in."

"Once again, I catch you touching things you shouldn't."

"My apologies. It won't happen—"

He smacks my ass again just as hard as he did the first time, but now he rubs the sting away with his cock. My eyes roll back. I shouldn't like this. I shouldn't like anything he's doing, and I need to stop him.

But I don't. I keep my hands on the bed and let him do what he wants to me because it's exactly what I want too.

"Somehow, I doubt that. I think we both know you like it

and would do it again if I hadn't caught you. You don't seem to be able to help yourself. Have you been this bad when cleaning other rooms?"

"No. I haven't."

"Good girl."

Jesus. The way he says this, the sound of his voice, that low, sensual rasp, is more than I can take. My mind grows fuzzy and soft. I think I'd do just about anything for him to call me that again.

"Why are you shaking like this? I won't hurt you, sweet-heart. At least not more than you'll want me to."

I suck in my whimper, refusing to allow it past my lips.

His hand drags up and down my side from my hip to the side of my breast. "You've touched my things. I think it's only fair I get to touch you in return."

I came up here to change into swim trunks. I've been restless all day, and I couldn't pinpoint why, so it was either go for a run, which I wasn't in the mood for since it's hotter than the blazes of hell out, or swim laps until my muscles ached and my mind quieted.

Then I walked in here and found Marcella's face in my pillow and realized why I was restless.

Her. Marcella Russo.

A fantasy. A preoccupation. A woman I promised I wouldn't touch, and yet here I am.

I press my hard cock into her ass and grip her long blonde braid so I can wrap it around my fist, and use it to wrench her back to expose her throat to me.

A strangled noise flees her lips that somehow manages to make my cock harder.

Fuck yes.

I greedily take advantage, licking and sucking at her skin. A low growl tickles my lips as my tongue flicks her racing pulse point. Her taste. Holy fuck, the way her skin tastes. I know this taste. I swear I do.

"Stop licking me," she demands even as she attempts to angle herself further against me, fighting the grip in her hair and the control I'm imposing.

I grin, my teeth sinking into her flesh, making her whimper and buck against me. I've got her held pretty good between her hair in my fist and her body caged by mine.

"This can't happen."

"It won't. I'm not fucking you."

She laughs. "Who said I was going to let you try?"

"Oh, sweetheart, if I wanted to put my cock in your tight little cunt, we both know you'd let me, and you'd love it."

She snorts. "So arrogant, *Your Highness.*"

I use my free hand to tear at her pants, ripping the button open and scissoring her fly before I shove the hem down past her hips. Her creamy ass is right here, and I smack it. Hard. She squirms and rocks away from me, but I can't have that.

"Say it again," I dare her.

"Your Royal Highness."

I grin like the devil. She thinks I'm going to spank her again, but I've got other ideas. I rip her tired, cotton thong down until it catches on her pants, locked right above her knees. Then I shove two fingers straight into her.

"Holy fuck!" she cries out, arching and attempting to move, to buck, but she won't go anywhere unless I allow her to.

"So fucking tight. So fucking wet for me, aren't you?"

I pound into her, finger fucking right against her front wall. She seems to like it rough, and my body blazes at the thought. At all the wicked, dirty, depraved things I want to do to her.

"I was wet before you came in."

I chuckle darkly. "You mean from smelling my pillow?"

"Fuck you!"

"Is that what you want me to do? Is that why your hot little cunt is gripping my fingers, practically begging for my cock?

You can lie and deny it all you want, but your body is all the proof I need that you want this."

"Ah! Rowan, please."

I lick her earlobe and bite the soft skin, dragging it with my teeth. "You say fuck you to me, and then you start to beg? Which is it?"

Her face pinches up. "I...I...I don't know. We can't do this, and yet if you stop..."

I continue to pump my fingers in and out of her, but I slow my pace, rubbing her, gliding them instead, making sure she feels everywhere I touch. "Let me make you come."

Now I'm the one almost begging.

"Oh god. This is a mistake. Such a big mistake."

"I'm taking the choice from you. You're mine right now. Mine to pleasure however I choose. Lower your chest to the bed, arms above your head," I command. "Palms flat. Don't move unless you're told, and do not disappoint me by attempting to say no."

To my astonishment, she obeys immediately.

I release her braid and run my hand down her back, pressing on her spine until her chest is flat against the bed and her ass is high. She shakes, her back twisting to fight me off her, but that won't happen.

I smack her ass. "You can't push me off, so stop trying."

I want to eat her out. I want to eat her ass and cunt, but I don't because I know if I taste her, I'll be done for. I won't get her naked either. I won't see or touch her tits. I won't kiss her. But fuck, I want that.

All of it. All of her.

This is scratching an itch and nothing more. A one-time momentary lapse in judgment that won't carry over. It's not as though she'd want that anyway.

My other hand wraps around her hip, and I rub her clit

while I finger fuck her pussy. She's so wet, and she smells so good, and I'm dying. Excruciating, crippling agony with the need to be inside her. To come. It's robbing me of my brain cells and blood flow. The visual of her like this is everything.

Her hips cant into my touch, seeking more, wanting me to work her harder. It makes me want to edge her. To keep her here like this all day, right on the brink. But time isn't on my side, and playing games isn't in my best interest for self-control.

I'm going to fuck my hand morning, noon, and night to her. It's going to be just one more time. It's going to be me fighting everything not to seek her out. Not to sneak down to her room at night, open her door, and climb into her bed to claim what's now mine.

Mine. Shit. No. I can't have these predatory, possessive thoughts about her.

My cock leaks in my shorts, and I rub it against the globe of her ass, anxious to touch myself but knowing that won't happen. My heart pounds and my veins thrum with liquid lust. She sets my blood on fire.

She feels like silk. Her clit pulses and is hard and slick from her dripping cunt. I rut and thrust and grind against her, dry humping her ass without even so much as a fuck to give about it. I want to pull my cock out and come on her. I want to watch the ropes of white coat her perfect skin. I want to mark her so she knows exactly what's happening and who she now belongs to.

I pick up my pace, feeling her pussy flutter and tighten against my fingers. Feeling her grow even wetter, hotter. Her moans fill the quiet of my bedroom, and if anyone walked by, they'd hear her for sure. What we're doing is incredibly risky. But it won't stop me now. Nothing will.

Sebastian, Althea, and Bellamy could walk in right now, and I'd still make sure my girl came. Arousal is so fucking beautiful on her. The side of her face is smashed against the bed and I have the most perfect view of her profile. Her cheeks are flushed, her lips parted, and her eyes are tightened.

I swivel my hips faster, fucking myself between the fabric of my boxer briefs, my shorts, and her sweet ass. I groan at the feel of her clenching, all hot and needy on my fingers. I rub her clit harder, adding more pressure, moving in tight, fast circles. Her nails scratch at the bed, but she doesn't move away from her position. She keeps herself locked in place, twisting and shifting, but obedient all the same.

It makes me deliriously happy.

I come down over her back and lick the shell of her ear. "So sweet. Such a good, sweet girl for me."

A shudder rolls through her, and her pussy clenches, holding my fingers in, refusing to let them go. I rub her front wall and press in on her clit. Her pussy is leaking all over my hand, soaking my fingers.

I can't bear it. Not another second. If she doesn't come right now—

"Oh god. Oh hell. Oh fuck!"

And that's when it hits me.

It's her. It has to be. I pull back and stare down at her face when she comes. The way she moves and responds. Her sounds. The words she just said—they're identical to the ones she said after I made her come the first time.

She comes all over my hand, tattered noises and strangled pleasure that nearly make me orgasm on the spot tumbling out of her. I watch with rapt attention, studying her in a way I haven't until now. The moment she goes limp, the tension on her face relaxing, I pull my fingers from her cunt and put them straight into my mouth.

I tasted her cunt that night. I know what my girl tastes like.

It's a revelation, and my throat closes around my gasp. She tastes like innocence and sin. Like temptation and ruination.

Exactly the way Ella did that night.

I may not have a ton of clear memories, but I remember how her pussy tastes. I remember how her face looked as I made her come. How she sounded when she moaned for me.

I use my other hand to unzip my shorts and pull my cock out.

Her eyes flash open, and she twists her head over her shoulder, but I shake my head, pull my fingers from my mouth, and reclaim her braid, stopping her as I give myself three firm jerks and come all over her ass and the back of her black shirt. Wordlessly, she arches so she can stare at my dick, which only makes me come harder with grunts and growls.

Maybe I'm going mad. Maybe it's delusion and insanity and obsession. One night shouldn't do me so hard. It shouldn't lead to something like this.

But it's her. I'd swear in front of a military tribunal to it.

All this time, I've ignored it and justified it away.

Rationalized its impossibility.

But no. Marcella is Ella. Ella is Marcella.

I slap her ass, jarring her forward. I do it again, and she tosses me a scowl over her shoulder. I stare down at her perfect profile. Her lovely lines. I'm fuming. Lost. Insane.

She's painted in my cum, the sight erotic and beautiful, like her, and without a word—because I don't think I'm capable at this moment—I head into my bathroom to retrieve a cloth while I tuck myself back in and zip up.

I take a moment to give my reflection a *what the fuck* glare. By the time I return, she's gone, and I lean against the doorframe, locked on the rumpled spot on the bed where she had been moments ago.

I don't know what this means. I don't know who she is or what she's doing here. I don't know if someone sent her or if she came on her own. I don't know if this is about me or if she's here to hurt my family. I don't know how she got past the facial recognition or security.

Her accent is different. Her hair is different. Her eyes are different.

The rest is her.

Now I have to figure out what I'm going to do about it. And how to prove it.

19

MARCELLA

I race out of the palace, my feet carrying me from memory down the stairs, through the great hall, and out the front door. Gravel crunches beneath my sneakers, and I take off at a sprint, racing down the long-ass side of the palace until I finally get to the path. I don't slow down. I don't look back. I just run. The temptation to keep going, to never stop, is compelling, but my lungs have other ideas, and I practically slam into a tree on the edge of the woods, panting for my life as I collapse against it.

Gasps flee my chest, one after the other, my hand covering my racing heart as if that'll slow it down. I have Rowan's fucking cum on my ass and the back of my shirt. Ugh. Gross. Sticky and gross. Jesus fuck.

Visible tremors rack through me, and tears I refuse to let have their fun burn my eyes. But holding them back brings on a new set of heaving breaths.

"What did I just do? What did I just let him do?" Fuckup after fuckup.

This isn't who I am. I'm strong because weakness isn't an option. I do what has to be done because I'm a survivor.

I should go. I should leave this place behind and never look back. Except the only documents I have bear a name Antonia and the Signoria know. They'd hunt me down. They'd have me killed. Tortured and killed.

But worse, they'd kill Jaqueline.

They'd break her more than they already have. There would be nothing left of her, and then they'd toss her off the cliff once they deemed she was no longer of use to them. I've debated selling the earring somehow, taking the cash, taking Jaqueline, and going...anywhere. I don't care at this point.

I'll do what I have to do. I'll hack the king's laptop, and I'll find out what Antonia and Signoria want to know. What *I* want to know. Then I'll take Jaqueline, and that will be that. We'll leave it all behind. I'll kill them if I have to—though I want my murdering days to be behind me. In the meantime, I have to stay away from Rowan. I can't let that happen again.

I've got this. I've always got this. Fierce, determined, inde-structible.

Pushing myself upright, I search around until I locate some leaves on the ground. I use them to wipe off the cum on my shirt. The wetness on my ass will have to wait for my shower tonight.

Veering off the path, I pass freshly mowed, manicured lawns, as well as flower and herb gardens. The air is sweetened with their earthy fragrance, and I suck in a deep breath, savoring it. Samil had sworn the king was dirty. Messalina, for not a huge country, is a wealthy and thriving country. Samil said it was because the king was involved in dirty deals with shady international corporations and world leaders.

I haven't heard a peep about any of this from inside the palace, nor have any sketchy dignitaries or men come through. That doesn't mean he's wrong, though. If I discover that the king isn't dirty, if everything Bellamy said to me about Samil is true, then I'll leave the family in peace it so richly deserves.

There are a million variables to this. None of them are easy. All are dangerous, no matter how you look at it.

My work phone buzzes with an incoming text, and I slip it out to see it's from the queen. She's never texted me before, and nerves instantly hit me. Does she know? Nothing like getting finger fucked by your boss in the middle of the day and having him jerk off on you. Talk about a fireable offense. It's not like you can fire the prince. The help is who gets tossed out with the trash.

> Bellamy: I could use some help if you're able. I don't want to take you away from anything, but if you have a few minutes, I'm in the nursery.

> Me: I'm on my way.

What Bellamy sees in me, I have no clue, but I'll gladly take the distraction for what it is. I go in the opposite direction, heading to the palace through the back and past the pool. The children are splashing around with Oncle Rowan. Our eyes meet, and I do everything in my power not to look at his wet chest. As it is, his presence overwhelms everything. His carnal masculinity echoes through my body in a dark whisper.

One I have no intention of listening to again.

I look away, instantly dismissing him as I straighten my spine and brush my long bangs back from my face. I head inside, winding my way through and taking the spiral staircase up to the family wing. I don't so much as glance at Prince Rowan's door, now closed. It was a moment. A lapse. I already have too much on my mind...and on my shoulders. I have no space left in me for anything else.

The nursery is a large empty room beside an empty suite. It surprises me that it's not closer to the king and queen's. When I enter, I find Bellamy in the middle of the space, one hand on her back, as she surveys the walls as if trying to picture something.

"Bellamy?" I call softly so I don't startle her.

She spins and hits me with a smile. "Thank you for coming. I have an ultrasound tomorrow, and it triggered the realization that I'm officially twenty-nine weeks pregnant with two months left to go before my C-section date. Sebastian and I have put off setting up the nursery, but I think we're at the point of needing to get that going whether we like it or not."

I step deeper into the room. "Do you mind if I ask why you've put it off?"

A flicker of unease creases her features. "It's been a rough several months," is all she says. "But part of being determined not to let this curse, whether real or perceived—I think the latter in case you're curious—is planning and doing the things that need doing without fear. So here I am."

I can't help but respect that and respect her. "What can I do to help?"

"I don't know. I have no clue where to start. I know there are designers and things for this, but I feel weird hiring someone to design a nursery. The people we met with wanted to do some elaborate thing with gold leaf and hand-painted murals, and that's so not me."

"What do you like?"

"I'm not sure. It all sounded so formal, and I'm not that."

"You prefer simple," I surmise.

"Yes. I haven't ordered cribs or bassinets. Nothing. We've been getting gifts"—she pans her hand toward the stack of packages in the corner—"but I haven't opened anything yet."

"They're your babies. What do you want for their first bedroom?"

I get a wan smile. "I want my dad here, but that's not an option. I love to read. I love books. I think I know what I want in here and what I don't, but I think I need a second opinion and maybe help with a color scheme."

I nearly laugh. "Your Majesty, you are the queen. It's okay to use designers if you think they'd help."

"I know. But it's not me."

I give her a reassuring look. "I get it. Let's go over what you want first. Then we can focus on the other things. Do you mind if I ask why this room isn't near yours?"

She looks away. "Nora's suite was the room next to this one."

"Oh—" I cut myself off. Meaning she and the king didn't share a room.

Did the king love her? The whole notion of him becoming a beast stems from him being racked with grief following Nora's death. I know that's not true. He hid out because of the curse. But to hear they didn't share a bedroom? Did he know about Nora's affair? Was he having one of his own? Did he care either way?

Why couldn't he just put his jealousies aside and let Samil keep Nora? None of this would have happened. None of us would be here in this mess. *I* wouldn't be here in this mess.

"Do you know what you're having?" I redirect.

"A boy and a girl. We're going to name the little boy Joseph for my father."

"I love that." And I do. I can't imagine ever having children. I'm not sure people like me get to be mothers. "Two cribs, I take it?"

"Yes. At least we should do two, I think." She paces toward the wall and leans against it. "I'm new at this."

"I'm sorry to say, but I'm not anymore experienced." I walk over to her and stand beside her, mimicking her position.

"Baby clothes. Baby things. There's so much to learn and get."

"I'm sure the king can help with that."

"He does. But as I said, he's superstitious. Or nervous. I don't know."

Or just a jerk who wants no part of planning for more children. I doubt he helped the first time, selfish ass that he is.

"Tell me about your dream nursery for your babies. Rocking chairs, an adult bed for you and the king, bookshelves, themes…"

"All of that." She laughs. "Tomorrow I'll order furniture and have it all set up. As for a theme, I think *Le Petit Prince*."

I tilt my head to her. "Pardon."

"My father read me that book a million times growing up. I want the different planets and stories and words of wisdom The Little Prince encounters spread throughout the room." She looks at me, her nose scrunched. "Is that lame?"

I give her a reassuring smile. "Not at all. I love that. What if you painted the ceiling like a night sky with tons of glowing stars?"

"I like that idea. I don't want the room to be dark, so the ceiling is a cool idea. Roses are a big thing in that book, so those would be pretty on the walls too."

"It sounds like you know what you want."

She beams at me, her eyes sparkling. "I guess I do. Sometimes I have to talk things out. For now, maybe we should open the boxes of gifts and see what we have to work with."

"Let's do it. You open them, I'll take notes on who sent what."

"Perfect."

For the next hour, we work side by side, sorting tiny garments into piles, and laughing at the number of silver rattles that seem nothing short of useless. She tells me stories about her childhood, living in the US until she bounced around Europe with her father after her mother died. I don't give her much in return. I can't. I make up bullshit stories, the lies prickling my heart. The more time I'm in this job, the closer I get to this family, the more I hate every word that comes from my lips and every action I take against them.

Now I'm questioning everything, and I don't like most of the answers I'm coming up with.

"Mommy!" Phaedra comes racing in wearing her adorable little gold bikini, with Arthur, also soaking wet, hot on her heels. "Guess what Oncle Rowan taught me?"

"Future queen, you're dripping water everywhere, and you look like you're freezing," she says, her tone holding more amusement than censure, only for all of us to shriek when Arthur shakes his fur out like a dog would, sending sprays of cold water every which way. Our hands fly out to ward it off. "Ah! Arthur. You're getting us soaked!"

"That's because they ran in here without wrapping her towel around them. And yes, I'm including the ferret in that statement." Rowan enters, flanked by Sabrina and Zayer. He chuckles, holding up Phaedra's towel that she gratefully takes. Arthur scurries up to Sabrina, rests himself against her, and nuzzles into her towel.

Rowan throws me a side-eye as he enters but almost immediately dismisses me as if I'm not here. Awesome. I mean, I don't want his attention. That's the last thing I want. But a girl still doesn't like to be cast aside immediately after a guy finger fucks her to orgasm. I, on the other hand, had every right to dismiss him. Naturally.

Not so charming anymore, are you, Prince?

"Better. Now, what did Oncle Rowan teach you?"

"How to do a flip off the diving board." Sabrina crows.

"Sabrina!" Phaedra cries, stomping her foot indignantly. "I wanted to tell her."

Sabrina simply shrugs in a *you snooze, you lose* way.

"Phaedra, come here and tell me about it." Bellamy pats her thigh, and Phaedra walks over and sits on the floor beside her.

"We did flips. I made a full circle on the last one."

Bellamy claps. "Amazing. That sounds so fun."

"I did it three times in a row," Sabrina chimes in.

"That's great, legendary princess. It sounds like you all had fun." Bellamy giggles. "Zayer, my love, that towel is for drying, not being a superhero."

"I'm not a superhero," he protests. "I'm a sea monster. Rawr!" He lunges toward me with his tiny fingers splayed like claws.

I playfully cover my head with my arms and scream in fear. "Ah! Oh no! Don't get me."

The wet little thing jumps on me, the water from his trunks seeping through my pants. It's cold and definitely unpleasant.

"I'll save you!" Sabrina declares, throwing herself at Zayer and covering him with her towel, which he does not like. "I'm a friendly shark and protect humans from sea monsters."

"Sabrina!" Zayer whines, pushing her towel off his face.

I've never had siblings. Not really. Not in this way where I'd play and fight with them. I'm much older than Jaqueline, and Samil was much older than me. But their dynamic is adorable and fun to watch.

"I'm a sea queen, and I declare that everyone has to listen to me and that there can be no monsters or sharks. Only mermaids and sea fairies."

My lips bounce at Phaedra's declaration, and I see I'm not alone in that as Rowan and Bellamy are silently laughing. No one else can feel the tension, but it buzzes and hums like its own entity. It's a lot of work not to look at Rowan, and I wonder if he's having the same struggle I am.

"I should get back to work," I declare.

Bellamy nods. "Thank you for your help this afternoon. I feel so much better about all of this."

"I'm glad. It was fun." I offer her a smile and shift Zayer so he's sitting on the floor and climb up to my feet.

"I want to get changed and have a snack," Sabrina states.

"Me too, me too," Zayer jumps in.

Bellamy slowly peels herself off the floor, and Rowan helps, taking her hand and hauling her up the rest of the way.

"Children, why don't you go to your rooms and get dried off? Zayer, I'll be up in a moment to help you change."

The children run out of the room, making a beeline straight for their bedrooms, and I curtsy at both Rowan and Bellamy and leave the room, only to stop when I hear Rowan speaking to Bellamy now that he thinks I'm gone.

"I don't know about spending all this time with Marcella. I'm not sure it's safe. We know nothing about her."

"Rowan, she's been living and working here for over four months, and there hasn't been an issue with her. Emily promoted her because she's the best housekeeper, and thus far, I haven't seen any reason to argue that. She's sweet and kind. Yes, she's very reserved and formal, but I can't blame her for that. It's her job to be that way."

"There are security concerns—"

"What security concerns? Do you know of a threat?"

He blusters out a heavy sigh. "Not specifically, no."

"You, me, and Sebastian looked over her background check. Over her family, who we also looked up, and they checked out without so much as a speeding ticket. She's not Charlotte. She's not trying to ingrain herself in our family or slide in between Sebastian and me."

"I know."

"Then what is this? Is it because you're attracted to her?"

He laughs mirthlessly. "No. It's not because of that, though that certainly doesn't help anything."

"What's the problem with that? I honestly don't get it. Is it because she's a housekeeper?"

He makes a dismissive scoff. "No. I don't care about that, just as Sebastian didn't care that you were a schoolteacher and a nanny."

"Then what is it?"

"Just be careful with her. That's all I'm asking."

She makes a noise, and I hear her move. "I will be."

What on earth changed in the last twenty-four hours for him to say that now? Is it because of what happened in his room? How exactly does that make me a security risk and a threat to Bellamy and the children? I mean, I guess I technically am, but I don't see how he could know that from one sexual encounter today.

I bet this is how he is with all of his lovers. Plays until he's satisfied and finds or conjures reasons to get rid of them. What an asshole.

Before they can leave the room to check on the children, I slink away, unease prickling at my skin and leaving me unsettled. I don't know how much longer I can stay here without everything falling apart around me.

20

ROWAN

It's been bothering me all day. Every waking moment, it's all I've thought about. The questions continue to mount, each with no logical answer I can find. Her palace persona doesn't lend itself to sneaking into a royal ball in disguise. The accent adjustment and ability to alter facial recognition are jarring and suggest she's a professional of some sort.

She doesn't seem violent, but again, neither did Charlotte, and that's what I keep coming back to. How easily we were duped and how dangerous that situation turned out to be. I might also be losing it. There's that possibility too.

I haven't gone to Sebastian about this. I haven't gone to Javier, who comes home tomorrow with Emily.

The truth is, I have nothing concrete to go on other than my gut instinct. I need something to prove it. Something real.

Dinner service for the staff is when I decide to sneak downstairs to the servants' quarters. It's quiet, the dim hall illuminated by a series of overhead lights that glow over each door I pass.

I had to do some digging, but Marcella's room is the last on the right—of course, because why should this be easy? Glancing around to ensure I'm alone, I turn the knob and find it unlocked, which surprises me. I assumed I'd be shut out before I could even get in.

Her room is small, consisting of a double bed, a nightstand, a dresser, a chair, and a closet. The window up by the ceiling is as small as the room and provides minimal daylight, but it doesn't matter because, to my surprise, the lights are already on.

I shut the door behind me and look around, wondering where I should start. I don't exactly make it a habit of sleuthing around people's bedrooms. Everything is impeccably neat. The bed is made without even the slightest wrinkle in the blanket, and there's not a scrap of paper or an article of clothing on the floor. I open the closet and find rows of shirts and pants, most dark-colored like she's been wearing, and two new gray uniforms that have the tags still on them.

On the floor is a line of shoes—an old pair of sneakers and the black nondescript work shoes she tends to wear. Nothing is nice. Nothing is extravagant. So unlike the gown she wore that night and the diamond earrings that I know to be real since I had it appraised.

The closet door shuts with a tiny squeak that makes me wince, but I continue, going to the dresser next. It's more of the same. Plain, brandless cotton underwear, matching bras, some T-shirts, shorts, socks, and not a lot else.

Fuck.

Was I wrong? Is my obsession that acute?

I shove the drawer of her dresser shut and move on to her nightstand. It's as neat, organized, and simple as everything else. There's hardly anything here. No books or an e-reader. Just an old beat-up first-generation smartphone I can't imagine works very well and her work phone. Both are plugged in and charging, which seems odd to me, but maybe she doesn't bring them with her when she eats.

That's it on top, and when I slide the drawer open, it's completely empty.

Frustration boils through me. I pick up her pillow, and there's nothing under it.

"Arg!" I run my hands up my face and back through my hair. "Fuck!" I hiss under my breath. I grip her mattress and lift, my last-ditch effort, but there's nothing here either. I go to set it down and get the fuck out of here when something in the far corner between the box spring and the mattress catches my eye.

A box.

I shift the mattress to one hand, holding up its weight as I reach underneath and strain for the box, fingering it and managing to shift it enough that I can grip it. The mattress falls back to the bed with a thud, the same moment I open the box.

The earring.

For a moment, all I can do is stare at it, my mind racing.

It's her. I knew it, but this confirms it. I'm not crazy. It's actually her.

A voice out in the hallway jerks me away from it, and I quickly close the box, lift the mattress, shove it back where I found it, and lower the bed, smoothing out the blanket to hide what I did.

I head for the door, pressing my ear to the wood and listening intently. Whoever was speaking is gone. I pull back and wait another moment to make sure, then I open the door and slam straight into Marcella, wearing nothing but a towel and a ratty pair of flip-flops. She's holding a shower caddy that starts to fall from her hand. The towel cinched just above her tits gets the same idea and goes with it.

Naturally Marcella goes for the towel, and I go for the

caddy, catching it right before it fully slips from her hand and crashes to the floor.

"What the hell are you doing in here?" she shrieks, fury staining her cheeks and brightening her eyes.

I wince at her loud voice, but she doesn't care.

"This is totally inappropriate and a complete invasion of my privacy."

She's not wrong, but I'm too fired up to care. She's Ella. The woman I met at the wedding. The woman I danced with and couldn't take my eyes off of for a moment. Not even a fucking moment. The way she kissed me, the way she moved, the sounds she made, her natural disdain for me, the way she tasted, how her virgin cunt felt.

I slam the door shut behind her and set the caddy on the floor, doing my best to ignore her wet body in only a towel, her wet hair, and her sweet face. She was beautiful that night at the ball. A showstopper. But the woman from that night has nothing on the woman in front of me. This one's a heart-stopper.

"Oh, you mean an invasion like cleaning my room and smelling my pillow, or going through a closed portfolio that was under a laptop and fishing through it?"

She looks away, her jaw locked tight, and her eyes narrowed. She tightens the towel on her chest, but she's breathing heavily, her tits rising and falling, making the knot of the towel precarious at best.

"I admitted to that and apologized. What are you doing in here?"

"I was waiting for you."

She laughs incredulously, her words accusatory as they slice at me. "Oh. And you weren't snooping?"

I sure as hell was, but something is holding me back. I don't know her motive. I don't know who she's working for. I just know something or someone sent her to the wedding and here, and if I have her arrested, we may never know. She could clam up out of fear or spite or any other reason, and then we'll never know what the true threat is. She could also lie to save her ass.

I can't find Desta. Marie is a dead end. I'm the reason my father is dead, but I will make damn sure no one else hurts my family, and that starts with her.

"Snoop?" I scoff. "There's nothing in here. A nun has more shit than you do."

"So you were snooping?"

"You mean, did I open your closet? Yeah. I did that. I even opened your nightstand. Sorry to say there's no vibrator in there."

"Me too," she snaps. "One has to have money to purchase such things."

"We pay you. We pay you well." Honestly, I have no idea what the staff earns, but it has to be decent, otherwise, they wouldn't stay, and we have staff who have been with us for decades. That goes above loyalty to country and the throne.

She huffs a breath. "Why did you come here? What did you think? That we'd pick up where we left off this afternoon?"

"No. Sorry to say, sweetheart, that's not happening again."

"Phew." She wipes fake sweat from her brow. "That's a relief. I'd hate to have to take another shower to clean your cum off me."

I wouldn't. I'd pay serious money to see my cum paint her ass again. But it doesn't matter.

"You don't eat dinner with the other staff?" I question, switching things up.

She folds her arms under her tits, making them hike up and the swell of her cleavage grow like an enticing treat. My stupid dick is loving this. Thankfully, for the moment, my brain is running the show.

"No. I shower when they eat because I don't want to wait to

get a shower. But you obviously thought I was eating dinner and came thinking I wouldn't be here."

Fuck. That was a dumb thing for me to say.

I snarl, getting right up in her face. "I want you to stay away from my family."

"On what grounds?" she challenges.

"On the grounds that I don't trust you."

"I know. I overheard you speaking to Bellamy earlier, and you haven't been shy about letting me know that even though I've given you no reason not to."

Now would be the moment to tell her, but I don't. Telling her relinquishes the upper hand. If anything, I should be nice to her. Charming. Get her to let her guard down.

I sigh in defeat. "You're right. You haven't."

Shock flickers across her face before her eyes narrow and become distrustful. "Bullshit. What's your angle?"

I hold up a hand, palm out. "No angle."

"Riiiight. One line from me is all it took for you to realize you were wrong?" She scoffs sardonically. "Please. I'm not stupid."

No. She's not. "I mean it. You're right. I'm being...prejudiced, I guess."

Her eyebrows shoot up to her hairline. "What?"

I feign nonchalance and pan a consolatory hand at her. "We trusted Charlotte, and she betrayed us, and until a week ago, we didn't know you. I'm wary. It's my family, and I love them, and Bellamy is overly trusting. I *won't* see her get hurt again. Or Sebastian." There. Take that for everything it's worth.

Her eyes shift about my face, measuring my sincerity.

"You haven't given me a reason not to trust you. Other than your snooping around and inappropriate touching."

That part is actually true, and it throws me into even more of a tailspin. She's been a perfect employee. Great with the kids.

A friend to Bellamy. Then there's the other side. The one only I know about.

She rolls her eyes at me, and I so want to spank her again for that. I wonder how rough she'd like it. If she's fucked anyone else since me, or if I'm still the only man who's been inside of her.

"Inappropriate touching? I think that's the pot calling the kettle black, Your Highness."

I crowd her, my body inches away, not touching but oh so close. A small duck of my head. A lift of my hand. As it is, I can feel the heat radiating off her and smell the heavenly scent of her bodywash on her skin.

My forearm hits the door above her head, and I dip in, my face hovering above hers. "Oh sweetheart, we both know you not only let me, you loved it."

She presses against the wood and glares fire up at me. "Yeah, and I just washed your cum off my ass, so clearly I'm not the only one. You caught me smelling your pillow and stealing a glance at your secret porn. Big deal. You're the one who lost control and shoved your fingers inside me." She smirks. "And now here you are. Can't get enough of me, can you?"

Her little taunt raises my blood pressure, and I get right up in her face, practically nose to nose.

"And I bet if I shoved my hand up your towel, I'd find you soaking wet for me. Again."

She laughs. "Oh, Your Highness, how sad that you think that was for you."

"Wanna bet?"

In a flash, I spin her around and pin her to the door, take both of her hands in mine, and shackle her wrists up high above her head. The towel falls, and she thrashes against me, fighting. But it's not the way she fought me earlier. This isn't *I hate you*, but *I want you to fuck me*.

She's actually fighting me.

It slows me down for a beat, and that's when I see it. The scars and welts at varying stages of healing crisscrossing her back. Slashes of white that make me freeze, ice over my blood, and slow my reflexes, not releasing her fast enough because my little siren drops her shoulder, twists her wrist, and nails me right in the gut with her elbow.

An oomph catapults from my lungs, and I stagger back a step. It's enough of a hit to snap me out of my shock and thrust me straight into rage. I grab her by the shoulders and push her back against the door, getting in her face.

Because what the fuck? What the absolute fuck?

There's so much more to her story than the bullshit lies she's fed us. And I intend to find out what it is. Right fucking now.

21

ROWAN

"Marcella," I bite through clenched teeth, panting for my life as I work to rein myself in while fierce protectiveness unexpectedly surges through me. "Sweetheart, I'm only going to ask you this once, and I expect a real fucking answer. Who did that to you, and where the fuck are they now?"

She snarls, practically baring her teeth. "Fuck off, Your Highness."

I grin. "I already did that once today. Now tell me."

She's lying to me, infiltrating my home under false pretenses, and yet the sight of those scars makes me want to destroy whoever caused them. Is that why she's here? Is she under someone's thumb?

"I thought you said you were only going to ask once."

I growl. "You're such a brat. Is anything about you real, or is all your formality just an ugly ruse?" Then something hits me. "I spanked you today. Hard."

Guilt gnaws at me, and my anger falters. I take a step back, pick up her towel, and hand it to her, doing my best not to look at her body as she snatches it from my grip and holds it against her chest.

"I'm not as weak or fragile as you think I am. Besides, why would a prince care about a servant's scars? Unless you're worried you fucked around with damaged goods."

The accusation stings, and I rub a hand along my jaw, trying to think, trying to calm down, trying to figure out just what the fuck is happening here. I stare down at the floor, at her adorable feet still in her ratty flip-flops.

"Is that what you think of me?"

"I don't think of you at all, Your Highness."

I lift my chin. "Liar."

She huffs. "You don't know anything about me."

That's probably the first real thing she's ever said to me.

I fold my arms across my chest, squaring my stance. "Then tell me."

"Your Highness—"

"Rowan. When we're alone, when we're like this, it's Rowan."

She smirks defiantly, knowing just how to push all my buttons. "And if I don't?"

In a flash, I'm back on her. My nose brushes hers, and I bite her lip, my teeth sinking into the plump flesh as I work to control myself. "Pretty girl, unless you want me to spank you again and force my name from your lips, I'd start calling me Rowan."

I reach around and grab her ass, feeling the soft, warm, supple globes and running my hands over them. Desire spreads through me like wildfire.

She glares, her eyes twin slits of hate. "I didn't say you could touch me."

I suck her top lip between mine. "You didn't say I couldn't."

"Don't fucking touch me."

But she's not pushing me away. She's standing here when I

get the impression that if she wanted to, she could easily beat the shit out of me. Or at least try to.

"Did I hurt you earlier?" I ask, moving to her neck and kissing the soft, sweet skin.

She pushes against me, but it's not much. Barely a shove. "Don't you dare do that. I'm not some fairy tale damsel in need of saving."

"No?" I draw back and meet her gaze. "Then who are you? I'd love to know."

She's naked before me except for her towel, which is hardly covering anything. Her chest is heaving as mine is, the minuscule space between us charged. Maybe this moment was a foregone conclusion. Me coming down here. Us standing like this.

I don't know what to make of any of it. I don't know what to make of *her*.

I should walk out of here and tell Gabe, my security detail, Javier, and Sebastian what I found in her room and have her arrested. But I don't. There's a vulnerability to her, same as there was the night at the chalet. It's as if she's actually one thing while being forced to be something else. The demand to tease and extract every secret she's keeping from me is pervasive.

I cup her face in my hand, my thumb dragging along her cheek. The way she's looking at me right now is meant to sear flesh from bone, but she's not fighting me anymore. She's not pushing me away. And there's that something beneath her steely gaze. That unmistakable softness she covers with pithy retorts and sharp sarcasm.

She's not going to tell me. I know that.

Past all her determined hatred and forced fervor is a woman who's scared. I've seen this look on Bellamy before, and I see it in Marcella now. She's strong. No doubt about that. You don't get those kinds of marks on your back and still fight if you're not tough. But never in my life has the need to protect someone and keep them safe been more pervasive.

With that, she's even more dangerous to me than she was moments ago.

But looking at her right now, feeling her body, the slight tremble she's trying to hide...

My lips sear down on hers in a kiss there is no coming back from. It happens the way lightning strikes—sudden, electric, and deadly. Every particle I'm composed of is tethered to her. It has been for months. Since that first giggle I heard. Since that first smile and dance and kiss. Since she gave me her first and made me hers.

A groan mixed with a growl climbs up my throat, and I squeeze her ass, lifting her with one hand and forcing her legs around me. I push her into the door, using it for leverage as I tilt her face with my other hand and take her from another angle.

"We can't do this again."

My lips trail kisses down her neck. "But we are, and this time, I'm not coming on your ass. I'm coming deep inside of you."

Her head falls back, giving me better access to her throat. "This is a mistake," she presses, even as she grinds her pussy against my pants. I'll have the smell of her cunt on them. With any luck, a wet spot from her, too. Fuck. My cock surges with blood. With the need to be back inside of her, this time with nothing between us.

Except the millions of lies we're keeping from each other.

She won't tell me who she is, who she's working for, or what she's after. I'm playing dumb and pretending that I didn't find the earring or know that she's Ella. Nothing good comes from this. Other than me fucking her brains out.

"Probably," I agree. "Definitely. I don't care. I will later, but right now, I don't."

Her hands go for my shirt, ripping at the seam and sending the buttons flying. Not exactly how I'll want to walk back across the palace, but again, I don't fucking care right now.

She shoves the fabric over my shoulders, where it snags at my elbows. I don't want to put her down. She'll run or we'll lose this moment if my hands aren't on hers, and I don't have her pinned to something. Still, I set her on her feet, drinking in the lines of her body, her large tits and smooth creamy stomach and pink pussy. She could barely stand when I ate her the first time. Her innocence radiated from her that night, but now there is nothing innocent about my siren.

My shirt hits the floor, and I take her hands and bring them to the belt of my pants to do this for me because I want to touch her. I have to touch her.

"Second thoughts?" I question when her fingers falter.

"A thousand of them." She pauses. Swallows. And hits me with those green eyes through her lashes. "I'm choosing to ignore them. For now."

"Good." My hands cup her tits, and I lift them to my mouth. I sink my teeth into her plump flesh, biting hard enough to mark her.

"Ah!"

"Shhh," I admonish. "I don't trust you, and you don't trust me. But I saw your scars, and you *will* tell me if something I do is too much."

"I already told you I'm not a damsel."

"No." I peek up at her with a smirk on my lips. My tongue comes out and rings her nipple. "You most certainly are not." I take her nipple into my mouth, drawing a gasp from her. Her skin tastes sweet. Addictive. I lave my tongue across her tits, licking and biting them, unable to stop. Her skin reddens so perfectly. My teeth marks are visible lines, and I suck harder on the side of her breast until I get a smack to my head.

"What are you doing?"

I chuckle. I can't help it. "Marking you without hurting you."

"You're giving me a hickey."

"Yup."

She smacks my face away, and I laugh harder, but the sound dies as her hands tangle in my hair and she jerks me back to her tits for more.

"Such a needy, bad girl." I trail a hand down her belly to her mound, where I cup her. "But can you be a good girl for me?"

A moan escapes her lips. Fuck yes, she can be because that's exactly what she wants to be. She'll hate herself later for it. I know that. But right now, my girl wants to be so good for me. She wants me to spoil her. To kiss her. To touch her. To make her come and her pussy drip.

My hand slides lower, and I caress her bare pussy, running my fingers over the silky heaven of her. She arches against me, her right foot going up onto her tiptoes and angling her knee out to give me access while I continue to abuse her tits in the best way.

"Marcella," I hum against her. *My Ella*. Is that what she's been called? Is the name she gave me her nickname? For some reason, that small thought makes me sweat. She gave herself to me that night. Did she know we'd meet again? Did she know we'd find ourselves here only months later?

I move lower, mapping her body with my mouth. Savoring the softness of her stomach. The jut of her hipbones. Then lower. Her right leg is placed on my shoulder to ease the tension in her calves, and I kiss her inner thighs, one then the other.

"What are you doing?" she asks, breathless.

I grin as I nibble on her pussy lips, making her yelp. "Taking my time. Taking what I want. In that order."

"You can't do either."

"Watch me try."

Before she can protest, I lean in and taste her. My tongue swirls in a fat circle on her clit, and just like the first time I did this, my balls instantly draw up and my cock pulses. *Shit!* She cries out, and I bite her inner thigh in warning. Her lips mash together, but she shakes her head at me, then shrugs as if to say *it can't be helped*.

"Try. You have to try."

I hold her thigh against the side of my head and dive back into her pussy, sucking her clit straight into my mouth. Her knees buckle, and she flattens her back against the door, angling her hips so I'm forced to take her deeper like that's a hardship. A hot ember of lust burns my throat, and I grip her ass tighter, shoving my face in as far as I can.

Tonight I want it all. I want her body. Her mind. Her fucking soul. Damn the consequences, though I know there will be numerous if I can't find a way to stop after this.

A gust of air escapes her throat, but she shocks me by covering her mouth with her hand. It won't be good enough for what I have in mind, but it'll have to be.

With her hand on her mouth, I bury my face, pushing my tongue up inside her and using my lips and teeth on her clit. She bucks against me, rubbing herself and ripping at my hair. Pulling me closer. Pushing me away. She can't decide.

Lucky for me, it's not her choice to make.

I shove two fingers into her, having them glide inside her along with my tongue.

"Fuck," she hisses. "God."

"Not God." I blow on her clit. "Your prince. Don't mistake the two because I don't intend to show you mercy."

I pump into her two more times with my tongue before I pull back and let my fingers continue their work so my tongue can play with her tight little clit. And play with it, I do. I suck on it, tease it, kiss the sensitive skin, and seduce uncontained frenzy from her.

"How many men have you been with?" The words slice past my lips unrestrained. But like everything else tonight, I don't care. Her answer is what I need.

"None of your business."

I blow on her, making her shiver. "Tell me anyway."

She sighs, but she's too turned on to deny me. "One person."

"Good stuff." I hide my smile in her pussy, but the truth is, I want her to come on my cock, and I'm too impatient to wait. With one last pump, lick, and kiss, I take her by the hips and lift her back up into my arms. Each step to her small bed across the even smaller room feels like it takes twenty years. I attack her mouth, ravenous, needing to taste her so I know this is happening.

I've never been this impatient before, but with her, this is months. Months of thinking. Months of fantasizing. Months of obsessing. I want to break her open until she's reborn on my cock. I want to mark the inside of her the way I did her tits.

The night I took her virginity, there was blood all over the condom and my fingers when I removed it, and thinking about that now, about how I wish it had been on my cock instead, makes me feral.

I set her down at the side of the bed and spin her around, one hand on her throat, my other going to her pussy. I bring her head back to my shoulder, and she flattens her spine against my chest. I can't tell if that move is so she can feel this connection too or if she's trying to hide her scars from me.

I kiss a trail up and down her neck, from her shoulder to the sensitive skin beneath her ear. Smelling her. Tasting her. Savoring this.

"I don't have anything on me, but I don't want to use anything regardless."

Her breath hiccups in her chest.

"Am I going to get you pregnant if I do that?"

That thought shouldn't make me harder than I already am, but the idea of forcing my seed into her and getting her pregnant isn't an unpleasant one. My heart stops, and my lungs cave in. No. That won't be with this girl. It can't be.

"You won't get me pregnant."

I give her neck a firm squeeze and use my grip on it to bring her forward. Her hands meet the mattress, and a choked sound comes from her.

"No. I don't—"

I clench her neck tighter and kiss the scar on her left flank.

A wounded cry makes my chest seize, and I move on to the next. One by one, I kiss her scars.

"I don't want your pity."

My lips dip in, and I lick along the raised, firm line. "Good. Because in addition to not getting my mercy, you won't get my pity either."

With that, I tear my boxer briefs off and shove straight inside of her. Exactly how I did the first time. She cries out, her body tensing against me. And fuck me to hell, she's just as tight. I've never fucked without a condom, and the pleasure, the feel of her, is unlike any other.

"So good," I rasp. "You feel so good. Do you feel that? How perfectly I fit inside you?"

My hand stays on her throat, my other wrapping around her to hold her hip bone. I kiss her face, moving her jaw to find my lips. But she's tense. Still. I smack her ass to get her to relax. When she finally does, I pull out and shove back in, reclasping her hip.

"No mercy."

"No pity," she replies.

I bite her bottom lip and pound into her, my pace relentless.

"Oh god!"

I squeeze her neck, pressing in on her carotids. "Who's fucking you, Marcella? Tell me."

"You are," she manages, though her eyes are back in her head and her voice is muted.

"That's right." I pummel faster, my pelvis slapping against her ass and thighs. "Your prince. Fucking say it."

"No."

I squeeze harder, cutting off more of her blood supply.

"Say it. I'll make you come so fucking hard," I pant against her ear, pounding her cunt, savoring the wet, hot heat as it coats my cock. "I'll give it to you so fucking good."

"You're fucking me. Prince. My prince." The words are a hoarse whisper, but I hear them, and they make me desperate. Unhinged.

"That's right. I could take anything I wanted from you right now. Every piece of you is mine."

I momentarily ease some of the pressure on her neck, licking, fondling, touching her everywhere I can. Her tits. Her nipples. Her clit. All the while I slice in and out of her, driving in as deep as her swollen pussy will allow. I surround her, every inch of us touching, kissing, fucking. With each pass inside her, I squeeze tighter, strangling her airway until her hand latches over mine. Then I relax it.

Over and over, I play with her breath. Her blood flow. I control her body. Possess it. And she knows it.

The moment her pussy spasms, I pull out. My wet cock slaps my abs, just as unhappy about it as she is. She whimpers in protest, but I spin her around and take her down to the bed.

"Look at me," I demand, but she closes her eyes and shakes her head.

Not fucking good enough.

I grip her throat tighter. "Look at me!"

Her eyes snap open, and I thrust back into her, pistoning and rolling my hips so I hit her front wall from the inside. My knees dig into the bed, and my hips pummel as I lean over her. God, she's so pretty like this. So fucking stunning with her face all red and her eyes gone and her body filled with me. *Only* me.

Reaching between us, I rub her clit.

"Don't close them. Keep them on me. I want to see your gorgeous eyes when you come for me. I'm fucking you so good."

"Yes," she manages.

"You want more, though, don't you, my good girl?"

Her eyes cling, her lashes wet, and when she swallows, I feel her muscles working against my hand.

"It's okay to tell me. I've got you."

More tears form in her eyes, but she silently nods.

"Sweetheart, I'm going to give you my world. Every piece of me. Even the ones I shouldn't."

Somehow, I fuck her faster, harder while I take her mouth, but just for a kiss. Just so I can taste her discordant moans and whimpered cries. Her cunt is slick and hot and feels so fucking right. My balls draw up, and pleasure mounts to an unbearable breaking point low in my belly.

But it's her face that's pushing me over the edge. Pupils blown, lashes at half-mast, wet hair a total disaster, cheeks flushed bright red, breathing labored, and utter erotic bliss.

"Fuck!" I bellow, only to catch myself and smother my moans against her lips. She shudders and shakes, her orgasm coming on strong, and I release her neck, forcing blood back up into her brain and her breath back into her lungs.

She screams, and I swallow it, grunting and growling as her nails dig into my back, scratching and likely drawing blood. It only surges me higher.

It's the most intense orgasm of my life, and I collapse on her, holding her here with my weight, never wanting to let her go. Knowing I won't get the choice.

After all, she's here for a reason. *La mia dolce piccolo vipera. My sweet little viper.* But more than that, she's *la mia stella. My star.* And that hits harder than anything else.

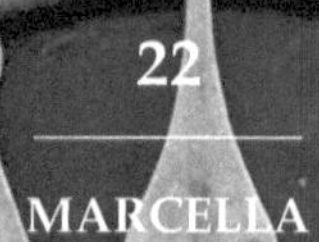

22

MARCELLA

Goddamn, I'm so fucked. Literally. Figuratively. Whateverly. It's all there, and it all boils down to one thing. One *person*, rather. Rowan.

He fucked me again before he snuck back into the palace. The irony of him sneaking out this time instead of me didn't exactly make me smile. Nor did the aftermath of what happened between us.

The throat. The eye contact. The kissing of my scars. Every encounter with him is more intense than the last, which I didn't think was possible.

He was snooping around my room, but I have to imagine that if he found the earring, he would have said something. Other than that, there's nothing in there.

But why is he so distrustful?

Is it the curse? Is it from Samil and Charlotte, and now he's naturally distrustful of everyone? He's not this way with any of the other staff on the family side. It's just me, and it doesn't quite add up.

I lock my door when I leave my room. Always and without fail. But I didn't last night, and I didn't because I was distracted.

I loved my brother. He was the only bright spot in my life after my father died, other than Jaqueline, and Jaqueline was often kept from me because of that. Samil answered to no one and did what he pleased, and that included spending time with me.

Every villain has a story, and sometimes that story isn't as evil as people imagine. His was baked in heartache. In jealousy. In grief and hatred. In a venom that necrotized his soul. But...I don't know if I want to seek his justice anymore.

I can't change the past. There is no revisionist history.

This is my life. I have to stop imagining what could have been. What I wish it were. I don't have a reset button as much as I wish I did. I could have been so many pretty things. A magical piece on the board that braved and vanquished adversaries. And I would have made it all better. I would have. No one's death would be glued under my fingernails. I'd have no sins to atone for.

But that's not how my story goes.

It's black and bleak. The crawling earth nightmares derive from.

But with that, I know who I am. Or more likely, who I want to be.

I don't want to snoop on the king's computer. I don't want to find secrets he likely doesn't have or plant ones he was never a part of. I don't want to destroy his family. I don't know if the girls are his or Samil's, but if they're Samil's, that would make them my blood too. More than that, I really like Bellamy.

That woman has been through it and yet somehow manages to greet every day, every interaction, with a smile and hope. It's magic. It's addictive. It makes me want to be...different. Have more. More than I ever thought I could.

So I was distracted last night and didn't lock my door. I was in the shower thinking about my next steps. The choices I have to make for myself, Jaqueline, and our future.

Then Rowan happened and fucked me into a coma. Or

maybe I simply needed a good night's sleep, which isn't something I've had for, well, likely ever but certainly not since I took over for Emily.

My day doesn't start any better than it did yesterday.

I rise early, eat quickly, and make sure everything is in line with assignments and staff. It is. But by the time I'm ready to head upstairs to start my morning cleaning, there's a text from Signoria Batorini.

S.B.: I want you in the king's computer by tomorrow morning. If you're not, this is only the beginning.

There's a video attached, and I find a corner, a tight alcove, and with tremulous fingers and my stomach in my throat, I hit play. I don't have to. I could delete it and move on. I know what it is simply from the freeze-frame image. Jaqueline is tied to a post in our basement while Antonia whips her back with her favorite cane.

Still, I hit play, and I watch in horror, unshed tears in my eyes, and resolve hardening in my gut. Antonia has that smile on her face. That sick, twisted as fuck smile. She loves punishments as much as Signoria does. I suppose that comes with their bloodline, and I'm grateful I'm not part of it.

Jaqueline's face is strained in agony, her screams wrenching the air, making a gasp and a cry shoot past my lips. The camera pans, the image changing, and there is Signoria, wearing an equally sadistic smile.

"Get it done," she says in Italian, and that's that. Video over.

My lungs cave. I have to do it. Whether I want to or not, I have to do it. Tonight.

I shove my phone into my pocket, wipe away the moisture clinging to my eyelashes, and press on, forcing one foot in front of the other.

I tell myself that I can see what's on there about Samil. Then I can discover if what the queen told me is accurate. I can search through videos and documents and whatever else I can find and learn his secrets. And if his secrets are as awful as Samil told me they were, then maybe my actions are justified. Maybe exposing him is mercy to the kingdom.

Maybe.

I don't see Rowan as I do my morning duties of tidying up, and I'm more than a little grateful for it. I change sheets, dust, polish, and scrub. It's mindless, tedious work, and I sing through it, focusing on the lyrics and harmonies and stretching my voice because I can't think about anything else.

Some people are born with a song in their heart, and others have to force it from their lips. I'm the latter, and I'll never be the former, no matter how much I'd like to be.

After I finish with Rowan's office—no smelling or snooping today—I head down and check on everyone else, and once I'm positive things are going smoothly, and half the staff is eating their lunch, I take to the path that's become my respite. My revival.

Today nothing feels open or safe or sacred.

The air is hot and dry, making me sweat, and the buzzing of cicadas gives me a headache. Even the earthy scent of herbs and the freshness of flowers are pissing me off. I read a book once a long time ago that I stole from Antonia, and in it the main character said there's nothing a drink and an orgasm couldn't fix.

The last time I had a drink was at the wedding. And last night's orgasm didn't fix shit. It only created more problems. Problems I have no choice but to fix myself, and that comes down to one simple truth.

I have to save Jaqueline.

I will do anything for that. Commit any crime. She's an innocent. A sweet girl who deserves better than the nightmare her entire life has been. She doesn't remember our father. She's never known happiness or peace. I will do what I can to protect those who deserve it, but she will be my endgame.

After that, I'll figure out the rest.

The path crunches beneath my worn shoes until I reach the edge of the forest, breathing out a sigh as the canopy of leaves shelters me in their cooling shade. I lean against the trunk of a tree and close my eyes. I don't have to be back inside for a little less than an hour. It should be peaceful.

But the tiny snap of a twig alerts me that I'm not alone.

It could be an animal—I'm hoping it is—but the hairs on the back of my neck have me on alert, and I slowly turn over my shoulder and lock eyes with Rowan. Motherfucker. He followed me out here, but he didn't want me to know it, judging by the *oh shit, she caught me* mien he has going.

"You need to work on your tracking skills, Your Highness. You should add that to your snooping skills."

I turn back to the woods as my ears search, finding him behind me and listening as he advances.

"I think we both need lessons then."

I laugh. I've had lessons in espionage my entire life. I've just gotten sloppy. A weird taste of freedom and an annoying curiosity can do that to a person.

"Why are you following me?"

He doesn't reply, and I'm not in the mood for his answer anyway. He continues to prowl toward me, now less than six or so meters away. I can tell from the sound of the ground he's walking on. I'm salty and defensive like a caged animal.

Which is why I say, "Fuck off and leave me alone. I'm on my break, and you have no right to intrude."

"We need to talk."

I shake my head against the tree and close my eyes. "We have nothing to talk about, Your Highness."

"Oh, I think we both know that's not true."

He'll have to catch me then. And hope I don't kill him with my bare hands.

On my next heartbeat, I take off at a sprint, starting on the trail but quickly veering off it, winding my way through trees and over brush and fallen limbs. The palace property is massive, and I could run at this stretch for two hundred kilometers at least without reaching anything else.

A laugh springs from my lips. The taste of adventure and the thrill of being chased making me go faster. I pump my arms and push myself to my breaking point. Only I'm not alone. A cursory glance over my shoulder reveals he's chasing me, determination on his face and in his stride, his eyes dark and predatory.

Shit! My pulse kicks up, and my baser instinct takes over.

"How far are you going to run?" he calls out at me.

I smile, even as my lungs burn, begging for air. "How long are you going to chase?"

"As long as it takes to catch you, mia stella."

Something about the way he says that and calls me *my star* in Italian, a word that rhymes with my name, makes my empty core clench and my stupid heart skip a beat.

"You should turn around now, You Highness. I'm not your star, and I'm definitely not someone you want to catch."

"No, you're la mia vipera, but that won't stop me." His voice is closer than I expected, and it catches me off guard. I twist my head back to him, but my bangs pick up the wind and snag in my eyes. I brush the hair back and continue to run, but it's a fatal mistake. It slows me down enough, and just as I go to leap over another branch, an arm bands around my waist and swings me around.

My lungs collapse as I'm slammed into a tree, but I don't have time to notice it because he's all over me, his ragged breaths panting down on me as he holds my chin and stares into my eyes.

"Why were you running?"

I can hardly catch my breath, my chest heaving as I try. "Why were you chasing?"

"Because you ran from me." He pauses, and something flickers over his features. "If you run, I'll chase. But I caught you this time, and now you're mine."

His lips slam down on me, angry and hungry and ready to consume. He bites my lip, the pain sharp and exquisite, the metallic taste of blood tickling my tongue. He licks it away, sucking on my lip, on my blood, as he pins me to the tree. I try to shove at him, but he's a wall of muscle and takes my wrists in his hands and locks them over my head, the same as he did last night.

It must trigger the same memory because he smirks against me before he tilts his head and kisses me harder. I twist my wrist and claw at his hands, making him bite my lip again. He shakes his head and uses his pelvis to hold me in place while his other hand gropes my tits.

"I'm not yours," I manage around a gasp as he pulls my nipple through my blouse.

"Your body tells me otherwise, mia stella."

"Stop calling me that," I snarl.

He jerks my chin with his hand. "It's what you are. My star. Beautiful and luminous, but too hot to hold in my hand and will most certainly burn me if I try."

"Then don't try."

Something hits him, his features serious and a little shaken. "I don't know how to stop. You're my star and my viper, beautiful and venomous. *La mia stella velenosa*. I tried to stay away, but you're all I think about, all I want, and now here I am."

With his hand on my jaw, he kisses me again, his tongue invading my mouth as his hard cock grinds into me. I can fight him as much as I want, but the truth is, he's all I think about and want too.

My leg climbs up his hip, and I use my heel on his ass to push him deeper against me. Right where I need it.

"Fuck yes," he growls, ripping at my shirt, trying to work the buttons but failing to do it one-handed.

"Release me," I demand, and to my surprise, he does. I should keep running, but I don't. It's too good. Too addictive. His mouth and hands and cock. I want them all. But only them. I won't dabble with the rest. The other things that tickle lonely, dark places within me. The ones he pokes at, whether intending to or not. He brought them to life that night at the wedding. He's good at using flowery words, but his words are meaningless.

Our hands fumble while our mouths move sloppily. A tug here. A rip there. A push aside, and his fingers are inside me, pumping up and down, forcing a moan from me, while my eyes close and I submit.

"Look at this," he says on a choked breath. "Christ, how your cunt takes me. And these are just my fingers. Greedy, dirty girl. You love how I touch you. How I touch you and no one else."

My arms wrap around the trunk of the tree behind me, and I lean back, angling my body and making it long, allowing myself to open up fully to him. His eyes are drugged. Black and inky like midnight.

"Say it, Marcella." He smacks my clit before he rubs it in tight, fast circles, pleasure building from within. "Tell me this is mine."

I shake my head even as I writhe into him. I made the mistake of calling him my prince last night, and I can't do that again.

He grins and spits, letting it trickle from his lips straight onto the top of my pussy before it dribbles down. His fingers rub it in, swirling his saliva around my clit before pushing it into me.

"Good luck selling that to yourself."

Flattening me against the tree, he kisses me, taking no prisoners as he continues to work me up, faster and harder by the second until I'm dizzy. Until he's everywhere and I'm nothing but heat. A fire he's stoking with oxygen and kindling. A blazing inferno with no way to stop it or put it out.

He feasts hungrily on me, licking and nibbling at my lips, jaw, and neck. But right before I come, he lines his cock up with my entrance and plows straight into me, slamming me back against the rough tree that scratches and abrades my back.

Despite the brutal intrusion, he winces and kisses tenderly up to my ear. "*Non ti farò del male come hanno fatto loro.*" *I won't hurt you as they did.*

My eyes cinch tight, and a strangled gasp breaks the air between us. I can't. It's too much. All of him is too much.

He spins us around, still inside of me, and takes me to the ground. I have one leg in my pants, and his are around his ankles, but neither of us cares. We're savage. Pumping hard in steady thrusts that have both of us grunting and groaning and moaning, begging for more.

He's shaking, hardly holding on. "Your pussy is so fucking wet. So soft and tight. I fucking love your pussy." His teeth graze my jaw. "And I know you love my cock, even if you'll never tell me."

His gorgeous blue eyes pierce into mine. I do love his cock, and he's right that I'll never tell him. I hike my knees up and spread my legs wider for him, needing to feel him deeper. As deep as he can go.

"Look at that. Fuck yes, spread that pussy for me." He slows, sliding out then in. Out then in. His hands on either side of me are pressed into the dirt and leaves, and he stares between us. "I'm going so deep. You feel that?"

Yes, I feel that. He's so deep he's practically in my stomach.

I hang on for dear life as he pounds and fucks.

I push up into him, meeting him thrust for thrust. I need him to go harder. Faster. And I tell him that, practically begging for it. The way his cock strokes me, the perfect friction of it, is something I could get lost in forever. He knows how to fuck. I may be inexperienced, but I know enough to know that.

"That's it. Take it. Fuck me."

Slap. Slap. Slap. It punctuates our growing symphony as his pelvis meets my thighs. As our bodies mix and become one over and over. My tits bounce. My hair is littered with who the fuck knows what. I don't know how long I've been gone or if anyone is looking for me.

But again, who cares?

That seems to be how it is with him. I lose all sense of reason, and he becomes my apex.

Our hips move faster, skin slick with sweat all over us. He drops to his forearms and kisses me, and I cling to him. Toeing that delicious line. The one I'm chasing yet dreading. I don't want this to end. I don't want reality to come crashing back down on me as it inevitably does once our passion is sated.

"Fuck. I'm gonna come. Come with me, mia stella velenosa. Let go and come with me."

With my new name as a whisper, a seductive purr, I'm pushed headfirst into another dimension. Waves of pleasure skyrocket through me, and I hold on for the ride. Jaw locked, his eyes entangled with mine, I let go.

He pants against my cheek, groaning and grunting as he shoots inside of me.

I have no idea how I'll ever go back to how things were before we started this.

I'm not sure it's even possible anymore. It's a recipe for disaster.

23

MARCELLA

The leaves and brush make a bed that's not the most comfortable to lie on. My body sags into it regardless, and my eyes close. I blow out a heavy breath, feeling a hand over my heart, and realize...

"Your heart is pounding," Rowan whispers.

A slow, easy smile curls up my lips. "Yep," is all I can manage.

One of his hands stays flat on my breastbone while the other glides down my stomach to my pussy. He cups me, and I squirm against him, my hips swiveling to shirk him off, my clit too sensitive, but he's not having it. He pushes two fingers into me, and despite myself, my back arches slightly.

"What are you doing?" I question, wanting him to stop but also not wanting him to stop. It's the paradox I live in with this man.

His fingers answer for him as they pump in and out of me. I peek open an eye and catch him watching himself finger fuck me again.

"I don't have time for this," I state flatly. "I have to get back."

"I don't care," he replies as he keeps going. "You work for me, and this is where I want you."

"I don't work for you."

His sharp gaze snaps over to mine. "You're a servant of the royal family, and I am the royal family. Therefore, as I've been saying, you're mine. Mine to touch, mine to keep where I want, mine to make come if that's what I choose."

His barbarian, caveman shit would be hot in a strange, alpha, dominating way if it weren't also absurd in the fact that I will never be his. Not in any real way. It's not even that he wants that with me. This madness is not exactly a fledgling relationship.

It's sex. Good sex, but still sex. Exactly what I said it was the night at the wedding.

He said the same bullshit to me that night and likely says it to every woman he sticks his dick into. I'm not special to him, and I have no illusions that I am.

"Rowan, we have to stop this. It can't keep happening."

He doesn't stop. His fingers keep going, and despite the fact that I just came, my body's already working itself back up. He has me on a hairpin trigger. He touches, I respond.

"I didn't follow you out here to chase you and fuck you." His voice is distant. Lost almost. His eyes locked on my pussy.

"Then why did you follow me?" I bite into my lip, trying not to moan.

"To watch you. To talk. I don't know. I saw you going down the path, and I followed you. It was instinct."

"It was curiosity because you still don't trust me." Nor should he, so I don't blame him for that. My voice holds no bite to it. I don't even know why I brought it up.

"I told you last night that I do."

"Yes, but we both know that was a lie."

He sighs and crouches between my spread legs so that he can see his fingers pumping in and out of me better. My pussy isn't just open or exposed, it's in his fucking face right there in daylight.

"Rowan, stop." I try to push his hand away, but he catches my wrist and pins it to my side.

"Don't push me away. Not again. Do you know how beautiful you are?"

The reverence in his voice catches me off guard. "No," I reply honestly and without much thought. It's not that I'm being self-deprecating or don't think that my face is pretty enough. It's just something that I never thought about for myself. One has to have a beautiful soul to be beautiful on the outside, and that's not something I have. I've killed people who may or may not have deserved to die the way I was told they did. I'll have to pay for that at some point, but I'm not beautiful.

My scars are my scars, but I know there's nothing beautiful about them either.

"It bothers me how beautiful I think you are. How I can't stop thinking about you. How you've become all I see when I close my eyes. I don't like it, Marcella. I don't like it at all."

"It's just my face—"

"No. It's more than that. It's more than your face or your body. I don't get it. I feel as though I know you, and yet I don't."

I huff out an annoyed breath. Right. It's sex. "That's another reason why this has to stop. This is the last time."

Rowan chuckles mirthlessly, but his fingers haven't stopped, and his other hand releases my wrist and glides to my breasts, where he cups and squeezes them.

"I think we both know that's not how this is gonna go. Maybe we fuck each other till we get it out of our systems. Maybe that's all this is. Just fucking. But I don't wanna stop. Not yet. Not until I have to. I care about the other stuff, yet it doesn't seem to be a deterrent."

"What other stuff?" I ask softly, wondering where his thoughts are. His face is chaotic and hard to read.

"I don't know, Marcella. I'm going crazy with you. I want you to the point of madness. Not just your body. Your mind too. But you hold it all back, and you're right, I don't trust you. I know what's written in a background report. I know what it says about your family, about your qualifications, but I don't know anything about *you*. You don't talk about yourself. You don't talk about your past, which we both know is extensive. You don't tell me anything."

Now it's my turn to laugh, the sound harsh and sardonic, even as his fingers have me breathless. "You want to know about me? You actually care?"

He glares up at me from between my legs. "Yes, mia stella, I actually care. In case you haven't realized it yet, I'm starting to care far more than I should."

That trips me up, and my eyes close and my hands cover my face. Because I want what he's saying to be true. It hits me like a sledgehammer, or a cane to the back as it is for me, but it's there. I want what he's saying to be real.

"I can't talk to you about this while you're doing that."

Surprisingly, he stops, his fingers pulling out of me, though he doesn't move his position or his hand from my chest, even if it's now just resting flat against me.

"Go ahead," he prompts.

"Rowan, I'm not somebody you want to get involved with. I don't know if this is just sex to you, if you're trying to fuck a servant and get that little piece of slumming-it fun out of your system, but I'm not the girl to do this with."

"Why not?" he asks softly.

My lips form a straight line. I'm already revealing too much, and it's likely because he's crawling into places he shouldn't be going, and I'm not talking about the fact that he's inches from my pussy in broad daylight. He's been crawling there for months. Even in his absence, in the months where I didn't see him, didn't speak to him, I still thought of him.

It was impossible not to. I knew I would, especially once the plan began and they brought me to the palace to work.

I'm a servant, and he's a prince. Cinderella to Prince Charming. Only there's no glass slipper or happily ever after for us. We're what happens when midnight never ends. There is no us in the light of day, out in the open for all to see.

The reality is, he'll outgrow me soon enough.

He's Prince Rowan after all.

He fucks his way from woman to woman without so much as a second thought. So I let my hands fall to my sides, and I push myself up onto my elbows and stare at him. Thankfully, he's stopped pushing his cum back into me. I think that's what he was doing. My possessive prince. It's unfortunately as seriously hot as he is.

"I was born on August 26. I'm a Virgo in a lot of ways. I'm practical, meticulous, and I usually have a strong desire to help. Regardless of the personal cost to me. My favorite color is blue. Not light blue. A deep, navy blue. My favorite food isn't salad. That was a lie. The truth is..." I trail off, staring up at the mantle of leaves overhead with sparkling rays of sunshine slicing through. "I don't know what my favorite food is. I don't know what books I like to read. I don't know what movies or TV shows I'd want to watch. That was never part of my life. I'm not sure who I am at this point other than a servant." I lower my head and meet his gaze. "That's what I am. Not exactly exciting, and definitely not sexy. You might like the way my tits and my pussy look and feel, but you're not going to get much else from me."

He takes his cum-covered fingers and presses them on my clit. He pushes in hard. Hard enough to make me gasp and attempt to scoot back from the infiltration. I get a warning look. Something that automatically stops me. He rubs in deep circles, and just like that, his fingers aren't playing, they're moving with purpose.

He shifts and catches the back of my head, holding me up so that our eyes are locked. "Marcella, you are so much more than that."

His lips catch mine, and he kisses me deeply. Fiercely. His tongue slices through my lips and swirls with my own before he pulls me up higher and presses our foreheads together.

"I don't know a lot. But I'll tell you what I do know. You're smart," he murmurs against my lips, the speed of his fingers increasing, making me breathless, making it difficult to concentrate on what he's saying, though I try. "You're fierce. You're loyal—to whom I'm not exactly sure. You're determined. You're a good liar, a little too good. You come close to crying when you don't think anyone is watching you, and you hate that you do. You hate crying, which is why you fight it so hard. You feel it makes you weak, and weak is the last thing you want to be. Weakness pisses you off. You do like taking walks. You like quiet. You like peace. You like roller coasters. You get excited by the notion of fun and adventure because it's all new to you and something you've never experienced before. You like children and want friends. And you're fearless."

My eyes pinch closed. "Shut up, Rowan. Just shut up and make me come and let me go!"

"There's so much more to you than you realize about yourself. And I think that's why I like you so much. I see you. I see all these things you work so hard to hide. But I don't know your secrets, and that's what worries me. That's the part I don't trust."

My head falls back between my shoulder blades and a shudder racks through me. He picks up the pace of his fingers, and I let him. I don't argue. I don't even open my mouth to say anything else about it. I can't. He has me completely overwhelmed, physically and emotionally.

There's no getting around him. He's everywhere inside me.

My orgasm builds, deep penetrating waves of pleasure that

start in my core and have my legs straightening and my pussy clenching against his hand.

"That's it, sweetheart. That's it. Come for me. I want to watch you come for me."

I don't have a choice. My body takes over, and I detonate. My orgasm cycles through me, not as strong as the first one, but definitely powerful enough to make a bellowing cry come from my lips. Rowan covers my mouth with his, tasting me, swallowing my moans of pleasure, and I kiss him back, allowing myself to feel this, to experience it.

The moment my body sags, his fingers pull away. He wipes them on the bottom of his pant legs slung round his ankles, and something about that makes me laugh. The state of our undress is ridiculous. We just fucked in the woods in the middle of the day. Anybody could have taken this path. Anybody could have come and seen us. We're not that far from the main grounds, from the palace, and I don't even know how loud I've been or how loud he was.

We get so wrapped up in each other that nothing else hits our radar.

He gives my boobs one last squeeze, and I slap his hand away. I get a dirty, flirty smile from him in return. The charming one. The one he gave me that first night at the wedding.

I stand, and he helps me get dressed, our eyes clinging to each other, our hands staying close. I don't know what this is. I have no words for what it could be. I just know it's not smart. I know it's going to cost me. Maybe cost both of us.

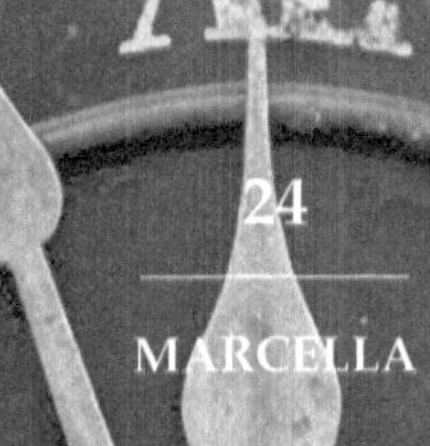

MARCELLA

Once I'm dressed, he picks leaves and debris from my hair, and I help remove the remaining pieces from my braid, only to undo it and re-plait it.

"Presentable?" I ask once I'm finished. He grabs me by the nape of my neck and hauls me in for a final toe-curling kiss.

"Perfect. Now get your adorable ass to work." He spins me around and spanks me, and I jump forward with a yelp. But there's no stopping my smile. There's no stopping the skip of my heart.

I leave Rowan behind and head toward the palace, skirting around the pool where I hear the children splashing. The afternoon is spread out before me, and I get back to it, anxious to make sure there are no issues and check in with the staff.

Marsha is in the hall when I pass through the servants' wings. I'm in no mood for her. My plate is already full, and she looks like she wants to add on a buffet.

She gives me a sneering look, and I mentally sigh. "Have something to say?" I question.

"Nope," she sasses. "Other than you're going down."

"Uh-huh. Spare me the '90s teen drama quotes. Did you do your work?"

"I always do my work. Better than you do. You never should have been promoted to this job."

I give her an indifferent shrug. "That's not how Emily felt. And I know it's you, Esme, and Raul who have been messing with things, changing orders and schedules and dirtying up rooms once I've finished cleaning them."

She snorts a laugh. "Why would we bother messing with anything of yours? I hardly even think about you."

"Uh-huh," I repeat.

She huffs. "It's not my fault you're incompetent, and it's finally coming out for others to see, including the king."

"Right. When I catch you, you'll be fired." I liked the idea of killing her, but she's not worth having more blood on my hands. Five people. I've killed five people at the command of Signoria Batorini. Two of those were at the encouragement of Samil. They were evil people who did evil deeds—or so I was told, or saw when I did my recon on them.

Still, I have to live with that. Marsha's not worth being number six.

"You don't have that authority. I know you don't. Besides, Emily returns tomorrow, and with that, everything is going to change. Especially when I tell her what's been happening."

"We'll see. Until then." I give her my back, walking away and dismissing her.

"You won't be here long," she yells after me as if she has to get the last word in.

That's my plan.

"I'm not the only one who's been upset with your work."

I turn back to her before I reach the hall that will take me toward my room. I need to change. I can feel the dirt and grime on me. "The sad thing about you, Marsha? It didn't have to be this way. You could've stayed my friend. All three of you could have. You could've helped me with all of this, but you didn't. You chose to be my enemies. And for what? Because I got the job and you didn't? Grow up. It's temporary, but memories aren't. And I will remember this."

"Ooh, I'm so scared." She smirks, rolling her eyes dramatically at me. "Real fucking scary, aren't you?"

I give her the same sadistic grin I learned from Signoria and Antonia. "You have no clue."

I continue toward the servants' area, listening as they finish up lunch. I enter the room smiling at everybody and checking in. Briefly, we go over afternoon assignments and any concerns anyone has. No one else seems bothered by my role. Everyone is greeting me with kind smiles and helpful suggestions.

After I'm done, I change out of my gross clothes and into something clean and dry, then head upstairs to the room where Emily is going to be coming home tomorrow.

My mind is racing, stuck in the woods, on the video of Jaqueline, completely lost in thought.

I have to get into the king's computer before Javier and Emily return home.

It has to be tonight.

I don't see Rowan for the rest of the day, and he doesn't come to my room tonight. I'm grateful. As it is, I'm wound too tight, and if I saw him right now, I'm not sure how I'd respond. What I'm about to do doesn't sit well with me. Quite the opposite, actually. I don't want to do this, but if I don't, if I don't go in and at least look and see what's going on, then not only will Jacqueline suffer, but I'll never know the truth about Samil.

The problem is, I don't know what I'm hoping for. The king's guilt or the king's innocence.

I'm not planting anything tonight. Signoria has whatever she wants me to put on his computer, and I'd have to meet up with her to get it. Tonight is simply recon.

I don't have access to the main cameras anymore, so everything I'm doing right now is a risk. And if anyone happens to be monitoring the cameras tonight, they'll catch me instantly, and I'll be put in jail, or perhaps the dungeons downstairs.

The king's study is on the second floor, and I know from my earlier recon after I moved into the palace that he goes to bed late. Or should I say he goes to bed with his wife, then goes to his study later. I don't know what he does in there. All I know is that he's in there usually late into the night.

The darkness of the palace surrounds me, the air thick and heavy with electricity and humidity from the storm outside that finally broke the summer heat. It's eerie. I've never quite believed in ghosts or scary stories before—certainly not the curse—but for the first time, I feel a presence around me. The creepy paintings with eyes that follow me aren't helping that. Outside, rain is coming down in sheets, the drops pelleting the windows, making me even more jumpy than I already am.

I slink up through the back stairs, my footsteps silent. It's been a long time since I've snuck around, not just the palace but in general, with the intent of doing evil deeds. The halls are empty. No one is around. The attendant sitting at his post in front of the cameras is face deep in his book, with only a small light to read by. I slip past him through the shadows, and he doesn't even so much as twitch or look up.

It's late, and as I reach the second floor. The grandfather clock sounds, startling me half to death. It pings one chime after the other, one, two, all the way up to twelve. Midnight.

I steady myself and continue on, prowling along the walls, mindful of where the cameras are, at least the ones that I've been able to note. I round the corner and pad to the junction where the floor branches off to the offices. For a moment, I stand stock-still, plastered against the stone wall, listening. There's no sound. The king's study is straight ahead of me, and I don't distinguish any light coming from beneath the heavy wood door.

I release a silent breath, roll my shoulders back, and move with purpose, on the edge of no return. My hands tremble ever so slightly, and I shake them out, pushing my nerves aside and quelling the adrenaline fighting to be set free. It won't help me. No second thoughts. No second-guessing.

I have to do this.

I roll my body up to the door and press softly against it. It's closed but not locked, and I twist the knob and let myself in, then slowly close it behind me with the tiniest of clicks. Lightning flashes across the sky, momentarily illuminating the room. It's closely followed by a loud clap of thunder that rattles the windowpanes.

I need to be fast.

A storm like this will wake people.

This would be so much easier if the king's laptop were in his office, but when I did evening rounds, I saw it was in here instead.

The laptop is sitting closed on the table in the back corner of the room. It's connected to two monitors, and I remove the connection because they'll cause too much light. I don't know the king's password, but I don't need it to get into his system. I'm skilled enough to use other techniques to bypass it and gain access, which is what I do all the while throwing cursory glances at the door.

I do a quick search through the king's most recent files, meeting notes, governmental emails, and drafted letters. I dig through his finances, and though I don't have hours or more like days to spend doing this, nothing appears to be out of order at first glance. There are no large sums of money moved anywhere. No offshore accounts. Nothing that jumps out and screams sketchy or illegal. I realize this is his personal laptop, and he could store these things elsewhere. In fact, only an idiot would keep them on their personal computer, where anyone could gain access.

The king is a lot of things, but he's not an idiot.

But as I'm digging, I uncover a folder in a private section titled S.B., the same letters I use for Signoria Batorini, though I already know it's about Samil.

My heart hammers, making my throat tight. I check the door again, then click on it.

The file is loaded with at least a hundred different items, ranging from documents to video files, the dates going back months to years. Samil became the prime minister roughly a year after Nora died.

At the time, his grief was consuming, and I remember asking him why he was running at all, plastering on a fake smile for the cameras and gladhanding contributors.

"One word," he said. *"Revenge."*

That was it, but I understood.

After he won the election, he didn't come home often, needing to stay in the capital for business, but we texted frequently, and on random nights, he'd call and talk for hours. Endless rants about King Sebastian. About how crooked he was. How he wished the curse would come and take him already. How bad he was for the kingdom. How untouchable he was in this palace, locked away with the children.

Endless tirades that fed an already poisoned well inside me.

I start with the documents, scrolling through the list of Samil's financial statements. All of these were obtained after his death, likely as part of an investigation. One particular document catches my eye, and I click on it, my brow furrowing as I scroll through line by line. It's a list of names, and next to them are monetary amounts and bank account numbers. Each of the sums is different, but not small by any measure.

After that is a notation of a correspondence date.

I take a picture with my phone and go back to the documents to search.

One by one, I find the people linked to each dollar amount. And what I discover chills me to my bones and has me staring at the screen, reading and rereading to make sure I have it right.

Each is a text message conversation logged from Samil's cell phone or emails he sent, all from the same IP address that's pinpointed on here as Samil's residence.

But that's not what's rattling me. They're bribes. Bribes offered to engage the king in shady business deals. Bribes to parliament members to vote against the king on laws and policies. Payments for attacking or kidnapping Bellamy and/or the children. Payments if they're able to get to the king himself.

Some of them are proposals or inquiries. Some of them, especially the bribes, were transactions.

I don't know how to make sense of this. Of the things he told me versus the things I'm seeing here. King Sebastian never made any of this public. And he could have. He could have said, *"Not only did the prime minister try to kill my future queen and me but look at all the evil he was attempting to do."*

He didn't.

And the only reason I can come up with is for the betterment of his country that was in deep turmoil after the assassination attempt and Samil's death.

On the flip side, Samil told me time and time again that the king was crooked. That the king was a liar. That he took bribes. That he was bad for the kingdom. How it was his job as the prime minister to stop him. That the king went after Nora simply to hurt him because he was jealous and spiteful.

But if he were spiteful, wouldn't he have posted all of Samil's wrongdoing?

Did Samil realize that the king wasn't any of those things, and in the absence of evil, did he work to construct it? Was all that orchestrated? His own attempt at a cover-up for his crimes or was it simply the madness and obsession of a broken man?

Looking at this, looking at these files, looking at some of those bank accounts and registries, it's not the king who was working bribes. It's not the king who was crooked.

It was the prime minister.

I don't know how to make heads or tails of this. I don't know how to compartmentalize or make sense of what I'm reading. Why would Samil lie to me? Why would he tell me all these things about the king if they weren't true?

Floored, I lean back in the chair and rub a weary hand over my forehead and across my mouth. I feel as though I've been rubbed raw with sea salt and left in the blazing sun to bake. I know Samil hated him. I know how venomous he was. But nothing he told me about the king was real, even as Samil tried to make it so.

Shaking my head, utterly gobsmacked, and frankly feeling ransacked and betrayed, I go on to the next file, and the next, and the next. It's more of the same. Samil trying to create crimes and pin them on the king. Samil trying to hurt the king. Samil trying to hurt Bellamy and the children. The fucking children.

He offered to pay a man fifty thousand euros if he killed all three of them at the holiday ball and made it look like an accident. That was the night he took Bellamy. That was the night he died.

My insides churn with sick turmoil, and bile climbs up the back of my throat.

Bellamy was right. He wanted them dead. All of them. Fresh sweat coats my forehead. All these years, all these lies, all the reasons I'm here...

I don't know how to make sense of this. Samil, my brother, my protector, the reason I'm still alive and breathing. He kept me safe. He cared when no one else did. I love him. I love him so fucking much.

But I don't know how to handle this.

Was it purely based on his jealousy? Was this simply his way of trying to get Sebastian out of the picture?

Was everything a lie?

And if it was, what does that mean for me?

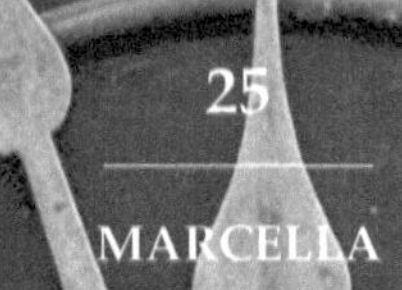

25

MARCELLA

I click out of the files and go over to videos, anxious to see what's in here. There are several with a multitude of dates, but the night of the royal engagement is what I'm after, and I click on that folder. I start at the top since they're arranged by time.

It's of Samil in the hallway, knocking one of the royal attendants unconscious and dragging him into a nearby closet. A moment later, Bellamy steps out of the bathroom and looks around, unease all over her. Then Samil is on her, brandishing a knife. There's no sound, but I wish there were. I wish I knew what he said to her that night.

He drags her through the hall, and the cameras on the video change one by one until they reach the library up on the third floor. I don't know if I can watch this. I'm terrified of what this will do to me. Samil wasn't concerned about the cameras. That doesn't surprise me. He knows how to alter them, same as I do. Hell, he's the one who taught me.

I click on the next set of videos, and he has the queen inside the crow's nest on the third floor of the library. It looks different from how it does now. They're going back and forth with each other, visibly arguing, and he presses a knife into her chin. Bellamy is crying, and I seize up, breathing heavily. He terrorized her. He slashed at her throat. Just like that. Malevolence all over his face.

A gasp flees my lungs, and my hands cover my face, emotion clogging my throat. Jesus Christ. Jesus fucking Christ. I shake with barely contained sobs.

I knew he did that to her. But it's one thing to know something and another to see it.

How can all the things you thought you knew about someone turn out to be wrong?

Bellamy is bleeding all over the place. She's pregnant. Neither knew that, but I know it watching this, and I can't...I just fucking can't.

A moment later, Sebastian comes roaring into the room and goes straight for Samil, attacking him. The king is barehanded. He doesn't even have a weapon, and the two go at it, yelling things at each other, saying things I can't hear. Samil's vicious, but the king is too. Fighting and battling to the death. Literally. In the end, the king tries to save Samil despite everything. He does his best to hold on and pull him back up, only to fail.

Samil falls out the window. I didn't know which window it was until seeing the entire video this way. I never watched it. I couldn't. I was told Sebastian killed Samil in supposed self-defense that the king manufactured, and that was that. But this...

The king collapses to the floor, bleeding everywhere, and I turn it off. I don't need to see the video of Samil fighting with Nora. I don't need to see him tampering with the helicopter. I know all about that. Samil told me every detail. In the end, what it comes down to is everything I thought I knew, everything I was told, everything I believed, is a lie.

How can one man be so good to some and so villainous to another?

Love makes us crazy.

It breathes madness in our minds. A four-letter word layered in complexities.

How am I supposed to ruin a man who's not guilty? Samil died, and while that was one of the worst experiences of my life, maybe it was justice. He's with Nora now. That's how I have to think of it. Samil and Nora are finally together. Although she likely wants nothing to do with him since he killed her and their unborn child.

The truth isn't so simple. It never is.

Rage and uncertainty war within me. A poorly constructed house of cards, and by removing one foundational piece, the whole thing is toppling down.

Conflicted, I close everything out just as a noise outside the study startles me. I shut the laptop and drop to the floor, crouching beneath the table and tucking myself behind two of the pushed-in chairs. I didn't have time to plug the monitors back in. Shit. Shit!

Blood pounds through my ears as the door to the study opens, and the king walks in. He's in a white T-shirt and pajama pants, grumbling under his breath in Latin as he walks past me toward the window. He's lost in thought, which is to my benefit, but if he comes over to the table, I'm done for.

He turns and moves in this direction, and I hold my breath, only to release it silently when he goes over to the bar in the corner, makes himself a drink, and starts to pace in the dark. I have no idea how I'm going to get out of here without being detected. It's not possible. He shut the door behind him. I'm stuck in here.

And while that should concern me most, right now his expression is holding me captive. He's tormented. Agony stretches along the lines of his face as he combs his fingers through his hair. He takes a hearty swallow of whiskey, only to tip his head back and swallow the rest of it. He sets the glass down on the bar with a loud clink and refills it before he returns to the window.

I don't know how long he stands there. Minutes. Hours. Every breath feels interminable. My heart is in my throat, and I have no clue what to do.

He turns around, and I hold still as his eyes glide right past me. Somehow, he doesn't see me as he heads over to a large chair in front of the fireplace. The king puts his head in his hand and sits in the dark as the storm rages outside the window. A moment later, there's a tap at the door, and the king calls out in French, for whomever it is to come in.

The door opens, and Bellamy enters. She doesn't search around the room. She knows exactly where he is, and he sits up, twisting to her.

"What are you doing up?" she questions, hovering by the door.

"Nothing, baby. Go back to bed."

"I can't," she tells him. "The storm is loud, and the bed is cold without you in it. What's wrong?"

She turns on a lamp, walks over to him, and climbs straight onto his lap. He gratefully takes her there, wrapping his arms around her and burying his face in her neck.

Her hands rake through his hair, and she kisses him.

He emits a peaceful sigh, and I feel wrong witnessing their intimate moment. Still, I can't help but envy what they have. Their love. How sweet and tender he is with her. Bellamy is magic, a balm, and even though she's a year younger than I am, I want to be her when I grow up. Spending time with her, seeing what they have, what's possible, it's changed core parts of me. Parts I don't want changed back.

"How are my growing babies?" he asks instead of answering her.

"Moving." She takes his hand and places it on her belly, and a hearty chuckle flees his lips.

He leans in and kisses her. "I love you. I love you so much."

"I love you. Now talk to me, Your Majesty. What are you hiding? We said we wouldn't do this again."

I hate being in here. I hate listening to their conversation. It's not right.

Bellamy left the door partially ajar, but if I move and open the door more, I'll be spotted for sure. Still, I have to try. The longer I'm in here, the greater the risk they'll see me. Especially now that the lamp is on. I'm not well concealed, and if she or he got up and came in this direction, they'd see me for sure.

I push myself up onto my hands and knees and crawl like a cat out from under the table when the king's words make me stop mid-movement.

"We have some movement on Marie," he says.

"Marie?" she questions.

"Yes," he replies, his hand rubbing her belly. "We received intel late this evening that she broke into a home in a small village in France."

Bellamy gasps, her hand covering her mouth. "Oh my god. Sebastian, are you sure?"

He kisses her neck. "Yes. Her fingerprints match."

"That's what had you and Rowan in here until it was time to put the children down."

"Yes. I believe Rowan is planning to leave in the morning to go see what's going on."

"Is Desta with her?"

Desta? And Marie? Holy motherfucking shit. Marie!

My jaw drops, and I gape. They're chasing Marie. I can't believe it. How do they know she was the one who took Desta?

Sebastian shakes his head, then shrugs. "We know nothing at this point. We've been quietly working with governmental agencies, and a set of fingerprints collected following the break-in triggered an alert."

"Wow. Do you think she knows we're chasing her?"

"I hope not. I hope she has no clue. But Bellamy, while Rowan is gone, I want you and the children to stay close to home. I know you wanted to take them to the children's museum in Tourin, but I don't think that's safe right now."

Bellamy releases an exhausted sigh. "Sebastian, following a lead on a fingerprint has nothing to do with us going to a museum."

"Just please."

"Honestly, nothing has happened when we've left the palace. If anything, everything that's happened occurred while we were in the palace."

He makes a turbulent noise.

"You know it's true. Whether there is a curse or not, we cannot allow it to continue to control us."

"I'm not. At least I'm trying not to. But right now, nothing feels good. Nothing feels safe. Just when we start to get a handle on things, everything spins out of control again. Please, just this once, listen to me. For my own peace."

Lightning flashes across the sky, immediately followed by a loud bang of thunder. It distracts them, and I take that as my moment to sneak out. Except my foot snags on a lamp cord, causing it to move and grate against the table it's sitting on. *Fuck!*

My heart batters against my ribs, and a cold sweat breaks out on the back of my neck.

"What was that?" Bellamy asks.

I don't stop. I keep going because it's too late now.

"Was that the lamp?" the king questions.

I reach the door and continue through it, getting to my feet and pressing my body against the wall. I don't know if they saw me or will get up to investigate. As it is, I unhooked the monitors and will have to sneak back in tomorrow before dawn to reattach them.

Shit. This is bad. This is really bad.

I don't look back. I push myself along the dark corridor when a sound behind me tickles my ears. Fuck. Adrenaline pumps a steady cocktail through my blood, and I crouch and move, keeping to the wall and the shadows.

Then I hear another sound. The door to the study closing.

They could look me up on the cameras now, and that will be that.

I continue along the hall and down the stairs, going faster and faster. The weight of everything is like an albatross around my neck, making my steps heavier. I don't want them to catch me. I don't want this to end. The longer I can drag this out, the more money I can earn. I can create a résumé and get Jaqueline and build us a real life.

She could go to school. Hell, I could too.

I make it down to the servants' area, but I keep moving, needing to get out, needing air, needing breath. The walls are closing in on me, and I pick up my pace. The servants' entrance that leads to the delivery area beckons me, and I plow into it, struggling with the lock for a moment, only to break through.

Rain instantly soaks me, the air balmy and electric.

I keep going, racing around the side of the palace and up the sharp incline, fighting slick grass and mud, the darkness and the rain, trying not to jump with each massive bolt of lightning that claws like the devil's fingers across the ink-black sky.

I stop when I reach the rocks, my chin lifting and my eyes blinking against the onslaught of rain as I search. The window. That's the window.

I take a step, the earth blanketed by jagged rocks, and I climb up the first tier.

This is where he fell. Where he threatened to push Bellamy to.

I run my hand along the shiny black surface.

Harrowing grief consumes me, staining my face in tears of acid.

I love him, and I hate him.

I hate them. I hate what they made me. I hate the neglect and abuse and toxic fucking poison. I hate the blood on my hands and in my soul. I hate that this family is hurting, and so much of it is because of mine.

A scream lurches from my chest, drowned by the thunder, but I don't care. My fists pound on the rock as blind fury consumes me. I rage, screaming and howling until there's nothing left of me except for a panting, sobbing mess.

I collapse against the rocks when a flash of lightning reveals that I'm not out here alone. Someone has been watching me.

26

ROWAN

I wasn't going to come down to see her. I held off all night and was more than a little preoccupied by the latest development on Marie Elonaise. It was the first thing to distract my thoughts from the blonde since I first laid eyes on her. It was welcome, and I pored over the intel from the French government. Fingerprints. That's it.

But Marie's still out there. She's still slinking around.

I leave in the morning, and I'm anxious to go.

Except I don't want to leave Marcella. At first, I told myself that the gnawing sensation was because I don't trust her, and I'm the only one here who knows she's Ella and is possibly up to no good. At least she could be. I honestly don't know.

It occurred to me that she could simply be running from something or someone—the person who did that to her back. The palace could be her safe haven from years of abuse. That's almost how this seems. But I don't know because she won't tell me, and because she won't tell me, I still don't trust her.

Tonight she ran right past me in the hall. I was still debating whether I was going to go to her room and had been standing outside, pacing the servants' quarters at midnight for longer than I care to think about. I couldn't decide if I was going to talk myself into her room and spend my remaining hours inside of her. Holding her. Talking to her.

Or if I was going to do the sensible thing and go back upstairs to bed.

I knew I was going to do the latter. But I resisted and tried to talk myself out of it all the same. The woman has me spun up. I'm a junkie in need of a fix, and she's the only drug I crave a taste of.

But when she ran past me, breaking before my eyes, I didn't question myself. I followed her out into the rain. I don't know what happened. What drove her to this moment. Why she wasn't in her room at this late hour. I doubt she'll tell me, but right now, I don't care.

Her body settles, collapsing exhaustedly against the rocks. Lightning flashes, and her head quirks up, catching me as I move toward her.

"What are you doing out here?" she yells, furious that I saw her, yes, but also to be heard over the pounding rain.

"That's my question to you." I take another step, climbing up the rocks and mindful of my footing so I don't slip. "What the hell are you doing out here in the middle of a storm like this?" *Screaming your head off and crying like no one is watching,* I don't add. I climb up to the next. This is where Samil fell to his death, so it's a bit ominous for me. Even more so because it's where he wanted to throw Bellamy to.

It's likely coincidence that she picked this spot to lose herself for a bit, but still, I don't like it.

"I..." She trails off and almost comically wipes her face. For what? So I won't know she's been crying? It's pouring rain. Who cares about tears?

I reach the large boulder she's perched on and crouch beside her. My hands cup her face, and I hold her steady, my eyes bouncing back and forth between hers. "Are you okay?"

She laughs, but there's no humor. "I'm great. Never better."

"Did someone hurt you?"

She pushes my hands away, ever the tough girl. "You need to stop trying to be my hero. I don't need you to save me. Hell, I don't even want you to try."

I stare into her. "Is that true? That you don't want me to try?"

She looks away. "Stop following me. It's creepy."

I chuckle. I can't stop following her, even if it is creepy. She's made me a stalker. Whether that's due to safety concerns or my previously mentioned obsession, I don't exactly care.

"No," I tell her bluntly.

She goes to argue, but a whole-body tremble hits her, and she's shaking. From the rain or from adrenaline or from her tears, I don't know.

"Shh. I've got you." I kiss her forehead and encircle my arms around her so I can tuck her body against mine. She's cold and shivering uncontrollably despite the warm temperature. I draw her into me, shifting us both so she's on my lap and I can hold her.

Lightning flashes overhead, and I want to get us out of here.

I take her face in my hand and lift it. I do it to gauge her reaction. To see if she'll let me take her inside, but the look in her eyes stalls my breath, and I dip in and kiss her instead.

I expect her to push me away or tell me this can't happen—as she always does—or possibly tell me to fuck off and mind my own business. What I don't expect is for her arms to wrap around my neck so she can hold me close as she kisses me back as if her life depends on it. I grip her tighter, my head tilting, and my mouth opens. Our tongues meet, and it's wet and warm, and she tastes like tears and sorrow.

My heart shifts in my chest. It becomes...well, it becomes hers. I could lie and say a million other things, but I know they'd all be exactly that. A lie. My heart is hers. I'm hers.

She fists the back of my shirt and my hair, and I kiss her as I lift her off the rocks and up into my arms.

She tucks into my chest, and I kiss the top of her head, breathing in the scent of her soaked in rain. The rocks are a motherfucker. The incline of the earth is too. It's slippery, and this storm is no joke. But I don't care. I shouldn't be here with her. I don't know who or what's compelling her. I know it's something. No one cries the way she was crying on their own. Someone did that to her.

She's not here by accident.

That should have me staying a million miles away from her. But I can't. I just...I can't. The scars on her back and the way she is with Bellamy and the kids and how she was losing her mind tonight. Hers is a heavy, tormented heart. A broken heart. But her soul is there. I know it is. She's fighting me, but she's not. She wants to push me away, but she doesn't.

She's conflicted, and if she didn't give a shit, that wouldn't be the case.

I kiss her head again. "I've got you, baby."

She sniffles and holds on tighter even as she says, "Don't be good to me."

"Marcella, I'm starting to realize that's all I want to be. Let me be good to you. Let me take care of you. It's okay to put your faith in me. I won't hurt you."

She shakes her head against me, but then we're walking inside, and I'm still carrying her, and this palace is huge, and we're dripping water everywhere, but so be it. I don't take her to her room. I want her in my bed tonight. I'm too big to share a double bed anyway, and I want to sleep with her. Not just fuck her. I want to hold her.

We reach the third floor, and her chin tilts up as if she's finally coming to and realizing where we are. "What are you doing?"

I smirk. "You're mine tonight, mia stella."

"Rowan. No."

Except it's too late because we're at my suite. "This way you can smell my pillows without having to sneak around about it."

I shut the door behind me and walk us toward my bathroom, but she wiggles, trying to get out of my arms.

"Put me down. I can't be in here."

I don't put her down. I walk us into the shower and turn it on to hot. She shrieks when cold water hits her, but I press her against the wall.

"I'm not letting you go." I take her mouth with mine, instantly splitting her lips with my tongue and tasting her once again. Her kisses are becoming something I can't give up—just like her.

"That's not going to be your choice."

"It's not going to be yours either."

The water turns warm, and with it, she melts against me, the tension in her muscles relaxing. I toe off my ruined shoes and kick them to the corner, then remove my shirt. Hers is next, and I have to pick her up again to get her shoes and socks off.

It's ridiculous and difficult with how wet everything is. She laughs when I struggle with her pants that are now stuck on her hips.

I growl in frustration. "This is impossible."

"I've been trying to tell you that, but you don't want to listen."

I chew on her bottom lip. "Still don't. Take them off. I need to be inside you."

"And if I don't? If I walk out of the shower and never look back?"

I spin her around and force her hands up against the shower wall, my mouth coming down to her ear. "I'll chase you. Then I'll spank you for running."

I press my chest into her back and grip the sides of her

pants before I yank them down her legs. I pull one foot out, then the other, until I have her naked before me.

I kiss a trail down her neck and along her back. Her breath hitches when I kiss and lick along her scars, but I continue down to her ass. I bite one supple cheek, followed by the other. She yelps as I do it again, harder this time, and I smack my hand over the indent of my teeth before I trace them with my fingers.

I want to be rough with her. I want to brand myself all over her skin. I want to fuck her so hard she feels me for days every time she moves. She makes me savage, and I like it. I like this feeling. This version of me. It's one I've never had with anyone else before. It's not charming or manicured. It's crude and unpolished.

It's as if she's waking me up, and now I'm the man I want to be instead of the prince the world sees.

My hand slides up her inner thigh, and I use it to spread her wider, making her take steps to accommodate me. The sweet pink of her pussy is right in front of me, and I bite her inner thighs, making her jump and move to escape me.

"My beautiful, sexy girl, you look absolutely stunning with these on your skin." I drag my fingers along the indents of my teeth and climb back up her body. My good girl still has her arms raised, and it shocks me how one can be so defiant and anxious to submit at the same time.

It makes me so fucking hard, I have stars behind my eyes from the lack of blood flow in my brain.

I turn her back around and kiss her with an all-consuming, *I can't get close enough* level of desperation. The heat of her mouth and the way she kisses me back, filled with longing and lust, makes me tremble. Our hands are everywhere, our mouths messy as we groan and moan and grind, wanting to fuck, needing to come.

She's sin racing through my veins and capturing my heart.

My fingers split her pussy lips and rub her clit. She moans, kissing me and rocking against my hand. Before her, I never kissed much. It felt misleading and intimate when I knew the woman was only going to be a simple fuck and nothing more. But from the night I first met her, all I want to do is kiss her. Again and again, over and over. Any distance between us feels like too much.

She rolls up onto the balls of her feet and pushes down on my fingers, rolling her hips as she fucks against my hand. Steam surrounds us, making me dizzy and high.

"You're so fucking wet for me."

"Rowan." My name is an expletive. A plea. More internal conflict.

"You can pretend you don't want me, sweetheart, but your hungry little cunt is grinding on my fingers, desperate to get more friction so you can come."

Her eyes clench, and she coils in, but I'm not having that. I pick her up, force her legs around my waist, and enter her. My lungs empty, and my eyes roll back. *Jesus.* How is it this good every fucking time? How is that even possible?

I settle into her as deep as I can go. All the fucking way until I'm practically in her womb.

"There. It's just us. Me inside of you, you surrounding me. I've never wanted anything as badly as I want you. I have you, and it's not enough. I keep needing more."

"Rowan, please."

I pepper her face with kisses and grip her ass, splitting her cheeks so I can really drive into her. I'm unyielding. I hold her steady and plunge in and out of her like the palace is burning around us, and this is my last chance to feel her.

Because that's what this is like. It's always like this. Every time with her feels like the first and last. Like I'm chasing her and will never stop because she believes she always has to run from me. It thrills and terrifies me all at once.

The piston of my hips doesn't let up as I move into her, sinking deeper, going harder.

I groan against her lips and kiss her sloppily. Her hands hold the back of my head, fingers knotted in my hair. Her pussy spasms and clenches, her breath seizing as she gets close. I nibble and kiss her wet skin, giving her every inch of me, burying myself, pounding, my breath shaking.

Her cunt grips me, squeezing me to the point where light dances behind my eyes.

"So fucking tight, sweetheart. Fuck, your pussy is amazing."

"More," she pants. "Rowan, more."

I'd do anything she asked. Fucking anything.

I work into her, hiking her thighs up higher, the slide so fucking good we're both loud. I get us both to the end, my orgasm racing up my spine like a shot. She rides me through hers, wiggling her hips and moaning and crying out.

I slow, savoring the feel of her as the tail end of pleasure holds me.

More kisses. More touching. More breathing.

I pull out and set her down, but I don't stop touching her. I can't. I wash her hair and body, and she only mildly protests, but the truth is, she's spent. Her eyes are heavy, and her muscles are lax. I dry her off and dress her in my clothes and tuck her into my bed.

"No sneaking out on me," I whisper as I hold her tight. She stiffens, but I simply kiss her neck and trickle my fingers along her skin until she gives up the fight and falls asleep. A few moments later, I do too, thoughts of morning on my mind and questions about whether my Cinderella will be there this time when I wake up.

I wake before my alarm. It's not dawn yet, and I'm groggy and have a mild headache, but I'm also smiling like the devil because she's still here. I doubt it's intentional. I'm positive she'll be angry about it when she wakes up, but for now...

I slip out of bed and gather her clothes, which I hung up to dry overnight. They're still damp, and I walk them down the hall to the linen room where the royal family's clothes and things are attended to. There are two washers and dryers in here, and I toss her things into one of the dryers and turn it on before I return to my room to get myself ready.

She's out, her breathing heavy, her body not even stirring as I skulk about my room. I grab a piece of paper from the desk and a pencil and do a quick sketch of her like this. It's not great. It's dark in here, and this pencil isn't what I'd typically use, but it's good enough.

The lines of her face develop beneath my hand. She's so pretty. So peaceful looking. It's the first time I've seen her like this, and it might be my favorite look on her yet. A thought occurred to me before I fell asleep last night. I finish up my very rough sketch, set it in my desk drawer, and pick up my phone to place a quick order for what I need. I finish packing, go retrieve her dry clothes, and return to my room. Just as I zip up my suitcase, her eyes flutter open.

"Morning," I drawl, and she jerks up, taking the sheet with her to cover herself. It makes me smile at how adorable she is. First, she's wearing my shirt, but considering I've seen and tasted every inch of her, modesty isn't exactly necessary.

"Shit. I can't believe I slept in here," she mutters in Italian as she inches to the end of the bed and gets out, frantically searching around. I step toward her and hold out her clothes.

"They were still damp this morning, but they should be pretty dry now."

She tilts her head and narrows her eyes. "How did you do that?"

"I'm a prince. I demanded your clothes dry, and they did. It's how I get everything done."

She arches an eyebrow.

"I used the dryer," I deadpan.

She snorts before she can stop it.

"What?" I bark, affronted. "I know how to use a dyer."

"Oh? How many times before this have you?"

Busted. I shrug. "It wasn't exactly difficult. You press power and start."

"The prince of Messalina used a dryer for the first time. Wonders never cease."

"You're very sarcastic for a woman wearing nothing but my shirt." It's the best thing I've ever seen in my life. Sexy rumpled hair, flushed cheeks, bright green eyes, hard nipples, creamy thighs, and my clothes on her naked body.

"Thanks for the reminder. I have to get out of here."

"You can use my bathroom. I have to leave anyway." I didn't get a chance to talk to her about this last night. Before I can, she scoots past me for the bathroom, and I grab her forearm to stop her. "Don't you want to know where I'm going?"

She shakes her head as she shakes my grip loose. "Nope." She makes for the bathroom with hurried strides.

"Don't you care how long I'll be gone for?"

"No again!" she calls to me from the other side of the now closed door.

"Fine! I wasn't going to tell you anyway." That part is true. I wasn't going to tell her where I was going or why I was leaving, and I have no clue how long I'll be gone for.

She laughs, likely because she knows I wanted her to care or at the very least ask while feigning she didn't care.

"You could at least try to pretend you're not so in love with me," I tease, except the words get drowned out by the sound of the toilet flushing and the faucet turning on.

A moment later, she comes flying out of the bathroom, holding her wet shoes because I had no idea what to do with those. I suppose I could have done an internet search to see if shoes can go in the dryer, but it didn't occur to me until now.

She blows past me like she's not even going to say bye or give me a kiss or anything, and fuck that. Fuck this. I grab her once again and haul her into me.

I kiss her deep and hard and a little miffed. "I'll miss you too."

"I never said I'd miss you."

I cup her pussy. "I was talking to her. She'll miss me even if you won't."

She pats my cheek. "Aw, is your ego bruised that I'm not like every other woman and hopelessly in love with you simply because you're Prince Rowan?"

Yes. "Pfft." I roll my eyes like a teenager. "Like I'd want you to be in love with me. You're mean."

"Yeah, but my pussy is sweet."

I can't argue that.

She gives my cheek another pat, then heads for the door and, without another word, sneaks out. Damn. I've got it really bad for the wrong woman.

I grab my bag, my backpack filled with my laptop and chargers and shit I'll need, then head out my door. Except instead of going to the breakfast room for a quick cup of coffee—stopping when you're the prince of a country isn't so easy, especially when you're trying to keep a low profile—or even going to the garage, I go to Sebastian's suite.

I listen outside the door because the number of times I've heard him fucking his wife makes me want to keep noise-canceling headphones on me at all times. Thankfully, it's quiet, and I tap lightly on his door.

It takes him a moment, but then I hear him bark, "What?"

"Kiss your children with that mouth?" I retort, keeping my voice low so I don't wake anyone else up.

He curses, but I hear him move, and a moment later the door opens. "What is it?"

"I need to talk to you."

He scrubs a hand up and down his face. "Now? What time is it?"

"Just about five."

"Fuck, Rowan. I didn't get to sleep until a few hours ago."

"Me too. It can't wait."

He nods and goes back into his room to throw on more than only the boxer briefs he was wearing. A moment later, he's back, and without a word, we go down the stairs to his study since it's the closest private room. Except as we round the corner, I hear what I think is a door closing, and a flash of something catches my periphery, but before I can make out what it is, it's gone.

"Did you see that?" I ask him because I'd almost swear it was Marcella.

"See what? No."

Huh. Weird.

We close the door behind us, and Sebastian immediately asks, "What's so important that you couldn't wait?"

"Two things. One, Marcella is Ella, and two, I'm sleeping with her."

Sebastian blinks at me, his hands going to his hips as he works through what I just said. "Rowan…" He trails off, releases a breath, shifts his weight, and drops his chin toward the floor.

"I found the earring in her room."

A gust of air exhales from him as if I just answered his unasked question.

"I didn't trust her from the start. There was something about her that triggered me. I told you this. I did my best to stay away from her and stuck to mostly watching her through the cameras."

"But that clearly didn't last long. Who is she? Why is she here, and why did she sneak into the wedding? And how the fuck did she make it past our facial recognition?"

"All excellent questions I don't have answers to, except I believe she was sent there or here or both by someone."

"Someone who, Rowan?" my brother roars, and I wave my hands for him to lower his voice so he doesn't wake the entire palace.

"I don't know, but she's either not here willingly or she's here to escape something or someone."

He growls and paces over to the window. "Why do you think that? Because you don't want to believe she's here to hurt us? Because your dick likes fucking her?"

"She has scars on her back. Lots of scars. They're not new, though some don't seem to be all that old either. She's tried to warn me off her a million times, but there's this…vulnerability to her. A conflict within her. She's tormented and breaking. I've seen it, Sebastian."

"All of that only makes her more dangerous. She's been

around my wife, my children, and you've said nothing to me until now."

"You have enough on your mind without me adding to it, but with me leaving today, I had to say something. I was handling it."

"You were not. You're fucking her, but more than that, you have a twisted fixation with her. You always have. It's clouding your thoughts and judgment."

It might be. I'm honestly not sure. I didn't trust her. Not even a little. But after last night...seeing her that way...I don't know. Something shifted inside me. Still, my truth is universal.

"I'd never risk Bellamy or the children. Not ever. Not for anyone or anything. I told Bellamy I didn't trust Marcella and asked her to keep her distance. This was before I found the earring. Bellamy argued with me and said she felt safe with her."

"We felt safe with fucking Charlotte."

I pan a hand out toward him. "I agree, and I said that. Marcella is a different situation than Charlotte."

"How do you know that?" he retorts, looking angry and frustrated. "You know nothing about her."

He's right. I know nothing about her. Nothing real. She's warned me off time and time again. Yet I'm so compelled, and I can't make heads or tails of it. Am I putting us at greater risk simply because I want her here? Because I want to solve her puzzle and unwrap her mystery? Because I want to be the man who saves her?

"Give me one reason why I shouldn't have her locked up immediately."

"Because if we do, we'll never learn her secrets. We'll never figure out the truth because she won't tell us. I know it. But if she believes we're not on to her, that we don't know she's the same woman from the wedding, and that we're suspicious of her, she might lead us to whoever is orchestrating this. Or she's genuinely hiding from someone who has been hurting her, and the palace is a safe place to do that. She's been doing her job, Sebastian. Same as she has for four months. Charlotte showed her hand much faster, and if I hadn't suspected Marcella was Ella from the start, we'd have no clue about any of this."

"It takes big money and resources to pull off what she did."

"Yes," I agree. "That's not her. She has nothing. Barely any clothing and no personal possessions. She's someone's captive, one way or another."

He rubs his scruffy jaw. "You realize that makes her even more dangerous."

I sigh and shift my weight. "Perhaps. I think she's conflicted. I don't think she wants to hurt anyone."

"A caged animal doesn't want to hurt anyone, but they'll do whatever they have to, to protect themselves."

I blow out a breath, my hands going to the top of my head, and I sit in a chair, only to stand back up and pace in a circle. Fuck if he isn't right. I meet my brother's steely gaze. "Sebastian, if you want to arrest her and have her questioned, I won't stop you. I love my family, and I'd rather die than hurt any of you. That's a fact. If something happened to you because I didn't act..." I can't finish that. It's why our father is dead. "Fuck. I'm a fool."

"Rowan..." He stops himself, breathing out harshly. "How deep does this go for you with her? Is this sex? Obsession? Or is this...more?"

I drop to the edge of the sofa, my elbows on my thighs, my head in my hands. "I think...how could it be? I don't know her. Yet, I still feel as though I do. I see her and...fuck, Sebastian, how did you know?"

He chuckles. "You told me."

I lift my head. "What?"

"You told me I was in love with Bellamy. You were right. I was. But I also trusted her."

"I'd be an idiot to trust Marcella."

"But something in you does anyway?" It's a question, and I consider it seriously.

"Something in me does. Or maybe sees there's something else there. I don't know what it is or why it's there. Maybe I'm lust drunk. Maybe this is my dick doing all the talking."

"Rowan, you've slept around plenty. You've never been like this."

"She walked out on me. Maybe that's why."

He gives me a pointed look. "Is it?"

"No," I answer honestly, feeling the truth behind that simmering in my gut. "But that doesn't mean that what I'm doing with her isn't fucking stupid either."

He walks over to me and sits beside me. "Emily and Javier come home today. She has a work phone with all the security features. We'll start tracking her, and I'll have Javier put an alert on her facial recognition in the palace. Certain locations at certain times will trigger it. And I'll have Bellamy and the children keep their distance unless there's a third party with them, but I'll add on an armed attendant to them."

I nod slowly, my head falling back to my hands. "You won't let your wife leave the palace, and yet you're willing to do all of this for me?"

"You told me you believe Marcella's a patsy or a victim. I'll give her and you the chance to prove that. But Rowan, I will say that my leash on this is extremely short."

"Yes. I agree."

"And if I suspect anything or fear for my family's safety in the slightest—"

"You act accordingly and do whatever you have to do."

His hand grips my shoulder. "Go find Marie. Then come home to us."

The drive to France is long and interminably boring. It's not exactly like I can do this alone as my own recon mission. I'm the prince of Messalina, and therefore I require security with me at all times. Technically we're also not supposed to drive ourselves. I have, and so has Sebastian on occasion, but it's rare and, for this, not permissible.

So it's me sitting in the back seat, drinking coffee and thinking about her. About all the things Sebastian and I spoke about this morning. I feel better for having told him, but I also realized my reasoning for not initially telling him was bullshit. I kept saying it was my responsibility to handle or that he had enough on his mind with Bellamy, the children, and the curse.

Thinking about it now, that's not true.

I was afraid of his reaction. I was afraid he'd arrest her or tell me unequivocally that I couldn't watch her or touch her. Truthfully, I'm shocked he didn't, but despite my desires, and possibly my fucking heart, I couldn't leave for who knows how long with a potential danger lurking in the mist.

But with that, I also need to dig deeper and harder. I need to uncover her secrets and the reason why she snuck into the wedding and now works in the palace. What happened to her last night that drove her over the edge?

My eyes close, and I replay the events as they unfolded. She wasn't in her room. It was the middle of the night. She also didn't have her phone—either phone—on her because when we came upstairs, I brought her into the shower and undressed her, and it wasn't with her.

So what the fuck happened?

I could pull up the cameras, but the palace is massive— seventy-five thousand square meters with over seven hundred and fifty rooms. Without knowing where she was last night, it would mean a lot of searching, and not all of the rooms have cameras in them. It's mostly the halls with the exception of the main rooms, several parlors, the library, the solarium, and other random areas. Private spaces don't have cameras in them for obvious reasons.

I blow out a breath and sink back against the seat, my eyes heavy and my mind foggy. All too soon, Gabe, my lead security, clears his throat, and I wake with a small start.

"Sorry, sir. We're here."

I blink, wiping the sleep from my eyes, and glance toward the window. We're on the outskirts of a French town not far from the Messalina border. It has the appearance of a suburb with rows of homes on neat streets.

Marie was here? That seems...odd.

I pictured her hiding in places like the cottage where the onesie and blanket were found. Then again, she doesn't know we're chasing her. She has no clue we know she's the one who took Desta because we never announced the fingerprints we lifted from the newspaper clipping. The only ones who know about that are Sebastian, Javier, Bellamy, Emily, Althea, and me. It's been over twenty years since that night.

Maybe she's finally starting to let her guard down.

The SUV stops in front of the address the local police gave us. There's a perimeter of crime scene tape linked from tree to tree. I scoot to the door and glance around the neighborhood. There's a woman up the block with a stroller and an elderly couple on the other end walking a dog. A few houses down, a gardener is mowing the lawn. It's as regular a world as it gets, and yet the woman who took my baby sister was here.

It makes me murderous.

She has no right to live when Desta likely isn't.

The door opens for me, and I step out, squinting against the blinding sunlight. I pull my sunglasses out of my pocket so I can slip them on. We're getting curious looks, and whether or not people recognize me remains to be seen. Right now, we simply appear like special police with our black SUV.

A police cruiser pulls up and parks in the driveway.

I scoot under the line of yellow tape, and two uniformed officers greet me halfway up the walkway.

"Your Highness," they both say, going to bow when I stop them.

"Please don't. I appreciate the gesture, but I'd rather not draw unnecessary attention."

"Of course, sir," one says.

I reach out and shake their hands, which surprises them, but they're letting me in here when they could just as fast tell me to fuck off. It is a crime scene. Someone broke into the house through a back entry point. The tenets were away on holiday when it happened. It's a rental, and the owners have several properties they manage.

"Thank you for letting me view the home today. Was anything taken?" I question.

"Not that the residents are reporting, Your Highness," the other officer states.

My brows knit. "Has anyone else entered the home?"

"Just the crime investigation unit, the homeowner, and residents, who were escorted by us, and we made sure nothing was touched. The residents are, as you can imagine, anxious to return home. We haven't told them of your involvement, and after your visit today, we're going to allow them to return."

"Right then." Who breaks into a home, likely knowing that the occupants are away, and takes nothing? "Shall we go in?"

They nod and lead me up the front steps to unlock the door for me. It's a quaint home from the outside, but the inside is a different experience and immediately raises new questions. The furnishings are high-end, and the electronics, including the large television, are top of the line. The lounge leads into a kitchen that would make Margarite, our chef, jealous.

On and on it goes. A home gym with state-of-the-art equipment, an office with monitors and computers that must cost a fortune. I open drawers and closets and anything I can think of. They don't stop me.

"This is quite the home to steal nothing from," I state.

"Yes, sir. We can't figure it out either. Neither can the residents."

"What do they do for a living?"

"Software engineers, I believe. They're two brothers."

Hmm. Okay. Gabe throws me a dubious look.

"And you're positive the fingerprints match the person in your database?"

"Yes," the first officer tells me. "It was double-checked."

"But they don't belong to the homeowner or tenants?"

He glances at his partner but shakes his head. "No. The fingerprints in question weren't discovered in the house. They came from a back fence leading to the home of the people who called in the break-in."

Weird. So she likely put on gloves before entering.

"How did she get in?"

"Through the back door," Officer Two answers. "She picked the lock."

No alarm. No cameras.

I continue on, visually scouring the home as I head upstairs. There are three bedrooms, but only two are being used as a place to sleep. The third bedroom has a sofa, but that's it. Or at least that's how it appears until you open the closet.

"Did the police or tenants come in here at all?"

The officer who came upstairs with me clears his throat. "Um, no, sir, we didn't. It's a practically empty room, and neither the homeowners nor the tenants came in here."

My head twists over my shoulder to him. "The tenants who had their home broken into didn't come into this room and open the closet to check on their safe after someone broke into their home?"

He looks almost sheepish. "No. They didn't."

I turn back to the professional-looking safe that's sitting ajar. She cracked it. There are no markings on it or evidence of forcible entry. "Fascinating." I can't see what's inside. "Perhaps you should dust for fingerprints?"

"Yes. Smart. Let me go get the kit. I'll be right back."

He leaves me like the fool he is, and I don't waste a moment before I put on my own gloves and open the safe door. And what I see inside makes me gasp and reach for it without thinking. It's tucked in the back, off to the corner, but it's impossible to miss with daylight streaming all over it.

It's not Desta's tiara, but it appears at first glance to be a diamond from it. Not one of the large diamonds that we already found, but one of the smaller diamonds. I remember what the tiara looked like, and we looked at pictures of it again when we found the loose diamond. This is one of the heart stones from the center ring. I'm positive of it.

It's pink, about ten carats, and rare.

Similar to the stone Bellamy wears around her neck, only this one is bigger.

Other than that, the safe is empty save for a few scattered hundred-euro notes. The house was robbed, but the thief knew exactly what they were coming for, where to find it, and how to get it.

I return the door to how I found it and remove my gloves.

A moment later, both officers, along with Gabe, are in the room, and I stand back. He shouldn't have let me stay in here. That's an error on their part, but this isn't my country, and frankly, I don't care about their crime scene. There won't be fingerprints anywhere on the safe.

Was the tiara here to start with, and a stone simply fell out of it as it had before? Or was Marie coming for loose stones? How did these people get it in the first place? Marie was hasty. She didn't put gloves on until she got into the backyard. She left the safe ajar and some money still in it. She also left the diamond.

It was a smash-and-grab job, but with more skill than an average thief would have. The police think she was in and out in under five minutes.

It's not the first time she's made mistakes. The only reason we found her is because she left the discarded baby items in the old cottage along with the newspaper clippings. Likely because she had to flee quickly. But as with everything lately, I have more questions than answers.

The police inspect the safe and dust for prints. Go them. I stay back and keep my mouth shut until we get back outside the home again.

"Thank you for your help, officers." I shake both their hands and give them my charming prince smile. "I appreciate it, and so does my country. I'll be sure to call your captain and thank him for all the diligent work you both have done on this case and your invaluable service. I don't think there's much more for me here, so our part in this is done."

Otherwise known as *please have the tenants return so I can watch them as best I can and learn more about them.*

It could be a long few days for me.

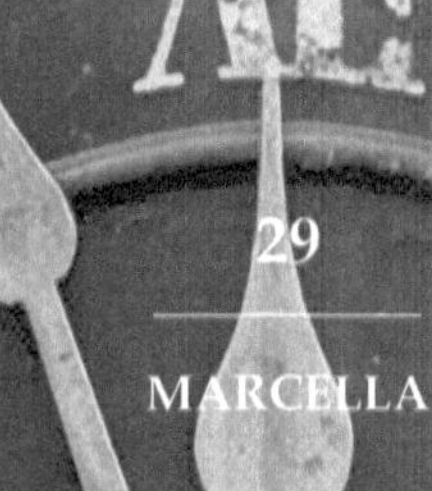

29

MARCELLA

The space that the royal family turned into a bedroom and recovery space for Emily is incredible. There's a large hospital bed, another bed for Javier that's directly beside it, a reclining chair, a sofa, and a dresser. The en suite bathroom has been outfitted with accessibility equipment. Then there's the rebab space attached to her new bedroom.

I'm going through her room, making sure it has everything she needs, including extra towels and linens, since this room has become part of my primary responsibilities, when Raul comes in.

He stops short when he sees me. "Oh. You're in here."

"Yes. What do you need, Raul?"

"I was just..." He trails off, only to snag on the items in my hand. "I was going to make sure Emily had fresh towels."

"No, you weren't. You were going to do something assholeish and underhanded to try to make me look like I'm not doing my job or I'm incompetent, as you have been since I took over Emily's role."

He squints at me. "We haven't been doing anything. You've been doing that all on your own, honey."

"First of all, if you ever call me *honey* again, you'll wake up without your fingernails. Second, you just said *we*, implying more than one of you has been messing with things, which isn't what I said, but I appreciate you confirming it all the same."

He blanches. Whether from my fingernail comment or from the fact that he's a moron and just outed his equally moronic partners in crime, I'm not sure. They're not the brightest bulbs, hence my calling them the three stooges.

"You can't talk to me like that. I'll file a complaint."

I smirk. "Go for it. When you do, I'll file a complaint backed by proof that you, Esme, and Marsha have been disruptive, unproductive, and malicious simply because you're children and can't handle your jealousies. Grow up, Raul, and get back to work."

I turn my back to him, and because he's all bark, little bite, and the dumbest of the three, he's out of things to say.

"Leave the spray bottle of whatever nasty shit you're hiding behind your back."

He makes some kind of aggravated shriek but shockingly sets it down and storms out. The moment his footsteps fade down the hall, I retrieve the spray bottle of brown water that looks like it was made with dirt and empty it into the sink before I wash everything down.

At least that's something he can't use in other parts of the palace.

Finished with that, I set the empty spray bottle beneath the sink, put the rest of the towels on the rack, and exit the bathroom only to have it be my turn to stop short.

"Your Majesty." I curtsy.

"Good morning, Marcella," he says in that stern way of his, his eyes scouring over me before they turn their scrutiny onto the room. "I came by to make sure everything is set for Emily's return home."

"Yes, sir. That's what I was doing as well. I hope everything is to her satisfaction. And yours, of course."

I'm like a cat in a room full of rocking chairs with this man. Has Rowan told him what we've been doing? Does he know I broke into his office last night? After I left Rowan's room, it was the first place I went, and I hooked the monitors back up and made sure everything appeared untouched, but you never know.

"Everything looks to be in order."

A prideful smile tilts up my lips. "Thank you, sir."

"Marcella, are you happy working here?"

Shit. Oh shit. What's worse is that there's no inflection in his tone or alteration in his features. He's stoic and completely closed off to interpretation.

"Yes, Your Majesty. I am." It's the truth. Minus the stooges and the prince who's determined to fuck up my world, I'm the happiest I've ever been. I'm contributing, I'm earning my own money, and most of the people are kind. I could do this job forever and be grateful for it. The only thing missing is Jaqueline.

He nods slowly, walking deeper into the room as if he's weighing my answer. "You've spent quite a bit of time with my family since you took on your new role. You taught my daughters chess and helped my wife get the nursery in order."

"I enjoyed both of those quite a bit. Your family is lovely."

"You're a very bright woman, Marcella. Is working as a housekeeper what you hope to continue doing?"

My brows crease. "How do you mean, sir?"

"I'm curious where your dreams lie."

"My dreams?" I almost laugh at the words. "Your Majesty, hope and dreams are not words I've allowed myself to entertain. Duty and service are all I know."

He stops walking and twists in front of me, his height and size imposing. He's intentionally trying to make me nervous, and with that, he knows something. Or at the very least suspects. Yet here I'm standing, so I'm not sure what his game is with me yet.

"Duty and service to whom?"

Brilliant question, Your Majesty. "At present, the royal family."

He's rough, but he's a good man. A good king. My brother... well, I have a lot of thoughts and feelings about Samil, most of which I haven't properly sorted through yet. I imagine mental peace where he's concerned will be a hard-won venture.

His gaze holds mine, firm and unyielding, and I match it. It's also the truth. I'm not sure where my loyalties lie. I'm not sure where my heart is taking me. But at this moment, with no one else's agenda but my own, I was hired to serve the palace and the royal family, and that's what I'll do.

"You know about the curse. You know what Charlotte and the former prime minister did to us."

My throat thickens. I try to swallow, but I'm paralyzed. I can't move. I can't even blink.

"We've seen our fair share of wolves in sheep's clothing. That said, my wife and children like you very much. They told me so just this morning." I drop my gaze, discomfort making it difficult to maintain eye contact. I understand his threat, and yet I can't help but feel joy and pride in hearing that Bellamy and the children like me.

"Sir. I like them very much as well." I swallow and lift my chin, giving him more of my truths. "I'm truly sorry for all you've endured."

I sweep my long bangs behind my ear, and he squints, tilting his head.

"You remind me of someone." He sounds almost surprised by this. "Or perhaps it's your hair color."

Yes. My hair color is a bit exotic as far as blondes go. It's a golden yellow with natural streaks of white when the sun bleaches it out. Samil had the same hair.

"She's here!" Bellamy calls out, popping her head into the room and interrupting this awful moment. "The ambulance is arriving now."

"I'm coming." Without another word or even a cursory glance in my direction, the king leaves, and I blow out a relieved breath. I can't tell what he knows, but he's suspicious of me. That much is obvious.

After one last visual inspection, I head toward the front door of the palace through a long corridor and into the entry foyer, which is more like a historical art museum than a foyer. There's a painting of the royal family with the previous queen in it. She's holding a tiny baby Zayer, and the two girls are young.

Queen Nora is beautiful. Stunning really. Her girls are so much like her.

I don't want to hate Nora.

I don't want to look at this beautiful queen, who was so beloved in this country and to her family, and think ill of her. I don't know what her relationship was like with the king, other than what Samil told me.

All I know is that Samil loved her. That their affair continued for years and years. That she's the reason all of this happened. She betrayed the king. Isn't that what the curse is based on? The betrayal of Messalina with her husband, Emperor Claudius? Maybe Nora started all of this again for them.

Bellamy mentioned that her love with Sebastian is what she hopes broke the curse. But what if there is no curse? What if it's just the follies of humans, their betrayals, their jealousies, their love? Enormous tragedies have befallen this family. But does that make them different than anyone else? Being hateful or furious with dead people is futile. But I'm furious with my brother. Possibly even a little hateful too.

I turn my back on the painting and saunter out the front

door to where the ambulance is. Emily is being carted off the back on a gurney, annoyance all over her face and in her folded arms. That only grows as Bellamy comes racing over to her, fussing over every small detail.

"I'm fine, Bellamy. I've been up walking and everything. This is just a precaution and a bit overdramatic," Emily says. "Honestly, all of this is ridiculous. They could have put me in a wheelchair."

"Let us take care of you," Bellamy admonishes. "You take care of everybody. We want to return the favor."

Emily sighs, finally giving in.

Javier snickers. "Naturally, you relent for the queen."

"I like her more than I like you."

"You must," he teases, an indulgent gleam in his eye. "She gave the nurses and doctors hell."

It makes all of us laugh.

"I did not. I simply don't like being fussed over. Ah, Marcella. Perfect. Just the person I was hoping to see. You'll talk work with me, won't you? Your texts have been vague and simply telling me what I want to hear. Don't think I wasn't on to you."

"You needed your rest with no aggravation or work on your mind," I reply.

She rolls her eyes as the paramedics wheel her along the gravel path. "Except I'm home now."

"And you still have to focus on your recovery."

"Has it been that bad?"

I laugh lightly. "Not at all. Honestly, other than a few small hiccups and a couple of situations, everything has been fine. I promise, once you get settled, I'll tell you everything. But just as the family needs you to take care of yourself, your staff does too. We need you to return to your job."

So I can take this as my résumé builder with a nice recommendation and leave.

"Okay, fine," she relents, allowing the ambulance drivers to push her in on the gurney until she reaches the front doors. "Please, please, let me switch to a wheelchair. I don't like being on this thing."

No one can say no to her, and a wheelchair is brought around. They help her down into it. Her movements are rigid and her body is stiff. Every time she winces, Bellamy, whose hands are clenched in tight balls in front of her mouth, does too. I suspect being in pain is relatively normal after having a hip replacement.

She's wheeled down the hall to her room, and we all follow her in there. Javier does a brief sweep of everything, and Emily starts to tear up. "I can't believe you did all this for me."

"I would have created a hospital in here if you had needed it," Sebastian tells her plainly. "Rowan wanted to, and he's also planning several improvements to the palace we'll tell you about."

The way Rowan takes care of his people tickles my heart and heats my cheeks. It's one of the things I love about him. Last night he took care of me. He carried me in from the storm and held me, and after we had sex, he washed and dressed me, then held me. It was the best night's sleep I think I've ever had.

But if it's love that drove Samil to madness, I'm not sure that's something I'd like to explore. His blood runs through my veins, and I'm already in way over my head with a man I have no future with. I'm bad for him. Poison for his family.

I'm the villain in the latest page of their saga.

For that reason, more than anything else, I say, "I'll let you get settled. I'll be back later to talk."

"Marcella?" the king calls out to me.

"Yes, Your Majesty?"

"My aunt has the children on the third-floor crow's nest. Would you mind going up there and asking her to come down and join us here?"

I nod. "Of course, sir."

"I'd also like you to stay with the children for now."

"Very good. I'd be honored."

Shocked, I curtsy to everybody and leave the room. So... maybe he's not suspicious of me?

Winding my way up through the palace to the third floor, a pang of unease hits me. I was only in this room once, and it was during my palace tour after I was hired. After last night, I know this is where it happened. Signoria and Antonia had said it was the library window he was thrown out of.

But now I know better. It was the third-floor crow's nest. A room that's been redone since that night. My breath settles in my lungs, and a fresh wave of sadness hits me. The room has been transformed from the video I saw last night. It used to be lined with bookshelves with an open floor area that was connected to the second and first floors of the library through a winding staircase.

Now the floor has been closed up and the bookcases removed. There are comfortable sofas in front of the fireplace, a large, open play space for the children, and an office area for the queen. It's cozy and pleasant. You'd never know that death happened here. That blood stained the floors.

The children are off to the side playing, while Althea reads a book in the corner on the window bench. Zayer is making a palace out of blocks while Sabrina and Phaedra are playing dolls, dressing them up, and having them do things in the massive dollhouse.

I clear my throat, and all the attention turns to me. "Lady Althea?"

Her head lifts from her book, and she sits up.

"Sorry to disturb your reading, but His Majesty is requesting your presence downstairs. Emily has returned home. They're in her space."

"Lovely. I'm so glad she's home. Thank you for coming to get me. Are you staying with the children?"

"That's the plan."

"Marcella, come play with us," Sabrina calls out.

"I want to play chess," Phaedra agrees.

Just as Althea reaches the door, an attendant enters. Althea looks surprised by his presence but doesn't question it. She may be surprised, but I'm not.

So much for him not being suspicious. If I were questioning it before, it's confirmed now.

The king doesn't trust me.

He knows something.

But what is the question? And what does Rowan know?

I do my best to shove down my nerves and ignore him as I take out the chessboard and lay it out, then set up the pieces.

"I want to be black," Phaedra demands.

"Then I get to be white." Sabrina snatches a white pawn from the box.

Zayer is too busy with his blocks to care. The three of us play chess, me helping both of them. My personal phone buzzes in my pocket, and I ignore it. I don't even so much as flinch or go toward it. If I learned one thing from the videos last night, there are cameras all over this room.

On one side of me, I have Signoria and Antonia orchestrating something I no longer want to be part of. On the other side, I have the royal family that I'm growing more and more attached to. Including the prince who surprises and thrills me in ways I never expected were possible.

All I know is that everything is becoming harder and more difficult by the second. And I'm not sure how any of us will survive unscathed when the end comes.

30

———

ROWAN

"Software engineers, my ass," I grumble, staring out the passenger window of a nondescript car from three houses down. "Gabe, tell me something."

"Yes, sir."

"If you had your home broken into, and the only thing ransacked in your ridiculous place was your safe that held a very specific diamond, would you be throwing a party right now?"

"No, sir."

"Didn't think so."

I sent the diamond to our special investigation unit. They're the ones who identified the bloody onesie, the blanket, and the diamond from the tiara. But I took a picture of it and sent it to Sebastian, and he just about lost his mind. He wanted to come join me here, but he knows he can't with Bellamy being so close to the end of her pregnancy, Emily just returning home, and Marcella being there.

"There." He points. "Look."

I watch as someone steps onto the front porch, smoking what looks to be a joint and talking on the phone.

"Fuck. Why didn't we bug the house?"

"Because the police were with us."

"Right. Them. Incompetent twits that they are. Thank God."

If they hadn't been, we might not have the diamond without anyone knowing about it. If word had leaked about that or our involvement, it would have set us back and likely wouldn't be as far along as we are.

Gabe takes pictures of him, but even with our windows down, we can't hear. We'd have to get out of the car and attempt to sneak close enough to listen, but with the tight proximity of the homes to the street—and to each other—there's no way that would work. This is the sort of neighborhood where everyone knows everyone else's business.

"We should interview the neighbors."

"They're being paid off."

I turn to him. "You think?"

He gives me a *what do you think* look and then nods back over at Smokey Joe getting higher than Everest. No one is calling the police. No one is complaining about the noise of the party in this residential neighborhood on a weeknight.

"If that's so, then why did the back neighbor ring the police?" I ask, rubbing at my jaw as I think this through. "Do we know?"

Gabe stops taking pictures and goes into some sort of crazy app he has on his phone. Likely something illegal that's hacked into the police, but I don't care, and I don't ask.

"They phoned at midnight that a person wearing all black terrorized their dog when it barked at them, and that they saw them walking through their backyard, opening their gate, and then entering the house through the back door. She said her neighbors were out of town and she was concerned."

"Hmm. So she knew that they were away and called the police. Do we know where these people were?"

"I'd need my computer for that, sir."

"That's your mission for tonight or tomorrow before we return."

"Yes, sir."

"Gabe?"

"Yes, sir."

"You know I hate it when you call me that, right?"

His lips bounce, the whites of his eyes gleaming against his dark skin. "Yes, sir."

"Fucking asshole."

He laughs. If Marcella has taught me anything, it's that people who don't want to be found aren't. We looked into her. It became part of my obsession, and it turned up dead end after dead end, almost as if she didn't exist. If someone is smart and has resources, they can evade almost anyone. But these people aren't in the shadows. They're right here, in everyone's face, loud and obnoxious with zero fucks to give about any of it.

They were robbed. An untold amount of cash was taken. A priceless diamond—and possibly the tiara—was too, along with who knows what else. Yet these people don't have a care in the world. Why?

"Tomorrow we speak to that neighbor. Not me, obviously, but you."

He chuckles. "Yes, sir. I know the drill."

"Why would people like this not have any home security? No door cameras, no alarm. They had a lock that was easily picked and a safe that was cracked. That's all."

"Arrogance, maybe."

"Or perhaps they thought no one would be dumb enough to try to rob them."

THE PRINCE of Messalina has to appear as though he's on some holiday that wealthy playboy princes take. Even when in suburban France. With that, we're staying fifty kilometers from the house at a luxury hotel. They've been annoyingly gracious and perfectly imperfect with their fastidious service. I want to be left alone. I want to be inconspicuous.

No such luck.

They've brought me champagne and chocolate-covered fruit and nuts and fucking mini cupcakes. Since we returned here for dinner, I've had three people knock on my door with various items. I'm gracious. I tip well. But fuck off!

I shoo the last person away, take a shower, then climb into bed. It doesn't take a genius to know where my thoughts gather, and I don't stop myself when I pick up my phone and press her number for a FaceTime.

The call is declined, and I swear to fucking God, that woman is getting the best spanking of her life when I get back.

I call her again. Then again. Finally on the fourth call, she picks up, but it's not her face I see.

"Do you have the phone stuffed into your blanket?"

"My pillow. Why are you calling me?"

"Marcella, *I don't even know your fucking middle name,* Russo, let me see your pretty face or I'll have Althea come down to your room, and trust me when I tell you, my aunt does not like to be up past nine, and here we are close to ten."

"I was sleeping."

A pang of guilt hits me. "Were you?"

"Trying to."

"I'm sorry. Let me see you, then I'll let you go to sleep."

The picture shifts, and she's there, on her side in the dark. A smile hits my lips, and my finger glides along the screen.

Fuck, the way my chest clenches and my heart flutters. "Hi."

"Hi," she replies even as she works to hide her smile. "Why are you FaceTiming me on my work phone?"

"Because your piece of shit regular phone is so old it doesn't have that capability. Come to think of it, I don't know the number for it."

I get an eye roll. "You know what I meant."

"I didn't want to go a whole day without seeing you."

She releases a breath, her cheeks pinking up, but I don't want her to withdraw, so I keep going.

"Tell me about the palace."

She licks her lips. "Emily came home. She was in some pain, and everyone fussed over her."

My fingers continue to run over the phone, tracing her face. "I'm positive she hated that."

I get a small, crooked smile as she shifts, treating me to the best angle ever. I prop my phone up against the wall behind the desk I'm sitting at, flip to a new page, and start sketching.

"Stop drawing me."

"Never. I see your face when I close my eyes, and whenever that happens with something, I have to draw it. I drew you this morning when you were still sound asleep in my bed."

"Your Highness—"

"Rowan," I correct as my hand continues to move, my eyes bouncing back and forth between the paper and the screen.

A huff. "Prince, what you're doing with me isn't smart. This has to stop."

"So you like to say, and yet here we are."

"I'm hanging up now."

"Please don't. I want to look at you for a bit longer. Talk to you. Pretend. Maybe even imagine."

"Imagine what?"

"That the world isn't as complex as it seems. That you're simply a woman I met and I'm just a guy and this isn't as impossible as it feels. I don't want it to be impossible. I want what I feel when I look at you to never stop."

Her eyes glass over, and she shifts again, pressing her head deeper into her pillow to hide it. "And what's that?"

"Hope. Excitement. Lust. Derangement." Love. I won't say it, and I barely allow myself to think it because it seems too soon and too insane, but it creeps into those dark, unruly recesses all the same. It's impossible for it to be that. I don't know her. There are all these things that make her everything I need to stay away from. But the thought is there. A truth that resonates through me and doesn't care about all the other bullshit.

I can't leave her alone. I think about her night and day. My moments are consumed with her.

She giggles, the sound like music. "You are definitely that last one, Your Highness."

"Don't pretend you don't like me too."

She rolls her eyes. "Good night."

"Will you sing for me?" I don't want her to hang up. Searching for Marie fucks with me. The diamond I found *is* fucking with me. I feel like I'm chasing ghosts, and when I get to the end of this—if I ever get there—I'm positive it will be with heartbreak.

I don't like to think about the curse because it's entirely out of my control. My nieces and nephew are my life. My brother is the only true family I have—other than Althea, but she's not of our royal bloodline—because our mother has little if anything to do with us. Bellamy is pregnant with twins, and the fear— the chronic fucking fear—keeps me up. I want to fix everything, and I don't know how, so looking at Marcella and drawing her and listening to her is a tonic to my ravaged soul.

She might prove to be the biggest curse of all, and maybe this is all part of it. The beautiful angel of death coming to claim its next victim—me. But I'd rather be destroyed by her than continue in the gray nothingness.

"Sing?" Her brows pinch in confusion as if I spoke to her in ancient Greek.

"Yes, my enchanting siren. I want you to sing something for me."

"And jump to your death?"

I laugh, my hand continuing to move across the thick sketch paper. It's as if she were reading my mind. "If that's how it goes, there are worse ways for a man to die than at your hands."

Her face pinches up for a flicker of a second before she evens it out and asks, "Sing what?"

"Anything. Your favorite song that you like to sing."

"I don't know a lot of songs. I only know what I grew up hearing."

I already figured that out, which is why she'll fight me on some of the things I'm sending her.

"I don't care. Pick something. Make it up if you have to."

Again to my surprise, she opens those full lips, and her voice is set free. It's incredible and sends chills racing up my spine. I don't know the song. It's some Italian thing, but she could be singing me the history of Messalina straight from one of the old tomes in my study, and I wouldn't mind.

She finishes the song, and I'm in some sort of trance state. My hand even stopped moving, and I hate that it did because I missed so much and could have drawn incredible things.

"You are so beautiful, Marcella. You make the sun rise even on the gloomiest day."

The phone pulls away from her face, and I'm stuck back in the darkness. "Don't say things like that to me. I should hang up on you. I never should have answered."

Yeah, yeah, blah, blah. I don't know who she's trying to convince with that routine, me or her. This is why I think she doesn't want to hurt us. This is why I think she's running from a past that won't let her go or is being manipulated by a hand wrapped around her neck.

"I'm sending you some stuff," I tell her.

And I'm back, this time treated with her annoyed scowl. "What stuff?"

"Stuff." But there's no hiding my smirk.

"I don't need you to buy me things."

"I know. I did it for me because it makes me happy."

She snorts a laugh. "Such a selfish, self-indulged prince."

"The worst sort." I sit up straighter, the charcoal in my hand moving quickly once more, nervous she'll ruin the image again, and I'll be forced to draw from memory. I hate that. I much prefer to draw from a direct visual.

"Do you draw all the women you sleep with?"

"No. I've only drawn two. Her and you."

She releases a heavy breath. "Her?"

"The woman you saw when you snooped."

"Why her?"

I suppress my grin. "Jealous?"

She laughs, but there's no humor to it. "Not even a little."

"Uh-huh. I met her the night of my brother's wedding to Bellamy. She saw how bored I was. How disinterested I was in every woman there who were only talking to me because I'm the prince and they wanted to be the next princess. That woman didn't care about any of that. Like you. But that night she gave me something, a piece of herself that was just for me and no one else. I liked her instantly. I liked her before I knew her secret. But after I had it as my own, she had me."

She swallows thickly and licks her lips. "What happened to her?"

"She ran off, and I haven't seen her since."

Marcella's eyes close tight, her cheeks flushed, and she moves the phone away, having difficulty hiding her expression.

"Then I met you," I continue.

Wordlessly, she shakes her head.

"My toxic trait is falling for women who want nothing to do with me."

"Rowan..." She bites her lip and puts the phone down.

"Don't do that."

She doesn't lift it from her pillow, and I'm trapped in darkness. "I'm not someone to fall in love with."

"So you keep reminding me. Fine. Warning noted. Now show me your pretty tits."

She giggles, and I smile like a stupid bastard. Her face is back, but the phone is moving, and so is her shirt. She lifts it up, shows me her pretty tits, then says, "Good night, Your Highness," and hangs up on me.

I can't wait till tomorrow when she gets the packages I sent her.

31

———

MARCELLA

"W hat's all this?" the king bellows as he walks into his study. I'm legit on my hands and knees trying to get a fucking bleach stain out of a Persian rug that's likely ancient and priceless. But it's bleach. Bleach doesn't come out. It takes everything else out of whatever it spilled on.

"I'm so sorry, Your Majesty," I start, not even knowing what to say. I'm going to get fired for this. Or stuck with a bill I can't pay. Then everything will be in the dumpster, including me, and Antonia and Signoria Batorini will take turns setting it on fire to char my remains. They might do that anyway once they realize what I'm up to now.

"How did this happen?"

I sit back on my haunches, black rubber gloves on my hands, holding a useless scrub brush as the overwhelming scent of bleach burns my eyes and nose.

There's a noise outside the study that catches my attention before I can respond, and I'd swear to all fucking God, I catch a flash of Marsha's lavender hair shooting away. Bitch is fucking dead. Her two buddies will go with her. I wasn't going to kill them because I'm trying to turn over a new leaf and all, but fuck that.

Emily praised my work yesterday, and this morning, shit has been all downhill. I don't take kindly to people loosening a wheel on my trolley so the thing topples over and everything spills out, or replacing my coffee with decaf and my sugar with salt—a lame fucking prank. They can't get away with the big stuff anymore now that she's back, but they also know that I didn't rat them out, so they think it's still game on for them.

Idiots.

I turn back to the king. "I don't have an answer for you, sir."

He tilts his head, his eyes narrowing at me before slipping back down to the odorous white spot in the center of what once was grays, greens, and gold.

"Marcella..." He trails off, studying me with a seriously furrowed brow.

"Your Majesty—"

"Did you do this?" he cuts me off. "Because I don't see a container of bleach on your trolley, empty or otherwise. Nor do you look scared or like you fucked up. You look...well, to put it in my wife's terms, pissed."

I choke out a laugh. I have no clue where it comes from, but the king of Messalina just said *pissed* in English to me, and it's funny. He's also not yelling and screaming and storming around as I expected the beast king would. Samil used to call him a total motherfucker, and I have no doubt that he was or at least was to Samil. Thus far, I haven't seen much of that.

"No, sir. I didn't do this."

"Do you know who did?"

I sigh. "I have my suspicions, Your Majesty."

He takes two steps back and sits on the edge of the sofa, legs crossed at the ankles, arms folded over his broad chest.

"You're not going to tell me, are you?"

"No, sir, I'm not."

Because where I was complacent before, trying to be the model employee and all that, I'm going to choke them to death and watch the life slip from their eyes. I'll enjoy it. I never enjoyed killing—it was horrible, and that's putting it mildly— but their deaths I'll enjoy.

He considers this for a moment and nods. "You realize I could command you to, or at the very least, check the footage on the cameras of who entered my study before you."

"Cameras, sir?" I question as if I didn't know. All he does is give me a simple nod. Smart man. "Yes, Your Majesty, I'm aware of all of that."

"But you still don't want to tell me." It's not a question.

I stand, depositing the brush back onto my trolley along with my gloves before I face him. "No, sir."

"Have things like this been happening to you since Emily left?"

"Am I allowed to lie to you, sir?"

He chuckles, a rare smile curling up his lips. "Not unless you want me to fire you."

"Yes, sir, things like this have been happening since Emily left."

"Things like my bedroom appearing as if you haven't cleaned it or dirty footprints on my floor."

I wince. "Yes. Once I saw them, I cleaned—"

He holds his hand up, stopping me. "How come you never came forward?"

Snitches get stitches. We don't talk. We don't rat. Not even when someone wrongs us. We're patient. We bide our time and retaliate. We handle it ourselves. "That's how I was raised, sir."

"I see. How you were raised. By your farmer parents."

I try not to react, and I don't respond.

"Hmm."

"Sir, if I may, I'd like to address it myself, if that's all right."

He runs a hand along his jaw to the back of his head, and I've seen Rowan do a similar move like that, and Jesus fucking Christ, I need to *stop* with him already. The sleeping in his bed and the phone calls and the drawings and the freaking boxes that are sitting unopened on my bed are messing with me.

"I'll permit that. For now," he tacks on. "But Marcella, this rug is three centuries old, and they ruined it to try to pin you with the blame. That's not the sort of thing I take lightly, nor is someone doing something malicious in my palace, where my children and pregnant wife are. Do you understand that?"

His pointed words don't go unnoticed.

A slick oil spill of dread coats my insides, making me feel greasy and all wrong. The king is on to me. I know he is. Why he's giving me latitude to stay, I don't know, but I won't take the risk of sneaking in here again. I've been working on a plan, going over the figures in my bank account and my earnings to see what I can afford and what I can't. At this point, it's not much, and I have no idea how I'll get Jaqueline even if I can manage to buy our way out of the country to somewhere safe.

I curtsy. "Yes, Your Majesty, I completely understand that."

"Good. I expect you to handle this matter quickly, and as part of your handling it, I want them fired and gone from my palace by this evening."

There go my plans for murder and retribution. Firing her won't go over well, but fuck it. If anything, hopefully it'll teach the other two a lesson. "I understand. If necessary, do I have access to the video from the cameras outside the room?"

"How certain are you of the person?"

"Fairly certain."

"Start with that, and if you need the video as backup, I'll have Javier get it for you. I also expect you to discuss this matter with Emily, as she's the one in charge."

I nod. "Very good, sir, and thank you."

He rises and heads toward the exit but stops. "I heard about your suggestions for improvements to the palace."

I don't reply. I simply wait him out.

"They're good, and we're going to be enacting some of them. Thus far, I've heard good things about your work. Keep it up, Marcella, and there will likely be other jobs and promotions here for you."

He leaves, and an odd sense of pride swarms me like a pack of honeybees, tickling my insides and buzzing through me. It's a sensation I haven't felt in years. Not since my father or Samil would praise me for a game of chess well played, or mixing up the right combination of chemicals to make an undetectable poison, or flawless execution of speaking another language. I thrived on that praise, on that feeling, even if I didn't know till much later what they were grooming me to become.

Now I have to fire one of the three stooges.

I'll speak to Emily about it first.

I head downstairs toward Emily's suite when my phone buzzes in my pocket. My personal phone. Shit. I pull it out and wince.

> S.B.: I will be in Tourin on Sunday at 10 a.m.
> Meet me at the café in the lobby of L'Hotel
> Louise, and I'll give you the drive. We're close,
> Marcella. No mistakes or you'll both pay.
>
> Me: I'll be there.

I have less than a week to figure everything out and create a foolproof plan. It's not enough time. But the longer I'm here, the more suspicious the king grows of me. And the closer I get to a prince who seems to be holding on to me with both hands. What he said about the woman at the wedding...about me...

God, the way my heart is starting to beat for him.

Emily is sitting in a chair, drinking some water, when I

enter the rehabilitation room. She's drenched in sweat, and her therapist is off to the side, taking a break as well.

"I'm sorry to bother you, but I wanted to speak to you about something."

"Absolutely. Come in." Emily waves me over, and I take a seat in a chair beside her. I regale her with the rug incident and who I strongly suspect did it. I also tell her about what happened while she was away because I don't care enough about these people to exact revenge. I don't care what happens to them either.

"You never said anything," she comments.

"Most of the time I didn't have proof it was them. I also didn't think much about them. Truthfully, I didn't want to start drama or have them create more disruption and scenes. It was easier to fix their sabotage than anything else, and I kept telling myself I'd handle them, and to a certain extent, I did. I managed the difficult situations they created, and I'm proud of that. The palace ran smoothly, everyone did their jobs, but the things they did this morning to get me fired went above and beyond to the point of malicious and destructive."

"Yes," she states, wiping her forehead with a towel. "I agree, and that's unacceptable. What they'd been doing likely would have resulted in some discussion, but not anymore. Imagine if the queen had walked in there and inhaled the strong scent of bleach? Or if someone had gotten hurt because of their care-lessness?"

"I should have done more. I know that. I don't know for sure who changed the menu order. After I changed my password on the iPad, it didn't happen again because they weren't able to get access."

"Which was smart thinking on your part, but they could have killed someone, and they need to go. All of them. Text them and ask them to come in here. We'll do it now, and we'll do it together."

"Thank you, Emily. You've been endlessly supportive of me since the moment I arrived, and that's not something I've had a lot of in my life."

"You're young, Marcella. This was your first time truly managing people, and much of that is a learned skill. It's not easy to call out colleagues on their behavior. But you learned a lot, and that's what's important."

She squeezes my hand, and a few minutes later, Larry, Mo, and Curly walk in, each with an *oh shit* expression while trying to be incredulous or irritated. It's a cute look on them. Emily nods to me, which sort of shocks me, but I guess I'm the interim head of house, so here we go.

"I wanted to let the three of you know that, effective immediately, your services are no longer required in the palace."

"What?" Marsha asks, not understanding.

"You're fired," I simplify. "All three of you."

"What?" That's Raul this time, and his comes with some venom attached along with a snarl.

I go through the laundry list of crimes and misdemeanors I know they committed.

"You're a lying fucking bitch." Raul again.

"We never did any of those things!" Marsha.

"It was all you. How dare you try to pin your incompetence on us?" Esme.

"We have video, fingerprint evidence, and this comes from His Majesty."

Now they turn into owls, and it's just kind of sad. I was plotting their deaths, and they're not worth much more than a small conversation. Clearly the life lessons I've been taught aren't ones to follow. I should have spoken up about them earlier. I should have asserted myself better. As Emily said, lesson learned.

Accusations are thrown. Nasty words are slung. In the end,

two attendants come and escort them to retrieve their belongings and make sure they leave the palace.

One issue is dealt with, and admittedly, that was the easiest of them.

I still have no clue what to do about everything else. And that's what's most troubling.

32

MARCELLA

My bedroom door shuts behind me, and I twist my back to work out the kink that just won't seem to go. Even my hot shower didn't help. My shoulders are bunched tight, and no amount of deep breathing or mental pep talks will unwind them.

Then there are the things sitting on my bed.

Jesus, Rowan. Really?

I let them sit for a moment, even as my curiosity is practically screaming at me. I brush my hair and get changed into my sleep shirt and shorts. Once I run out of things to do, I sit on my bed and stare at them.

"This prince is going to break my heart." Whether that's because I walk away or he does when he discovers the truth, I don't know, and it doesn't matter. It's going to hurt like a motherfucker.

Nothing real can happen between us.

I'm a palace servant. A slave to a family that won't even allow me the respect of their last name. A prisoner to lies and secrets I don't want to keep, but still have to. I don't know what a relationship is, but I know enough to know that they don't survive the secrets I'm holding or the lies I've been telling.

I rub at the pang in the center of my chest.

With an annoyed shake of my head, I tear into the first box and find...a fucking vibrator. Seriously, Rowan! There are two, actually. One is a wand of some kind, and the other is hot pink and curved, one side thicker than the other. There's also a water-based lubricant in the box.

A laugh slips past my lips. He bought me sex toys, knowing I don't have any, because the asshole snooped around my room. I glance toward the back corner of my bed at the invisible earring beneath the mattress. He didn't find that, though. If he did, I can't imagine I'd be sitting here. He has the other one, and if I can steal it back from him, I can sell them, and that will more than pad my wallet for a while.

I shake that off and go for the second box. This one has two sets of headphones in it. One goes into my ears, the other over them. They're both expensive, but why would I need two pairs?

A text comes through my work phone, and I reach for it, thinking it's Rowan, but it's not. It's a message from a music app letting me know that my six-month subscription is ready for me when I download the app to my phone.

He bought me music and a way to listen to it.

The third box is the largest and—fuck. This asshole. This perfect, amazing asshole. He bought me clothes. New sneakers, new work shoes, new shirts and pants and fucking panties and bras. Sexy ones too. Pretty ones. Ones I'd pick out for myself if I had money.

Tears burn the back of my eyes, but I won't let them fall. I can't.

I pick up the phone and call him. He answers on the first ring with, "You must have opened the boxes."

"How did you know that?" I flop back, my head bouncing against the pillow before it sinks in.

"Because you would never have called me otherwise."

Fair. "Your Highness, I can't accept these gifts."

"You can. I wasn't sure what kind of listener you'd be, so I bought you both kinds of headphones."

"Why are you doing this?" I whisper, my voice cracking on the end.

The phone makes a ringing noise, and I peek open an eye to see he's FaceTiming me again. Nope. I hit decline, but he calls again, and on the third try, I relent and hit accept. I get under the covers and pull them over my head.

"Where are you? Or I suppose the question is, where am I?"

"In my blanket. I can't accept the gifts."

"I want you to have them. It's nothing extreme. I didn't buy you diamonds or extravagant designers, though truth be told, I wanted to. I bought you things that most people have. Things you should have. Things I want you to have."

I shake my head, my hand over my eyes. "And the vibrators?"

He chuckles, the sound warm and enticing as it curls through me. "Have you tried one yet?"

"No. Nor am I going to."

"If I were there, I'd start with the Hitachi." His voice drops, the sound low and gravelly. Rough and unrefined.

"Which one is that?" I ask, though I already know. It's on the box.

"The white wand. I'd turn it on and run it all over your body, along your muscles to relax you, and across your nipples."

My eyes pinch tight, and I bite into my lip. "Are you trying to have phone sex with me?"

"Video sex, and absolutely."

"How many women have you done this with?"

"Just you. Come on, torture me a little. You know you want to."

I pull the blanket off. "How is it torture for us to have video sex?"

He smiles, and that fucking smile and those motherfucking dimples. Damn him for being so good-looking and charming. "I can't touch you. I can't smell you. I can't taste you. That's torture. Watching you pleasure yourself when I can't be there to do it myself is agony."

"You're way too into me."

He tilts his head. "Baby, my obsession with you has its own definition because the current one doesn't do me justice. Come on. Torture me. Make me hurt with how badly I need to fuck you."

After the day I've had, I could use a good orgasm. Fuck it.

I sit up and open the white box, pull out the long wand, and hold it in my hand. It's decently weighted, and just looking at it is already making me wet.

"Take off your shirt and panties," he demands.

I shiver, biting into my lip to cut the tension. "Sit and watch." I prop the phone up against the bedside lamp and remove my clothes, then set them at the foot of the bed.

A deep groan echoes through the phone, and I lie back, holding the wand in my hand and touching my breasts.

"Fuck, mia stella, you are exquisite. Turn it on."

A thrill runs through me. I want to do this for me, but I'd be lying if I said I didn't want to do it for him too. I want him to watch me. I want him panting and begging and touching himself because he's so turned on and wild with the thought of me that he has no choice.

It's why I peek over at him on the screen, and he doesn't disappoint.

Jaw locked tight. Blue eyes nearly black and afire with uncontained lust.

I lick my lips and continue to touch myself while looking at him. I can't pull myself away. His intensity holds me captive. I'm a slave to him, but this time a willing one.

"Turn it on."

I gulp as a bubble of nerves hits me.

He must read it because he says, "Don't worry. You'll like it. Go on the lightest setting to start. I've got you."

My eyes close. It's what he said to me the night he took my virginity. He had me then, and he has me now. I trust him with this, and so I turn on the vibrator. It makes a buzzing sound and pulses against my hand.

"Yeah. That's it. Start touching yourself with it."

"Where?" I ask softly.

He growls. "Fuck, I love that you just asked me. Run it over those sweet tits for me. I want to see how hard we can get your nipples. How good it feels when they're stimulated just right."

It tickles at first touch but immediately turns pleasurable. The vibrations hum along my skin, making my breasts feel fuller and heavier. My nipples get impossibly hard, and the moment I touch the vibrator to them, a moan hits the air.

"Does that feel good?"

I nod, my eyes closing and my back arching. "So good. Oh god. How does it feel this good? It's not even on my pussy yet."

"Christ, you're making me sweat."

I glance at the screen. "Are you jerking off?"

He nods. "Starting to."

"Can I see it?"

"Shit, sweetheart, you're going to make me come way too fast if you keep asking for things like that. Drag the wand to your pussy and show me, and I'll show you just how fucking hot you're making me."

I pick up the phone with my other hand and trail the wand as I run it down my center to my pussy. The moment the head of the wand hits my clit, I cry out and grind into it. It's intense, but god, it's so good. Sweat breaks out on my forehead as heat consumes me. Unabashedly, I plant my feet into the bed and spread my knees, needing more contact, more vibration.

"Oh fuck!" he bellows.

Rowan is standing completely naked, with one hand on his lower abdomen and his other moving on his cock. It's insanely hot. Not something I never expected would be, but holy shit, it has me pressing the wand in deeper.

"That's the hottest thing I've ever seen."

Funny, that's exactly what I was just thinking.

I bring the wand lower and press it against my opening, getting it wet before I roll it back up to my clit. I run it in circles, pressing it in deeper. My thighs tremble, and I set the phone back against the lamp so I can play with my tits.

"Talk to me," he commands. "Tell me every thought you're having."

"I'm picturing your face between my thighs," I admit. "Your fingers inside of me. Your tongue on my clit, the way the vibrator is."

He grunts. "You have no idea how much I love eating your cunt. The way you taste and smell is too perfect for words."

His hand is moving on his cock, jerking it forward and back, rubbing his thumb along his head that's red and glistening with precum.

I lick my lips. "I want to taste you too. I haven't done that before." I blink at him. "Would you teach me?"

"Would I teach you how to suck me off?"

I bite my lip and nod.

He chuckles mirthlessly. "Sweetheart, I'd fucking love to teach you how to suck me. I bet you'd be amazing at it all on your own."

His cheeks are flushed, and the motion of his hand is driving me higher. I pull on my nipple and run the wand up and down my pussy, going from my opening to my clit and back.

"I want to be inside of you so badly. It's all I can think about. The way you feel on that first thrust. The way your cunt grips my cock. The sounds you make. How beautiful you are when I'm as deep as I can go."

"Rowan. Oh god!" My toes curl and my spine arches as pleasure pulses through me.

"Shit, Marcella, what are you doing to me? I'm going to come," he rasps. "I can't hold off."

"I'm going to come too."

His groan prickles the hairs on my skin. "Come with me, mia stella. My beautiful goddess. My siren. Come with me. God, I wish I were inside of you. I wish I could fill you up and after fuck all my cum back into you over and over—"

"Oh fuck!" I cry only to muffle my face with my pillow. My orgasm sweeps over as my thighs clamp around the wand and I fuck it, rolling my hips and grinding into it. My pussy is leaking. I can feel it everywhere, including down into my ass. It's wave after wave of unbridled pleasure.

The moment my clit becomes too sensitive, my legs fall heavy against the blanket, and I pull the wand away, shutting it off and panting beneath the pillow.

"You still with me?"

A giggle bursts from my lungs, and I pull the pillow away. My phone is face down on the bedside table, having tipped over, and I pick it up and bring it up to my face. "No. I don't think I am. I'm somewhere else entirely."

"Me too. Damn." He gives me that soft, dopey smile that never fails to make my heart pitter-patter. "I wish I could hold you and kiss you. Sleep beside you."

I shake my head. "Not happening again."

He rolls his eyes. "Uh-huh. You haven't asked where I am or what I'm doing."

"It's none of my business."

"You're not the least bit curious?"

I smirk. "Curious would mean I've been thinking about you, which I haven't."

"Liar." He sighs. "I wish you would tell me."

"Tell you what, Your Highness?"

I can tell he's running his finger over the screen by the way he's looking at me. "All your secrets. All the things you don't want me to know."

I stiffen as a gnawing chill sweeps through me. I tuck myself under my blanket, covering my body from his view. "What makes you think I have secrets?"

"Just a hunch."

"I probably should tell you. Then you'd finally listen and stay away from me."

He frowns, and I wish I hadn't said that. His hand is moving, but now all I see is him from the chest up. Ferocious sorrow has me rolling to my side and tucking in on myself at the truth of my words. All this is so fleeting. This joy. This excitement. This...*feeling*. The one that resonates in every fiber of my being when I look at him. When I think about him. When my careless mind gets swept away and imagines my life as something other than what it actually is.

I clear all of that away. Antonia always told me emotions are useless and make us act hastily and carelessly. She's not wrong. Everything I'm doing with him is utterly reckless. My midnight prince.

"Are you drawing me again?"

"You're the most beautiful thing I've ever drawn."

"Rowan..."

"Mia stella, you can tell me. I swear you can. I'm safe for you. I'll never hurt you. Not ever."

"Rowan!" I gasp and cover my face with my hand. "Please."

"I care about you. I haven't been shy about letting you know that."

"But why? Why do you care about me? You've known me for like three weeks. This has to be about the sex."

"Look at me, Marcella."

His voice is commanding, and I obey, needing to hear him, to see him.

"The sex with you is incredible. Best of my life. But it's because it's you that it's that good. We could have something. I know it's new. I'm not a fool. But I also know if we gave it the chance, it would grow into something real. Something incredible. I've never felt this kind of spark with anyone before. There's a reason for that."

I feel it too. I know it's there. "We can't be together. This won't turn into a relationship or anything real."

"There are only two reasons to put that sort of limit on us. One, you're hiding something from me that you believe would change the way I feel about you. Two, you're scared for whatever reason that I'll hurt you. Which is it?"

I can't answer him, but I don't have to. He knows it's the first.

"I'd take care of you. I'd protect you. I'd keep you safe. But at some point, you have to trust me in order for that to happen. Think about it, okay?"

He disconnects the call, leaving me reeling. I want to believe him. But I don't see how any of that will be possible. Once he learns the truth, he'll hate me.

"No one knows who they are or what they do," Gabe tells me as he gets back in the car and starts it up. "But the neighbors who called the police were scared. I know that much. They didn't answer many questions, and their eyes kept shifting about. She said she wished she hadn't called the police."

"Interesting. So they're likely drug dealers, mafia, or professional thieves..."

He nods, his dark eyes shifting about as he puts the car in drive and takes us out of here. "One of those would be my guess."

"Lovely. They're smart, but not smart enough if Marie was able to break in, get into their safe, steal whatever she wanted, and leave without being caught. We have her fingerprints, but that's only because we have them from the cottage. Otherwise, they'd be useless to the police."

"Yes."

I stare out the window, lost in thought. "What we need to figure out is how they got the crown and how she knew they had it. Was this a recent theft or something they did before?

And why now? The onesie and the blanket were mentioned in the news, so she must know the investigation was reopened."

He rubs his jaw. "She would have needed money after taking Desta, and keeping it would have been a liability. But these people are in their early thirties and were kids when Desta was taken. Truth be told, I don't think anyone would want to be in possession of Princess Desta's tiara, considering she was stolen."

"Yes, except it's priceless."

"It still shocks me that your mother handed it over to her without even seeing the princess."

I've thought of that too. She went alone to meet her. No security. No safety provisions. Things could have been done. Arrangements put in place to follow Marie after. None of it makes sense.

"Is there a way to trace these people's phones? Find out more about them?"

We come to a stoplight, and he rests his forearms on the wheel. "I looked into their phones. They're burners, so untraceable. The house is rented and not owned by them. They own a private software company that doesn't produce any software and has no clients. They're shadows."

"Can we put a team on them? Something inconspicuous, obviously."

"That's my plan, sir, but I'll be honest and say I'm not sure what information we'll get that they're not willing to let people know. That said, they obviously feel invincible since they're throwing another party tonight and the police didn't do anything with the house or even question them all that much."

I rub my stubbly jaw. "I suppose. Either they knew it was Desta's tiara or they were clueless. No way to know. That aspect aside, how did they get it, and how did Marie know they had it? The tenants said nothing had been taken but never opened the closet in that empty room when the police were with them.

They had no clue if it had been robbed until we discovered it and the police told them, but I'm sure they likely suspected or at least worried about it since nothing else was taken."

"They didn't want the police to know about the safe or what was in it," he agrees. "These people are running something illegal. I have to believe if you obtain something like a priceless tiara, you know what it is."

I nod. "I'd say so too. They held onto it and put it in a safe for a reason and didn't mention it to the police." The village sprawls around us as we enter, winding our way toward the hotel, but I'm too lost in my thoughts to see any of it. "They're too young to have had anything to do with Desta's disappearance. It was a big risk for Marie to go in and steal it back. Why would she do that?"

"Maybe she knew exactly who these people were."

My brows furrow at him. "Meaning?"

"Meaning they don't handle matters like this through the police. They handle them privately."

"If they know who stole it. The police aren't revealing Marie's name or that fingerprints were lifted. They could be clueless."

"If we're lucky, they are."

I sigh and sink down into the seat. "Imagine if she'd been caught. If the police had arrived faster. We could have her. Finally have answers. It was a dumb thing for her to do, but I'm so grateful she did."

"It was worth the risk for her, despite her carelessness. Maybe she needs the protection, and that's why she went for it?" he muses, and my head swivels over to him.

"Protection?"

His eyebrows lift. "Yes, sir. The Eye of Egypt is in it."

"What?"

"The Eye of Egypt. You've never heard of it?"

I shake my head, but his incredulous face isn't comforting.

"It's a famous stone that the ancient Romans took from there centuries ago. It was said to have powers of luck, protection, and prosperity, giving great fortune to anyone who possessed it. It was owned by Messalina herself and stayed in the country after her execution. It's a forty-carat flawless emerald. Your mother had it fashioned into Desta's tiara."

I stare at him. "She didn't mention it to us when she told us she gave the tiara to Marie. I didn't realize that was the primary stone in the picture. Sebastian's crown has a flawless diamond. Mine a ruby. I never thought about it."

He's quiet for a minute as we get closer to our hotel. "It's priceless, and yes, the diamonds and other stones are rare, but that emerald has as much power and lore to it as the curse itself. If you're at all superstitious in that way."

A shiver runs over me.

I didn't use to be. I never believed in any of it before. Nor did Sebastian. Not even after our father was murdered and Desta taken. We were young and believing in such a thing felt like believing in our own inevitable untimely demise.

Then Nora dropped out of the sky, and our worlds changed. Even more so when Samil attacked Bellamy and Sebastian. Since then, it's been one thing after another. A darkness we can't escape. And it feels like only the beginning.

Honestly, it feels like it's been coming for Bellamy.

AFTER DINNER, I call Sebastian, and the two of us talk for the better part of an hour. He vaguely remembers hearing about the emerald but didn't realize it was in Desta's tiara. It's creeping us both out, but one thing is for certain: Marie is still around, and she's not done.

It has me questioning who Marcella is even more.

I wasn't going to call her tonight.

I said a lot of things to her last night, and I'm already putting myself out there too much with her. I know she won't call me. I know she won't tell me her secrets, even if I suspect part of her wants to. Sebastian told me about the rug and how she fired three people today. I was shocked he did it that way, trusting her to that extent.

"What if she works for Marie?" I questioned him.

"It's a possibility, but why would Marie risk anything inside the palace? And why now? She doesn't know we know about her."

I step out onto my balcony and sit in the lounger. I pull out a cigar and light it, puffing black smoke into the sky. "I don't know. The questions are mounting one by one."

"One thing at a time. The cameras didn't get any visual on Marie, so we're forced to go by her old employee picture. With that, Javier is calling in favors and likely breaking laws I don't want to know about. He has a hundred kilometers periphery from the break-in home on any public cameras."

"Except the facial recognition is reading a face that's twenty years younger than it is now and taken from a picture that's twenty years old."

I take a smooth drag and blow out two smoke rings.

"It's a long shot. The truth is, we're going to have to get lucky like we did with the fingerprints. I'm not saying we give up this chase, but I don't want this to consume you more than it already is."

"I want that tiara back. I want that emerald."

"It's not going to break the curse."

I close my eyes and nod. I know that. But I still want it back.

"What do I do about Marcella?" I ask, changing the subject. "Should I confront her? Tell her that I know she's Ella, and see where the chips fall?"

"I don't know. At some point, if she won't talk or lead us to her true intention for being in the palace, we have to detain her.

I know you care about her, and I don't take that lightly, but I know you understand what I'm saying."

"I do." I take two more puffs and stub the burning end into the ashtray. The moon is high in the sky, the hour nearing midnight, and all I want right now is to see Marcella's pretty face. "Why couldn't I have fallen for a Bellamy? Someone sweet and easy—"

He chuckles. "There's nothing easy about Bellamy."

"There is, though. The only reason she was difficult was because you were a beast and worked so hard to resist her for as long as you did. Marcella warns me off at every turn, yet she talks to me, sleeps with me, teases me, and gets vulnerable with me. I see so much when I look at her. I don't want to stop. I don't want to go back to how my life was before."

"But her warnings have meaning behind them."

"Yes." I stare out at the small village sprawling around me, most of the lights in the buildings and homes out. It's quiet and dark and peaceful. "That's what I fear. Her warning is real. She told me the night at the wedding that she wasn't safe. So why can't I do the smart thing and let her go?"

"Because she's under your skin and you don't think she's dangerous. Maybe I'm daft, but I don't see it either. I didn't with Charlotte, though. Not until it was too late, so perhaps our instincts are off. I have an attendant on her, and her face is set up to trigger notifications in our system. She's in her room, and in the three days you've been gone, she hasn't gone anywhere she shouldn't or done anything she shouldn't."

"That's a relief."

"Call her and see what she's doing. You won't be able to sleep until you do."

He's right, and I disconnect the call. She may be under my skin, but this Marie thing has me spooked. The tiara has me spooked. And there's a woman who promises me she's dangerous.

I press her number and video call her.

This time, she doesn't make me call her three times. She picks up on the second ring, her sleepy face front and center on my phone.

"Couldn't stay away, could you?"

I chuckle, smiling like the fool she makes me. "Me? You're the one who picked up."

"Because I knew you'd keep calling until I didn't."

My finger runs over my screen. "Smart girl." Why do I feel better when I look at her? When I hear her voice? Why does my world fit and my insides click into place when that happens? She's going to ruin me for any future I might have otherwise had. It'll always be her. No matter what. Even if she betrays me, I'll still want her. How fucked up is that?

"I already used your vibrator tonight, so no show for you."

My lips twitch. "Believe it or not, I was calling to talk, not video fuck you. Did you think about me while you used it?"

"No," she answers quickly, and I frown before I can stop it.

She giggles. "So down bad, Your Highness."

She has no idea.

"You did, didn't you?"

She sighs, but she's smiling, her expression light and sweet. "I might have."

"Then I'm sorry I missed it." I walk back inside and over to my bed to sit on the edge, my elbow on my thigh, the phone in front of my face. "I'm coming home tomorrow."

She sucks in a breath. "Your Highness, we need to talk."

I nod. "We do."

"Then you know we have to stop this. I realize I've said that a hundred times, and each time I give in, but I...I can't do it anymore."

"Because you're starting to have feelings for me?" I don't know why I ask her. It won't help me. Or maybe it'll be everything I need to know.

"Because we both know this isn't going to end well. We have something. I won't deny that. But I have to start thinking about my future and what I have to do for that."

"You're telling me I don't enter into that equation."

She laughs. "You're the prince of Messalina, and I'm a palace servant. I think we both know what this is and what this isn't between us. There is no glass slipper. There is no happily ever after. It's not a fairy tale."

She's likely right, but that doesn't stop the way my stomach knots, and my chest feels like someone is poking it with a million needles. This isn't the kind of feeling that will dissipate with time or be eased with alcohol or placating words. This is heartbreak, and it sucks.

"You could choose me," I say, the words escaping, but I don't retract them either.

She releases a shaky breath and looks up at her ceiling, away from me. Her chin quivers. She feels this too.

She clears her throat and returns to the camera. "I can't. I don't want to."

"Yes, you do. You're a terrible liar."

"Please don't make this worse. Please let me say goodbye."

I don't want to. Goodbye is final. Forever.

"You're not going to tell me your secrets either then," I surmise.

"The world's not so black and white. My story isn't a good one. I'm not a good person for you, Your Highness. The best thing I can do for you is to let you go. The best thing you can do for yourself is to let me." She sniffs and wipes under her eyes and nose. My girl is crying. She's breaking before my eyes, but she's still telling me goodbye.

"Marcella, the glass slipper will fit. There is a chance."

She sobs and bites into her lip to stifle it as tears drip from her eyes. "Please, Rowan. Please. I don't want to hurt you. Not any of you. I don't care about you that way. Not at all. For me, it was sex. I'm sorry if I made you believe otherwise. We had some fun, and now that's over. Let me do the right thing for once."

I blink, my stupid eyes burning. She's lying, and I don't know why. It's insanely obvious. You don't cry if you don't care, and she always fights her tears. Always. But she's more than crying. She's distraught. It wasn't just some fun. It was a hell of a lot more than that.

I wanted to be her hero. The one who saves her from whatever it is that's haunting her and holding her captive. Maybe she's right, and I need to listen. But I already know that's impossible. She can say whatever she likes, but we both know the truth. And that's the one I'll stick to.

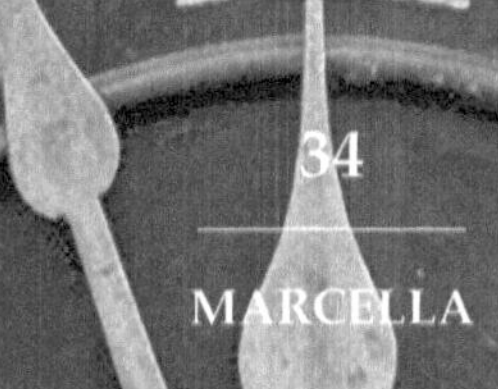

I slept like shit, tossing and turning, my heart heavy and my thoughts chaotic. I'd doze and dream about him. Dreams that would start wonderfully and turn ugly and dark. He's supposed to come home today, and my plan is to keep my distance. He said he'd let me.

That's how we got off the phone.

It's over now, and I have to accept it. Hell, I made it so.

At least the three stooges are gone, and I can work without having to worry about them. I text Jaqueline to tell her that I love her and that I'll be home soon. I don't dare text her more than that. Antonia monitors our phones.

I can't stomach food, but coffee is a must, and after I've downed my second cup, I head upstairs to start on the royal bedrooms. Except when I get to the king and queen's, I find Bellamy still in bed, which is rare.

"Oh, Your Majesty, I'm so sorry. I didn't mean to intrude."

"No, it's fine," she says. She's on her left side with a large body pillow tucked around her. "I have a bad headache and didn't feel like yoga this morning."

I enter the room and shut the door behind me to give her privacy. "Can I get you anything?"

"No, but thank you. This pregnancy is kicking my ass. Along with this headache. It feels like a migraine. I used to get them as a kid but haven't had one in years. I'm nauseous, have blurry vision, and the light hurts my eyes." She laughs lightly. "I'm a mess. My legs are swollen too. I'm a whale and can barely walk because of how swollen I am! Plus, one of the babies must have settled under my right rib because the pain there is wicked."

"Maybe we should ring your doctor."

"I'm seeing her tomorrow, and I was there two weeks ago. All she said was that my blood pressure was a little high and that we'd monitor it. I'm fine. It's just a rough da—"

Before she's able to finish her thought, her body jerks, and she lurches as if she's going to launch herself out of the bed before she starts violently vomiting.

I fly toward her, grab her hair, and hold her body up, which is no easy feat with her large belly. She cries out in pain as more vomit covers the bed and floor.

"Oh god," she wails between heaves.

I climb up onto my knees and hold her with one hand. With my other, I reach into my pocket and pull out my work phone. We have an emergency app, and I trigger the alarm.

"It's okay," I tell her. "I've got you. Help is on the way."

"No. It's just a migraine. It's not a big deal."

"We'll let your doctor decide that."

"No, no."

"Bellamy, stop arguing."

She sags and finally nods. "You're right. I'm being dumb."

Not even a minute later, the door bursts open, and two royal attendants are there with their freaking guns drawn.

"Whoa! Put those away! Her Majesty is very sick and needs to go to the hospital immediately. Please ring for an ambulance and get the king here."

Guns are holstered and they speak into their wrists.

Bellamy collapses, and I gently set her down away from the mess before I race into the bathroom for a washcloth. I run it under cold water and return, clean up her face, and press it to her forehead. She's not speaking, her eyes are closed, and her face is tense.

Panic consumes me, and I press two fingers to her wrist. Her pulse is racing.

I keep the washcloth on her forehead, whispering soothing words.

"I'm not dressed," she mumbles. "I need to get dressed."

"You're wearing a shirt. What if I find you some sweatpants?"

She gives me a weak nod, and I go to her dresser, locate a pair of soft leggings, and return.

"Turn around," I tell the guards. They obey, and I slowly help Bellamy to sit up. She sways in my arms, and I steady her, watching her face, which is paler than a sheet as I carefully slide her away from the vomit.

"I'm so sorry," she says.

"No apologies, Madam."

I help slide the pants onto her, noting just how swollen her ankles and calves are.

"I feel awful. My head is pounding, and my right side really hurts." She emits a sob, trembling. "The twins. Oh god. They have to be all right. Sebastian is going to lose his mind with this."

We finish getting her pants on, and her face falls into my chest as she openly weeps.

"Ambulance is fifteen minutes out," one of the attendants tells me.

"His Majesty is—"

"Here. I'm here." A frazzled king thrusts his way into the room, his eyes manic as he searches and finds me holding

Bellamy. "What happened? You were sleeping when I left you this morning." He climbs on the bed behind her and runs his hand over her face and hair before he kisses her forehead. "My love, what's wrong?"

His eyes seek mine, demanding answers.

I go into a quick account of how I found her, what she told me about how she was feeling, followed by the vomiting. He curses in Latin and picks her up, holding her in his arms. She melts into him, clinging tightly as she cries. He looks so helpless, and she looks afraid. It breaks me.

"What can I do?"

The king looks at me. "The cloth in your hand. Hand it to me."

"Of course!" I can't believe I didn't. "I'm so sorry!" I hand him the wet cloth, which he puts on her forehead. "I'll go grab a wheelchair."

"No. I'll carry her. It'll take too long for you to do that with the current elevator system. Which is likely why you suggested we upgrade it." He kisses her forehead. "My sweetness, I'm going to take you down to the ambulance. Javier will follow."

"The children—"

"I can help with them," I offer. "I'll clean everything up in here, and between myself and Lady Althea, we'll make sure the children are occupied all day." I meet the king's eyes. "I swear, I'll take care of them. I swear."

"Don't tell them anything is wrong," Bellamy pleads.

"I won't," I promise her. "I've got them, Your Majesties. Take care of yourself and your twins."

"Thank you, Marcella," Bellamy sobs as Sebastian lifts her off the bed, tucking her gently against his chest. "Thank you so much."

The king throws me a grateful look. One I don't expect. "Yes, thank you. Please let Althea know the plan."

I nod.

"Marcella, I'm trusting you with this."

"I understand, sir. I won't let you down. I swear it."

He nods. "Would you do me a favor and let Rowan know as well?"

I blanche. He knows about Rowan and me. It's obvious he does. It shouldn't shock me. They're very close. But I had hoped our secret hadn't gotten to the king or queen.

"Of course, Your Majesty."

Without another word, he leaves the bedroom with Bellamy in his arms, the attendants following him. I ring Lady Althea, who tells me she has the children and will take them to the big playroom after breakfast. I promise to join them shortly. I send a large group message with a change of schedule for today without stating why, then with a pit clogging my throat, call Rowan.

It rings and rings, but he doesn't pick up. I leave him a message asking him to call me immediately and get to work on cleaning up the vomit that's little more than bile. I'm going against everything Signoria and Antonia want. It feels good. I helped the queen when they would have wanted me to brush off her symptoms and keep her here, potentially putting her life or the life of her unborn children at risk.

It was instinct that had me helping her.

But I'm not the monster they tried to make me. I won't ever be her again.

A sense of pride rolls through me. Where there is kindness, there is goodness. I have to believe that.

Once that's finished, I head toward the playroom when my phone rings.

"What's wrong?" he asks the moment I answer.

"Your Highness, the queen was very ill this morning and is currently on her way to the hospital with His Majesty. He requested that I call you to inform you of the situation."

"Fuck," he swears. "Is she okay?"

"I don't know any of the details, sir—"

"For fuck's sake, Marcella, don't speak to me like that and tell me what the fuck is going on!"

"One moment, sir."

I open a random door, which turns out to be a small parlor, and shut it behind me.

"I don't know if she's okay," I tell him honestly. "She had a horrible headache and was still in bed when I came in to clean the room. She complained of abdominal pain and generally not feeling well. Then she started vomiting, and I hit the emergency alert on my phone. I don't think she wanted me to, but I had to. She was so sick and didn't seem right. By this point, she's likely in the ambulance. Lady Althea and I are going to watch the children and keep them occupied until we get further word."

"Jesus. I can't..." A loud breath echoes through the phone. "I'll leave for the hospital now. You might have saved her, you know."

"I hope there's no saving required. I hope it wasn't anything more than a migraine."

He's moving around, things banging, zippers zipping. "Not quite the evil woman you want me to think you are."

"Rowan, don't."

"I'm not doing anything other than stating a fact." A pause, but I hear him moving, likely leaving the hotel. "Hold on. Don't hang up," he says to me before speaking to someone in French about how they have to leave immediately. "Okay, I'm back. Are we still broken up?"

"What?" chokes past my lips.

"You broke up with me last night. I was checking if you'd come to your senses while you were tossing and turning all night."

I close my eyes and lean heavily against the door. "What makes you think I was tossing and turning?"

"A hunch. I was, too, in case you were wondering."

"I wasn't."

"You're smiling."

Damn him.

"I am not."

My smile grows.

"You are. I can hear it in your voice. I make you smile. I bet I even make you happy."

"Don't push your luck."

"It's all I've got with you. So...our breakup?"

I huff, tucking down the butterflies the man never fails to give me, along with my inane smile. "I didn't break up with you because we were never together."

"Oh, mia stella, we were definitely together. You're my first girlfriend."

I snort. "That's present tense when you just told me I broke up with you. And at thirty-three, that's sad. Especially since I wasn't your girlfriend. Your delusions aren't doing you any favors."

"Either you broke up with me or you weren't my girlfriend. Which is it because you just contradicted yourself."

Crap! I totally did. Ugh. "The latter. I was never your girlfriend."

"It was a trick question. You were my girlfriend, but I've decided that I don't accept you breaking up with me."

"Pardon?"

"I don't accept."

I shift my stance and lean all my weight against the door. "It's not up for negotiation."

"Ah, so you admit we were together."

I bump the back of my head against the wood. "No. That's not what I meant—"

"All the same, I thought about it, and I'm not allowing you to let the best thing to ever happen to you go. You said last night that you were doing it for me, but I'm doing this for you. You're welcome."

An incredulous laugh bursts from my chest. "Oh my god! You are so conceited!"

"Am I not the best thing to ever happen to you?"

He is and then some, but I'd rather die than tell him that.

"No. Your vibrator is."

He laughs, and yep, my smile is back in full force along with those stupid butterflies.

"But you thought of me while you were using it," he protests. "You told me that last night before you tried to break up with me. And because I'm such a great guy—a total catch, I mean, I am a prince—and you're so crazy about me, I'm informing you that I don't accept your breakup and we're still together."

I sigh. "I'm hanging up on you now, Rowan."

"Sounds good, baby. I have to get to the hospital, and our GPS says we're three hours away, which means it's time for me to talk shop with my trusty driver. I'll see you soon, though."

Before I can argue further, he disconnects the call. I need to get to the playroom and help with the children. I need to come up with a solid plan that keeps everyone safe.

Except part of my tossing and turning last night, as he said I did, had me come to one brutal realization.

The only way to keep everyone safe is to eliminate the threat.

I wonder how fast the prince would change his mind if he knew the woman he's calling his girlfriend is a lying murderer sent here to destroy his family.

ROWAN

The moment I hung up the phone with Marcella, I called Sebastian. He was a mess. They were working Bellamy up, trying to figure out what was going on with her and the twins. I didn't keep him on the phone long. I simply told him I was on my way.

But I could hear it in his voice.

He was thinking one word over and over: curse.

How much is Bellamy going to have to go through? What happens if she dies or the twins are lost? Sebastian won't come back from that. The children won't either. I'm not sure I will. It'll be the final straw in our family's story. The nail in our coffin.

Dread tears through me with the speed and precision of a bullet. This car ride feels never-ending as the minutes tick by with impossible slowness.

Gabe is quiet. He didn't ask me anything about Marcella, and I didn't offer, but he heard the end of my conversation with her. He worked late into the evening, searching for anything that could relate to Marie and the tiara.

But like a ghost, Marie materialized and was gone without a

trace. No more fingerprints. The camera images we have of her aren't much to go by. She was wearing all black, had her hair off her face, and had a hood over her head. She kept her head down as if she were aware of where the cameras were.

All we have is her old employee photograph, but that's more than twenty years old. She's aged. She could have had plastic surgery to alter her appearance. We don't know what type of car she was driving or what alias she goes by now. All we know is that she's alive, knows how to stay under the radar, and stole back Desta's tiara.

It's maddening.

Yet I can't stop. I have to keep searching for her.

It felt less tangible before.

The onesie, the tiara, the blanket, even the newspaper clipping were old. They were discovered recently, yes, but they were from the time right after Desta was taken. After that, I was following small leads. Tiny events that made me think I was onto tracking Marie, which I likely wasn't.

But this is real. It's renewed hope.

This is her right on the edge of my fingertips but just out of reach.

Gabe enters the hospital ahead of me, and I keep my head tucked down. Sebastian told me they have Bellamy on the labor and delivery unit in a special room, and when we arrive on the floor, it's easy to see that the word is out that the queen is here. Two attendants are stationed down the hall, but the whispers aren't quiet. Neither are the looks we get as we walk down the hall.

I give a nod to the nurses, noting a few blushes and flirty waves.

The old me would have loved that. I might have even taken a few of them up on that to cut the edge off all this shit inside me that I can't control or stop. But now the thought of sex with anyone other than Marcella feels empty. Flat. Wholly unappealing.

Sebastian is out in the hall on the phone when I approach, but the moment he spots me, everything I heard in his voice on the phone is right there in his features.

"Thank you, Aunt. I'll keep you updated." He ends the calls and puts his phone back in his pocket. "The children are happy," he says instead of a greeting. "Althea just informed me that she and your Marcella are taking them swimming and after that, they're going to bake something with extra chocolate. I didn't ask what, nor do I care."

I grasp his shoulder. "Tell me what's happening with your Bellamy."

He cracks. Right here before my eyes, my older brother, the king of my country, my eternal rock, cracks. It breaks me apart. My stomach twists painfully, and my breath is robbed from my lungs. I heave out breath after breath, and fuck, I'm legit about to cry.

"They think she has something called HELLP syndrome. It's rare, but it can happen with twins. It affects her blood and liver. They were surprised it came on so fast for her."

I curse under my breath in Russian. "But she's here. They caught it."

"She complained of a headache last night and went to bed early. But she's had a lot of headaches, so I didn't think anything about it. This morning when I got up to work out, she was still asleep, and I didn't wake her, figuring she needed the extra rest. She's been swollen and having some rib pain. Bellamy told me it was likely typical end-of-pregnancy stuff. Especially with twins. I didn't question it. I have no clue what Nora went through when she was pregnant. We didn't...I mean, I was there during the pregnancies and part of them, but she and I..." He ends it there. "I'm not sure what would have happened if Marcella hadn't been there and triggered the alarm."

I shake my head. I can't think about that.

"They have her on some medication that's making her miserable," he continues. "She says she's hot, but also it's making her sleepy and a bit lethargic. And they...they gave steroids to help the babies' lungs mature because the likelihood that they'll have to deliver the twins in the next day or two is very high. They said they can treat the syndrome, but they can't reverse it. The longer this goes on, the greater the danger for all of them. The only way to fix this is for Bellamy to deliver."

I gulp. "This early?" She's barely thirty-one weeks.

"They're trying to hold off, but yes, this early."

"Fuck" slips out before I can stop it.

"Yes. Fuck is right." His hands go to the top of his head. "Rowan—"

"Don't. Don't say it and don't think it. It won't help anything."

He swallows thickly and nods. "I love her more than my life. I can't lose her. I can't lose them."

"You won't."

"My children can't lose another mother."

"They won't."

"If it's not real, why is it one thing after the other? Why are they all happening to her?"

"I don't have an answer for you, but there is no satisfactory reply. What if I said, yes, it's real? What will that change? You said you weren't going to let it control you again, and now you have to prove that to Bellamy and to your children."

"I brought her into my life. I did this to her."

"Sebastian, what is that going to change or fix? You just said you love her more than your life, and she's the mother of your children. She's part of this now. No changing that. But she's so strong. A fucking fighter like no other."

He nods slowly, pacing in a small circle. "You know, there might not be a way to break this thing. If that's so, then my children will be subject to this."

"Sebastian…" I trail off. He's scared. I know that. I can't imagine his riotous or violent emotions right now. I'm positive that if I were him, if I were the king and my wife and children were at risk, I'd be much worse off than he is. I'd be losing my mind to the tenth degree. "What can I do? Name it. I'll do anything."

He stops, and his eyes meet mine, resolute and intense. "I want Marie found. I want the tiara returned. I want to know what happened to our sister. If we can do all of that, perhaps we have a shot at ending this. But with so much unresolved, maybe my loving Bellamy wasn't enough. Maybe we have to close the loopholes and put that chapter to rest."

"I've thought the same thing," I admit.

He scrubs his hands up his face, releases a strained breath, and heads for Bellamy's room. "I won't be home tonight."

"I know. I intend to spoil your children."

He twists back to me. "Thank you. I don't know where I'd be without you."

"Can I see her?"

"Yes, but she's in a gown and very out of it with the medication they're giving her."

"I won't stay long. I just want to give her a kiss on the forehead. Then I'll go."

"Rowan." He stops, his hand on the lever of the door. "We need to find out who Marcella is. I feel you're right about her, but I also believe those who sent her won't stay hidden for long, and we need to be a step ahead of them."

"I'm on it," I promise, feeling a pang of guilt. I don't want to let her go. I want to hold on with both hands. But this is about a hell of a lot more than just me. It always was. It's easy to forget that when I'm with her or hear her voice. But the time for playing around is over.

BELLAMY WAS PRETTY OUT of it, as Sebastian said, flushed and complaining of being hot. The nurse who was in there said the medicine prevents seizures, which is terrifying to even think of. They're also debating if they're going to give her a transfusion. Sebastian climbed into bed beside Bellamy and held her, which was a relief. I know his instinct is to pull away to protect her, but he's not, and I give him credit for that.

If what happened with Charlotte taught him anything, it's that they are in this together and he won't be parted from her again.

The moment I get home, I change into swim trunks and go out to the pool. The kids are running around, having a contest to see who can make the biggest splash. Althea is sitting in the shade, and I head toward her even as my focus is glued to the woman wearing the most basic and boring bathing suit on the planet and yet somehow managing to make it look sexy with the hint of her breasts trapped beneath the fabric and her blonde hair twisted on top of her head in a messy bun.

She glances up when the kids call out to me. I throw kisses and waves at my nieces and nephew and a smile at the pretty blonde who is trying to show just how unaffected she is by my shirtlessness. Newsflash: She's failing. I wink at her, and she rolls her eyes and returns to the children.

"You're drooling, Rowan."

I chuckle under my breath. "I see there are no secrets in this palace."

"Sebastian told me about her, so I would keep extra close watch."

I take the chaise beside her and toss an arm behind my

head. I can't blame him for telling Althea. In fact, I could use her wisdom.

"What do I do?"

"I'll admit, I haven't spent a lot of time with her," she says, keeping her voice low so it doesn't carry. "I looked into her family. Or at least the family she claims to have come from."

"And?"

"And her documents are pristine, Rowan. They passed our every inspection."

"Meaning they're expensive to obtain."

"If they're not legitimate? Extremely expensive. They're legal documents as far as I can tell. Government-issued. The family are farmers with a small bed-and-breakfast that hasn't been particularly lucrative. That was part of her story for coming to the palace to work. She claimed she had to send money back home to help her family."

"But?" I press when she doesn't immediately follow that up.

"But no money has left her account. None. I questioned the bank manager this morning. She hasn't moved a cent in the nearly five months she's been here. She hasn't spent anything either. On her days off, she stays in the palace or on the palace grounds. She hasn't gone to see any of her supposed family. She's isolated here. Friendly but not friends with other staff. She does her job well, is polite and professional, which is why Emily gave her the role. But there are large gaps, Rowan, and that concerns me. We don't know her real name. Her fingerprints and facial scan were clean because it's as if she has no history, or any history she does have was wiped by very talented people."

All of that is a kick in the teeth and makes me angry that I didn't do my due diligence with her. I was blinded, and hearing this makes me feel stupid and weak.

"I should ask her. I've avoided it because I was afraid we'd never get answers, and she wouldn't lead us to the people behind this. Or at least that's the story I fed myself. But if you're telling me in five months of being here we have nothing to go on, then maybe it's time I press her."

"Sunday is her day off, and right now we have enough going on with Bellamy and the twins. Let's see what happens over the next few days. If she stays here as she's done, you'll confront her. If she leaves, we'll have her followed. Something is going on with her. I believe that much is clear. Whether she's hiding out or here at someone else's hand isn't, but I'm inclined to believe the latter given what we know."

I nod in agreement because that's exactly how it seems. "I don't think she wants to do ill by us." I don't. Maybe that's more of my stupidity with her, but it doesn't fit the woman I'm looking at, who is playing games with the children and Arthur.

"Maybe yes, maybe no. People can hide almost anything with the right motivation."

I sigh. "The next few days will tell a lot, and I'll watch her until then."

"I had no doubts that you would. Just be careful. The heart is quick to turn our heads so our eyes don't see what's actually in front of us. Don't let her blind you."

She's in her room. She spent all day taking care of the children without a break, then retired to her room. Sebastian texted to inform me that they're likely delivering the twins tomorrow evening. He's a mess. We're all a mess. The twins will be very premature and will have to stay in the NICU for a while after they're born.

I don't know what to say to the children. We had them very busy today, so they didn't ask a lot of questions other than at dinner and bedtime. I'm going to have to tell them some version of the truth tomorrow.

Fear grips me by the throat. Once again everything is spiraling toward a dangerous and deadly path, and I have no control over how to stop its trajectory.

I just want to see Marcella. Talk to her. I could hand her the diamond earring and ask a simple *what the fuck is going on*. But we'll see what happens on Sunday. It's only a few more days to wait.

I pull up my text stream, hardly fighting it.

> Me: I want to see you.

Marcella: No.

Me: Why not?

Marcella: I broke up with you, remember?

The first real smile I've had in days hits my lips.

Me: And I told you I didn't accept that. I want to see you.

Marcella: It's not a good idea.

Me: Tell me why not. The truth.

Marcella: I'm not right for you. We're not right for each other.

I sigh. She's right. But I don't care. I wish I did, but I don't.

Me: One last night. Give me one last night. Please come to my room.

Come on, Marcella. Give me something. Something you haven't yet. I've chased and pushed and forced my way in, and all this time you've given me these tiny pieces I didn't have to steal from you. Show me there is a piece of you that cares.

She doesn't reply, and I chuck my phone in frustration. It bounces off the floor, and I wince. Shit. I need my phone in case Sebastian rings.

I pick it up, toss it on my nightstand, then go get myself ready for bed. She's not responding because she's not coming. She's told me no and to fuck off countless times, and I haven't listened.

I climb into bed, the blankets around my waist, my hands behind my head as I stare up at the ceiling. The alarm on my phone pings, and I bolt upright and grab it. She left her room.

Her face is triggering the cameras. My breaths quicken, and my heart picks up a few extra beats.

She's coming here. She's coming to my room.

Elation sparks through me like an unruly child I can't contain. I get out of bed and go to my door, waiting, watching her on the cameras as one flickers after the other, all cataloging her face and tripping the sensor. Uncertainty is all over her. Her inner conflict is clear as day. Yet she's coming, only to stop outside my room.

She doesn't knock, and I don't open the door. I wait her out. I let her decide.

Finally, the tiniest tap stirs me away from watching her on my phone to my door.

I open it, and there she is. What's happening behind those pretty eyes, I can't tell. She's bottling herself up, but she's here, and I don't care about the rest. This woman puts the air in my lungs and fire in my veins.

I don't say anything. I don't hesitate either. My hand cups the back of her neck, and I haul her into my room. The door gets kicked shut, and my lips are on hers. She whimpers as I kiss her with an intensity I've never experienced before. It's that electric moment right before the storm hits.

With my hands on her ass, I pick her up and force her legs around my waist, grinding my cock against her. Her hands find my hair, and she arches her body up so she can angle her head down and kiss me deeper. This is what I needed. This connection. This moment to tell me I'm not fucking crazy. There is more here.

I'm in love with her. It hits me like a wave. The kind that tickles your feet and splashes up your body, shocking you with the cold but making you laugh a little with giddy excitement because you knew it was coming. I'm so in love with her, I don't know what to do with myself. There's no answer. I see my brother with sweet Bellamy, but that's not us. Marcella's not sweet. She may even have an evil streak I can't begin to fathom.

Catching her bottom lip between my teeth, I suck it in my mouth, exhaling hard as I go crazy, kissing her like this truly is the last time. I trail kisses everywhere, from her cheek to her ear to her neck to her jaw, getting lost in her scent and warmth.

She tastes so fucking right.

"Such a good girl for me," I whisper, flicking her tongue with mine. "Say it. Tell me you're my good girl."

She moans, sending all the remaining blood to my cock. "I'm your good girl. But only for tonight."

I smile. My feisty girl always has to drop the caveat. Fine. "Then I don't have a moment to waste."

Diving down, I drag my teeth along her jaw to her tits heaving out of the top of her tank top. I bite the plump tissue. She's so fucking soft. So absolutely perfect. I've never felt lust like this with anyone, and I'm on fire with it. Totally gone. Lost in her mouth and skin and scent and body.

I never want to let her go.

Nothing—fucking nothing—has ever been better.

I rip the top of her tank top down to expose her tits to me.

"Jesus," I gasp when she grinds her pussy in only her little sleep shorts against me. My heart pounds like a fucking drum, and I cup her breast, squeezing until she moans for me again. "You're going to be screaming my name in your sleep for the rest of your life. You'll wake up hot and flushed and soaking fucking wet. I will haunt your dreams. You may think you can be rid of me after tonight, but this is endless."

We're connected. She moves, I feel it.

"Christ, Rowan." Her hands grow possessive, one sliding under my shirt to run her palm up my abs, her other gripping the back of my hair, holding me tight to her. I shiver against her touch. She'll haunt me too.

She flattens her back against the door and rips my shirt

over my head. I do the same with her tank top and press our naked chests together.

Hell yes.

She wiggles out of my arms, and I set her down to tug down her shorts. She's wearing the panties I bought her. Pink fucking lace that feels like a sweet little contradiction to the black cat wearing them. Goddamn, she has a beautiful body.

I slide my hand down over her ass and squeeze as I bring her back into me. Her soft tits press against my chest, and my mouth reclaims hers. I rub the center of her thong up into her pussy, and she moans, rocking into my hand. It's exactly what I was hoping she'd do. She's not holding back tonight. She's giving herself to me.

Her cunt is warm and wet, and when her panties are exactly as I want them, drenched in her, I rip them straight off.

She gasps. "What the hell?"

"I'm keeping these. I'll end up wearing out the smell in no time with how many times I'll jerk off to them."

"Jesus, you're dirty."

"Like you."

I spin her around and press her into the door, licking along her scars, feeling their texture. As always, she shudders and shakes, but she's beautiful, and these scars are a part of her. If she'd let me, they'd only be her past. I reach her ass and yank it back, biting and nibbling and squeezing. My hand slides between her cheeks, and I ring her wet opening before I slide my finger back to her asshole.

She squirms, and I give her ass a hard smack. "Mine. You're here, and this is mine tonight. All of it. Whatever I want, however I want it, it's mine. If you run, I'll chase you and take it anyway. You know I will."

She trembles, so fucking wet it's practically spilling out of her.

I split her cheeks and ring her virgin asshole, sliding a

different finger into her pussy. "Oh god," she groans. "Fuck, Rowan."

"So fucking hot. So fucking tight."

I lick her ass, swirling around the muscles and shoving my tongue in, getting her nice and wet there. She rocks into my finger, whimpering and rolling her hips, frustrated that I'm only giving her one finger and nothing on her clit.

I pull back and spin her around, pushing the finger that played with her ass back in it as I kiss her bare pussy. My cock twitches painfully, and I look up. With my eyes on hers, I tongue her clit. My finger pushes deeper into her ass, pumping in and out, and I cover her with my mouth. I suck on her clit and drag my tongue up her dripping cunt.

Pushing up her thighs, I put both on my shoulders, forcing her to grab onto the door handle and lean hard into the wood for support. I bury my face deeper, shoving my tongue into her as my finger goes in knuckle deep.

"Please," she begs, her body shaking and her breath shallow.

Just as she reaches her orgasm, I pull back and blow cool air on her pulsing clit. She whimpers and writhes, jutting her hips as if she's seeking my mouth.

"Shh," I admonish. "Only good girls get to come."

"Oh god. Fuck you!" She smacks the top of my head, grips my hair, and tries to push my face back into her.

I chuckle, nibbling on her pussy lips and blowing more cool air on her overheated flesh. Even my finger in her ass is still, and it's driving her crazy. Like what she's doing to me.

I hold her hips firmly with my other hand, then slowly play with her clit again, kissing it gently, licking it lightly.

"Fuck," she hisses. "Rowan, I can't take it."

"You can take it. You will take it."

"You're punishing me."

I glance up, glaring at her. "Damn fucking right I'm punishing you, Ella."

She stills, her eyes going wide and her lips parting. She pulls her legs from my shoulders, plants her feet back on the ground, and my finger slips out of her ass.

She trembles and covers her tits with her arms as if that'll help anything. "You knew?"

"Of course I fucking knew." And I can't hide it anymore. I can't keep playing cat and mouse or whatever fucked-up, twisted version of it this is. I can't keep pretending or lying. I have to push her because if I don't, if I don't test her and see if she'll meet me on the other side, she'll never be mine.

Her bottom lip quivers, and her eyes glass over. "How long?"

"I suspected almost immediately, but then I found the earring."

"The night you were in my room. You've known all this time?"

"I've known all this time." I grab her hips and bury my face back in her pussy.

"Rowan, no." She tries to push my head away as the first of her tears hits her cheek and rolls down her face to her chin before it plummets and lands on my cheek. I swipe it with my finger and tuck it in my mouth, tasting her salt and agony.

"Shut up, Marcella," I growl. "Don't tell me no. Is that even your real name?"

"Yes," she cries. "Please. Oh god. You have to stop."

A laugh rips from my lungs, and I pick her up so she's in my arms. I hold her tight as she fights me until we land on the bed, and I pin her arms down at her sides. "You said I get tonight with you."

"That was before." She shakes her head, her hair flying everywhere. "We can't. Not like this."

"Then tell me how. Tell me who you are."

A sob rattles her, and her eyes pinch tight. "I can't."

I start to lose it. I drop to my elbow and cup her face, holding it until she looks at me. "You can, baby. I told you this once, and I meant it. I'm the safest person in the room. I'm safe for you."

"I'm not safe for you."

My anger fuses anew. "Tell me why. Tell me!" I demand when she mashes her lips together. I'm losing it, and I can't stop myself. I can't hold back. "I fucking love you. Don't shake your head at me. I do. You know I do."

She sobs, and I push into her, rocking my hips slowly so she feels me. Feels what I'm telling her.

"I've been watching you and waiting for you." *Thrust.* "I know next to nothing about you, and yet I feel like I already know everything." *Thrust.* "I see you." *Thrust.* "I love you." *Thrust.* "How could you think I wouldn't know it was you?" *Thrust.* "That I wouldn't remember you?" *Thrust.* "I searched for you for months." *Thrust.* "Dreamed about you every night." *Thrust.* "But you were here all that time." *Thrust.* "What are you after?"

Her eyes are closed, and tears leak from them, but she's rocking into me as I thrust my hips, sliding my cock inside her tight little pussy. Her tits bounce back and forth as I increase my pace, slamming in and out of her, burying my cock to the hilt every time. Punishing her for shutting me out.

My forehead meets hers, and I bite her lip. Hard. I make her bleed, and I lick that too. Rough and gentle. "What are you so afraid of? Do you not know I'm the fucking prince? I can help you."

She shakes her head. "You can't, Rowan. Please."

"Tell me you don't love me."

She whimpers, and my walls start closing in.

"Tell me. Please fucking tell me." I hate the desperation in my voice, but that's how I am with her. Desperate. Unhinged.

Cageless. "Tell me you don't, and I'll stop. I'll climb off you, and that will be that."

Except she doesn't say anything.

Her tongue flicks my lips, and I growl, pummeling into her, slicing her body in fucking half with how hard I'm fucking her. Her pussy clenches around my cock, squeezing it like a fist, but still her lips stay sealed. Even her moans are silenced, and it's driving me crazy.

"You can trust me," I whisper against her lips between bites and licks and kisses. "I'm safe. I'll never hurt you. Choose me, and I'll always take care of you. Trust me," I pant in time with my breaths. "Choose me. Trust me." Despite everything, pleasure skitters across my skin, my balls draw up, and my abs tighten.

But I can't come in her. Not this time.

She's not mine. She'll never be mine.

And I shouldn't want her to be.

It shreds me apart, and I slam into her and push a finger between us to rub her clit. She's going to come, even if I have to force her orgasm from her.

"Ah!" she cries out, and there it is. She comes so fucking hard. Her neck arches, going taut, and her face is flushed and pinched up in painful ecstasy. She's so beautiful, and devastation twists in my gut. I watch her the entire time, rubbing and fucking her through it, savoring and mourning the feel of her around me one last time. The moment she's done, I pull out and come across her stomach and tits, bellowing out a thunderous roar.

I fall to the bed beside her, my hands on my face, my breathing ragged.

I hear her get up, feeling the dip and rise of the bed, but I don't move. To my surprise, she goes into the bathroom, and the door shuts. A moment later, the toilet flushes and the tap turns on. The door opens, and I still haven't moved, the air too still, the room too cold. I'm naked and exposed and endlessly fucking vulnerable, but I don't move.

She brushes past the bed, and slowly I sit up, forcing myself to see her. To watch as she gets dressed, her tears all dried up now. She meets my eyes once she has her clothes back on and walks over to me. Her lips press gently to mine, then she's gone. I keep myself rooted in place as she walks out the door and shuts it behind her. This time, I don't chase. I let her go. Steeling myself to do whatever I have to do going forward.

Even if it means I have to take her down.

I don't bother getting back into bed. Instead, I break all the rules, get in a car by myself, and drive to Tourin to the hospital. I park in the garage like a normal human and make my way up and through the hospital. They try to stop me at the entrance of the labor and delivery ward, but I simply lift my head and let the nurse see my face, and that's all it takes.

But the pitying twist of her mouth she tries to hide tells me just how rough I look.

I walk down the hall, keeping my head low and my arms heavy. It's quiet and dark on this end, and I don't want to go into Bellamy's room. That feels like an invasion. I don't know why I'm here other than I had to leave the palace and have nowhere else to go.

I lean against the wall and sag to the floor, drawing my knees up. My forearms fall across them, and I bury my face. I can still smell her everywhere on me. Can still taste her. I thought there was good in her. I thought whatever she was there to do, she was losing faith in it. I was wrong.

I have two guards on her room, and the tracking on her phone is turned on.

Sunday is her day off, but if she's not gone by the end of it, I'll have her fired and thrown out. Or thrown in jail. I can't be stupid anymore. I have to protect my family. No more fighting her and the curse together. Or maybe she's its weapon. Maybe that's how the curse sinks its talons into me. Through her.

I must doze off because the next thing I know, there's a scream and a flurry of footsteps and shouts. I jolt awake, my head slamming back against the wall. Dazed, I shoot up to my feet, nearly toppling over as nurses and doctors rush past me into Bellamy's room.

Sebastian is shouting, Bellamy is screaming, and my heart takes flight.

"What's happening?" I ask, but no one spares me a glance. There's a team of doctors and nurses in her room. Words like *placental abruption* and *fetal distress* fly around. Things like *crash C-section* and *propofol*.

A half-second later, Bellamy is wheeled out of her room, an oxygen mask on her face, and tears all over her. Sebastian is right beside her, his expression harried. Our eyes briefly meet, but he doesn't stop. He stays with the gurney, holding Bellamy's hand as they run her down the hall.

I follow after them, unsure what to do, my legs shaky, barely able to keep me upright.

Fuck you! You don't get to take them. Not any of them. They're not yours to claim.

I pick up my pace to a run, chasing after the gurney, but I'm stopped by a hand in my face as I approach the OR.

"I'm sorry, Your Highness, you can't go in there."

The nurse goes to the OR, and that's when I see Sebastian standing by the door, trying to peer in. Silently, I walk over and stand beside him, my hand on his shoulder, and my heart in my throat.

"Your Majesty, you shouldn't be—"

"I'm not going anywhere," he clips, and the nurse nods. He's the king and Bellamy's husband, and good luck trying to fight him.

She enters the OR, leaving us here alone in the hall.

"It came out of nowhere," he mumbles. "She was asleep. The babies' heartbeats were fine. Then her back arched and she tensed, and a second later, she screamed. It was like something went into her body and ripped her apart, and now she's in there, and I can't be with her. I can't be with them."

I hiccup a silent sob, tears tracking down my cheeks.

"They're putting her under, and she won't get to see them. What if she never wakes up? What if she dies on that table and she never gets to meet them?"

"She won't," I tell him emphatically. "That's Bellamy on that table."

He doesn't reply, and I don't blame him.

"How..." I gulp. "How far along are the twins again?"

"Thirty-one weeks. They'll be small. One baby would be small at that age. Twins will be even smaller."

"But they gave them steroids," I persist, though I don't know why. There is no comfort right now.

"They told us yesterday that they wanted at least twenty-four hours for their lungs to mature. It hasn't been that."

I swallow and hold still as they cut into Bellamy's stomach. She's unconscious on the table, a mask still on her face to help her breathing. Sebastian is shaking and turns around, putting his back to the door.

"I can't watch them cut her. Can you...can you?"

"I'm here."

"What are you doing here, Rowan?"

I would laugh at that question if I had an ounce of humor in me. "That's a discussion for later."

"Tell me now. Distract me."

"I told Marcella I knew who she was. I told her I love her and that I was safe. I asked her to choose me because I'm a fool.

She didn't. I was inside of her and begging her, and then she left."

"Rowan—"

"I have two armed attendants on her room, and tracking on her phone is turned on. I don't care if it's a violation of her employee rights or whatever. She can sue me over it."

"Anything else?"

"Sunday is her day off. If she's still in the palace by nightfall, I'll have her detained."

"If she's not?"

"The guards will follow her from a distance, and I'll track her like a bloodhound until I learn each of her secrets. No one will hurt us, Sebastian. Not ever again. Not even now." I suck in a rush of air and blink twice. "Jesus, the first twin."

He spins around and races over, his hands planted on the door.

"Coming through." We jump out of the way as a team of doctors and nurses with two incubators come bustling in. The moment the doors swing shut again, we're back at the glass.

"There's the second one. Aleah."

"What?"

He smiles, his eyes sparkling with tears. "Aleah. Our little girl. I can't see Joseph."

"You never told me that's what you were going to name her, only him."

"Joseph is for her father. Aleah is after Althea."

A smile lights up my face. "Does she know?"

He shakes his head. "Not yet. It was going to be a surprise."

"She'll love that."

"They're working on them. They're helping them breathe." His breath hitches high in his throat. "My god, they're not breathing on their own."

The doctors are putting tubes down the twins' throats and

pumping air into their lungs while they hook them up to tubes and wires, and what the fuck?

"Rowan..."

"I know. I'm here. They're alive, Sebastian. Look at them. Your son and daughter were just born."

He breaks down, grabbing for me and hugging me against him. I hug him back, both of us weeping and not giving a fuck about it. It's just us out here, somewhere in the darkest depths of the wee hours of the night.

A few minutes later, just as we're getting our shit back together and wiping our faces, the doors open and there are the twins, tiny little things in incubators. Sebastian sucks in a rush of air.

"They're doing okay," the doctor tells him. "They're a little over one point five kilos each, and the steroids helped their lung function. We need to keep them intubated for at least the next twenty-four hours, but then we'll evaluate extubating to BiPAPP. They will have trouble controlling their body temperature and functions, so we'll do that for them."

Sebastian shakes his head, and the doctor chuckles.

"My apologies, Your Majesty. Your twins need a bit of help from us at the moment, and I can't guarantee anything, but right now, for thirty-one weekers, they're looking good, and all appears very promising."

Sebastian blows out a strained breath, his body sagging. "What about my wife?"

"She's in good hands, Your Majesty, and her doctor or a nurse will be out shortly to update you."

He looks utterly lost. "Where should I go? Who should I be with?"

"Go with the twins," I tell him. "Bellamy will hand you your ass if you don't. I'll stay with her, and the moment she opens her eyes, I'll text you."

Sebastian gives me a brief hug, slams his fist into my back, then leaves with the twins, a hand on each of their incubators.

I'm back at the window when the door practically opens in my face. I stumble back a step, and the nurse apologizes profusely.

"It's fine. How's my sister-in-law? How's the queen?"

"Her placenta tore away from her uterine wall, and she lost a lot of blood. Part of her condition thinned it, so we had to give her a transfusion, and she'll also get platelets to help."

"All right. But she's okay?"

"Yes, Your Highness. We're moving her to the PACU, and she'll be groggy and in some pain when she wakes up, but she should be just fine."

Relief as I've never known shakes through me. "Can I see her?"

"Of course. I'll bring you to her. They're moving her now."

I follow the nurse but send Althea a text letting her know where I am and what's going on. My phone informs me it's three in the morning, so I don't expect her to reply, even though she doesn't have her do-not-disturb on. I also text Gabe, asking him not to kill me for leaving on my own. I need to talk to him more about Marcella. I haven't done that because she felt like mine to look into and no one else's, but that was the possessive caveman in me talking.

Javier never found anything on Ella, and he knows the situation because he put the tracking on her face. Everyone has held back because of me, but no more.

The PACU is blindly white and startlingly empty. Nurses and aides curtsy as I pass, but I can't remove my eyes from Bellamy. She's as white as the walls, her chestnut hair sweaty and tangled around her, and she has deep purple bruises beneath her eyes, along with a nasal cannula in her nose.

I snap a picture of her that I'll no doubt get hell for later from her and send it to Sebastian, letting him know what the nurse told me about her condition. She has a blanket over her lower half, her belly still large and protruding, but empty now.

I lower my forehead to the side of her bed and close my eyes.

She's still here, and the twins are fighting.

"Your Majesty, you're fierce," I murmur to her.

"And you look like shit," she whispers in English. The sound of her gravelly voice has me sitting up, laughing.

"*I* look like shit?" I parrot in English.

She blinks at me, her pretty blue eyes glazed, her expression sober. "Where are they?"

"Upstairs in the NICU with Sebastian."

She starts to cry, and I run my hand over her cheek. "Don't cry, Your Majesty. They're doing okay. That's what the doctor told us. They're just over one point five kilos and—"

"Kilos? Rowan, my brain can only comprehend English right now. What is that in pounds?"

I do some quick mental math. "Somewhere above three pounds, I think."

"So small."

"But mighty. Like their mother."

More tears fall. I can't tell if she's in pain. I imagine they gave her something for that in the OR before they cut, but I have no clue.

"I want to see them."

"I don't think you can yet. Let me ring your nurse—" Before the words are fully out, the curtain is drawn back, and two nurses are there. They kick me out so they can examine her, and I text Sebastian. He tells me to come to the NICU so we can swap places, and I head upstairs. I'm handed a gown and mask to wear and told to scrub my hands, which I vigorously do.

Sebastian is standing over the twins, who are side by side with each other.

"Bellamy wouldn't stand for them to be alone," he says as if he had to explain himself.

"I'm happy to stay with them."

"They're so tiny, Rowan. Look at them. Tubes in their mouths and noses and through their umbilical cords. I've been talking to them so they hear my voice."

"They're hanging in there."

"Yes," he agrees before he looks up at me, sincerity dripping from him. "Thank you for being here."

"I'm glad I was."

I sit in the rocking chair by their incubators, and Sebastian leaves to be with Bellamy. I must fall asleep once again because when I wake, it's daylight, and the NICU is buzzing with life. I sit up in the chair and get treated to the best sight ever, Bellamy holding one of the babies and Sebastian holding the other.

Except. "Oh fuck," I hiss and turn away, my eyes closing.

Bellamy laughs, then whimpers. "Don't make me laugh, Rowan. I had my stomach cut open not long ago."

"You could have warned me you were...what the hell are you doing?"

"Pumping. I can't feed them yet as they still have tubes in their mouths, but they encouraged me to hold the baby against my skin and pump, as it'll help stimulate my milk production."

"Keep your eyes off my wife's breasts."

I hold up a hand. "Gladly. Jesus." I sit up a little straighter and scrub my hands up my face. "What time is it?"

"A little after six," Sebastian tells me. He has one of the twins on his bare chest with a blanket over them. "Althea got your text, and so did Javier and Gabe."

"Good. How are you feeling?" I ask Bellamy in English since that's all she's speaking right now.

"Like I've been cut open and had my insides ripped out of me. But I'm okay. Better now that I can hold them."

"You're a natural. And how are you?" I ask my brother.

"Exactly as Bellamy said."

I nod, not the least bit shocked by that. "What can I do?"

"Go home and shower," Bellamy teases. "You look like crap."

I smile. "I see we're careful with our colorful language now that we're around the twins."

"Yes, we are," she asserts.

"Good luck with that, Your Majesty."

"No making me laugh, Rowan!"

"Right." I hold up a hand. "Sorry. Apologies."

"Why don't you stay a bit longer, at least through rounds, then go home? The children will have a lot of questions. And so will Gabe and Javier."

38

MARCELLA

When I step out of my bedroom door, the palace is buzzing. People are in the halls talking, and there's movement everywhere I look. It's odd for a Saturday, which is typically a quiet day. I switched my day off with Astrid, one of the other servants. Signoria Batorini texted yesterday evening, telling me she was going to be in Tourin this morning at eight instead of tomorrow at ten and that I had to meet her.

I don't stop to talk to anyone. I don't listen to the chatter. I make my way upstairs to the royal side and go straight for his room. It's in the same disarray it was in last night when I left it, and my heart lurches.

Trust me. Choose me.

Oh god. He has no clue. I bury my face in his pillow and take a quick inhale. One last breath of him. I made a decision last night that solidified when I got the text. He'll hate me for it, but the truth is, it'll save them. All of them.

I set the items he bought me—including the vibrators and underwear—on the bed and grab the diamond earring from the drawer. In its place, I leave him the note I wrote this morning and go. Even when it feels as though it might physically kill me to do so. My heart stays here. It's his to keep. The thing never did me much good anyway.

With my backpack on, I walk the mile and a half in the early morning heat to the nearest bus stop. My thoughts frequently drift to Rowan, to last night, but that won't help me now. It'll only hurt what I have to do.

The bus into town isn't long, and my gaze stays glued to the window, watching the pretty landscape of Messalina pass. Tourin sprawls out before me as I climb down the three steps from the bus onto the sidewalk. Determination holds my spine and head straight as I walk the streets, up two blocks, and down three. On and on I go, following the GPS directions on my work phone until I reach the edge of town where L'Hotel Louise sits. It's a posh hotel on the hill with a view of everything, including the river. It's also near the hospital, and I wonder how Bellamy is doing. How her twins are.

I have no right to ask. No right to know.

I enter the lobby and take in the elegant vibe with its crystal chandeliers and velvet couches with white roses in bud vases on small tables scattered around in the lounge. Signoria sits at a table with her back to the room, her blonde hair pinned up in a perfect chignon. In years past, she would have been front and center in the café, her face a beacon to the room. Shame has done funny things to her, but her soul was black well before Samil died.

Ignoring the host, I breeze over to her table, drop the coin into her purse that's hanging off the back of her chair, and take the seat across from her.

A server comes by, and I order myself a coffee and a croissant without asking if I'm allowed. It makes Signoria scowl, the lines of her face stressing the Botox doing its best to keep them smooth and in place.

"Were you followed?"

I shake my head. It's just us in here, and the staff is giving us our privacy, no doubt tipped very well to forget they saw Signoria Batorini speaking to anyone.

"No one knows I left. No one cares that I did." They will tomorrow, though when I don't present for work. By that point, my work phone and everything I need it for today will be dead. I left everything else that wasn't mine there. I'll send Emily an email or a text letting her know that my sister or family needed me emergently and that I'm sorry I had to go, blah, blah, blah.

By the time she gets it and looks to do anything about it, Signoria and Antonia will be dead, and Jaqueline and I will be out of the country. I know the people who got me the IDs, and I'm hoping they'll trade their work for diamonds or cash if I can sell the diamonds first. Then we can start fresh. Away from Messalina. Away from nightmares and memories.

The evil deeds we commit cannot be erased by others' bullshit revisionist history. Wrong is wrong, no matter how you try to dress it up and make it look presentable. With that, I'm done doing the evil for others who have the luxury of pretending they're above it simply because their hands aren't dripping with blood.

My coffee and croissant arrive, and I take my time adding milk and sugar, stirring it around and driving Signoria mad.

"What did you find on his computer?" she snips, her impatience getting the best of her.

"Nothing," I tell her bluntly after I take a sip. "There was nothing on there. He did no wrong. He's not part of any schemes. No blackmail or manipulation." I stir my little spoon around. "Your son, on the other hand, was tied up in all kinds of both."

Her lips purse to the side as if that tidbit were boring and useless to her. "I have what I need you to plant on his computer," she continues, dismissing my narrative. "Do it tonight, then leave tomorrow."

"Of course," I tell her, my gaze not wavering, not even as I take another sip. "Samil loved Nora, and I understand his hatred of the king. The king won, and Samil lost. Still, you're aware you're going to ruin an innocent man."

Rage colors her face. "Do not speak to me about innocence you know nothing about. He killed my son. Your brother. The only reason I've let you live. You will do this, Marcella, or I will kill Jaqueline while you watch, and then I'll kill you."

Not if I kill you first.

Except this is part of the game.

"I'll do it. You know I will. I love my brother, and the king deserves to go down for what he did, but I want my freedom. I want Jaqueline's freedom."

She's quiet for a very long moment, and this surprises me. I expected her to laugh as she's done every time I've made that request. This time she doesn't. And it chills me further. It also solidifies my resolve, knowing full well what her plan is for me.

She appraises me, taking me in from head to toe. "You look different."

"Different?" I parry, taken off guard by her topic changer.

"Yes. There's something about you now, isn't there?"

"Signoria, since I could barely walk, I've done your bidding. I've taken your punishments, and I've accepted your torture. I've never let you down. Not once, and I won't now. Do we have a deal? Our freedom for the king's."

"What if I asked you to kill him? It's what Samil wanted. Would you deny the only person to love you their dying wish?"

I harden, my eyes narrowing. "I thought you wanted me to plant evidence. Now you want him dead. Which is it?"

"Both," she tells me in no uncertain terms.

Fuck me. I stare up at the ceiling, blowing out a harsh breath. I pretend to mull this over, allowing unease to hit my features. Finally, I drop my chin and nod. "All right. But if I do,

Jaqueline goes free whether I make it out of the palace alive or not. Do we have a deal?"

"I have her locked up at an undisclosed location. Antonia will kill her if I don't call in or if I don't return home. She'll also kill her if the files aren't uploaded by midnight or if I get the slightest inclination that everything isn't going perfectly."

Jesus. I should have known. She always has an insurance policy. That changes things up a bit, but it's not insurmountable.

"That's not necessary."

"It is," she assures me. "I've waited five months for you to do this. Antonia repeatedly told me to be patient. To give it time. In all this time, you've done nothing. You broke into the king's computer once, and all you have to tell me is that he didn't do anything wrong?" Her voice climbs before she evens it back out. "This is unacceptable, Marcella. I want it done tonight, or you both die. Jaqueline's life in your hands will motivate you."

"Signoria," I press. "Our freedom?"

She squints at me. "If you put these files on the king's computer by midnight and kill him, I will allow you and Jaqueline your freedom."

She's lying. She's going to kill us both. I'm a liability, and Jaqueline is inconsequential to her. Not that I'd make it out of the palace alive if I tried or actually did kill the king.

"Thank you, Signoria." I smile. "I'll do whatever it takes for you, then Jaqueline and I will leave and never look back."

"If you don't do what I ask—and be warned, I will know when the files are uploaded—then I will kill both of you." She leans forward. "And Marcella, I will make it hurt in ways you never imagined possible."

That she's not lying about. "Yes, Signoria. I understand. I won't let you down."

She nods, satisfied. She puts her giant designer purse on

the table and pulls a drive from it. It slides across the table, and I quickly snatch it up and pocket it.

"You'll return by dawn tomorrow, and we'll progress with the next steps."

"Yes, ma'am."

I rise and leave her behind. Part one of my plan is in play.

Now I need to get to her car and hide myself in there before she sees me. I'll send the drive to the king after I'm out of the country. He should have it. He should know what she was planning to do. It's likely a virus. Some kind of malware. Or perhaps it's simply files she wants on there, but that would be entirely too traceable unless set up properly.

I exit the hotel and veer right, heading toward the garage, when I slam into a hard wall. Except it's not a wall. It's a man. I draw back, but his hands capture my shoulders, and his face is right in front of mine.

No.

"What are you doing here?" I glance over my shoulder as panic skitters through me. She won't come out this way. She'll go to the garage, but fuck, she could see him if she decided to go for a walk or shopping.

"That's my question for you. Imagine my surprise when I get a notification from the palace that you left and then I see you walk into this hotel."

"Rowan—"

"Who were you meeting?"

"No one." I shove him off me. "And none of your business."

I try to move around him. My window for making it to her car undetected is growing slimmer by the second.

"Oh no, sweetheart, it is my business." He glances over my shoulder, and I twist back to find a tall Black man right there. I didn't even hear him approach. "Bind her wrists."

Jesus. "No! Rowan, you can't. You have to let me go."

"Not this time. You told me you're dangerous. I believe you."

My wrists are forced behind my back and locked together with a zip tie.

"Let's move," the man behind me says.

I nearly trip over my own feet as I'm pushed forward. Rowan puts his back to me as he moves toward a black car. Sweat clings to my brow as the back door is opened and I'm thrown inside, falling into the well between the seats. Awkwardly, I do my best to get myself up, but bound the way I am, it's not the easiest.

I'm pulled by my upper arm and placed on the seat, shoved to the opposite window as Rowan gets in. He buckles both of us up, and we set off.

"You have to let me go. I was leaving! I wasn't coming back."

Both men ignore me.

I glare at the side of his face. "You have no grounds to detain me."

Rowan chuckles, but there's no humor in it. "The fuck I don't, *Ella*."

"Now? You do this now? You've known who I am for weeks."

He glares enmity at me. "You see, that's the funny thing about this. I *don't* know who you are. But I know that you left the palace and just had a clandestine meeting with an unknown woman."

Fuck. He saw her. Yet he doesn't seem to know who she is. Whether that's because he didn't see her face or because he doesn't know her is unclear, and I don't ask, but one thing is certain. There's no way I'll get access to the king's computer by midnight or be able to kill Signoria and Antonia.

Which means Jaqueline is dead. And I'm next.

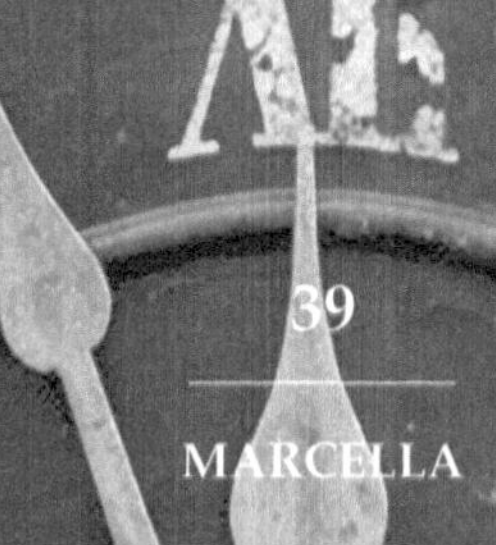

39

MARCELLA

Rowan doesn't speak to me the entire drive back. I don't know what to do. If I tell him about the Signoria and they go after her, Jaqueline is dead. If I don't get to the king's computer, she's dead. If I tell him the truth, he might not believe me. At the very least, he'll have to investigate, and that includes looking into the drive. But the moment it's inserted into anything, it'll notify the Signoria, and she'll know I've been compromised, and again, Jaqueline will die.

I don't care about me in this. I never looked at my life with any longevity in mind. I'm far from innocent, and I deserve whatever I get. But Jaqueline doesn't. She's so young. There's still a chance for her in this world. But I have to get her out.

For all I know, Signoria could have seen what happened outside of the hotel, and it's already too late. Dread pools like boiling oil in my gut. All I wanted from this was to save Jaqueline and save the royal family. Now everything is sideways.

But the facts remain the same. If I want to save Jaqueline, if I want to save the king, I have to act. I just don't know how to make it all work now that I can't track Signoria since they confiscated my phone, and I'm trapped here.

We arrive back at the palace, but I'm not brought in through the front. We drive around to the side, stopping before the garages without pulling in. The car shuts off, and the driver gets out. My door is opened, and he uses my bound wrists to haul me out of the car. Rowan follows. The sound of car doors slamming shut behind me is deafening. There's a side entrance over here that I never paid much attention to, except that I know where it leads.

The door is unlocked with a code, then we're walking down a steep flight of stairs. The cellar is dark and has an earthy undertone to it. Probably because it's ancient and it shows it. The floors are stone, the doors are short and metal. This is one of the original palaces built in this country, and it's centuries old.

We reach a room, and I frown at the sight of it. There's a bed, a table, a chair, and nothing else. No bars either. Just a heavy, old door.

The man holding my wrists, whose name I still haven't gotten, walks me in before he releases me. The door shuts, but I'm not alone. My backpack is tossed onto the table, but it's useless to me now. Rowan takes a seat while the large man stands at the door.

I might have better luck without him here, but it seems I don't get the choice.

"Rowan—"

"What do you know about Marie Elonaise?" he cuts me off, and I startle at the question, my eyebrows taking a nosedive.

"Why are you asking me about Marie?"

His jaw locks, and his eyes harden. "Tell me!" he shouts, shocking me with his vehemence. I sit on the bed, my wrists behind me since they haven't cut the ties.

"She took the princess."

His eyes widen, and he exchanges glances with the man before he returns to me. "How do you know that?"

I tilt my head, squinting at him. "How did you know about her?"

"I'm asking the questions, Marcella. Was that Marie you were meeting with?"

"No."

His arm slashes the air. "Don't lie to me. We have people arriving at the hotel now, ready to intercept and bring her in."

My stomach plummets, and my eyes close. Fuck. "Rowan, you can't. Please, I'm begging you not to."

He ignores that, and a sob locks in my throat.

"Who was it then? Who are you working for and what are they after?"

"Let me go, and I'll give you everything you're after. I swear I will. Please. It's the only way to save everyone."

I get a wry smirk. "That's not how it works, sweetheart. You're not going anywhere other than to prison after we interrogate you."

I don't care about prison. He can threaten me all he wants, but I've lived in one my entire life. "Don't intercept her. Please. Please, please, don't. If you do, a young girl will die. Follow her all you want, but please don't confront her."

With any luck, she left before their guards got there, but I don't know for sure, and I can't check my phone since it's in my backpack.

He stares me down, then, after an interminable minute, gives a short nod. The guy pulls out his phone and texts someone, and I breathe a little easier, but not much.

"Tell me how you know about Marie."

I fall back on the bed, my hands beneath me, and I twist my wrists while I look up at the stone ceiling. "What's the deal for me with this?"

"Pardon?" He laughs the word. "I'm sorry, you think you get

something out of this? You know about the woman who took my sister. That's treason, Marcella. Punishable by death."

I sit back up and meet his gaze head-on. "She's thirteen. Has no birth certificate. No national identification number. No last name. Same as me."

He blinks at me. "Same as you?"

"Rowan, I will tell you everything because I want you to know it. Because holding onto these secrets isn't going to help or save anyone. Not even Jaqueline. But she's only thirteen." A tear hits my cheek that I can't wipe away. "She has a good heart, and she will die tonight if we don't stop it."

"Who is she?"

"My half-sister."

He pauses for a moment. "What are you asking for?"

I look up at the ceiling, willing the tears back. I blow out a heavy breath, then say, "If by some miracle she doesn't die, if she's able to be rescued, get her real paperwork, find her a good home where she's loved, and educate her. That's all I want."

"You're not asking for anything for yourself?"

My lips twist into a rueful smile. "I think it's pretty obvious my life isn't going very far from here. It likely never was."

He looks like he's about to break in two. "It didn't have to be like this. You could have come to me. You could have said something. I would have helped you and her."

"You wouldn't have once you found out who we belong to."

He rises and cups my face to wipe my tears, standing over me. "Who do you belong to?"

"Signoria Batorini."

He stiffens.

"That's the woman you saw me meeting with today. Samil was my half-brother. Jaqueline's half-brother. We share the same father. Signoria Batorini is my stepmother."

His hands drop from my face, and he steps back like he's

been struck, and any love and softness I saw in him a moment ago are gone. Just like that. As I knew it would be.

"You broke into the wedding..."

"For intel. Not to harm anyone. Signoria and Antonia—"

"Who's Antonia?"

Jesus, this is complicated. I lick my lips, tasting the salt from my tears. "What do you want to know first?"

He glances over at the man but just as quickly returns to me. "The wedding. Tell me about the wedding, I guess."

"They wanted intel on what people were saying about Samil, if the queen genuinely loved the king or if she was after his money and title, and if we could use her against the king. We also wanted to know how easy it would be to break through your security and gain access to the royal family."

"We?"

I swallow and nod. "Yes. We. That includes me."

"And me?" he barks, heat rising up his face. "What was fucking me? What about giving me your virginity, or was that part of the act and all bullshit too?"

I glance at the man by the door, and this pisses Rowan off.

"Don't look at him," he snaps, his tone mocking and mean. "He doesn't give a shit about who you fuck or how you use your body to get what you need. But I do."

Ouch. Not that I can blame him for that. "I didn't use you, and my virginity was real. I had no intention of even meeting you that night. I was to break in, blend in, listen, watch, then leave with intelligence we could use."

"And after that?" he growls.

"I hacked into your system, changed my face on your videos and how you had it in your facial recognition software. I was given a set of IDs that could pass any security. A family that owes the Signoria a lot of money became my family and references, and I started working in the palace."

"With the goal of..."

I swallow. Here it comes. "With the goal of taking down the king."

"Jesus fucking Christ." He paces away from me and collapses back into the chair, his elbows on his knees, his hands over his mouth as he appraises me with disbelief and anger. "Jesus fucking Christ, Marcella. I'm the dumbest motherfucker on the planet. I knew you were dangerous. Hell, you told me you were, and I was stupid enough to believe that there was good in you. That you were under the thumb of someone else. Love and lust really are blind, aren't they?"

I can't stop my grimace or the way his words sear through me. My insides rattle, and my heart that was barely held together comes apart, bleeding me dry with no way to hide it. I could tell him I changed course after getting to know the family and him. I could tell him that I wasn't going to do any of it. That I was going to kill the Signoria and Antonia.

But what's the point?

It's better if he hates me. Nothing was ever going to come of us anyway. Obviously. I mean, how could it?

"I knew you broke into the wedding. I knew you were up to no good. And yet I allowed you near my family."

"I wasn't going to hurt them," I whisper under my breath, though I don't know why I bother. Maybe because I can't stand to see him blaming himself for the position I put him in.

He laughs bitterly. "Right. Just my brother then. The king of my country."

"Is there a reason the woman wanted to meet you at the hotel today?" the man asks, his voice rich and deep.

"Yes. I have a midnight deadline to plant something on the king's computer." And kill him, but what's the point in saying that? I wasn't going to do that part of this anyway. Hell, I wasn't going to do any part of it.

"You have to plant—" Rowan's phone rings, cutting him off. He checks it and answers immediately, his eyes on me. "Hey. I have her in one of the prisoner rooms. Sebastian, this is so fucked I hardly know where to begin." He listens for a moment. "No, you're not coming back here. Bellamy had surgery not even six hours ago, and the twins are in the NICU."

I gasp. Oh my god. "Are they okay?"

He scoffs at me. "Like you give a shit."

My chin drops, and shame spirals through me along with a bone-deep sadness.

"Fine. I'll see you soon." He ends the call. "Congratulations. You've pulled my brother out of the hospital and away from his wife and newborn children."

He stands, his gaze colder than ice and filled with a loathing there is no coming back from.

"You can explain the rest to us when he returns. As for your Jaqueline, she's likely as evil as you are. Right now, I see no reason to help you with anything. If she dies, it'll be on your conscience, not mine."

He nods to his security guy, and the two leave me here alone, taking my backpack with them. The metal door grates as it locks me in here, and all hope dies.

Gabe closes the cell door, locking her in, and my fist slams into the wall. It's fucking stone, and it hurts, and I likely broke something, but I don't care. Gabe doesn't react, and it's one of the things I like most about him. He only speaks when necessary and never with disdain or judgment. He's a facts guy, and that's what I need right now.

I got the notification that she went into my room this morning. Then one that she left the palace. I called Gabe, and he tracked her. But I'll be fucking honest, in all of the scenarios I conjured up, this isn't it.

"How the fuck is she Samil's half-sister? How the fuck did she get into the wedding and our palace, and how in the motherfuck does she know about Marie?"

I have a million more questions for her. A fucking million. But I had to get out of that room. Her tears were challenging me. The look of genuine concern over Bellamy softened me. For a moment, I saw her again. The woman with the scars on her back who would cry and rage and fight. Who had these moments that made me swear she wasn't a monster.

But she is.

She's my curse. I have no doubt about that in my mind. Because despite everything, I still fucking want her. I still want to take her in my arms and hold her and promise her everything. Despite all I heard in that room, I still want to be her hero. The one who fixes everything for her. But it's a ridiculous notion. She doesn't need me to fix anything. She's the one in control. She always has been.

I was her pawn while she played me like a queen.

I can't be alone with her.

My hand throbs, my knuckles cracked as I rub it up my face. I'm bleeding, and I don't care. Why her? Why not any of the countless women who have thrown themselves at me for years? Why is she the one I noticed? The one who saw beneath the crown? The one who got to me?

"She said she has no last name, had no IDs or documents. Same for the girl."

"Yes."

"Rowan, she doesn't fucking exist. She's a shadow. Their assassin."

Pain twists my gut as I've never experienced before. His words hit me on an entirely different level. Her backpack sits on the floor by the door, and I pick it up, unzipping the threadbare thing and finding...all of her shit. Her entire life fits in this small backpack.

I would have given her the world. Dressed her in expensive clothes that only I would get to take off. Covered her in diamonds and filled her with my babies. That illusion of happiness is just that. An illusion. I knew it all along, but that pervasive hope kept me going. That ridiculous and dangerous four-letter word.

I drop her bag to the floor and storm down the hall only to twist and return. The children are upstairs with Althea and two attendants. I don't know if the attendants caught up to Signoria Batorini or not, but I'm sure Gabe will check in. We didn't bring extras. Gabe flew out of the palace and met me. Dumb fucking mistake.

At the very least, the children are safe, as are Bellamy and the twins.

So I have to focus on Marcella. On saving my family. On keeping us all safe and alive. Twenty minutes later, my brother's shoes tap on the stone. I'm leaning against the wall, where I've been since I punched it, waiting on him.

"How's Bellamy?" I ask before he can speak. "The twins?"

"The same as when you left them this morning." He stops in front of me, and I can tell he's noting my hand, but he doesn't ask. He doesn't have to. "Tell me everything."

I blow out a breath and lift my chin. "Honestly, I think she needs to tell you."

He searches my eyes. He's calm. Eerily so, but I know him enough to know that the beast is raging right now. He should be furious with me. I hope he is.

"Okay. Let's go in."

Gabe unlocks the door but stands outside. He can see and hear everything in here, as it has cameras with audio. Sebastian enters first, his eyes on Marcella, who no longer has her wrists bound. She's sitting on the bed with her legs folded as if she doesn't have a care in the world. Holy shit. How'd she do that? Fucking assassin indeed.

I cock an eyebrow at the discarded zip tie on the bed.

"I have small hands," is all she says, and I tuck in my smile. My fucking siren. A woman with the face and voice of an angel and the heart of a monster. Still, she shocks us both when she stands and curtsies at Sebastian. "Your Majesty, I'm sorry you had to leave your family. I know I have no credibility right now with anything, but truly, I hope Her Majesty and the twins are doing well. I was terribly worried yesterday morning."

Sebastian takes the seat I was in before, and I hold the post Gabe had by the door.

"Marcella, who are you?"

She glances at me, confused that I hadn't told him yet, then returns to him. "I'm the half-sister of Samil Batorini."

Sebastian, for how shocked I was, somehow isn't. "I knew you looked familiar. Your hair is the same color as his. You also have a similar face shape." He crosses his legs, his ankle on his opposite knee. "I knew Samil nearly all my life. How come I never heard about you?"

Marcella swallows and looks down, retaking her seat. "I was the bastard offspring of an affair his father had with one of the house servants. My mother died during childbirth, or Signoria had her killed. Either way, I don't know, but I was a secret. I was never given their last name. There is no record of my birth. I existed in their house and didn't know better until my father died and I became the charge of Signoria and Antonia. The Signoria wanted me dead, but Samil stepped in."

Sebastian rubs his jaw. "He had you made into this. Into the woman in front of us who breaks into royal weddings in disguise and into palaces as servants under false pretenses with the plan of hurting others."

"Yes, sir. He helped make me into this..." She laughs lightly, but a tear falls down her cheek as she does. "I thought he was saving me. That he loved me. He would spend time with me. Fencing, playing chess, teaching me how to code and hack. How to hold my breath under water for minutes. Yes, he was training me."

"But you loved him as a brother."

It's not a question, but she nods all the same. "Very much so. And with that, I hated you."

He leans back and places his elbow on the table. "I'm not surprised by that. I stole Nora from him."

"They loved each other."

Sebastian chuckles bitterly. "Not quite."

Marcella tilts her head. "I met your former queen, Your Majesty. I can tell you, she loved him."

Sebastian looks like he's been struck. "You met Nora?"

"Yes, sir. Several times. She came to our family's home frequently, both before you were married and after."

Sebastian peeks at me, and I shake my head. This is news to me. He turns back to her. "Are you suggesting they had an affair?"

She holds her hands in her lap, her spine straight, her gaze steady and unwavering. "Yes, Your Majesty, they had an affair. Your entire marriage, she was having an affair with my brother. She was pregnant with his child the day she died."

Sebastian shoots out of his chair and flattens himself against the wall. "You know this as fact?"

"How else would Samil have known where Nora was that day? Gained access to her family estate so easily?"

Sebastian's jaw drops, his mind working overtime.

"Holy shit," I murmur, my hands on my head. "She was pregnant with his child?" They had been having an affair the entire time. I look at Sebastian. The girls. Sebastian and Nora rarely slept together. Zayer is the spitting image of Sebastian, but the girls look like Nora and Nora alone. Blonde hair and green eyes. Nothing like Sebastian. I can see he's having the same thought, and my heart breaks for him for that.

"Now you know why I hated you," she continues. "My brother, the only person in the world who loved me, was broken. You stole Nora from him, and he filled my head with what a jealous, spiteful man you were. If you hadn't done that, if Samil had married Nora, I used to imagine he would have taken me with them, and I wouldn't have..." She pauses, then redirects. "I understood his hatred of you. Anytime we spoke, it was all he talked about. How he loved Nora, how she wouldn't leave you. He was obsessed. The morning she died, they fought about that. He begged her to choose him, and she wouldn't. Not even with the baby. He was going to kill you to get her, but I didn't know until Bellamy told me that he was going to kill your children with you. He never told me that. He told me Nora was going to have you come alone so the two of you could talk."

I release a breath and shift, edgy and antsy and not knowing what to do with myself. Sebastian is frozen. I've never seen him so still.

"My daughters?" he asks finally.

She shakes her head, clearly reading his question. "I don't know, sir. He never said anything about them."

"I killed Samil."

"Yes, Your Majesty, you did. I never saw the video of it, though. I was simply told that Samil was trying to get back at you the only way he knew how by taking Bellamy. Then the two of you fought, and you threw him out the window and were hurt during the skirmish."

He folds his arms across his chest. "I see. What's your purpose here?"

She holds his gaze. "To take you out. Signoria wants me to destroy you by planting files on your computer that likely implicate you in illegal doings, and then I'm to kill you. That edict came down to me this morning when I met her in Tourin."

I can't handle how calmly she's talking about this. The words are hardly affecting her at all.

"Were you going to do it?" I ask, sick to my stomach with all of this.

"No. I was going to sneak into her car and wait there as she drove me home or wherever she was going. Then I was going to kill her and Antonia, take Jaqueline, and leave the country for good."

Leave the country for good. After she killed two people. Jesus fuck. I don't know which to focus on. I'm being ripped apart from the inside out, pulled in every direction. That's why she had her backpack full of her things. She wasn't coming back, but not for the reasons I thought.

Sebastian peers down at her. "You realize all of this is treason? Everything you've done is grounds for us to lock you up and throw away the key. *If* we decide not to see you executed for your crimes."

"Yes, sir. I'm well aware of that, and if that's your choice, I won't fight it. I'll plead guilty and take my punishment. Lord knows I deserve it for the crimes I've committed. But my younger half-sister, Jaqueline, is thirteen. She's not a monster," she says, her eyes flicking over to me before returning to Sebastian. "I will do anything you ask, give you any information I possess, but please, please don't let her die."

He ignores that. "Did you play my brother for a fool?"

"Sebastian—" I bark, but he holds up a hand, cutting me off.

"I have to know, and it better be the fucking truth."

"No, Your Majesty. The only fool was me." She turns and looks at me, tears lining her eyes that cling and don't fall. "I tried to stay away so many times. I told you I wasn't good and that it couldn't happen between us. I was trying to protect you, but I was also trying to protect myself." She swallows audibly and returns to Sebastian. "I fell in love with your brother, and it was the best and worst mistake I've ever made. I don't want to hurt you or your family. I want..." She trails off and looks up at the ceiling before she laughs ruefully. "It honestly doesn't matter what I want at this point. I never expected to be a princess. I didn't give in to him time and time again with ulterior motives. Sometimes feelings and desires are bigger than us and override the path we're set on. That's all I know."

Before she can utter another word that would eviscerate me further, I leave the cell. I have more questions. A ton of fucking answers that I need. But after hearing that...I can't breathe through my shredded lungs to even ask them. I need a break from her before I lose myself further. Sebastian follows as I hear the door shut and lock behind me.

"Watch her cell," he says to the attendant before he walks past me, knowing I'll follow. "Gabe, can you check on my children and stay with them for a bit as an extra precaution?" That puzzles me, but Gabe wordlessly goes to keep an eye on the children.

We have a lot to talk about. But I'm stuck.

She loves me. I believe her. And it's fucking killing me.

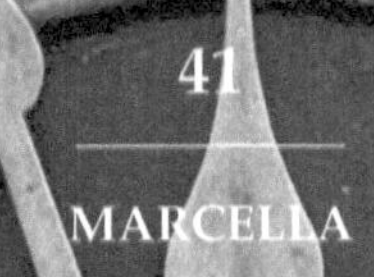

41

MARCELLA

The door closes with a resounding bang, the lock clicking into place, and my heart plummets into my feet. I can't stay here. Every minute I'm here is a minute closer to Jaqueline being murdered. Rowan hates me. That's not going to change. I told him how I felt, and he looked like he was ready to douse me in gasoline and set me on fire. Not that it matters. It doesn't.

I was going to leave. I *have* to leave.

There's no future with the prince of Messalina.

I'm not the girl who gets the guy and the happily ever after.

I have to get out of here. I have to stop Signoria.

I walk over to the door and press my ear against it. There's no sound, but that doesn't mean someone isn't on the other side. There's also a camera in the corner, but fuck it. I'm out of options.

I test the door, already knowing it's locked. But much like a lot of other things in this palace, it's old and in need of updating. Unfortunately, I don't have a lot in here to work with. The chairs, table, and bed are all fixed to the floor, and even if I could free them, the door is thick and won't be broken down.

It's going to either have to be the hinges or the lock. The lock is the easiest, and I grab the zip tie since that's all I have—oh shit. I have the drive in my pocket. They took my backpack, but they didn't frisk me.

It's not a pin or a wire, but I bet between the two I can pick the lock.

I slip the drive into the lock and leave it in place. Then I bend the plastic in half and slip it above it to create a makeshift key. I twist the two but...nothing. Fuck! I try two more times and get nowhere. I need tools to pick the lock.

Frustrated, I bang on the door.

"Yes?" someone answers from the other side, and I practically cry out in glee.

I press my mouth to the door and speak against it. "Um, hi, I need to use the restroom. It's an emergency."

A silent beat. Then, "I'm sorry, mademoiselle, I'm not allowed to let you out. His Highness's orders."

Of course.

"I understand, but please, I really need to use the restroom. Surely by law, you have to allow even prisoners the ability to use the bathroom, and there isn't one in here."

More silence.

"Please. I'll be so embarrassed if I have an accident. Not to mention the mess of it and—"

"All right. Stand back. Don't try anything funny. I'm armed."

"Thank you. I understand." I grab the zip tie and drive before he can open the door and take a step away with my arms behind my back. The ancient door creaks open, and in walks an attendant who can't be any older than I am. He's tall but thin, and it's almost unfair. Especially when his eyes go wide.

I smile a flirty smile, and he blushes ever so slightly. Cute. "Thank you. You're my hero."

His gun is pointed at me, but the fool has the safety still on. Before he can step foot in the room, I swing up, and I kick the gun out of his hand. It bangs into the wall before it skitters across the floor, and the guy shouts, trying to dive for it. I drop an elbow to the middle of his back, knocking him to the floor in a sprawl.

He grabs for my legs, managing to catch my ankle and jerk it up. It's enough to throw me off balance, and I fall back, the air shooting from my lungs as I hit the stone floor. He takes my moment of stun and attempts to crawl over me—again, rookie mistake—and I throat-bar him with my forearm, thrust up, and push him off me.

I throw a punch that hits him in the jaw and hop to my feet. He groans and swipes at me, and I nail him in the ribs with my foot when he tries to catch my ankle a second time.

"Help!" he cries out. "Help. She's trying to escape."

Asshole, shut up!

But he doesn't stop. He doesn't give up. He stands and comes at me, shouting at the top of his lungs while his hands fly about, trying to catch me. I twist to the right, ducking under his arm grab, rear back, and punch him in the face. It knocks the poor guy off his feet and to the ground. He hits the back of his head, rendering him unconscious.

I listen to his chest. His heart is still going strong. But shit. I really got his nose.

I place my thumbs on either side of the bridge of his nose and, in one swift move, I crack it back into place. He whimpers and jolts, but it doesn't wake him. Still, he'll be happy he doesn't have a displaced nasal fracture tomorrow.

I grab his gun, slip it into the back waistband of my pants, snag the key from his pocket, and lock him inside the room. I glance down the hall. No one is there. So much for people manning the cameras or the prisoner. It's almost as if they want me to escape.

And best of all, my backpack is sitting on the floor right beside the door. I snatch it up and toss it over my shoulder. I don't hesitate. I don't think twice. My feet carry me on instinct, and I race toward the stairwell that they brought me down. I slam through the heavy door, staggering back into the blinding sunshine and pervasive heat.

There's no way I'll be able to make it out of here on foot. It's impossible.

The garage is on the left, and there's a side entrance that will get me inside it. It's my best option. I break through the unlocked door and quickly survey my options. I need something inconspicuous but fast enough to get me there. Two large, black SUVs that I know they use when the family goes out, which are equipped with tracking, take up the first two bays. After that, it's the SUV they brought me back here in, a smaller SUV, and a couple of expensive sedans and sports cars.

I don't know which car to take.

Down on the end is a small sedan, not as flashy or exciting as the others. I grab the keys hanging off the hook on the wall and race down there. The garage door opens, and my heart hammers faster with every second it takes for it to slowly ascend. At this rate, I'll have a heart attack before I can even get out of here.

"Come on!" I growl impatiently.

The moment the door is up, the car roars to life, and I peel out, swiveling around on the rocky driveway and speeding toward the gate. This is another issue. They could have been alerted that I broke out. If the guards attempt to stop me, I have to keep going.

I shift the gun out of the waistband of my pants and put it into my backpack on the front passenger seat. I approach the exit and wave at the guards with a pretty smile. They give me a nod and a wave and open the gate. Just like that. They've seen me before walking the grounds and when I left this morning on foot, but that feels too easy.

Then again, who cares?

I drive away from the palace as fast as I can while I pull up the tracking on my work phone. It's the only one I have with active internet access. She's in the car, heading southeast. The attendants must not have gotten to her in time, or they're tailing her. Either way, it doesn't matter. I head in that direction, going down the long, winding road that will take me to the autoroute to intersect her path.

She's ahead of me by at least forty-five minutes, and that terrifies me.

A lot can happen in forty-five minutes.

I glance in my rearview mirror, but I don't see anyone behind me.

I told Rowan I loved him. Well, I told the king that I loved his brother. I love him, and I'm leaving him behind, but it has to be done. That's what I keep telling myself. My whole life has been have-to, and maybe that will change someday, but that day is not today.

The road winds and curves, taking me around quaint countryside and small villages. I don't see any of it. I'm hyperfocused on the path ahead of me and the view through my rearview mirror. She's driving in the direction of the palazzo, but before she can cross to the route that will lead her there, her car takes an exit off the highway and goes a different direction, due south.

It takes me a moment to figure it out until it all clicks into place. The bay house.

She's going to Samil's bay house. I know it. That's the only thing in that direction that would compel her there, and it's the perfect place to keep Jaqueline. It's been abandoned since Samil died. For all I knew, they had sold it along with many of his other properties and possessions, but clearly she's held onto it.

I pick up my pace, praying I don't get pulled over for speeding, but breaking every speed limit and law by at least thirty kilometers an hour and pushing this car to its max. The bay house is a large, sprawling mansion of windows and balconies, overlooking the bay that leads out to the sea, with conservation land on all other sides. Samil took me there years ago after our father died, and we went out on his boat. He taught me to fish and how to use a knife to skin and debone.

The house sits three stories high up on stilts, and it'll make getting in and out tricky. I can only pray that Jaqueline is still alive and I'm not too late to stop Signoria from having Antonia immediately kill her. I have the gun I took off the guard and the knife Samil gave me. A double-sided switchblade with a smooth edge on one side and a serrated one on the other.

The gun's my second choice. I want them to feel their deaths, knowing there's nothing they can do about it. I want to make them hurt.

I see the turn off to the road that leads to the bay house up ahead, and I pull along the side, tucking the car behind a bank of bushes and shrubs. I get myself ready, putting the gun back into the waistband of my pants and tucking my phone in my pocket. I keep my knife in my hand, ready to open it at a moment's notice.

It's a kilometer-long path that leads down to the house, bracketed in by thick marsh and wetlands. Birds fly high in the air, and the sound of insects is thick in the air. It's hot and humid and a little miserable, even this close to the water. I haven't been here since I was twelve or thirteen, and I don't know if Samil has cameras. If he does and they're monitored or even set for motion alerts, I'll be made before I get close to the house.

The house appears ahead of me, and I keep low and tucked to the ground, edging the border of the tall grass. Signoria's car is parked along the side of the house beneath one of the pillars. It's not just Signoria and Antonia I have to deal with. It's her driver, Cristo, too, since she never drives herself anywhere.

Sweat glides down my forehead and back. My heart bangs painfully against my ribs, but I tuck away my nerves, knowing that they won't help me. The back entrance is up a deck that leads to the first floor. My sneakers make no noise as I climb the steps, my eyes tracking every window for movement. I crawl up to the back window and peer in, searching around. I don't see anyone here. Just a bunch of furniture covered with sheets.

Slinking over, I test the back door, but it's locked. Because of course it's fucking locked. I check under the mat, but there's nothing. There's a small pot with a dead plant to the left of the door, and I search in that and find a small key hidden beneath it. Bingo.

Unlocking the door, I let myself in and shut it behind me. It's quiet in here, which automatically sets me on edge. Reluctantly, I put the knife back in my pocket and remove the gun. I flip off the safety and tip it down at a forty-five-degree angle. Blood thrums through my ears as I take slow, even steps.

I move along the first floor, my ears searching, only to catch Signoria's voice on the other side of the first floor. I move in that direction, my finger on the trigger of the gun.

I don't want to shoot her, but I keep it ready all the same.

"What do you mean she went out?" Signoria yells.

"I don't know, Signora," Jacqueline whines, her voice carrying, even three rooms over. "She didn't tell me where she was going. Only that she would return shortly."

A loud *clap,* followed by the sound of Jaqueline whimpering, hardens my jaw.

"Insolent girl. I don't want to hear your useless excuses. She's not picking up her phone, and I need her here."

Yeah, to do your dirty work.

"I'm sorry, Signoria, I don't know where she went."

Jacqueline's voice is filled with tears, and I put my gun back and take out my knife, flip it open and handle it so the smooth side is facing out.

Movement catches my attention, and my head whips around, my knife pointed out, ready to strike. Rowan is standing there along with his bodyguard, both with guns pointed and murderous expressions.

Fuck. They followed me. Goddammit! How? I didn't see them behind me. Then I mentally kick myself. Of course. My stupid fucking work phone.

Vehemently, I shake my head, waving my hand for them to leave.

What the fuck is he doing here? He's the prince.

They're going to ruin everything.

Rowan motions for me to get behind him.

"Go," I mouth. "Leave."

Does he have any clue how dangerous him being here is?

Rowan attempts to grab my arm, and I shirk him off, pointing the knife at him. His bodyguard raises his gun at me, and I flip him off.

"Get him out of here," I breathe.

The unmistakable sound of a gun cocking makes me wince. Especially when I see the barrel is pointed directly at Rowan's head.

"Tell me where your head is with this?" Sebastian asks as we reach a parlor on the main floor.

"She's Samil's sister," I state, ire lacing my voice as I walk to the window and give him my back because my face is likely saying too much. "She's an assassin." And I fell for her. I shouldn't feel betrayed, but I do.

"Do you believe she was going to follow through with the plot against me? That she wasn't going to kill Signoria Datorini and this Antonia woman instead?"

I hitch up a shoulder. "The woman is skilled. I think at this point, that much is obvious. Her words could all be lies."

"You don't believe that," he says, his voice dropping a notch.

"I don't *want* to believe that. There's a difference."

"I believe her," he throws out, and I turn, surprised by that. My brother looks tired. Like he's aged ten years overnight. I hate that he's here. I hate that this called him back to the palace when his focus should be on his wife and children. He hasn't even seen Phaedra, Sabrina, or Zayer to tell them the news.

This is fucked all around.

"It doesn't matter, Sebastian. She was going to kill two people. Hard to glance over that. It's not exactly something we can ignore."

"No," he agrees. "And it will be dealt with, though I wonder if that would be considered self-defense more than anything."

"Self-defense?"

"You told me of the scars. I think we know where she got them."

I release a weighted breath. "Trusting her is a trap." *Part of the curse*, I don't add. "Marcella went to the hotel willingly to meet her. She only fessed up to everything once we caught her, and we already know how skilled a liar she is."

"Do you believe that or are you just angry with her?"

It's a valid question.

"She knows about Marie," I tell him, changing course since I can't answer that. "When I saw her in the hotel meeting with that woman, I thought it could be her. When I questioned her about Marie, she told me that she took Desta. I asked how she knew that, and she was surprised by my question. She asked how I did."

Sebastian pales. "She doesn't simply know about Marie. She *knows* Marie. Or at least someone who is very close to her and the situation."

"Yes," I agree.

"Did you ask her about Desta? If she knows about what happened to her?"

I shake my head, my hands going to my hips. "We didn't get that far. But it seems she has other secrets we don't yet know."

"She loves you."

I scoff out a bitter laugh and roll my eyes. "It doesn't matter."

He nods, his stand firm. "It matters."

I shift my weight and clench my shirt under my folded arms

so I don't pummel my fist through the window behind me. "It's not as though I can marry her. She doesn't exist. She's Samil's half-sister. She's a goddamn assassin. I'd never be able to trust her, and frankly, she can say she loves me all she likes, but all of her possessions were in her backpack. She wasn't coming back."

There's nothing left for us.

I'm glad she was leaving. I never would have had the strength to let her go. I would have fought heaven and hell to keep her. Chased her to the ends of the earth. Even now, the urge is compelling. But if I had come home and found her gone...

"She wants us to save this thirteen-year-old girl? How fucking sick is the Batorini family that both she and this girl don't have last names or identities, and they not only beat young girls but also plan to kill them?"

"I think we already know the answer to that. You have scars from that family under your shirt."

He nods, running a hand over the top of his head to the back of his neck. "I think Marcella would have killed the people who want to kill me, and after, we never would have seen her again."

"I agree."

He lifts his chin until our eyes lock. "It wouldn't have stopped at me, you know."

"How do you mean?" I ask, my brows forming a V.

"Signoria Batorini wouldn't have stopped at my death. She would have continued. She would have eliminated my entire family."

A chill runs up my spine. "Perhaps." I can't deny the plausibility of that.

"The girls are mine," he says.

"I have no doubt that they are." And I mean that. They're his. Even as I ache for him that the question is there.

He releases a breath and stands. "The girls are mine," he repeats. "I don't need a blood test. I don't need proof. They're mine. I held them when they were first born. Hell, I remember the nights we conceived them because I didn't exactly sleep with Nora often."

Shit.

"I'm not surprised she was sleeping with him," he continues. "She would always tell me she couldn't stand him, but she was gone a lot too, coming up with different locations and excuses for things she had to do as queen. I didn't challenge it because I didn't care all that much. I neglected her in a lot of ways. I don't blame Samil for hating me, especially if she was pregnant with his child. I'd hate me too. I'd want me dead. If it were Bellamy, I don't know what I would have done if she belonged to another man."

"Love breeds madness. I have firsthand knowledge of that now, but I didn't before."

"Yes, it does. I don't know how I would have reacted if I had known about the affair, and I can't change the past. Nora made her choices, and Samil made his. He took Bellamy with the intention of killing her, and for that reason alone, I will never regret his death. But it seems as though, at least according to Marcella, that accidentally killing Nora and his baby broke him, and after nearly losing my wife and children, I can't begin to imagine that sort of agony."

I release a breath, my head bowing.

The door slams open before I can say anything, and Gabe is there. "She's escaped," he announces. "I just got a notification that Marcella worked her way out of the cell, knocked the guard unconscious, took his gun, stole a car, and fled the palace."

"What?" startles past my lips.

But Sebastian isn't surprised. He simply checks his watch. "That was faster than I thought it would be. She's very good, your Marcella." He meets my eyes. "She didn't come after me. She stole a gun and left." He walks over to me and clasps my shoulder. "If you go after her, keep that in mind. I'm going to kiss my children, tell them about their new brother and sister, then return to my wife. Keep me updated and keep yourself safe above all else."

With that, he leaves, and I can't believe it. I can't believe he knew this would happen and allowed it. Now that I think about it, we didn't have anyone watching the cameras and only one young guard on her cell. This was intentional.

I look at Gabe. "Let's go."

"Your Highness—"

"It's not up for negotiation. I'm going." Because I have to save her. I have to make sure she's okay. I will take down Signoria Batorini or anyone else who hurt my girl, but I will fucking make sure she's okay, and when this is all over, I'll hold her captive in my arms and make her tell me all her secrets, and we'll see where we come out.

EXCEPT NOW THERE'S a man on my right holding a gun to my temple. This wasn't the most well-thought-out plan, and that seems to be how we do things lately. Unwisely. Rushing into a situation and praying it all goes to plan. That's how we did it with Samil, that's how we did it with Charlotte, and now this. Fuck!

"Marcella, what is this?" the man with the gun asks. His fucking hand is shaking, which isn't what you want when you're the one whose head it's pointed at.

Marcella doesn't look scared. She looks furious.

"Cristo, what are you doing?" she hisses under her breath, keeping her voice low. "This is the prince. Lower your weapon. I brought him here."

Cristo's eyes widen before he looks at Gabe, me, then back at her. "No."

"Sì," she persists, speaking in Italian with him. "Come on, Cristo. You know me. They've been digging into me. I lured them here so we could torture secrets out of them, and after, I was going to kill them. But if you shoot him, we won't get any of those secrets we so desperately need."

The man stands still, except for his shaky goddamn hand. "You brought them here for this?" He's incredulous because it doesn't exactly make a ton of sense.

She scoffs and rolls her eyes indignantly, working to sell it. "Yes. Of course I did. How many jobs have you been my driver to? You know how I do things."

I don't know how she does things. Jobs? What jobs? What the actual fuck is going on and who is this woman?

"I kill everyone. Don't I? No loose ends. No trails."

Jesus. Is that true?

"I know," he agrees, and hell. I can't begin to wrap my head around this. She kills people? I mean, Gabe called her an assassin, but I thought of that more as a term, not a fact.

She holds up her knife but fishes out her gun from her back waistband. "Let me finish it. It's my right after what they did to Samil."

The man gives her a very long look, and she must see something in his eyes because I hear him intake a sharp breath a second before his face is blown out the back of his skull. Blood and bone and God only knows what else are sprayed across my face and side, and I collapse to the floor from the force of everything, unable to breathe, unable to fucking think.

That bullet was so close to my face I felt the goddamn air displace and sweep along my cheek from it. I wipe my face with the sleeve of my shirt, but it doesn't matter. It's everywhere. My eyes clear, and Marcella is holding a gun, a pissed-off scowl on her face.

She just blew the guy's face off because he had a gun to my head and was about to kill me with it. Or was about to out her. I honestly don't know what she's doing or what she's capable of or how she's even thinking of me in this situation.

"Hide your weapons," she hisses hastily. "Hands behind your backs, and don't argue with what I say. Do it now! Signoria!" she cries out.

I get to my feet, but before I can go to her, the woman I saw this morning from the hotel appears, and instinctively, I put my arms behind my back. Gabe does the same.

Marcella sighs dramatically and lowers her gun. "Fucking asshole," she gripes.

"Marcella? What on earth? What is this?" The woman waves a disgusted hand toward the dead man before her eyes widen as she takes both Gabe and me in.

Marcella faces the woman. "The king is dead," she announces without preamble. "And can you instruct your henchmen in the future not to point guns first and ask questions later? It got his head blown off."

She brushes back her long bangs from her face with her gun hand. The knife is still open in her other hand, down at her side.

The older woman is completely perplexed.

"What is happening? What are you doing here, and why is Cristo dead?"

Marcella scowls. "I killed the king. He caught on to me the moment I returned to the palace, and I slit his throat. The prince and his man chased me out of the palace, and I took them down, used their zip ties to bind their wrists behind their backs, and brought them here for us to dispose of after we torture secrets out of them. Then fucking Cristo had to point a gun at me and go to shoot."

Cristo has a gun in his hand, and since he's dead on the floor, he's got no argument.

"Marcella, how did you know we were here?"

"Antonia," she replies as if the answer should be obvious.

"Antonia?" the lady parrots, incredulity in her tone.

"I called her and told her what happened. She told me to come here to regroup and await further instruction."

The woman eyes both of us with our hands behind our backs. "You brought them here?"

"To kill them. I had no choice. Believe me, it wasn't my first option."

Fuck, is she deadpan. Shit. I believe her, and it's rattling me.

"Did anyone else follow you?"

She shakes her head. "No. It was only them."

"You won't get away with this," Gabe snarls.

Marcella snorts a laugh. "Honey, it's done. No one is coming for you. There is no rescue."

"But you killed my driver?" The woman is all but ignoring us.

Marcella pans a hand at the man on the ground. "Signoria, he's had it coming for a long time, and we both know it. But he pointed a gun at me and went to shoot. So yes, I killed him."

Signoria doesn't look upset, just annoyed. "That's a ten-thousand-euro rug he's bleeding all over."

Marcella curtsies, just as she always did for us. "My apologies, Signoria."

The woman huffs. "And the king's computer?"

Marcella bows slightly. "That's where he caught me. I was uploading to his computer when he entered. He came after me, and I sliced his throat."

She hisses something under her breath. "But it's done?"

Marcella nods. Then smiles gleefully. "It's done. I was able to get the file on his computer, and the virus will upload tonight at midnight. More importantly, the king is dead."

"Good. Excellent. Bring them in here and tie them to the chairs. Where is Antonia?"

"She said she's on her way back, but her phone cut off on me. She had bad service," she explains.

"Fine. But now you have a prince to kill, and I'd like to get it done."

Marcella comes over to me and grips me by the back of the neck. "Move," she barks, but her thumb drags along my skin. I'd be more afraid if my hands were actually bound. "This is gross." She takes the hem of my shirt and pulls it up to wipe the side of my face. "I don't want to see Cristo's blood anymore."

She faces me, her eyes boring into mine.

"Do as I say," she mouths.

I narrow my eyes at her. "What kind of future do you think you'll have after killing the king? After you kill me?"

A smile curls up her face. "Whatever I want. Unlike you, I'll still be alive. And free."

Free? There are so many things I don't understand right now.

Once she's finished cleaning me, she grabs Gabe and hauls the two of us into the room, pushing us against the wall with our arms—and guns—still behind us and invisible to this crazy fucking woman.

Sitting on a chair with her arms bound behind her is a young girl who eyes us as if she doesn't know what to make of us. She has a busted lip and a bruise beneath her eye, but her features are so startlingly similar to Marcella's that I instantly know this is the Jaqueline she was talking about.

Marcella crosses the room and cups the girl's face before she kisses her forehead, mumbling something against her skin I can't make out.

The girl gulps but nods.

And because I'm so focused on the girl and Marcella, it takes me a half beat longer to realize everything in here is covered in plastic. Not like the sheets in the rest of the house over furniture. This is completely different. It's a killing room. I know nothing about any of this, but I've watched enough horror movies to know one when I see one.

What kind of sick, twisted people are these?

I love this woman, but I can't reconcile anything I'm seeing with the woman I thought I knew. But that's the irony of this, right? I never knew her. Not really.

The woman comes and stands before me, her gaze cast up into my face, and she studies me before twisting her head over her shoulder to eye Marcella.

Then she laughs. Loud and rancorously.

"He's why you look different," Signoria says, her voice dripping in bitterness and censure.

"What?" Marcella draws back.

"You love him. He loves you. I see it in both of you. Do you not think I know what love looks like?"

Marcella's breath hitches, and she shakes her head, but there's no hiding the light flush on her cheeks.

"Signoria, I can assure you—"

"Don't lie to me!" The woman lashes out and strikes Marcella's face. I jolt, going to intercept her for hitting Marcella, but Gabe, ever so subtly, shakes his head at me. Fuck! I can't let her hurt her.

Marcella's head dips, blood dripping from a cut on her

cheek. "I'm not lying. I don't love him. I fucked him, yes. He fell in love with me, but love isn't something people like us get." She lifts her chin. "Is it, Signoria?"

The woman's lips purse. "Perhaps not. If that's so, prove it to me. Kill him."

Marcella goes rigid. "We haven't interrogated him yet."

A knowing smile that chills my bones curls up the woman's lips. "It's as I thought." She turns back to me. "Sometimes, Your Highness, a woman has to take matters into her own hands when others fail her."

Her hand lifts, and in it there's a small vial with a sprayer on it. She holds it in front of me, and Marcella screams.

"No!"

Before I can make sense of what's going on, two things happen at once. One, Marcella throws herself at the woman and knocks her to the ground. The second is that Gabe takes aim and shoots, narrowly missing Marcella.

He also misses the woman because Marcella has her on the floor. The bullet whizzes through the air and smashes the wall, splintering sheetrock everywhere.

Marcella is on top of the woman who is clawing and scratching at her, trying to force the spray bottle up into her mouth. Marcella twists the woman's wrists until she cries out in pain. The bottle is shoved in the woman's mouth, and she chokes and shrieks, thrashing violently, as Marcella works to spray whatever is in that into her mouth.

She must get enough in because the hand she was scratching at Marcella drops to the floor. Her body seizes, her eyes round as yellow-white foam froths at her mouth. She chokes, gasping and sputtering and writhing around. Marcella falls to the side, panting heavily, but keeping her body above the woman, her eyes pinned on her.

Signoria Batorini is dying, and the girl in the chair is screaming and fighting, desperate to get free.

"Marcella, no! You have to find it. You have to take it now!"

I don't know what that means. I'm stuck on the woman dying on the floor, but then Marcella collapses, and she starts seizing.

What the fuck is happening?

I drop to the floor and try to pick her up when Gabe stops me, turning her onto her side and pushing me back.

"Is the stuff airborne?" Gabe asks the girl.

"You have to help her!" the girl cries, openly sobbing.

"Is it airborne?" Gabe yells, holding Marcella with one hand while looking like he's about to get up in the girl's face.

"No! She must have breathed in the spray. Please help her. She's going to die," the girl wails, twisting and trying to get free. "Marcella!"

I look up at her, frantic with panic. "What do I do? Tell me how to help her."

"There's an antidote."

"Where?" I bellow, shoving the woman's dying body out of the way so I can hold Marcella's face. "Fuck, she's not breathing. Holy shit, she's not breathing."

Her eyes are open, but they're fixed, sightless, and her body is spastically jerking, but her lips are blue, and there's blood trickling out of the side of her mouth onto the plastic. She put her life in danger for me. That's twice now that she's saved me. I have to save her.

"It's in her bag. In Signoria's bag!"

"I need a medivac at Samil Batorini's bay house," Gabe says into his phone. "I have the coordinates. I'll send them. We need it here immediately. Send ambulances too. A young woman has ingested poison."

"Where's her purse?" I shout at the girl.

"Over there." She wrenches her body, her arms still bound, but she nods her head. "It's in the other room on the table. Hurry. It won't take long."

I get to my feet and sprint into the room where the dead man is on the floor. Frantically, my head swivels about, my eyes searching.

"We're losing her, Rowan. Hurry!"

Jesus! I can't. My body is shaking, my bones rattling, and my heart can't take this. Not any of this. I spot Signoria's purse on the far table, and I race to it, opening it as I speed back into the plastic room.

I fall to my knees and dump the contents out. A litany of female shit spreads across the floor. Gabe has Marcella on her side, holding her body as she continues to seize. Her eyes are closed now, her face ashen, and her lips caked in blood. Holy shit. She's going to die. She can't fucking die, and there are about four bottles of random shit in here.

"It's the blue bottle. The blue one. Spray it into her mouth."

My hands fumble as I pick it up and uncap it. I get right in her face, open her mouth, and spray.

"How much?"

"Four or five sprays, I think."

I don't know if it's five or six I end up doing. I can hardly count, let alone think. I simply spray the antidote into the back of her throat. Can I give her too much? What happens if I give her too much?

"Come on! Fucking work!" I growl.

It does. She stops seizing, her body sagging into the plastic. Thank fuck.

Gently I roll her onto her back, but something isn't right. Gabe is on it, same as I am, checking her pulse.

"Fuck!" He starts doing chest compressions, and my world spins. No. This was supposed to fix her. Not kill her.

I glance to my side, but Signoria Batorini is dead. Her eyes are open and fixed, and her body is still. She, too, is caked in blood and foam, but I don't care. She deserved worse. I hope that hurt like fuck and she was scared.

"Come on, sweetheart." I cover Marcella's head with my arms and press my mouth to her forehead. "Come on. Come back to me."

Except I can hear that she's not breathing. I pinch her nose and blow into her mouth to inflate her lungs.

"Gabe?" I rasp, barely able to make a sound as fear thunders in my chest as I've never felt before.

"No pulse. Compressions only."

"She needs air," I fire back.

He shakes his head as he pumps her chest. "Compressions are more important. And she likely still has the toxin in her mouth. Don't do that again. Switch."

He pulls back, and I take over, knotting my fingers and thrusting down into the center of her chest over her breastbone. I don't know how long I go for before Gabe pushes me off and continues compressions.

I kiss her hair, her forehead, her cheeks, her nose. "Come on, mia stella. I love you. I fucking love you!" I rage. "You can't leave me. We have so much to figure out, but I'm not giving up. I'll keep chasing you. I'll always fight for you. Please."

Tears course down my face, dripping onto her cheeks.

Just as I'm about to give her another breath, Gabe fucking be damned, a gasp startles all of us. I fly back and cup her face, searching it. Her eyes stay closed, but her color is improving.

"We've got a heartbeat. It's weak, but it's there. She needs the hospital, though. I don't think it'll last without intervention. Is she still breathing?"

"Barely. It's shallow and sporadic. Marcella, baby? Can you hear me?"

She doesn't reply, and I press my fingers into her neck, searching for her pulse. I find it, but it's as Gabe said, barely there, like her breathing. Then it fades.

"Fuck, I lost her pulse."

"Shit," Gabe hisses. "Is she breathing?"

I hold my ear to her lips. My eyes pinch shut. "No. Maybe she needs more antidote."

"Or maybe it's not strong enough," Gabe challenges, once again doing compressions.

In the distance is the sound of a helicopter, but they're too late. We're too late.

I shake, holding her, kissing her, begging her, pumping her chest and blood through her body to spell Gabe. I can't let her go. The girl in the chair is wailing, calling out to Marcella. This can't be happening. I can't lose her. She can't lose her.

My chest hollows, and shudders rack through me. She has no pulse and no breath. She's limp in my arms. Dead. Agony is its own heartbeat, pulsing through me and filling my veins and organs with bottomless grief.

"Helicopter is landing. Rowan, go let them in."

I shake my head. I can't leave her, but Gabe is doing compressions again, and the girl is tied up, and I have to save Marcella. I kiss her forehead and crawl up to my feet before I sprint across the house.

"She's in here," I call out to them as I open the door, waving desperately for them to hurry the fuck up.

"Your Highness!" The two paramedics gasp and go to bow, but fuck that.

"Move! She's dying."

"Sir!" They hop to attention, and I fill them in as best I can. There's a man with a gunshot wound to his head and a dead woman on the floor beside Marcella. It's as fucked as a situation can get.

The girl tells them that it's a concentrated form of cyanide and that the antidote she was given was an oral hydroxocobalamin.

The paramedics set to work. "No pulse. Get the paddles on her. I'm going to intubate."

"IV is in. First round of epi on board."

I don't know what they're saying, and I don't interrupt. I stand back as they put a tube down her throat and attach a large bag to it that they squeeze to give her air. The other paramedic is placing pads on her bare chest.

"Charged. Clear."

They stand back and shock her. And fuck. Her body spasms, and her back tenses. They just shocked her heart. I turn around, pounding my already aching fist into the wall.

"Anything?"

"Pulseless V-tach."

"Restarting compressions. Let's move her."

I turn back around as they get her onto the gurney. I glance over at the girl whose face is bruised and bleeding. "We'll get help for you too."

She simply looks at me, her expression calm yet distraught, with tears quietly flowing down her face like a river. "Will they put me in prison?"

"Prison?" I question, my thoughts too chaotic to make sense of anything.

"That's what Signoria and Antonia always told me would happen if I were discovered. That I'd be put in prison. A worse prison," she amends.

I can't begin to imagine the torture this girl and Marcella have faced. I've seen it on Marcella's back, but that doesn't speak to what they've endured.

"You're not going to prison," I promise her. "I'm the prince of the country, and I won't let that happen. No one will ever hurt you again."

Isn't that what I told Marcella? That I wouldn't let anyone hurt her again? That I'd take care of her? Now look. I couldn't save her. I couldn't protect her. My heart can't take this.

She licks her lips, and more tears fall. "You have to save her."

"She needs an IV antidote," the paramedic informs us. "The

oral form isn't enough. We were able to shock her and give her some medicine. It's keeping her heart going, barely, but it's not perfusing her tissue."

"Then give her the IV form," I demand.

"We don't have that in our med kit. This level of cyanide poisoning isn't common."

"I'm going to give her another round of epi and shock her," the other paramedic states. "Charged. Clear."

Her body jolts and spasms on the gurney, and they return to squeezing the bag to give her oxygen.

"Sinus brady at thirty-two. It's thready and won't last. We have to move. She ingested too much of the toxin. Her vitals are fading. She doesn't have long before the antidote completely wears off."

The gurney lifts, then they're wheeling her from the room, running her through the house.

"I'm going with you."

One of the paramedics shakes his head. "I'm sorry, Your Highness, we can't allow anyone else in the helicopter."

Then they're gone. Just like that, they're taking her from me. I follow them out of the house and watch as they load her up into the helicopter. A moment later, they take off, and that's it. I don't even know where they're taking her.

"The closest trauma center is Mercy West in Catalia. They'll do everything they can to save her."

I swallow my grief. It's a big hospital in a big city. But I already know there's a very strong chance she doesn't make it. Even if they get her heart beating again, she might never wake up.

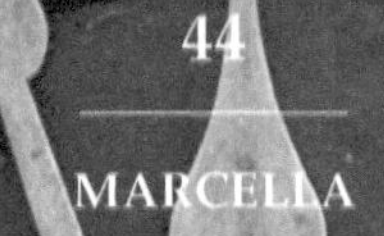

44

MARCELLA

"Marcella? Marcella, can you hear me, baby?" The voice is soft and sweet and a little rough. It also sounds distant, but it's growing closer. And I'm warm. Something brushes one cheek, then the other. "You moved. Are you awake?"

My arms are heavy and so are my eyes, but I'm awake. I know I'm awake. I force my eyes open, blinking slowly. Blurry amorphic shapes obscure my vision before they slowly solidify and come into focus. Blue eyes hold mine, and my heart flutters. Rowan.

"Hi," he whispers.

"Hi," I rasp, my voice sounding like I swallowed sand and chased it with burned cotton.

He smiles as he glances up in the direction of a beeping sound. "I knew I made your heart beat faster. Now I have the proof."

I try to clear my throat, but it's raw, and I wince. My chest hurts like hell, and I'm already exhausted and want to go back to sleep, but I force myself to keep my eyes open. It's dark everywhere. The room, out the window, everything is dark.

"Where am I?"

His fingers drag along my forehead and across my cheek. "The hospital, because the doctors wouldn't let me move you to the palace. It seems since you're not my fiancée or wife yet, I don't get to make medical decisions for you."

There is so much in there for me to focus on, but I'm stuck on that one tiny word. Yet. Is he crazy?

"What..." I trail off as visions and memories fill my head. I'm foggy, and it's a struggle to hold them but... "She's dead. Signoria is dead."

"Yes. You killed her in self-defense."

My brows tighten. It wasn't self-defense. She was going to kill him, and I had to stop her. Hell, I was going to kill her regardless. I should have. I should have shot her immediately after I shot Cristo, but I didn't know where Antonia was, and I wanted to learn what else was up Signoria's sleeve before I did that. She always has something, a plan B, and now I'll never know what it was.

"Jaqueline?"

"She's at the palace getting spoiled by everyone. Incidentally, she makes a great babysitter, and the kids love her."

A cracked smile attempts to tug at my lips but quickly gives up. My chest shakes with tears that won't fall. "I'm sorry."

His hand brushes hair back from my face. "Don't be sorry. You saved my life. Twice."

"And put you in danger."

"I did that. I tracked you, knowing it would be dangerous. If she had come closer with that bottle, Gabe was going to blow her head off."

"Now you tell me." My eyes close.

"Marcella, you saved a lot of people. You went against everything you've been trained and raised to do. Then you selflessly threw yourself at her. Give yourself some credit."

"Not so easy."

"I thought I lost you," he chokes. "You were seizing, and I sprayed the antidote in your mouth, but then your heart wasn't beating, and you stopped breathing. I didn't know what to do, and Gabe and I took turns with compressions. You came back for a minute, but then you were gone again. I thought I lost you," he repeats. "I thought that was it." His chin dips and his eyes hold mine, fiercely determined. "I'm not letting you go. Not again. Not ever."

"Rowan—"

He presses his lips gently to mine. "Only you would wake up after a near-death experience and immediately argue. Woman, shut up. I love you."

My heart ties itself into a thousand knots. "I love you too, but—"

He kisses me again. "Every time you try to argue with me, I'm going to kiss you. It's the only thing that stops you. We'll talk, okay? I know we have a lot to discuss, and I'm not shirking that. But you're alive, and I thought I lost you. Nothing else matters to me right now more than having you awake in my arms."

My eyes close. I don't have the energy to fight him, but it'll come. It'll have to come. He can say whatever he likes, but there's a reality to us that's undeniable.

"I have a lot to tell you, and I know you have a lot to tell me, but I should probably get your nurse. She said it could be any minute after they removed your sedation, but it's been six hours. I was worried you might not wake up. They said…" He makes a fractured noise. "Never mind. It doesn't matter. You're awake."

He kisses my forehead and climbs out of bed, taking his heat with him. I don't want him to go, but it's too late. I lift my hands and flex my feet, testing my strength. I don't have much, and even those small movements take the wind out of me. It also feels like someone broke my chest open.

A moment later, the lights flip on, and I squint.

"Sorry," a woman in blue scrubs says, but she doesn't turn off the light, so maybe she's not at all that sorry. "Glad to see you're awake. I'm Julia, your nurse. I'm going to examine you. I've notified the doctor that you're awake, and she'll likely want to come in and examine you as well. How are you feeling?"

I lick my dry lips. "Tired. Sore."

"You have two fractured ribs in your chest near your sternum from when they did CPR. Your body is tired and sore because they had to resuscitate you after you were poisoned. Do you remember anything?"

"A little," I hedge, not wanting to tell her anything. Talk about a loaded question.

"Well, you're very brave." She comes over and shines a light in my eyes and listens to my heart with her stethoscope before she feels around on my chest and belly.

I don't feel brave. I feel broken and off balance.

I don't know where Antonia is, and there will be a reckoning there. I'll have to answer questions about my past. About Signoria. About everything.

The nurse finishes, declaring me one lucky woman, then leaves me, but I'm not alone. Rowan is back, and I sigh.

He chuckles. "Always so happy to see me."

He climbs into bed beside me without invitation. His arms wrap around me, and he pulls me ever so gently closer, kissing my forehead. "Get some sleep, mia stella."

"Rowan..." I don't know where to begin.

"Tomorrow, okay? Tomorrow when you have more strength. The nurse told me you need rest, and so do I. But no more pushing me away. I need you. I need you every minute of every hour of every day, and that's not changing. It's only growing stronger. Get used to it. Get over it. You're mine. My girl. And I want to sleep holding you."

Damn him. I have no defense.

"Don't run out on me again." He stops breathing, looking pained, and everything in me melts.

"You might want me to." I bite my bottom lip, tears welling once more. The thought is devastating, but I also know I have to brace for it.

"Nah. I think I'm gonna always want you to stay." His fingers drag along my cheek, and he holds my face, staring into my eyes.

"I'm not a good person. I haven't been a good person. I haven't done good things," I amend because maybe the things I did weren't entirely my fault. I don't know. My thoughts are manic.

"The last one and not the first two. Glad you're getting there." A soft smile lights his features. "From the moment I saw you, I knew I wanted you. I can't imagine a world where that's different." His lips press to mine. "Hell, I'm breaking a million rules by being in your bed right now, and I don't care. They'd have to physically remove me to get me to leave you. So go to sleep."

"I want to deserve this."

A kiss to my nose. "Me too."

My eyes close, and I snuggle into him, taking the comfort he's offering and getting lost in his smell even though it hurts like hell to move even an inch or take a breath, for that matter. But Jaqueline is safe. I'm safe. We don't know where Antonia is, but I'll think about that tomorrow.

"He had it coming," she said in no uncertain terms. "Marie got Desta, and I was left with nothing. Worse, it was all taken from me. The king had it coming, and so does the rest of his family for what they did to mine."

Warm kisses trail along my forehead and cheek, and my

eyes slowly open. I blink and move at the same time, and it's a horrible mistake. A pained gasp rips from my throat, and I still.

"Fuck. I'm sorry! Hold on." He moves and pulls up a remote with a button on it. "Here." He clicks the button. "Give that a minute, it'll help."

Slowly, I relax, sinking back into the bed. It is helping, and my eyes close as I release the breath I was holding. Rowan sits up, twisting his back and neck to work out stiffness. I can't believe he slept in my hospital bed with me. That couldn't have been comfortable.

A piece of my dream flickers back through my memory, and I twist my head to him. "You asked me about Marie. I never told you."

He stands and runs his hands over his head, tousling his already sleep-mussed hair more. He picks some sleep out of his eyes and drops into the chair beside the bed. "How do you know about her? How do you know her name and that she took Desta?" he asks instead of answering my questions.

"Because she's Antonia's half-sister. I've met her."

All the color drains from his face, and his hands fall limply in front of him as he gapes at me. "You've *met* her? When?"

I'm so confused right now. "Um...I don't remember exactly. The last time I saw her was two years ago, maybe."

He blinks at me and shoots to his feet, his hands interlocking behind his head, and he breathes hard as he paces my room.

"Marcella..." he starts, then stops. "Fuck. Two years ago? Are you sure?"

"Yes. Why? What is this?"

"Was Desta with her?"

"No."

He spins and stares me down. "Do you know what happened to my sister? Is she alive?"

Now it's my turn to blink, utterly at a loss for words. "I don't know. All that was ever said about her to me was that Marie took her and Antonia hated her. Twisted. Antonia kept saying everything got twisted up."

"What does that mean?"

I close my eyes as I think back. "I don't know. They screamed at each other, and Marie made a lot of threats at Antonia that Antonia threw back in her face. It wasn't anything specific. That was it."

He gulps, looking wrecked.

"Rowan…" I don't know what to say.

"I'm sorry. It's just shocking to me that I've been searching for the woman who killed my father and took my sister, and you've met her."

My eyebrows take a nosedive, and I tilt my head, my confusion growing. "Marie didn't kill your father. Antonia did."

"What?" he bellows, startling me.

The door flings open, and a nurse walks in, her gaze casting back and forth between us. "Is everything all right?"

"Yes," I tell her. "Everything's fine." Except the look on Rowan's face tells me that everything is not fine.

"Okay." She looks nervously at Rowan, then back at me. "I'll return with your breakfast soon and to examine you. We'd like to get you up and get that catheter out of you."

"Wonderful. I'd like that too." Because peeing into a bag isn't my favorite thing. "Thank you."

"Press the button if you need anything." Her tone is pointed, but Rowan isn't going to hurt me.

The nurse leaves us, and Rowan comes straight over to me and holds my face in his hands, his eyes directly in front of mine. "Repeat what you just said to me."

"Antonia killed your father."

His expression crumples, and he collapses back into the chair, covering his face with his hands and breathing through his fingers. "How do you know that?"

"I overheard her and Signoria talking about it before, but she had also mentioned it a few times in passing over the years."

His hands fall to his lap with a thud. "You're telling me the woman who killed my father was literally within my grasp yesterday? How was she involved?"

"Because she worked for your father and was one of his mistresses."

He gulps. "Why would she kill him?"

"I don't know all the details. Only pieces I overheard. There was resentment. I think your father dumped her for Marie and fired her. She knew Marie was going to try to take Desta and she hated the king."

"My father broke up with one sister to fuck the other?"

There's nothing funny about the way he says that, other than his deadpan expression and tone. "Yes," I say apologetically.

"So she killed him out of what...jealousy?"

I shift ever so subtly. "I guess. Antonia is big on hate and retribution. She loves to make others suffer the way she says she has."

"Jesus," he hisses. "How is there such evil in this world, and how has it all found my family? I can't begin to fathom how you lived in that world with them."

"I'm sorry. I know this is a lot to hear and must be very painful." Something is sticking with me, though. Something the king said when I was in his study. "I have to ask, why are you searching for Marie?"

"Because she took our sister," he says simply. "We want to put her away for life and hopefully find Desta."

"She doesn't have her. I mean, I don't know where Desta is or if she's still alive or anything about her specifically. I only know that Antonia stole her from Marie shortly after Marie took Desta all those years ago, though I don't think Marie knows it was Antonia who did it. Marie has been searching for Desta since. Same as you have."

His jaw unhinges, and he stares unblinkingly at me. "What? Why would Antonia do that?"

"She hates Marie. She did it to punish her."

"How would taking Desta punish her?"

"Because Desta was Marie's and the former king's biological daughter."

My head is spinning so fucking fast and hard I feel as though I'm going to pass out. Desta is Marie's daughter. How the fuck did we not know this? Our mother sure as hell had to have, same as our father. So now we're not only searching for one person, we're searching for two. One killed my father, the other stole my sister, but I'm not sure I blame Marie so much for that anymore.

Antonia is a special brand of evil. She's also dangerous for Marcella. Marcella killed Signoria Batorini and knows Antonia's secrets. So yeah, not good.

I also have to imagine my sister is dead. Why would Antonia keep her alive? Any hope I had for Desta is now shriveled into nothing, and it hurts so acutely there's hardly a name for that sort of pain. She was a baby, caught in the middle of betrayal, jealousy, and venomous hate.

But speaking of betrayal. My father was a real piece of work. Is he the one who brought the curse back to us? Is he why all of this has happened, and then Nora's affair with Samil brought it back to us? One betrayal after the other.

My father is dead. Samil is dead. Nora is dead. Signoria is dead. I need to get Antonia. She needs to be killed. It's the only way any of us will ever be safe again, and the curse will die.

I hold Marcella's sweet face in my hands. "We need to get you out of the hospital and back to the palace."

THE HELICOPTER STARTS its descent to the private airfield two miles from the palace. We technically have a helipad at the palace at the back of the grounds, but after what happened to Nora, I don't think any of us have the stomach to land there, and I'd never want to traumatize the children with that sound.

The nurse came back a moment later, and I told her we were having Marcella moved to the palace and that they needed to make arrangements for that immediately. She tried to fight me, but Marcella told her that was her wish, and that was all it took.

They got Marcella out of bed, cleaned her up, and removed the catheter. She was in a good amount of pain, but when I asked when she'd be ready to leave the hospital and travel, she told me immediately.

The hospital wasn't happy about it, but the room Sebastian was in following the attack from Samil is essentially a hospital room, equipped with anything we should need for her, and we'll have our own set of private doctors and nurses come to take care of her.

I went out into the hall and called Sebastian and Javier. Gabe, who has been here the entire time, was with me. I very briefly explained what Marcella told me and what I knew of the situation. We all decided this had to stay between us as we dug deeper.

That said, Marcella is still very weak, and I won't rush what she needs to heal simply because I can barely contain myself.

We touchdown, the rotors of the helicopter slowing, and I remove the cans from my ears. Marcella has a lot on her mind. What should be the end of something now, once again, feels like the beginning.

I help her down, holding her weight with my hand on her waist. They gave her some pain medicine before we left, and not only has it made her drowsy, but it also hasn't touched her pain the way the IV stuff did. The doors of the SUV slam shut, and Javier throws me a look in the rearview mirror.

"We need to talk about Antonia Albini when you get back. We've done some digging," he says, and I sit up straight even as I keep Marcella's head on my shoulder.

"What did you find?"

He doesn't reply at first, his eyes dashing to the side, indicating Marcella.

I smile. "You can talk in front of her. She's the one who brought us this information, remember?"

He frowns and sets off. He doesn't want to do that, and I get it. But I trust her. I trust her with my life. And I know Sebastian trusts her.

"It's okay," she says softly. "You don't have to speak in front of me."

I drag my lips along her forehead. "I think we'll need to. I think you have more information than any of us combined."

Her eyes close, and her head rests on the space between my shoulder and chest. The drive to the palace is short, not even five minutes, and the doors are opening for us again.

Marcella is out on her feet, and I have her put into a wheelchair despite her protests.

"I think you should rest for a while before we all talk more."

"No," she says sternly. "I can rest later. I want to see Jaqueline, and I want to tell you, the king, and your security team anything that might help you."

"Are you sure?" I press, not wanting her to overdo it.

She glances up at me and squints against the sun to hold my gaze. "I'm positive. These aren't my first broken ribs. Trust me, I can take it."

I wince and press my lips to hers. "No one will ever hurt you again. I mean it. I realize I said that before, and then this happened, and there are no actual promises or guarantees in this world, but I will spend my life making sure no one else does."

She smiles softly up at me. "That's what I want to do for you and your family."

I kiss her a little harder and deeper than I should, but I have to. She's alive, and she's here with me, and despite everything, there is no fighting my joy with that. I take her hand and have the attendant wheel her to Sebastian's study.

She winces. "I broke into his computer," she admits, and points over to the table on the other side of the room. "I knew you and he had been working in here earlier that day, and Signoria wanted me to get into his system and see what was on it." She pauses. "She and Samil told me over and over again that the king was corrupt. That he had been taking bribes and misappropriating funds. I didn't find any of that on there. I found that in Samil's folder instead, and I watched the videos of the night he attacked the king and queen." She releases a breath. "That was the moment I decided I no longer wanted to be part of their scheme. I had been wavering, and it ate at me. The children were innocent, and so was Bellamy, and she was just lovely. I didn't want to hurt them. I hated the idea even though I felt like a traitor to my brother. But the evidence was indisputable. I realized I was a pawn for him too. It broke me. He only saved my life so he could use me."

I run my hand down her hair. "I'm sorry. I didn't know him well, but I'm sure he loved you, even if he did use you. Not everything was bad, Marcella. He was obsessed, and obsession breeds madness." I wink at her. "I should know."

She smirks and slowly pushes herself to stand, not wanting to be in a wheelchair. I help her to the sofa and prop her up with pillows. A half-beat later, Sebastian, Althea, Javier, Gabe, and Jaqueline come in. Jaqueline races over to Marcella and throws her arms around her, making Marcella cry out in pain.

Jaqueline bursts into tears. "Oh god! I'm so sorry!"

Marcella kisses her cheek and wipes the tears. "You just have to be gentle with me for a while. I'm fine. We're fine now."

"Sorry about the cracked ribs," Gabe says to her. "Those came from me."

She shakes her head. "I'm not. You saved my life." She turns to Sebastian. "Your Majesty, I'm—"

"Alive, which we're grateful for," Sebastian cuts her off. "The rest isn't important. Well, except what we're here to discuss."

She swallows and nods. "Yes, sir."

"Sebastian," he corrects. "Please call me Sebastian. My brother is in love with you. The formality feels weird."

A blush tints her cheeks, and I'm not sure I've ever seen her blush before. I sit beside her, and Jaqueline takes the other side. Bellamy is still at the hospital with the twins. It was announced last evening that they were born and that everyone was stable. It's been all over the news and social media.

Sebastian has been bouncing back and forth between the hospital and the palace, and that's on top of everything else that's been happening. Sebastian takes a seat on the sofa across from us, beside Althea. Javier and Gabe are at the table with their laptops open and ready.

"Marcella, I know you've been through unspeakable trauma, not just over the last few days, but over your lifetime. I also understand your loyalty to your brother and what you told me about him and Nora has shaken me to my core. I can't go back in time. But if I had known sooner, well, maybe many things would be different now. I don't know. I don't regret marrying Nora. She was a good woman and a good queen and my friend. She was also the mother of my children, and for that, I'll always be grateful to her. That said, I have so many questions, I hardly know where to start. I suppose my first question is, do you have any idea where Antonia could be?"

Marcella glances at Jaqueline. "I heard Signoria asking you about her when I arrived at the house. You said you didn't know where she was."

"I didn't," Jaqueline states. "Antonia drove me to the bay house, tied me to the chair, and said Signoria would be back. That was it. She left, and I haven't seen her since."

"She knew Signoria was coming to meet me in Tourin," Marcella picks up, though she's deep in thought. "I don't know where she could be. As far as I know, she doesn't own any property. She lived with us at the Batorini estate and would go visit her mother overnight once a week."

"Her mother?" Gabe questions.

"Yes. Um, Signoria's much older sister. She's an Albini. I think she lives near Carona, maybe."

Everyone exchanges glances, and both Gabe and Javier type away.

"Maryanne?" Gabe asks.

She nods at him. "Yes. I think that's it."

"She's dead."

Marcella's jaw drops. "You're sure?"

"Died about six years ago."

Marcella's eyes close and she sighs. "I don't understand. That's where she told us she went every week. I have no clue about anything else."

"We searched Signoria Batorini's home," Javier explains. "All of Antonia's things are gone, as well as Signoria's jewelry and some other expensive items that were listed on her insurance forms."

"Then she's gone. She was either planning that from the

start, thinking I was going to kill the king, and then Signoria would kill both Jaqueline and me, or she discovered something that made her do that. I don't know."

"Althea, did you know Desta wasn't our mother's child?" I ask.

Althea is visibly distraught. "No. Your mother was pregnant. The last time I saw her before Desta was 'born'"—she puts air quotes around the word—"was when she was seven months along. I wasn't living in the palace then, and your mother and I were never all that close. Shortly after that visit, she told me she was going to stay at a wellness retreat for the remainder of her pregnancy because she needed to get away from the stress and to relax. Then three months later, she came home with Desta."

"I remember her being pregnant," Sebastian says. "That's why I couldn't understand."

"She must have lost the pregnancy," Althea speculates. "Then stole Desta from Marie, knowing she was the king's child and therefore of royal blood. Losing a pregnancy that late in term had to be horrific. Your mother was never the same after Desta was born. We thought it was postpartum depression. She was on a lot of medication to help it. After your father was killed and Desta was taken, she withdrew completely."

"Marie still worked there, though," I state. "Our mother didn't fire her until a few weeks before Desta was taken."

"Maybe Marie started making threats," Althea suggests. "The baby was hers and being raised by another mother. Maybe it got to be too much for her, and your mother fired her to get rid of her."

Sebastian stands and goes over to the bar and pours three large tumblers of whiskey. It's the same thing he did after my mother left the last time. "You're on pain medicine," he says to Marcella. "But would you like one?"

"No. Thank you for offering, though."

"Gabe, Javier? I think I already know what you'll say, but I'll offer anyway."

Both shake their heads and Sebastian returns and hands Althea and me our glasses, and I take a hearty sip despite how my stomach is roiling.

"Antonia worked in the palace," Javier states. "She was the king's assistant. He fired her a year before Desta was born."

I lean back against the sofa, my hand on my forehead as I think. "Why would he fire her? Because he wanted Marie instead of her?"

"I told you what Antonia's like," Marcella says in a low tone. "She wouldn't have handled the king ending it with her for her sister well."

"Tell us about Marie and Antonia," Althea requests, finishing off her drink and setting the crystal on the small table beside her.

"They hated each other," Marcella explains. "They had the same mother and got the job at the palace from her. That's all I know. Marie came to the palazzo twice. The first time I was very young. I only remember she was sobbing. She kept saying, 'She's gone. Where is she? Who took her from me?'"

"She talking about Desta," I manage. "Jesus." I swallow down the rest of my drink, and Sebastian does the same.

"The last time she came was two years ago, and they fought. This time I didn't hear them."

"I did," Jaqueline whispers. "I snuck outside the sunroom and listened. Marie was looking for something and accused Antonia of taking it. Antonia denied whatever it was. They screamed, and Signoria had Marie escorted out. After Antonia told Signoria she had the piece stolen from Marie but didn't have it as the thief ran off before she could get it and kill him."

"The piece?" Sebastian asks.

Jaqueline shrugs. "That's how they referred to it."

I exchange glances with Sebastian, Althea, Javier, and Gabe.

The tiara. It had to have been that. And the thief who took it and ran off before she could kill him had to have been the ones from the house in France.

Now it seems Marie stole the tiara back. And Antonia is nowhere to be found.

"You need to rest," I say to Marcella because she does, and there's not much to follow that up with. We have to sort through these details, and fuck, if there aren't a lot to sort through.

More questions.

But it also feels as though we're getting closer to unraveling everything and finding the answers we've been searching for.

I can tell Marcella wants to argue but ends up nodding.

I help her up, gently wrapping my arms around her and walking with her to the wheelchair.

"I'll catch up," I tell the room.

"Can I go back and play with Phaedra, Sabrina, and Zayer?" Jaqueline asks, and I catch the smile on Marcella's lips.

I walk us out of the room toward the elevator to go up to the bedrooms. "She's going to fall in love with being here," she says quietly.

"Is that a bad thing?"

"I don't know, Rowan. I don't know what's happening or what will happen next for us."

"For starters, you're sleeping in my room, which is now our room."

She sags. "Rowan, we need to talk."

I reach around and kiss her lips before whispering in her ear. "Remember what I said about fighting with me. I want you in my bed. I want it to be our bed. Regardless of that, I know one thing to be true. There is no way I'm letting you sleep on your small bed in your small room with your shared bathroom after what happened to you. Please. Do it for me if not for yourself."

"Fine, but only because your bed is comfortable and I'm tired."

"And because you love me."

A smile curls her lips. "Don't push your luck, Your Highness."

"It's what I live for with you." I give her one more kiss, and we get on the elevator. Work has begun on some of the improvements to the palace, but the new elevator system will take a while.

"How are you still here? Is it because I saved your life? Because I gave you information?"

I laugh because that's a good one. "Not even close. You need to escape the toxicity of your thoughts. I know you're overwhelmed and don't feel as though you belong here with me, but you do."

She nods slowly.

This palace is entirely too big, and it takes us forever to get to my room. I help her up, get her undressed, and into bed. I climb in beside her and hold her, making sure she sees me.

She leans in and kisses me. "I love you."

My heart takes flight, and there's no stopping my elated smile.

"I don't feel like I deserve you or this, and it terrifies me, but I want you anyway."

"I love you too. I loved you before all of this happened. I loved you even when I knew I shouldn't. I trust you. You know I didn't before, and I had no reason to because you were lying to me and hiding your identity. But I trust you. You were going to leave me, and I understand why you felt like you had to then. But those reasons are gone. I don't want you to leave me. Not ever. I want to do this with you. I want to start fresh and build us into something incredible."

She sucks in a shaky breath. "I don't...I've done horrible things. I don't have a last name. I'm the illegitimate half-sibling of the man who tried to kill your brother and sister-in-law and your nieces and nephew."

"You're not Samil, Marcella. Or Signoria or Antonia. They tried to make you into something, and yes, you did some bad things, but I'm not sure you had much choice in that. You were abused—mentally, physically, and emotionally. You're not that person anymore. You're your own person, and I'm not sure you ever knew what that felt like until you came here. But now you do, and you can do and be anything."

"You're too good to be true," she whispers, losing steam, even as tears glisten in her eyes.

"It's the truth, sweetheart. Every word." I kiss her lips. "Jaqueline deserves that too."

"I'm working on making myself believe it. On believing I'm not evil and I am worthy."

"You're not evil, and you're more than worthy." I kiss the tip of her nose. "Get some rest. You need it."

She nods slowly.

"I want to stay with you. Is that okay?" I don't want to let her go. Since the moment I got to the hospital, I can't handle any distance between us. And until we figure out this situation, she could still be in danger.

Her eyes close, and she sags into the pillow. The one I caught her smelling all those weeks ago. "Go talk to them," she mumbles through heavy lips. "You have a lot to figure out."

"Marcella, something feels off about all of this."

"I think there's a lot more going on than any of us know, and we're here trying to complete a puzzle that's missing pieces. If I knew more, I'd tell you. I wish I did. I wish I knew the way to end all of your suffering."

I smile and relax my body behind hers so I can kiss her neck. "You have no idea how much you've already helped." I kiss her again, my nose and mouth resting against her sweet skin. "Stay with me," I whisper into her. "You know I love you. I know you love me. I also know you're reluctant because part of you still doesn't feel you can have everything. But we can. I want you. I want you as mine. Stay this time. Don't run."

"You're the prince. I've killed people, Rowan. Likely people who didn't deserve to die, but I honestly don't know. I killed them because that's what I was trained and ordered to do. But that doesn't make what I did right or okay. How would you explain me to the world? There is no explanation."

"I don't have to explain myself to anyone. I'm the prince, not the king. We can say whatever you want or not say anything at all. You're Marcella Russo now until you're Marcella of the house of Alerie. Jaqueline's guardian with your own last name."

She releases a breath and moves gingerly to touch my jaw. "I like that idea. But I worry Antonia will try to strike at you and your family because she knows I know her secrets."

"We'll figure that out as we go. It's not a reason for you to leave. It's a reason for us to find her."

I run my fingers down her hair and across her jaw as her pretty green eyes hold mine. "Your past doesn't scare me. I have a curse to fend off, remember? I need a woman who can stand by my side and fight the darkness with me."

"Women like me don't become princesses. That's the stuff of fairytales."

I chuckle. "Wow, so presumptuous. Now I know you're after my crown."

She tries to scowl as she says, "I hate your crown."

I grin. "But would you wear it with me if I put a ring on your finger and promised you always? All of my love. All of my obsession. All of my protection. My heart. My body. My mind. My soul. All of it is yours if you say yes."

"God, Rowan." She takes my hand and squeezes it to her chest. "I love you. I love you so much. You're the prince of my heart. The one who kept it beating when others tried to kill it. I don't feel like I deserve this, but I don't care enough to fight it anymore. Maybe people like me get second chances. Maybe sometimes, the glass slipper fits."

"Or we princes find the other earring."

She smiles, and I kiss the corner of her lips.

"Is that a yes? You'll stay? You'll be mine?"

"It's a yes. It was never a no. Even when I tried to make it one. It'll always be us."

EPILOGUE

MARCELLA

After four weeks of rest with a lot of restrictions and being homebound thanks to my prince, I'm starting to go insane. Rowan has been dividing his time between me and searching for Antonia. I've been rehabbing with Emily, getting stronger as my ribs heal and the full extent of the toxin works its way out of my system. Per my doctor, given the concentration of the cyanide, it could take a couple of months.

The twins are set to come home, hopefully next week, but Bellamy is here today, spending time with the children even if I can see she hates being away from the twins.

The children, including Jaqueline, and I are all in the pool while Bellamy sits on the edge with her legs dangling in. She's still recovering from surgery but has started light yoga with Althea, which is helping her body and her mind recover.

There's recovery needed for all of us.

Jaqueline and I have started therapy. She was having nightmares, and I clearly have a lot to work out from my past. We've been doing it three days a week to start, and so far, it's been immensely beneficial for both of us.

"Mommy, watch!" Sabrina cries from the top of the high diving board. "I'm going to do a flip!"

"I'm watching, legendary princess!" Bellamy calls back with a wave. The renovation plans are in full swing now that parliament has approved the ones for the palace, and Rowan and the children signed off on the ones for the pool. "Sebastian mentioned a nanny to me again last night," she murmurs to me.

This is where I attempt to hold in my smile. Ironically, I mentioned this to Rowan the other night, and he thought it was brilliant but wanted to mention it to Sebastian first.

"Oh? And?"

"And he said I need a nanny, but I trust no one. Especially not right now. I mean, think about what's happening. Charlotte was Marie's daughter. Who knows how far and deep this all goes?"

That was a kick I hadn't known. Unfortunately, we have no leads on Antonia. She's slipped into the void and disappeared completely, but that won't stop them. Not ever. They'll find her. No one can stay hidden forever.

"Rowan was supposed to talk to Sebastian, but you're here now, so I'll just bring it up, and you can tell me no and that'll be that."

Her brows furrow and she tilts her head. "Huh?"

"What if I were the children's nanny? At least for a little while or until you find someone better. Jaqueline is going to be starting school this fall here at the palace, but she can help me with them—I know she wants to—and the three of us can go from there."

Bellamy blinks at me, astonished. "You're serious? You'd want to help me with the children?"

I gnaw on my lip as my hands move in the water. "If you're comfortable with that, yes."

"Oh my god! I'd fuc—er, I mean, I'd really, really love that. Like, seriously love that. The children already adore you and feel so comfortable with you, and Jaqueline is so sweet and helpful. Yes. If you're sure, it's a big yes from me."

I laugh. "I'm sure."

"Oh hell, Marcella, you're going to make me cry. These freaking hormones are a beast. I'm so happy. I'm going to call Sebastian and tell him—"

"Tell me what?" comes from the sliding doorway that leads to the pool area. Sebastian and Rowan close the slider behind them and head out toward us.

"Marcella wants to be our nanny with Jaqueline as a nanny helper."

Sebastian appraises me. "You do?"

"I was going to mention it, but never quite found the right time," Rowan says. "I love the idea."

"I do too!" Bellamy states, standing up to face him.

"What about you, Marcella? It's a lot of work, and I don't want you to do this out of a sense of obligation."

I shake my head and climb out of the pool. "Honestly, it would give me so much joy, and I think taking care of children in a happy, positive environment would be good for my soul."

A smile cracks across his face. "Perfect. Thank you. That's a huge load off my mind."

Rowan wraps a towel around me and tugs my hand back toward the house. "Great. You start tomorrow."

I laugh. "What are you doing?"

"Taking a lunch break." He winks at me and pulls me inside and up the stairs to our bedroom. Not that I had a lot of stuff, but he moved me into his room before I woke up from my nap that first day. He announced to the staff that we were together and in love, and that was that. Good thing my stooges were gone. Who knows how they would have reacted?

We've been careful with sex. I mean, we've been doing it— we can't keep our hands off each other—but he's been very careful with me. The look in his eyes tells me that might all be over now.

Honestly, these last four weeks have been the best of my life. Being with him is like living in an eternal dream. We talk about everything, holding nothing of ourselves back. He's gone to some of my therapy sessions, and with that, we both have a deeper understanding of what I endured at the hands of Antonia and Signoria and even Samil. I've made my peace with him. It's all I can do.

Rowan strips me out of my bathing suit, his eyes fierce and hungry as he guides me to the bench at the end of the bed and sits me down. "How are you feeling?"

"Good. Strong."

"Any pain?"

I shake my head. I wouldn't call what I have pain. Just occasional discomfort, but it's nothing I can't manage.

"Good. Spread your legs for me."

I do without hesitation, opening myself up fully to him. He licks his lips, then flicks his tongue against my clit. I moan, already so wet and ready for him, I can hardly stand it.

"You're still dressed, Your Highness."

He gives me a wicked smirk as he reaches behind his back and pulls off his shirt, treating me to a sinful view of his tanned shoulders and arms. So perfect. So mine.

"Speaking of Your Highness, I wanted to run something by you."

He blows cool air on my pussy, and I shudder. "Hmm?" I ask absently, watching as he stares ravenously at my cunt. "Rowan, give it to me," I whine when he rings my entrance without pushing a finger in. "Don't tease me like this."

He chuckles and kisses my clit. "I'm not sure how to do this. I've thought about it. I thought about tying you up and making you come, and then doing it. I thought about bringing it up over dinner. I thought about waking you up with it. I can't decide because I don't think you'll be happy with me."

I push him back, and he lands on his haunches. "What are you talking about?"

"Do you remember when you mentioned you didn't want to be a Russo? How it felt wrong and weird since they were blackmailed by Signoria?"

"Yes." I shake my head. "Why are we talking about this now?"

"You mentioned your father's middle name to me. Alexander."

"What about it?" I whisper, closing my legs and drawing them up to my chest, suddenly feeling vulnerable. Except Rowan isn't having that. He puts my feet back on the floor and wraps his arms around me, putting us chest-to-chest and face-to-face.

"Your last name, as well as Jaqueline's, is officially Alexander. You're Marcella Alexander."

Tears prickle my eyes. "I am?"

"You are. It's legal. We had a judge sign off on it. You have a birth certificate. A national identification number. The works."

"I'm real?" I swallow. "We exist?"

"Yes."

Oh god. A sob clogs my throat, and my eyes shudder shut. My forehead falls to his shoulder, and I let go, crying my eyes out. "I didn't know you were doing that."

"I wanted it to be a surprise."

"It's a surprise."

His hand runs down my hair, and he holds me to him. "Good surprise?"

I cling to him. "The best. Thank you. Thank you so much." I can't even begin to describe what this feels like. To be shed of the past and born anew. What it will mean and do for Jaqueline and her future.

He pulls back and wipes my tears with his thumbs. "Marcella Alexander, will you do me the enormous honor of marrying me?"

My eyes bulge. "What!"

He smiles at my reaction, but there are nerves in his eyes. "You're my girlfriend, and it's been fun and all, even when you tried to break up with me. But you're more than just my girlfriend. You're what makes the blood pump through my body. Every cell I'm comprised of has your name on it. I love you. I want you to be my princess. I want us to chart our new future together."

More tears fall, but before I can respond, he pulls a box out of his pocket and opens it. Inside is a large pink diamond heart on a solid platinum band. He stares down at it as it glimmers up at me.

"This came from Desta's tiara," he explains. "I found it in the safe after Marie broke into the home and possibly retook the tiara. Maybe it's weird to make your engagement ring out of that, but I wanted to make something beautiful from something tragic. Bring hope and love from something lost and broken."

I cup his cheeks and stare into his eyes. God, this man. How did I get so lucky to find this man? So beautiful. So charming. My midnight prince.

"Yes, I'll marry you. I'll be your princess, though I can already tell you I will never want to be called that."

He laughs, the sound jubilant. I draw his face to mine and kiss him with everything I have. Everything I am. Everything I want to be.

He pulls the ring from the box and slips it onto my finger before he kisses me again. Then it's nothing but breath and lust and love. His shorts hit the floor, and his body crawls over mine. He interlocks our hands, and with his eyes on mine, he pushes deep inside me. My back bows at the intrusion, at the fullness of him. My eyes close but only for a moment. I don't want to look away from him.

Not for another second.

I want to feel him inside of me always. Knowing this connection, this love, can never be severed. We've been through hell together. Tested our limits. And came out indestructible on the other side.

He pumps into me, filling me up, making me feel every inch of him. His head dips, and his mouth takes mine. I climb my leg up to his shoulder, setting my calf there so he can fuck me deeper. Kiss me harder. Bend me in fucking half.

"Marcella," he whispers. "I need you."

"You have me. I'm here. I love you."

He growls, pummeling his hips harder into me. My hand with the ring is still locked with his, but his other hand plants into the bed beside my head, using it for leverage. But he wants more. We're not close enough.

He rolls us over until I'm on top and he's sitting against the headboard. His arms wrap around me, and I sink back down on his cock, moaning at how fucking perfect that feels.

"Only me, mia stella. Say it."

My head falls back as I start to bounce on him. "Only you. My prince."

He groans and thrusts up into me, making my eyes roll back into my head.

His hand is all over my tits, squeezing and pinching and pulling. He drags one up to his mouth and sucks my nipple in hard.

Oh fuck, yes.

Heat is already curling up through me, growing stronger with every pump and push of his cock. His tongue dives back into my mouth, making me groan, and the heat between my thighs burns hotter. I'm on fire. My clit pulses as I rub it against his pelvic bone every time I come down on him.

He presses me down harder, shoving himself in more and more to get to that exact spot. The one I need him to hit.

"Yes!" I cry, especially when I feel his finger on my asshole. He loves to play here, and he hasn't taken it yet. But I know it's only a matter of time. I haven't sucked him off yet either. All these things we have yet to do, but now that I'm healthy and strong again, I know there's no limit. It shoots a thrill through me and has me moaning.

He smiles against my lips. "What are you thinking about?"

"Sucking you off. Having you fuck my ass."

He groans, low and loud. "Shit, sweetheart. You're going to make me come." He pants against my mouth as we rub and grind and ride.

I hold the back of his head and kiss a trail up his neck. "Not yet," I tease. "But after you do, I want those lessons. I want to put you deep down my throat."

"Oh fuck!"

I laugh. "Still quick to shoot your load, Your Highness?"

"With you? Always."

He thrusts a finger into my ass, fucking me with it as his cock fucks my pussy.

His other hand comes between us and rubs my clit, and it's so intense, all the stimulation, feeling my pussy and ass full.

I grind into him, seeking more, wanting it all deeper.

"How's this?" he rasps against my mouth as he adds another finger to my ass. Holy shit! A moan rips from my lungs, and he smiles against me. "That's it. Take it. Stretch yourself on me, baby, because after this, I'm going to put my cock in your mouth and you're going to get me nice and hard again. And after that, my cock is going here." He pushes his two fingers knuckle-deep.

"Yes," I cry. "Please."

"Such a good girl, Marcella. Such a good princess for your prince."

That's when I lose it on him. He presses his thumb harder on my clit, and his fingers fuck my ass, and my pussy fucks his cock, and I'm done. Just so done. I come harder than I've ever come in my life, my face against his neck, my arms slung around his shoulders as I surrender and take wave after wave of endless bliss.

Just as I start to come down, Rowan pounds up into me three times and comes on a roar. I pull back and watch him, mesmerized, the same as I was that night all those months ago at the wedding. Except now there will be no running out, no clock striking midnight. It'll only ever be us. From now through all eternity.

THANK you for reading Midnight Prince. There is more to come in this world with the next book, Stolen Princes.

END OF BOOK NOTE

If you're here, you're likely looking for the list of content warnings. Please keep in mind that these contain spoilers.

WARNING: This book contains darker themes and elements as well as suspense. You will find beatings, torture - including that of a minor - enslavement, guns, knives, murder, poisoning, recussitation, pregnancy with emergency delivery, stalking vibes, chasing (minor primal play), and obsession.